THE NEXT WOMAN

ALSO BY CAROLINE CORCORAN

Through the Wall

The Baby Group

Five Days Missing

What Happened on Floor 34?

Tiny Daggers

THE NEXT WOMAN

CAROLINE CORCORAN

This is a work of fiction. Names, characters, organizations, places, events, and incidents are either products of the author's imagination or used fictitiously. Any resemblance to actual persons, living or dead, or actual events is purely coincidental.

Published by Thomas & Mercer, Seattle

www.apub.com

EU Product Safety Contact:
Amazon Media EU S.à r.l..
38, avenue John F. Kennedy, L-1855 Luxembourg
amazonpublishing-gpsr@amazon.com

ISBN-13: 9781662528200
eISBN: 9781662528194

Cover design by Dan Mogford
Cover Image: © Maria Heyens / ArcAngel Images;
© Kuznetsov Dmitriy / Shutterstock; © Sebastian Staines / Unsplash

Map design by Emma Ledger

Printed in the United States of America

This is a book for the magazine journos.
Always the funniest, always the smartest ♥.
Definitely not moustache-twizzling meanies.
We had no idea how magical those times
were, did we?
Lots of love,
Caroline xxx

Map Design by Emma Ledger

PROLOGUE

At the beginning of this summer, I thought my best friend disappearing on her birthday was the worst thing that could happen.

I had no idea.

No idea how catastrophic life on our island was about to become. No idea that Aurora would go from being unknown, a tiny dot on a map, to infamous and gigantic; the first thing people read about when they checked the news in the morning.

And I had no idea that my own story – that one I had tried so hard not to tell – would be central to it all.

The last thing Alice said to me was: 'Got to go, Lily – I'm about to drop the Waitrose duck spring rolls.'

'Bloody hell, Alice,' I said, laughing. 'Not the *Waitrose* duck spring rolls.'

Waitrose had only recently landed on our little island, and we were discombobulated by it. Not long ago, we were more a builders' tea and chip shop kind of place. *You've changed*, we could hear the other islands whispering to us.

Aurora is not a tropical island but a British offshoot, a little bit of the UK that came undone somewhere back in time. An island that drifted away, teenager from its parents. Our landmass exists entirely on a soft curve. From space we look like the letter C.

Living here means feeling, always, that the rest of the world just might have stopped existing. That you are alone, a French dessert. *Île flottante.*

Living on Aurora Island means that the zeitgeist skates to a halting stop when it reaches the coastline. That it puts its hand to its forehead and checks out the horizon, then says, 'Nope. Don't bother sending the memo on the new trend. They're content. Leave them to it.'

Now, I stand at the highest point of the island's highest hill, my smooth coat collie, Jake, panting hard at my feet. I stare across the sea at the mainland and listen to a collective deep and guttural croak. The cormorants. Native to Aurora and ruling the roost. Wings spread wide, perched on long branches that look like witches' fingers, right on the edge of the sea.

Hello over there. It's us.

There are practical things to take into account when you live on an island. Living here, for example, means that when the weather is terrible, the ferries stop running. You're cut off and you can't leave. Even if you're desperate. Even if a panic so great that it threatens to engulf you like a wave rises up, up, up your diaphragm.

Not that I leave much anyway. Still, it's how it's framed in your head, isn't it? The same outcome feels worlds apart to the human brain depending on one thing: whether we have control over it or not. If we do, fine. If we don't, the wheels come off.

The rest of the time I *could* leave, if I wanted to. And now, after what's happened, I would like to stand up and run off the island and away, free as the cormorants.

That's how I would do it: running. Not in a taxi that could break down, or a bus I'd have to wait for, but on foot – running as fast and as far from here as I could, entirely dependent on my own body for escape even if that body struggled for breath and its heels blistered and sweat oozed from its armpits.

I can't leave, though. And this time, it's not because of the weather. It's because no matter how much I want to run again, I owe it to them to stay.

I owe it to the Alphabet Women.

PART ONE: LILY

A

AURORA ISLAND ECO WELLNESS RETREAT, FINAL FRIDAY OF MAY

I'm taking my lunch out of our tiny work fridge when I hear a plop through the open window.

A swimmer.

I look up.

Outside is where the guests are. They come to swim in our manmade natural lake before hopping into one of the hot tubs, filled in advance with their choice of either natural mineral salts or personally picked seaweed.

The guests are the ones whose tiny vintage cars – with the roofs down – or huge 4x4s loaded with their outdoors kit fill the car park, and who pay £1,000 a night for a wooden cabin and £450 each to have Tomas, our chef, and his team cook them an eight-course tasting menu. Sommelier and wine pairings optional – although they often bring their own, shipped from Châteauneuf-du-Pape during a family trip out there last Easter.

The guests would never be seen in the black polo shirt, comfy black slacks and maroon tabard that I am currently wearing. They opt for Lululemon leggings, expensive trainers. Tailored shorts and a silk shirt. A swimsuit that looks like it was moulded to their shape.

The guest I'm watching out of the window is in the manmade lake now, after a dive performed so neatly she could have been mistaken for a pencil.

I hold my lunch in my hands as I watch this guest swimming in rhythmic lines like she really is a 2B, drawing columns in the lake.

I take the lid off my Tupperware.

The sign on the wall in the office says **AURORA ISLAND ECO WELLNESS RETREAT**, and underneath that there is a small placard announcing that we were the winner of the UK's Premier Wellness Holiday Destination, 2023 (luxury category).

The eco element of our name is there as a virtue signal. The hot tubs use more than three hundred gallons of water each per day. The salmon is flown in from Alaska. I've learned over the last two years, though, that eco is not something you quantify via an official body, and being 'more eco than a lot of other places' is enough eco for most people. We have water butts! Seven different types of recycling bin!

As the guest's pale shoulder nudges one of our rowing boats, I give her a name – let's go for Allegra – and I invent her a husband, Jasper. The children are probably being looked after by the nanny they've brought on holiday with them. Let's call them Ottilie and William.

The window is open and I hear the swell of Allegra climbing out of the water. She is immediately handed a robe by one of the pool boys, Ryan, to put on over a black bikini that manages to be obviously expensive despite being the simplest item of clothing I've ever seen.

From inside, still watching her, I harbour an odd feeling that the black bikini is a bit mean. That it would laugh at me if I turned my back on it.

Allegra's feet slide into arrived-this-week Birkenstocks, and she wafts over to the wellness centre, where she will most likely be loading the sauna rocks up with water in ten seconds while thinking about her pores. Later, she will slip on an Edeline Lee dress and a thin knit and take an evening walk down to the stretch of private beach that is owned by the retreat and that is out of bounds for islanders.

I shake my head.

Now Allegra's left my eyeline, it's time to flip back to the reality of being the office manager at Aurora Island Eco Wellness Retreat. To sandwiches and Tupperware.

My lunch today is packed in a leftover takeaway carton that is slightly stained by turmeric from a recent (alright, not that recent) chicken curry. Inside the turmeric-y container is the crunchy, brown buttered roll I made in my bread maker last night, loaded with hummus and salad.

I stick my head out from the back office to the front desk. 'Ten minutes,' I tell our junior admin assistant – and my surrogate little sister – Zadie Christmas, through a mouthful.

'No rush!' She carries on typing but I can see her smiling from the side, cheeks squeezable as a toddler's. 'Had a bag of salt and vinegar for breakfast!'

I lock my eyes on to hers. 'Zadie. I despair.'

At Aurora Island Eco Wellness Retreat, guests usually stay in wooden cabins, the fanciest of which jut out on to the lake. Inside, the ceilings curve to make them feel cocooned as they read self-improvement books under lamplight, or have a bath in the freestanding rolltop at the foot of a bed that is probably more comfortable than the average womb.

In The Barn, our on-site restaurant, guests eat organically sourced chicken and beef carpaccio and poke bowls loaded with that far-schlepped salmon, and in here, I eat this same roll most days, but that's okay. It's not like it was before. These days I like habits. These days I like blending into the background, a magnolia human, hoping that people forget my name and – even more importantly – forget my face.

Finishing my lunch, I watch a second guest dive neatly into the water – this time a man in a small pair of black shorts. It's only sixteen degrees, but they do it when it's far colder than this too. When there's ice on the ground.

What being rich seems to make you these days – I've learned in this job – is a masochist. There's a snug café here serving coffee from Panama that's the best I've ever tasted. There's an indoor pool that's not far off the temperature of a bath. Each cabin has its own Swedish wooden hot tub on its decking. These people's lives could be so *easy* and yet they spend the majority of their time chanting or walloping a crystal singing bowl at 6 a.m., or drinking shots containing actual *salad* and freezing their nether regions off in the ice of the lake or the even more brutal cold of the sea.

When I've swallowed my last mouthful and put my turmeric-y container into the North Face rucksack in my locker, I head back out to the front desk.

'Right, my love, you're free,' I say to Zadie. 'Get your lunch.'

She spins her chair round and stands up in one movement.

'Tell me that's not crisps as well?'

'Nope, Bob made me a packed lunch. She's on one about UPFs.' Zadie rolls her eyes.

I sigh with relief. 'Thank God for Bobbi. Tell her I'm bringing you a homemade roll tomorrow.'

'Ham?' she says hopefully.

'Also ask Bobbi her thoughts on your processed meat consumption.'

Bobbi is Zadie's landlady, an Amazonian blonde badass with tattoos all over and a little gold nose ring, and the local GP. She's also mum to four-year-old Bertie.

As I sit down in the seat next to Zadie's, dusting crumbs from the maroon tabard, the phone rings.

'Hello, reception.'

'Butchery this p.m., please. Two spots if you have them.'

They talk like this a lot, the guests. Perfunctory. Efficient. Like they're still at work.

'Not a problem. Can I take a name?'

'Fitzroy-Ferguson.'

'Got it.'

Butchery's one of the classes we offer at Aurora. The guests can also 'work on' themselves with hatha yoga, local landscape watercolour painting or bookbinding.

'All booked in for you. Anything else I can help with?'

But there's a shrill tone and Fitzroy-Ferguson is gone. Immediately the next guest is calling though, asking if I can source him size-eleven walking boots for tomorrow.

'Not a problem, sir.'

I'm clicking a link while he's still on the phone. It isn't the first time I've dealt with this request and I know what he's after, it's a website I have saved. He'll want to do the coastal path loop. A lot of the guests tackle it while they're here, heading to the more remote parts of the island, tracing the clifftops and then veering inland to Lake Maddock, before looping back towards the coast. The views are one of the island's biggest draws. That moment when you look out to sea from the cliffs and realise you're a dot is more effective than therapy.

There's a reason the man on the phone can't source his own walking boots. Our USP at the Aurora retreat is a no Wi-Fi policy – except for in the office – and a requirement for each guest to put their phones, iPads and laptops in a locker for the duration of their stay.

Each cabin is fitted with a landline, so they can be contacted in emergencies.

Most of our guests are CFOs, CEOs, or various other job titles with a big C at the front. Often their therapists have recommended that they take some time out. Log off. Disconnect. More often, their wives have insisted on it, wielding an expensive divorce as an alternative.

While they're here, we function as their Google. We book their on-site activities and we liaise with local organisations to hire them an e-bike or send them on a sailing adventure in the bay, followed by the on-beach sauna. We order them things that they've forgotten, whether it's walking boots, swimming goggles or seven pairs of –3.75 daily contact lenses.

'Khaki or navy, sir?' I say, back to the boots.

'Let's take the navy, I think!' this man – Jonas – says, laughing at random in a way that suggests he hit the rosé hard in The Barn at lunch.

The moment after we hang up, my own phone vibrates.

'Hey Evan.' Evan is my best friend Alice's husband. It's unusual for him to call. For *anyone* to call, actually.

Zadie must hear me. She sticks her head round the door from the back office. 'Need me to cover?' she mouths.

I shake my head. If Richard walks in, I can make it sound like I'm booking a fish-gutting masterclass.

'I can't hear you, Evan,' I tell him.

'SORRY!' he shouts. 'IT'S THE HELMET! Let me just . . .' There is another rustle. 'Bike helmet's off now, that better?'

He is slightly out of breath, and I picture him walking while steering his mountain bike. Ginger beard crackling against his phone.

'Much better.'

A gull shrieks; it must be close to him, and I flinch. 'You're not with Alice, are you?' he asks.

'No. I'm at work. She's sorting party stuff today?' Tonight is Alice's thirty-fifth birthday party. I sigh. 'She'll be at the shops, Ev. Grabbing emergency ice or something.'

After we ring off, I don't think about the conversation. Instead, all my attention goes to an eight-year-old who's rummaging in our mini kids' reading corner.

'Leave this one to me,' I tell Zadie.

We find him *Kensuke's Kingdom*. I read it to Alice's daughter Florence a few months ago. She's the reader in the family; her twin sister Freya's more likely to be found drilling penalties into the goal in the garden before playing out an intricate 'celebration' involving a forward roll and three cartwheels.

'Does it have *Star Wars* in?' the boy, Barnaby, asks.

'Well . . .'

The hint of a pout. '*Cosmic* was my last book. *Cosmic* had *Star Wars* in. Any Ninja Turtles?'

I shake my head.

'*Framed* has Ninja Turtles.'

'I know,' I say solemnly. 'Frank Cottrell-Boyce is a genius.'

He nods. Correct.

'Look,' I tell him. 'If it's not a ten out of ten, I'll give you free olives in the shop.'

A little palm covered in yellow pen is thrust out. 'Deal.'

'Is it cake time yet?' wheedles the voice behind me as Barnaby and his dad leave.

I turn to Zadie. 'Go on then.'

Most days at 3 p.m., someone sticks the kettle on while I dole out apple and cinnamon muffins or squidgy raspberry blondies or overweight slices of ginger loaf.

Today, I've baked chocolate school cake. I made it for Freya, who will turn her freckly nose up at the red velvet drip cake I've made for her mum's birthday.

Not that the girls will be at Alice's party, but they'll attack the leftovers tomorrow and Freya would be appalled if all she found on offer was red velvet. For Freya, desserts must be 'chocolate everywhere'. That means you can't even *think* about adding caramel or a sliver of biscuit, let alone a piece of fruit. She'll leave the red velvet for her sister.

'What can I say?' shrugs Alice. 'The girl's a purist.'

A few minutes later, I am at my desk with a slice of cake in front of me.

'Do you miss it?' asks Zadie. 'The library?'

'Every day. But we did our best.'

Aurora Island library was closed in a round of cuts a couple of years ago. We campaigned and we presented arguments and we even stood with placards outside the local MP's office, but we couldn't save it.

Our beating heart of a library, where the kids came every Friday to pick up their *Beast Quest*s and Jacqueline Wilsons for the weekend, and the dementia group met on the first Tuesday of every month, and the toddlers sang 'Five Little Ducks' every Thursday.

'Mini version here, though,' Zadie says. 'That kid was so happy.'

I smile. It slips off my face when Zadie leaves and I take my phone out of the drawer.

I have seven missed calls – all from Evan – and one voicemail.

'Alice is missing,' it says. 'Call me back.'

B

My eye-roll, as I call Evan back, is mean. But bloody hell, the fact that when Alice is anywhere other than where her husband expects her to be, he reacts like *this*, tells you everything you need to know about Evan.

If Alice goes out for dinner, he eats honey nut loops and doesn't wash his bowl. At our last book club, he phoned her five minutes after she arrived to ask where the remote control was.

When he answers, I speak on an exhale: 'Evan, she's not *missing*. She dropped some spring rolls, her phone probably slipped when—'

He cuts me off. 'She left a note saying she'd be twenty minutes. It doesn't take five effing hours to replace spring rolls, Lily.'

He's whispering, and between that and the 'effing', I know the girls are close by. It's 3.40 p.m. School's done.

'Who brought the twins home?'

'Their friend's mum who's a TA at school.' He pauses. 'Give me a second.' I hear a door close. 'Lily, Alice wasn't at pick-up.'

Now there's nothing to roll my eyes about. My breath pulls in. If you meet Alice after 2 p.m., she has one side-eye on her watch. If her car crashed, she'd run to that gate and still be first in the queue. She builds in contingency; stays in a safe radius. She also has back-up options – me included – and if all of that failed, she'd call them in.

'Could she have . . . In the car . . . ?'

'We'd know about an accident by now, wouldn't we?'

He's right. It's a small island.

I look out of the window, and see a woman walk past wearing only a thong bikini and kaftan. I glance at my watch. 'Traffic? Ferry would have just got in and it is a Friday. I bet the roads are gridlocked with all the second-homers arriving.'

Even in the middle of this conversation, my belly drops at that thought. We are sparsely populated; I don't like it when more people come. Forests don't recognise you and mountains can't make eye contact. People, though. People are different.

'Maybe she left the island and got stuck coming back? Have you checked the ferries are running? Then if she lost her phone . . .'

'She wouldn't have gone to the mainland. Not with her party tonight.'

'Exactly, there's the party! Well, she'll be back in time for that.'

'But if . . .'

'She will be.'

Of course she will be. We're a safe island. Nothing is dramatic on Aurora Island, except our waves.

Over the next hour though, I check my phone regularly. I'm vague with customers, and in our tiny shop off the side of the office, I charge a man named Donald with a florid face and a belly that looks like an inflatable too much for a bottle of Viognier and a large bag of truffle crisps. He's livid and rude. I refund him the whole lot and give him a free black pudding. *Hopefully that's enough saturated fat to finish him off.*

All the time, though, I'm waiting.

Waiting for the news – inevitable, surely – that Alice has turned up with dim sum under her chin, shouting at Evan to add ABBA to the playlist and squeezing the girls tight and saying, *Sorry, I'm so sorry, I'm so sorry I wasn't at school.*

It doesn't come.

By the time I knock on Alice's door at 5.15 p.m., my heartbeat is skipping somewhere near the top of my throat. Evan answers and shakes his head.

Nothing.

He goes to hug me, then remembers: not my thing. I tap him awkwardly on the arm.

'Are the girls here?'

He shakes his head. 'They were going for a sleepover while the party was on anyway, so I just . . .'

'In that case.' I nod to his phone, clutched in his hand, and he googles the number for Aurora Island police station.

'I need to report someone missing.'

As he speaks, my brain sends the most selfish of memos. *Run away from this. This is attention. This is visibility. Run.*

'Her name is Alice Fox. She's my wife.'

Surely this isn't real anyway, though? Not on this island. Aurora is wild and feral and the air's clean and it smells of trees and horse shit and salty sea and then, briefly, of elderflowers, abundant, that we pick and turn into cordial – quaint, in tiny bottles.

We are a small crew. We have a population of less than ten thousand people, and most of them live in the same two settlements, Port St Joseph and Syford, in the same corner of the island.

The rest runs wild.

But things have changed since the retreat arrived. More second-homers have landed; house prices have rocketed. Some people are furious. How can they get on the property ladder when someone who already owns a million-pound-plus house in Surrey is paying cash for the only thing on the market in their village?

Mostly though, our core is as it always was. On Aurora, we're a team. We float, alone, and we're 10 per cent beach and 40 per cent forest. We're isolated. Vulnerable. We have a shared style

– an *Aurora look* of walking boots and waterproofs – that comes from need.

You don't end up here if you need regular hits of culture; if you need art to get you going.

You end up here if letting your dog off the lead as the sea roars in your ears or scrabbling up a cliff face as your legs turn to jelly is what makes you feel like you're living. Kids play out; sliding down sand dunes on their bums in summer and pulling siblings in sledges down barely driven-on lanes when it snows.

We're only a mile off the mainland. I love that it feels like further. I love that, at times, it can feel like I've run away to the ends of the earth.

There is the sea, half crazed.

The boggy arduousness of the woods, rudimentary tyre swings slung up between the trees. The scent of pungent cheese and onion pasties from the hundred-year-old bakery. The farm shop whose opening hours are erratic at best.

At the heart of Aurora is the green, where, on summer evenings, the local band performs rock classics. Steve is the lead singer. He has a long and grizzly grey beard and rides his motorbike in leathers around the island with his dog, Boris, in the sidecar, waving to all the kids he passes.

The nights are organised by the owners of the best of the eight pubs on the island, The Dolphin, where Steve's wife, unbearably cool New Zealander Eleri, is the manager.

'Lily?'

I jump. Look up. I am at Alice's kitchen table with a tepid milky tea sitting in front of me.

'Lily, I said that's the door,' says Evan, standing up next to me. 'They're here. Police.'

'Sorry.' I push my chair back. 'I'll go.'

He lays a hand on my arm. 'No, I should get it,' he says. 'I don't want them to think . . .' He trails off.

Oh. Yeah.

Because they *will* think. They *will* judge him. They look at the husband. Especially now, the first time they meet him, when his reaction will tell them the most.

It's not just him though, is it? Being looked at is what could topple *my own* life over like a Jenga tower, and they will look at me now too.

'Evan Fox?' asks a young, slight police officer, with a face that looks skeletal. He has a Scottish accent. 'Police Constable Campbell from Aurora Island Police.'

Evan shakes the police officer's hand briefly then steps back. I see him wipe his palm on his shorts. 'Come in. Can I get you a drink?'

Nothing bad happens here, I repeat to myself as he sits down with tea and questions. *Nothing bad happens here and no one is looking at you.*

We tell them everything we know.

He tells us he'll be in touch. My eyes dodge his. Travel instead to his armpits; to dark patches of sweat.

'You need to give me some numbers,' I say after Campbell leaves, walking into the kitchen where Evan is slumped in a chair staring out of the bifold doors at the long, narrow back garden that's been taken over by the girls' stuff. Swings and trampolines, footballs and frisbees.

He nods.

On the wall next to me is a hessian sign, a little frayed at the edges, which I've seen hung up so many times in this house.

HAPPY BIRTHDAY.

Between us, sitting silently at Alice's beloved second-hand oak kitchen table, we message everyone who was due to come to her birthday party and tell them it won't be going ahead, because Alice is missing.

The buzzing starts immediately. Calls – all ignored – and a flurry of concerned messages.

'You head home,' says Evan, after we've contacted everyone. He drums his fingers on a pile of records next to him. On top is *Waterloo* – Alice's adored ABBA – ready to be played on one of Evan's prized record players tonight even if Evan, music snob that he is, would have rolled his eyes at it. A sob seizes my throat like a hand.

'I can stay tonight?'

'I'd like everything to be as normal as it can be. You never stay over.'

At home though, I can't sleep, thoughts on loop. We should have been at your party now. We should have been singing 'Happy Birthday'. We should have been regretting that last duck spring roll, spilling out into the garden. I may have even had a glass of wine.

Alice – where the hell *are* you?

The next morning, I walk up the path towards the Foxes' indigo-blue front door after two hours' sleep. I slow. The door is open.

'Evan?'

Panic rises more quickly than it normally would, like it's been waiting, primed in my oesophagus like a big cat.

'Evan!'

But it is okay.

It's okay.

He is there, sitting at the top of the spiral staircase in the same clothes he wore yesterday. His shoulders bounce up and down and a noisy, mammalian cry comes through despite his mouth being muffled by his hands. I close the front door behind me and walk up the stairs to sit next to him. There's no point speaking.

After a while, my eyes scan upwards. When I come to Alice's house, I sit in the kitchen drinking tea; I haven't been up here since the girls were babies and I would check on them sleeping when I babysat. I've never seen it like this. A spectacle.

Wall to wall, floor to ceiling, are the contents of Evan's vinyl collection. Rows of shelves full of records that he brought home in his Aurora Records van the day the shop stopped trading. Twelve-inch albums that can career you high and plummet you low, rip your limbs off and fix you.

'Death by internet' is what Evan called the record shop's closure in the low, depressive weeks that followed, as the van was sold and the music was silenced and Alice tried to rally him.

They'd house all the records here, she told him. It was a treat. *They'd* get to be surrounded by them for a while, play songs they hadn't heard in years, enjoy music again rather than seeing it through a work lens. And then, when they found the right spot, he would start again, invigorated.

'You can open another record shop!' she told him. 'We just need to wait it out.'

When her eyes met mine, I saw it: *Tell him what he needs to hear. The reality can come later.*

But Evan knew it was a fantasy. Record stores weren't what the high street craved. Second-homers and retreat visitors with disposable income spent a fiver on a latte but recoiled at putting down the same for music. Their soundtracks came from Spotify.

'My dad would be gutted,' Evan says now, following my eyes to where the records surround us, neat and alphabetised. Evan takes them out often but they always go back in the right place. 'The only thing he looks after,' Alice once said. 'The only thing he keeps neat.'

She wasn't wrong. It's immaculate. Almost obsessive.

He stares up at the Ps. 'Thirty-three years, Dad kept that place going. And I fucked it up in two.'

I shake my head. 'Different times, Ev. Nothing you could have done.'

It's been a year and a half since Aurora Records closed. Evan does shifts at the bike shop a few days a week and spends a lot of time out on his mountain bike, but mostly I have no idea how he fills his time.

In the midst of it all, Alice – who used to be the manager at a big city park on the mainland – started a landscape gardening business. After the second-homers bought the fancier stuff with the mature gardens, next went the old buildings in beautiful spots, gardens neglected and overgrown.

Alice designed a garden for a second-homer she met at book club, that woman recommended her to a neighbour; soon Alice had a year-long waiting list.

Evan sighs. 'And now this.'

'Two separate things.'

'Both me. Swear to God, I attract chaos. Swear to God, bad things come to me.'

When I finally persuade him to move to the kitchen, all I can do is refill his coffee cup. Coffee. Coffee. Coffee.

'How about one of Alice's ginger teas?'

'Coffee.'

'Glass of water there for you.'

'Can I just get a coffee, Lily?'

I see his foot tap, tap, tap, faster and more urgent, under the table.

'That police officer called first thing,' he says, when I put another coffee down in front of him. 'Gave me his direct line to phone if we hear anything or if we remember anything.' He pauses.

'He's sure she'll turn up – they usually do – but if there's no news by tomorrow, they'll talk about doing a press conference.'

A response comes from my gut. A press conference is attention. A press conference is eyes.

'I can't do that,' I say, a panic sweeping across my body. 'I can't. I don't . . .'

'No, me,' interrupts Evan, frowning at me, curious. 'Not you. If we go ahead, they want me to do it.'

The relief is short-lived. He can seem cold, Evan, when you don't know him. Removed. A little rude. How do I tell him to watch his facial expressions, if he's going to go out in public and do a press conference?

That he should make sure he never smiles, not even if someone says something kind.

How can I tell him to watch his tone?

Always the husband.

Things feel like they can't get any worse.

Until ten seconds later, when Evan takes a phone call.

'Her name's Beccy,' Evan tells me, frowning as he hangs up.

It's only been a day since Alice disappeared.

But now, another woman has gone too.

C

Clearly, now that two women are missing, this is being treated more seriously, because when I answer Alice's front door the next day, there are two police officers standing there.

They are the requisite opposites for a duo – skinny Campbell from yesterday paired with a man with a belly similar to the retreat guest Donald's. The before and after on a WeightWatchers advert.

The bigger one holds a hand out. 'Inspector Winterbottom, Aurora Island Police.'

A more senior officer now. I think about how the girls would laugh at his name, then worry that the smile has shown on my face.

Winterbottom nods towards Campbell. 'And I believe you've already met my colleague.'

'That's right.'

Campbell is standing behind him, looking like the work experience kid now. He's scruffy: shoes scuffed and old; auburn hair in need of a good trim.

'Still here, then?' he says.

I bristle. 'Not still. Went away and came back.'

'We had an email we wanted to ask you about,' says Winterbottom then, with a cough. 'Alright if we come in?'

As they step through the doorway, they glance up the stairs at Evan, who is in shorts and bare feet, pulling on a fresh t-shirt over his pale chest as he comes down.

'Sit down,' I say, gesturing to the living room and noticing my shaking hand – I see Campbell notice it too. I glance back up at Evan, and Campbell follows my eyes, then looks between the two of us, frowning. 'I was about to make coffee if you'd like one?' I ask.

'Lovely,' says Winterbottom. 'Milk and one sugar, thanks.'

'Aye, black and two sugars for me,' says Campbell. He looks exhausted. Possibly hungover. Impressive, I think, if you've found any decent nightlife on Aurora Island.

I put two mugs – one with a garden trowel engraved on the side, and one with an array of bikes throughout history – down in front of them a couple of minutes later, along with the cafetière for a top-up.

'Oh, will you look at all this!' exclaims Winterbottom. 'Instant would have been fine.'

I touch my neck, self-conscious. *For God's sake, Lily, stop drawing attention to yourself. That's the last thing you need. What was wrong with a non-descript instant?*

'You're round here a lot then, I take it?' Campbell says, looking between Evan and me again. Evan doesn't notice but I suspect a subtext. Campbell can see how nervous I am and is wondering if that's because Evan and I are more than friends. If that's got something to do with this. If I'm more involved in this than I'm letting on. I've seen it happen in other missing women cases. I shift awkwardly.

'A normal amount,' I say, hearing my voice shake. 'It's my best friend's house.'

When I look down, I spot a tiny smudge of chocolate on the arm of the sofa. *Freya.* I fight the urge to nip to the kitchen and get a cloth to wipe it off – for Alice, because that's what she would do – but it feels like another thing I shouldn't be preoccupied with.

Look at her, fussing around with her cafetière and her cloths, when her best friend is missing.

Or worse.

Already moved in to take the wife's place.

Narratives stick.

When I look at him, Evan is staring too, but not at the stain. Instead, his eyes gaze off into the middle distance. However much I want to disappear into a wall, or run, run, run, I'm going to have to steer this.

'You said you'd had an email?' I ask, quietly.

'Yes. It mentioned Alice came into a lot of money lately.' Winterbottom raises his eyebrows in a question.

'Oh. Yes.' A notable thing that happened to Alice recently: she inherited a little more than half a million pounds. I feel stupid now, for not bringing it up on Friday.

'I wasn't trying to . . .' I say; kid in detention. 'I forgot to mention it. It was a weird day.'

Cafetière, cloths and now this.

Evan's not apologising though. 'An email from who?'

I sit down next to him and put a hand on his arm. *Steady.* Campbell looks at my fingers.

'She did, yeah,' I say, snatching my hand away. 'Her dad died and she was an only child so . . . you know. God bless the boomers.' I attempt an awkward laugh.

Winterbottom must be over sixty himself. His face reddens. Campbell suppresses a smirk.

Evan doesn't notice that either. Instead, he has drifted again, staring out of the open window. He nods to where he's facing. 'That's why we're on the move.' There's a sign for Weavers Estate Agents shoved into a flower bed packed with rows of peonies the colour of a nail bed, and extrovert sunflowers. The purplest gladioli, with their strong spears, sit either side of the narrow winding path that trickles up to Alice and Evan's front door.

It's her job, so Alice's garden is pure science. Things bloom at the right moment. Nothing's ever barren. It's not big but it's thriving; everything it could be in this space. Disney World for the bees.

Evan's still facing that way when he speaks, defeated. 'Do they think it's me then? That I did it for the money?' He puts his head in his hands.

'Evan! Of course no one thinks that, bloody hell.' I look at the officers and wait for them to agree, but they're silent.

Doesn't matter. Evan has an alibi. It was one of the first things the police asked. When Alice went missing, that six-foot-three ginger big kid was out on his bike in the woods with a whole crew from his cycling club, who were willing to clip-clop into the police station in those funny little cycling shoes to verify his story.

'They're good friends,' Evan tells the officers as they stand up. 'The alibi? The cycling guys?'

They say nothing.

'They're my mates.'

'Good to know,' says Winterbottom, but he exchanges the briefest of glances again with Campbell, who's looking perkier after his coffee.

I see them to the door. 'Where are the wee girls then?' Campbell asks. 'Twins, right?'

'They're at a friend's house.' Then it sneaks out. '*Can* you tell us who sent the email?'

'We can't, sorry,' says Winterbottom.

When they leave, I search the kitchen cupboards until I find a cloth to scrub the sofa with.

I'm out of breath by the time I sit back on my haunches on the floor and look at the chocolate stain. I've spread it out. I've not made anything better.

In fact, I've made everything worse.

Again.

The next day, I've only been at work for a couple of hours when Evan calls.

I snatch up my phone.

'The police are sending me a picture of this Beccy. See if I recognise her.' I hear the coarse rub of his beard. 'In case there's a connection.'

'Can I see it too?'

I'm more likely to recognise the face than the name. I met eighteen Williams last week. A clause built in when planning permission was granted for the Aurora retreat means that all island residents – including (and this was controversial, because why the hell did *they* need it?) the second-homers – can use the heated Olympic-sized swimming pool, gym and beach, as well as the café, within specified hours and on specific days. When the retreat's not busy.

Between the guests and the locals, then, I see a lot of faces. I'll notice the large birthmark between their eyebrows, or the trace of dark hair dye around their temples. The Botox that's gone a step too far, the wiggle of an upper lip, ears that are a little elfin.

Messy human faces; far more memorable than names. I touch my own face. Would mine spark a memory in anyone?

The retreat was controversial when it arrived, big and brash and – despite our eco boasts – positioning itself right on the edge of swathes of green belt. There were protests. It was approved anyway.

Two years later though, I think most people would say it's been good for Aurora.

Bringing those numbers of people – *rich* people – to our island has pumped cash into our community and businesses. The initial contracts handed local businesses work – if not as much as some people wanted. When it opened, islanders scrubbed the loos, played *Baywatch* at the lifeguard station, and waited tables in The Barn.

For me, it was a lifeline. Just as the soon-to-be-opened retreat was making the front page of The *Island News*, the library I worked at on Aurora was closing. I had a month's salary saved. Jobs on the island were scarce. I'd started making plans to go back to the mainland. Then the job ads went up.

'Hold on . . . picture's through,' says Evan. 'No . . . I don't recognise her. Sending to you now.'

I refresh my email, and there is Beccy.

Beccy has so many freckles that they cling to one another and cover her skin, so that they almost give her a tan. Down one side of her face ropes a long, meandering plait. It's a mucky mid-brown and has little flyaway tufts sticking out. She keeps the rest of her hair off her face with a thick mustard-coloured hairband. Her face isn't mud-splattered but looks as though it should be. She would suit a coating of mud.

Mud. I know her. Like her.

'Oh.'

'What is it?' In those three words, I can hear that Evan is clinging to this, to a connection between Beccy and Alice, as the key to getting his wife home, and I'm desperate to find it too. To get my best friend home but also, if I'm honest, to get myself out of this goldfish bowl. To get back to normal life. To hide away again. 'You know her?'

But even though I've pinned down a gut reaction to Beccy, I can't pin down who she is.

'From the retreat?' Evan pushes.

'No. Not from work.'

Then I get it.

Beccy runs a glamping site in the most rural part of the island, deep in the forest. We went there for Alice's birthday last year. Beccy homeschools her three kids. A year ago, she laughed with Alice, me and a group of other women while we sharpened our knives, opened and cleaned the scallops, shucked the oysters and cooked it all up on a fire for tea. While we chucked mighty axe after mighty axe. While we drank thick hot chocolate in the outdoor kitchen.

'Alice knows her.' I say it victoriously, like it solves the mystery of two women on one tiny island going missing, when all it does is lead to more questions. 'She runs Wild Women.'

'Wild Women?'

'Place we went for Alice's last birthday.'

They'll look at Alice and Beccy as a pair now, I presume. Try to find a link.

'We can discuss it properly tomorrow,' I say. 'I can't leave until Zadie gets here at one but that will give us plenty of time.'

We're heading to the press conference together.

There's a pause. 'I need to warn you, Lily. For tomorrow, when you get here. There are people outside the house now.'

'People?'

'And . . . drones.'

I feel my heart rate speed up.

People.

Drones.

Jesus.

After everything that's happened, how the hell have I got myself involved in this?

◆ ◆ ◆

It's Tuesday and I'm at work, Zadie's soft hand squeezing mine.

'Sorry!' she says. 'So sorry. I didn't mean to make you jump, coming in like that. Your body's probably chock-full of adrenalin too.'

She has the wisdom of a great-grandma in a rocking chair, Zadie. In reality, we just got her a Colin the Caterpillar cake for her twenty-fourth birthday, and she's so Gen Z she wears Crocs with trainer socks to the pub.

'It's fine,' I say, though she's right and I jumped out of my skin when she came in. I stand up. 'Thanks so much for covering this afternoon. I just don't want Evan going to this press conference on his own.'

She squeezes harder. 'Absolutely. It's fine. Go.'

It must be unsettling for Zadie: her boring colleague with the sensible haircut, involved in this. It's unsettling for me too. I like to be in bed at 9 p.m. with an Agatha Christie audio book. I made a vow to stay away from all drama. Now I appear to be living in an ITV six-parter starring Sarah Lancashire.

I remember what Evan said yesterday.

People . . . and drones.

'I'm sure this'll get them back, Lils,' she says.

She lets go of my hand. I want to beg her to keep hold of it. I can't imagine Evan is a natural public speaker and I'm terrified of the press conference being a car crash.

I'm terrified of the press conference, full stop.

But I'm the grown-up here, eleven years older than Zadie, so I force a smile. Lift my head.

'It'll be fine.' I put my phone into my backpack and shove my giveaway shaky hands into the pockets of my work trousers. I shrug my backpack on. 'Come on, Jake.'

I don't have a car but it's rarely a problem. I have an e-bike for when I need it, but mostly I don't stray far. Half an hour later, as Jake and I round the corner at a fast walk to Evan's house, a Land Rover flies past at the kind of speed that would soak me to the bone, if there was a puddle on the road.

I hear something that sounds like a shriek.

A drone.

My breath becomes shorter, rasping, as Jake and I walk beneath the drones. He looks up at me.

What's happening here?

'It's okay, Jake. It's okay.'

I touch the soft fur on top of his head and his ears, exposing the white and grey underneath that dark sheen. Feel myself cower and duck as the drone swoops and soars.

A bird, and I'm prey.

Then voices land behind me. People I don't recognise clutch phones and hold them towards me like offerings. They swarm around us – human wasps.

'Who are you?' one of them asks, phone in the air to film me. I bow my head, my eyes. Photos, no. And do they mean . . . ? *Messy, human faces. More memorable than names.*

'Do you know Alice? Do you think Evan is an actor?'

An actor?

What the hell?

I put a palm across my face and pull out the latch of the country gate and barge through it, before pushing it back into place. They could open it – there's no fancy electric lock, no passcode – but they must know that they would be trespassing then. On the pavement, they break no laws. *Scaredy-cats*, I think, picturing Freya and Florence chanting it. All that bravado and *you're just scaredy cats, scaredy cats.*

As I'm about to ring the doorbell, head still low and hidden, the Foxes' deep blue front door is flung open and a long, slim arm coated in ginger fuzz yanks me inside like a fairground claw machine.

The door bangs behind me and I stand, trying to slow my breathing for a minute. I bend to pull off my trainers with hands that vibrate.

'You okay?' says Evan from the darkness of the hall. 'It's a lot. Did they come at you with the conspiracy theories?'

'Yeah,' I say, a hand back on Jake now, trying to pretend I'm reassuring the dog when it's me whose nervous system is drums and shrieking and chaos. 'Yeah. It's a lot.'

We stay in the hall, instead of heading into the kitchen for a cup of tea or getting comfy on the sofa. It's like we're hunkering down in the core of the house, the hall a windowless bunker.

Then I think of something else. 'The girls . . .'

'They're not here,' says Evan. 'They haven't seen this.'

A relief. But it's only delaying things, isn't it? It's their home.

And imagine arriving home to *this*. Wrestling your rucksack and your spelling list through a gaggle of angry strangers. Taking on a mob just to twizzle your spag bol for tea, when your world's already spinning off its axis.

They're seven. Those girls still believe in the Tooth Fairy.

'They wanted to go to school, and I thought it might help? Routine? Swear to God I have no idea if that's the right call or . . .'

'But they know?' I assumed . . . Not yet.

'They know a version. *Mum's got a bit lost. We're looking for her.*' His voice cracks on the last few words.

I ask the world's stupidest question. 'How are they?'

'Very upset. Freya particularly is taking it badly. But they don't get it, not really.'

'And school are . . . ?'

'Super supportive, yeah. They're safe there, and distracted. They're with their friends and with each other.'

I nod. 'Alice always says that's the bonus of twins. All the way through school, you've got your family with you.'

He smiles, wry. 'I can remember her saying that at the first scan while I was still staring at those two embryos, thinking *holy fucking fuck it's twins.*'

Glass half full is Alice's thing.

'We have to go back out there,' I say, staring at the door and made of dread.

Evan is on the floor now, slumped against a wall, his large body crumpled like paper. He bends at odd angles, grotesque.

'You don't,' he says. 'You could wait until I leave. They'll go when I do, no point hanging around if they can't torment me. Then you can get away quietly without them hounding you.'

Every instinct tells me to follow his advice. But how can I turn my back on this? It's for *Alice.*

'I said I'd come with you to the press conference. I'm coming with you to the press conference.'

He says nothing.

'Let's run through your statement one more time. Then we're going. Together.'

When he looks up, his eyes flash gratitude and I feel something I'm not used to feeling. I feel important. My shoulders rise and my spine straightens.

'Now get up. Alice needs you.'

At the station, the police whisk Evan away for a briefing before the press conference. I fan my t-shirt away from my back, damp with sweat from the walk. It's a warm day.

'Tea machine there,' Campbell says to me, coffee stain on his shirt. He points down the corridor. 'Or canteen down that way, they'll do you a cracking bacon sarnie if you're peckish. We'll be about twenty minutes.'

I nod. Then I sit down on a blue plastic chair and close my eyes. Jake settles himself at my feet.

I haven't slept much since Alice went missing, and despite this chair being as comfortable as a flip-down on a bus, I drop into a half-sleep, weird dreams and semi-reality.

'Is it Lily?'

I jump. Blink. A man I don't know is in front of me. My body curls in on itself.

'Who are you?'

I rub the corner of one eye.

The man pulls a chair over and sits next to me in the corridor. One leg dangles over the other and I look down. His socks, between slim jeans and white trainers, are a ridiculously bright neon yellow. He reaches down to give Jake's fur a stroke but I feel it: my dog's anxiety around new people. I cuddle him in close.

'Sorry,' this man says, pulling back. 'And sorry to wake you up too. I didn't realise you were sleeping.'

'Only because I . . . I wouldn't normally sleep here but . . .' Then I look at him again. Why am I explaining? My guard goes up. 'Who are you?'

He isn't from the island, that's obvious.

His accent is broad Manchester. His trainers are too white for our mud and too leaky for our rain. I'm also pretty sure that he is wearing socks whose primary aim is to be *fashionable*. On Aurora, we don't entertain such things.

I look up at him. His dark brown beard is neat, and the way he rubs at it as he thinks reminds me of Evan. Plain-clothes police from outside the area, I guess. Brought into help.

I sit up straighter.

'Can I help you?'

'I hope so, yeah.'

When I turn to look at him again, he's watching me too closely.

'It's about Alice. And I suppose now it's also about Beccy and Corinne.'

Even as I say it, I know. Still, the words come out: 'Who's Corinne?'

He nods towards the phone in his hand. His voice takes a step back, becomes gentler. 'Just came through.'

Definitely police, then, if he's privy to that information.

'She's just gone missing.' He pauses. 'Corinne Sanchez.'

He shows me a photo.

A fist to the belly. Not my best friend this time, but someone else I know. Someone else I like. Someone else who lives on our small, un-notable island.

How to sum up Corinne? Bare legs and turned-in toes. Sand in a ballet pump. A look that was born in East London but migrated with her, no matter how impractical it is, no matter how much of a bitch that sand must be to get out of those shoes.

I love chatting to Corinne.

'Did I ever tell you about the time we lost Britney in Paris?' I remember her asking me as she worked in The Barn, that shimmer in her eyes, as 'Baby One More Time' played low in the background. She used to work as a music PR in London. Arrived on the island a couple of years ago.

I was only in the café picking up some change, but while I waited for it, I sat down. She sipped hot coffee and winced as it burned the roof of her mouth.

'Okay, so there's fifty journalists waiting for their press conference. For "Toxic", maybe? Or "I'm a Slave 4 U". One of them. Anyway. They're all waiting for Britney, they've literally come to

Paris *for Britney*, some of them from the States, one from Kuala Lumpur, but we've got no Britney.'

I stayed sitting, even though the mention of London made me nervous. Even as I watched Corinne for signs. *Can she know? Does she?*

She shrugged. 'So I did what you always do when you're a PR with a load of pissed-off journos on your hands. Took them to a club in Montmartre and got them shitfaced.'

Corinne is human. Corinne drinks her coffee before it's cooled and then winces, and she is a natural storyteller. Corinne is more than a missing woman.

But all I say is: 'Yeah. I know Corinne, a little.'

A population of less than ten thousand people. A time span of four days. And *three women* have gone missing.

'Alice. Beccy. Corinne,' he says, looking at me, and waiting. Then he says it slowly. 'You get it, right? A, B, C.'

It's the first time I meet him. And it's the first time I give them the name in my head.

Alice, Beccy, Corinne.

From then on, they are the Alphabet Women.

D

'Sorry, I forget that here . . .' His cheeks collapse. 'I forget that . . . with a population this size . . . I guess you're pretty likely to know these women.'

He tries again. 'I live in the centre of Manchester, it's typical city-anonymous . . .' And again. 'It's different on the island and I should have been more sensitive. Was . . . Is Corinne a mate of yours?'

I bristle at the past tense he tries to gloss over. Shake my head. 'No. But she brings her laptop into the café a lot. Works from the retreat, where I work.'

He nods. 'What does she do?'

I carry on. 'She hosts a podcast. I help produce it sometimes.'

I used to produce a books podcast through the library. An attempt to make some money when the cuts were coming, I suppose. Corinne knew that and asked me to help on hers – *Playlist Refresh*, aimed at people whose playlists were full of stuff from their teens or twenties, who hadn't added anything new in decades and didn't know where to start. After I helped Corinne, a few other islanders asked me to work on theirs. We don't have a big pool of podcast producers on our sleepy island, funnily enough.

I think about Corinne again.

'*Singing*,' my colleague Joy mutters every time she sees her. 'Why is that woman *always singing*?'

Singing is the sort of life-affirming activity Joy can't stand. See also: growing something in your garden; voluntarily baking a cake instead of buying the cheapest, blandest one you can find in a supermarket; going for a – words can't describe how much she hates this – bike ride, when 'you could just go in your flamin' car'.

I picture Corinne, striding across the courtyard past our office when it's two degrees outside, in bare legs and ballet pumps. I would recognise Corinne's gait anywhere: those toes turned slightly inwards; long, pin-thin legs. Her chin is up and out, huge headphones plunging her into her own musical world – her walk is a dance.

I don't think Corinne notices that people stare at her, but they stare because Corinne's a rock star. Big, bleached hair that you'd see from the other end of the street. Eyeliner thick like tagliatelle. In Hackney, no one would look twice, but this isn't a standard visual for Aurora. In Aurora, we dress for need. Thick gloves for chopping wood, and wellies to stop the sand sneaking into our socks. Leggings to tackle the hills, wetsuits to take on the sea.

Corinne, though, never dresses for need. Everything about Corinne shouts *want want want want want*.

'Luna flamin' Lovegood over there,' Joy will mumble, peering out of the window at her.

'I like Luna Lovegood?' I ventured once.

'Oh you *would*.' People not joining in her loathing of most things is one of Joy's biggest bugbears.

'A, B, C,' this police guy says quietly to himself now, pulling me out of my thoughts about Corinne. 'Be relieved your name's not Doris.'

And as he says it, the thought drops, *thud*, into my head. If there is A, B, C, will there be more letters? *All* the letters? Is that what happens next? Twenty-three more women?

And selfishly, I think about what that means for me too.

I look at the poster of Alice on the wall, the one that's being used everywhere. The picture was taken before she got the Invisalign on her teeth after her dad's money came through. When her smile was still a little crooked.

Evan must have given them the picture, and now Alice – human Alice, with a bunion on her left foot and long legs and a strong aversion to mushrooms – has been turned into a poster, stuck with Blu Tack on to the wall of the police station. Frozen.

Just a face.

If it gets to my letter, my face will be used in the same way.

I can't let that happen.

I look this man up and down, something dawning on me as I glance again at his socks.

Shit.

'You're not police, are you?'

'No!' A beat. 'Sorry, I didn't mean to laugh. I just didn't think I gave police vibes.' He sticks out a large hand. Hairy knuckles, no wedding ring.

'So how do you know all this stuff? How did you know about Corinne?'

He digs into his pocket for a wallet and flashes a card. National Union of Journalists. 'I'm Ross,' he says.

Oh God. Possibly worse. I picture the people in Evan's driveway and Ross reads my mind.

'*Investigative* journalist.' He puts his card away and his hands up, palms out in surrender. 'Freelance. No tabloid shit, promise. Long-form features and podcasts. I know all this stuff, and about

Corinne, because it comes through first on the wires – from news agencies. Via the emergency services' media alerts.'

I eyeball him and feel my shoulder muscles tense. 'Did you know I work on podcasts? Is that why you came over?'

I sound suspicious but he nods, matter-of-fact. 'Yep! It is, yeah. Could we talk?'

I don't say anything. Recoil.

The journalist guy doesn't seem to notice. 'I want to do a podcast about Alice. Well, about all of the women now, I guess. This has moved fast since I . . . Anyway. I'll host it, I'll write it, interview, but I need a producer and I could also do with having someone local on board for this, because this is so absolutely tied up with the island.'

I pull a face. 'Like true crime?'

He leans back. Puts his chin in his palm and frowns.

'That's not what I would call it, no.'

'But that's what it would be?'

'No. It's a news podcast. It's called *Gone Girls*. You know, like the book? The first series was based in Oban, looking at the case of three teenage girls who went missing up there when they were camping after their A levels.'

I raise an eyebrow. 'True crime, then.'

He ignores me. 'In real time, as news is. I've been looking for the right story for series two and this happening on this island – which is such a wild, unique place, Lily, I'm obsessed with it – is fascinating to me. And will be to listeners.'

He waits.

'I'm not an idiot,' he continues, on a sigh. 'I know how close communities work and I know you'll be wary. But this could be . . .'

The surrendering palms stare at me again.

'It's not gratuitous, I swear. It's journalism, like me writing a piece for a supplement, just in a different form. A contemporary form, that people want to consume. They aren't keen on newspapers anymore – I don't know if you'd noticed that.'

I try to remember the last time I saw someone buying a newspaper. The man – clearly a second-homer – was coming out of Waitrose, in his seventies, and wearing boat shoes, no socks, and tailored shorts on pale, bandy legs. Under his arm he had the *Sunday Telegraph*.

Good, I think. *I'm glad they're dying*. None of my memories of newspapers are tied up in anything good.

'I understand the concept of a podcast, Ross, thanks.'

'Sorry. Yeah, of course. Sorry.' He shifts awkwardly in his blue plastic chair. He's a big man – not overweight, just . . . big – and his legs are struggling for a home in the narrow corridor. 'But not news stuff, right? You've not worked on a moving news story before?'

I say nothing.

'Okay, well – tell me if I'm being patronising, Lily, but I just want to make clear what I'm doing. How this works. News podcasts are a specific ball game. It's using the medium to get the story out there, like newspapers used to do. We're not analysing this twenty years after the fact; it's not a cold case. So this is going to surprise us and keep moving and we'll be working fast. In real time. Getting new episodes edited fast and up overnight, so that people are informed and kept abreast.

'The podcast does the reporting. Tells the story of what's happening so that more people know, so that more people can – potentially – come forward with information.'

'And you couldn't do this from Manchester?'

He shakes his head. 'No. I don't think so. It's hard to get a feel for what's happening without anchoring yourself to the place.'

'Until our island's overrun.'

He raises eyebrows that need a trim. 'Well, ideally not. But there's no doubt about it – you will have people turning up, when something like this happens. Especially now there are three women. My aim is to make sure some of them are useful people. Professional. Not conspiracy theorists filming for their social media and spouting conspiracy theories and garbage.'

I think about those people in Evan's drive. *Do you think Evan's an actor?*

I want to run as fast as I can away from this man and his – whatever bloody sell he puts on it – true crime podcast. To look away from his earnest eyes, half lost under tortoiseshell glasses, eyebrows sprouting over the top like weeds.

'I'm not interested.'

He leans forward, keen as a kid.

'It could help to find Alice.' His voice softens. 'She's your best friend, right?'

Alice, Beccy and Corinne. A, B, C.

'If you're on board, it'll be done your way,' he pushes.

'Isn't that how the tabloids out gay celebrities?' I snap. '*Tell your own story.* Blackmail by stealth?' My stomach plummets with a memory.

He winces. 'Oh God! Sorry, Lily. No, I didn't mean to sound like I was doing that.'

He leans back.

'Okay, let's start again.' I feel him shift awkwardly next to me in his plastic chair. 'Tell me about Aurora. How long have you lived here?'

I say nothing. Stare at the wall. Wait for my heart rate to slow.

'How do you get over here in between ferry crossings?'

I frown at him. 'What?'

'Canoe?' he asks, and I see the creep of a smile. 'Paddleboard? Particularly impressive front crawl?'

I shrug. 'You just wait until the next one, unless you come by private plane or helicopter.' I look at his slightly stained Pulp t-shirt. 'And you don't give helicopter vibes.'

'Ouch.' He grins. 'Do people actually *do* that?'

'Some guests at the retreat, where I work.' I wince. 'We have our own landing pad. And there's an airstrip at the top of the island.'

He whistles. 'How often does it happen then? That you're cut off?'

'Couple of times a year, maybe? Storms, extreme weather. Why are we talking about this?'

But he persists. 'And is it scary? Being trapped?'

I shrug. 'Not really. We have what we need.' I don't tell him that what's scary to me isn't Aurora being isolated. What's scary is Aurora being surrounded. 'Look – are we done here?'

He sighs. 'I need a new story for my podcast and I think this is interesting.' When I turn, he holds his hands up again. *Not me, guv.* 'Awful, obviously, first and foremost, and I'm sorry about your friend. But it's an odd crime, it's a bizarre story, getting more bizarre by the day and the setting . . .' His eyes drift out of the window. 'The Oban investigation got a lot of traction from *Gone Girls*. This case could use that, I think.'

Ross rubs his glasses on his sleeve. He has one of those faces that needs glasses. Without them his eyes blink, confused, like I've woken him up at 3 a.m.

'Well, good luck with it,' I say, lips pursed. 'But I can't help.'

'I think you can.' He reaches out to touch my arm. Pulls back as he sees me flinch. 'Sorry. I just . . . I think you want to do anything to find your friend. She's a mum, right? Two little girls?'

I turn and glower at him.

Ross nods and stands up. Glances at his watch. 'Got it. But if you change your mind . . .'

He drops an old-school business card on to the chair he's just stood up from. His right jean leg has edged up and I can see his bright yellow sock again. A little bit of thick hairy leg. I would guess he's in his mid-thirties, but somehow Ross has the air of a student at a 9 a.m. lecture, still breathing last night's tequila fumes.

I look down at my own clothes. I make no effort to elevate my awful work uniform with earrings or good shoes. Instead, I accessorise with ugly flats and pulled-back hair, like I'm working at B&Q.

When I look up, Ross has one hand on the door to the room where the press conference is being held, about to show his NUJ badge and take a seat. He raises his right hand in the air as a goodbye then opens the door, shaving a couple of inches off his six-foot-plus height with a hunch.

He heads inside.

'Lily, hey.' Evan is standing in front of me and Jake a few minutes later. He bites his lip. 'Right. I'm going in now. Time to do this.'

I stand up and crane my neck; child to a full-grown adult. 'They won't let me come in. But I'll be right here. Good luck.'

And he nods and opens the same door Ross went through, to take his place at the desk and ask people for information.

The door closes behind him.

I sit back down but only for a few seconds, because suddenly I can't stay in that corridor a second longer. I fling the entrance door open, Jake following after me, and the air doesn't change, as still outside today as it is inside.

A, B, C. But while Beccy's disappearance is public knowledge now, I don't think people know about Corinne yet. Which means they're not watching for this pattern.

I lean up against the pebbledash exterior of the police station and slip my phone out of my pocket. Scroll to the letter I'm looking for.

Look at who I need to call.

Danielle is a lifeguard at the retreat's private beach and in the indoor pool. She answers on the fifth ring, when I'm about to hang up. '*Lily?*'

She's at home in bed having an afternoon nap, after a few vodka tonics at The Dolphin last night, but she answers because it's surprising for me to call her. Because it might be a work thing.

'I'm sorry,' I tell her. 'Called you by accident.'

Next, I call Donna.

Donna works in the town I live in – Port St Joseph – at the GP surgery on the reception desk, and has a pretty, round face that's framed as perfectly as a print with shiny dark ringlets.

When I call, her singsong Welsh voicemail answers. 'Hi babes, this is Donna. Leave me a message. Big hugs.' I picture her in the rugby shirt she usually wears.

I listen to it twice.

Hi babes, this is Donna. Leave me a message. Big hugs.

Then I make a snap decision and call Donna's wife, Lois.

'Lily! All okay?' She answers straight away, sounding like she's on speaker.

'All fine. Just wanted to chat to Donna. You're driving?'

'Yeah. Travelling back from a work trip, though. I'm not with Donna – sorry, Lily.'

'Where are you now?'

'Driving down our road! Home straight. Two minutes from proper coffee and getting out of this sweltering car and eating an early dinner on the decking with Donna.'

I picture her, turning past Syford's Art Interiors and Gifts shop on the bend, and into the quiet winding lane where she and Donna live in the end terrace they've been renovating for the past year. 'I was supposed to come back the other day but I had to stay for work and . . . anyway, you don't need to know my dramas.' She chuckles.

'Oh, that's lovely.' Pause. 'So you've not spoken on the way? To Donna?'

'Nope, it's a surprise that I can make it back today,' she says. 'She thinks I have to stay another night now. Dinner ingredients in my bag. Slightly concerned about the eggs going round these bends though . . .' She trails off, and when she speaks again her voice softens. 'Anyway, is this about Alice, love?'

I only know Donna and Lois through Alice, who's friends with them both. We were in a group chat for her birthday arrangements last year, which is how I have Lois's number. 'I'm so sorry, I just can't believe that . . . Have you heard anything?' she says.

Of course that's what she thinks I'm calling for. What else would it be?

'And I heard another woman's gone missing too?' she adds. 'Horrendous.'

'Yeah. Beccy.'

But like most people, she has no idea yet about Corinne.

'Has something else happened, Lily?' she prompts, when I'm quiet. I look down and make eye contact with Jake. Bury my hand in his fur.

'I just couldn't get hold of Donna, that's all. But she's probably just busy.'

'Oh yeah, don't worry.' A beat. 'Though she didn't answer when I called last night.'

Just a gentle quickening, but I feel it in my chest, as I move my hand round to Jake's ears. 'Is that unusual?'

'It is a bit.'

It's awful to hear the moment that Lois realises what I'm getting at.

'Hold on, I'm pulling into the drive now.' I picture Lois, swinging from the relief of nearing home after a trip away to a face contorted with anxiety as her slight arms turn her car into their drive.

'I'm sure I'm being . . .' I start to say, feeling a weight of guilt at causing this panic, but then I stop as I hear the engine turn off. There's no point talking now.

I wait.

A key turning in a lock. The happy but slightly resentful mew of a cat who hasn't seen its owner in a few days.

I hear Lois take the creaky stairs of their old house, and I picture the gorgeous dark wood panelling Alice has shown me pictures of and their fireplace and their sheepskin rug, and I hear Lois's breathing becoming faster.

'Donna! Donna!'

Just her breath now. Panting.

'The bed's not been slept in, Lily.'

I hear doors open and a desperation enter Lois's voice, as she shouts her wife's name over and over again.

And I hear something worse. No matter how many times she shouts, no matter how loud she is, what comes back is silence.

There is no response. Donna is gone.

E

When Evan comes out of the conference room, a police officer I've never seen before follows. She offers us a lift home.

'Thanks, but we'll walk,' Evan says. His forehead glitters with a streak of sweat. His neck is flushed the brightest of reds.

When he rips his suit jacket off, the blue shirt underneath is damp under the armpits, and all across his back.

'I know it's warm but . . .' He rubs at his temples.

'It's fine,' I say, a light hand on his arm. 'It's not too warm, we can walk. Jake will prefer it anyway.'

While Evan was still in the press conference, Lois rang off to call friends and family. To ask if they'd seen Donna. I sat down on that chair in the corridor again, staring at my phone. I didn't move until Evan appeared. I've heard nothing else from Lois.

Come on.

'Fresh air's probably a good idea anyway,' I tell Evan. And how *novel* to walk without the Aurora wind playing its usual whistle. Without it stinging our teeth and reddening our ears, after months of what's felt like an eternal winter.

'They told you about Corinne?' I ask.

'Yeah. The inspector announced it in the press conference too. What the hell is thi*s,* Lily?'

I open my mouth to tell him about Donna but change my mind. What's to tell, yet? A woman didn't answer her partner's phone call and slept in someone else's bed. There are more everyday conclusions to reach from that than a missing person.

Evan and I turn left out of the police station into the centre of Port St Joseph, both of us silent.

Outside, a guy in his twenties in a Puma vest holds his phone up and scans it round, filming the police station and then himself, talking. I don't catch what he says.

I bow my head low and hope Evan hasn't noticed. I can't read his mood and don't know that he wouldn't lose it, if the guy pointed a phone at him. If he said anything about Alice, or started spouting conspiracy theories.

I walk fast.

'How did it go, then?' I ask, when we're far enough away from the TikTok guy to talk freely.

He takes a few seconds to answer. 'D'you mind if we don't go over it? I'm exhausted. It's done.'

'Sure. Of course.'

We walk in silence.

I stop at the turn-off to the retreat. 'This is me, then.'

He nods. 'Lily, thanks for today. I appreciate it.' He hugs me, and I pat his damp back awkwardly.

I watch him as he walks away, hunched and low for a man of six foot three, hands deep in his pockets. I mirror him, heading in the other direction.

It's 4.30 p.m. now – barely worth going back to work. But I know there are things that need doing before tomorrow. Plus, the thought of going home to an empty house and having time to *think* is terrifying. I want to keep busy.

'You sent the email about the midsummer menu at The Barn?' I ask Zadie as I walk through the door, and she nods.

'Done. Hi to you, too.'

'Hi. The new yoga timetable went up?'

'Yep.'

I nod and feel her eyes on me as I tidy the shop shelves, then the books in the kids' library. Finally, I head into the back.

'Earl Grey?' I ask Zadie, sticking my head round the door.

She looks at the clock. 'Yeah, go on then.' She pauses. 'I heard about Corinne.'

She twirls her seat round and sticks her leg out to prop the door open.

I nod. What is there to say?

'How did it go then?' Zadie asks. 'The press conference?'

I think back to the journalist guy and the way he looked at me and a wave crashes in my stomach.

'They wouldn't let me go in. Spaces all needed for the journalists. But I think okay. I don't know what the reaction was . . .' I trail off.

I don't have social media but you can't really opt out, can you, when the rest of the world opts in? I avoid Zadie's eyes, in case she's seen things online that I don't want to hear about.

We drink our tea and talk about work stuff, and Zadie leaves at ten past five to pick Bobbi's son Bertie up from nursery and watch *Alphablocks* with him while they eat fish fingers, like I know they do every Tuesday.

At half past five, when I'm still there finishing work off, there's a hesitant knock on the locked reception door.

I swear under my breath.

These bloody customers: the opening hours are right there on the door. Outside of that, it's the out-of-hours number for whoever is on call. We tell them that; they just don't listen.

Still, I unlock the door and open up, ready to be polite.

'Hi, Doris.' Big grin.

Oh, for God's sake.

'Journalist guy.'

His laugh is a chuckle. 'In case you're making a joke to cover up the fact you can't remember my name, it's Ross.'

'In case you're making a joke to cover up the fact you can't remember *my* name, it's Lily. What are you doing here?'

I don't wait for him to answer.

'I'm not being on your podcast.'

'Not *on* it. Just producing it. I don't need a host, I need a producer.'

'Great. I'm sure there are plenty for hire.'

'Not that have local knowledge.' He pauses. 'Not that are as invested in this as you. Podcasts have form, Lily. Look it up. When they're done well, lots of them have helped to solve cases.'

I scoff.

'Isn't it worth a punt? To find Alice?'

I move out of the way.

On Ross's back is a rucksack that's not made for walking along coastal paths or through the dense forest that fills 40 per cent of this island. This rucksack is made for walking a little stretch of a high street between River Island and Pret, where I imagine this guy would pick up an expensive cheese and pickle baguette, a bag of crisps and a can of Coke.

'Five minutes,' I sigh.

'Not a second longer,' he says, taking the city backpack off by the sofa in reception that the guest husbands often wait on while the guest wives nip into the store to pick up the pre-supper olives and crisps and gin. 'Is here okay?'

'Sure.'

Ross turns over a non-fiction book on mindful drinking that's on the coffee table. It was a deliberate choice, made because our guests love declaring that they don't drink much anymore (the recycling bins paint a different picture, but we humour them).

Before I sit, I look down and see, over the rim of his tortoiseshell glasses, a glimpse of very long dark eyelashes. Jake – who comes to work with me every day – follows and stations himself at my feet.

'Go on then,' I say, pulling out a stool across from Ross and sitting down. My palm goes to Jake's ears, instinctive. 'If you're so sure your podcast can solve this, what's your theory?'

'I don't have a theory.'

More of my vertebrae slouch.

'That's what I want to avoid,' he continues. 'Two plus two equals seven, and the next minute, someone's been lynched online and their life ruined. You've seen it happen.'

I nod. This has been my worry for Evan.

'I'm not interested in sensationalism or trying to make news where there isn't any. I want interviews and facts. I want the listening figures of a true crime podcast but backed up with proper journalism.'

He ignores my silence and carries on. 'We'd interview people who are relevant, who have insight, who are *local*, a lot of the time, then collect everything together in one place. Report the latest developments. Spread the story far and wide. Someone has to know something. That makes your odds of finding them much better.'

'I wouldn't *speak* on it.' I recoil.

He shakes his head. 'No, I wouldn't expect you to.' He frowns at me and says slowly, 'Jesus, you make this . . . Look, I don't need a host or a writer. I'm a journo, I can do that part. What I need is someone to edit and upload it and sort the sound out and stop it being tinny and make it, you know . . . slick.'

'Anything else?'

'Sort of . . . project-manage it, I guess?'

'But I don't work for you.'

'You could. Freelance contributor contract. We can sort that out quickly.' He eyeballs me. 'Look, in short, I need a producer. *You're* a producer. Eleri in the pub told me you're good but she also said that you'll never say you're good – in fact you'll probably tell me that you're awful.'

I raise an eyebrow. 'Oh, you know *Eleri* now.'

'Cool chick.'

I stare at him. 'You've made podcasts before. You must know producers.'

He shrugs. 'Sure. But like I say, local will make a huge difference on this.' He pauses. 'And when I say project-manage . . . I could do with someone who can tell me who would be useful to speak to. Places it might be good for me to head to. Someone who can help me make sure the geography works, that we're painting a proper picture of what it's like living here. So that the podcast feels authentic.'

'What do I get out of that?'

He nods, like he was waiting for that question. 'I'm sourcing advertisers. I want some of them to be local too actually, to give back to this community. But I'm expecting big numbers. It's a proper operation, Lily. We'd sort a day rate you're happy with.'

He sighs.

'I guess also a feeling that you've helped to find your best friend and these other women?' he says. 'That there's something you can do when maybe you – like everyone on the island – feel a bit redundant.'

'Mm-hmm.' I look at him closely. Everything in me is screaming at me to walk away. But I could do this. I could do a good job of it. And it could help to find Alice.

I picture the twins.

'Tea?' I ask him, eventually.

He looks at me, confused, but recalibrates quickly. 'Never not amenable to a brew.'

I stand up.

'I have it very milky,' I tell him as I walk to the kitchen. 'Say now if you hate that.'

'You're my tea twin, Lily!' He's a puppy. 'Exactly like that, please.'

I come back a few minutes later with two cups of childlike tea and a Tupperware box full of cinnamon cookies I baked yesterday.

It was a ridiculous thing to do when my friend had just gone missing and there was a red velvet drip cake that could feed twenty-five people baked and uneaten in my kitchen. But I couldn't eat Alice's birthday cake without Alice, and my hands had twitched to bake.

'You know there's confirmation that Donna is gone,' he says, through a mouthful of cookie. 'Wow, are they cinnamon? They're incredible.'

I nod. Earlier, I had a message from Lois confirming that she had been in touch with everyone she could think of and no one had seen Donna. Her phone is still going straight to voicemail. The police have been informed.

'A, B, C, D missing,' mutters Ross. 'What a USP. There's such *planning* to it.'

He thinks.

'What bothers me most is what that means. You don't start this unless you're planning to go all the way to Z. And though I hope to God it's not the case, if these women *are* being killed, then A to Z would be one of the biggest mass—'

'Can you stop, Ross?'

Can you stop so I don't have to think about it? Alice, dead. Alice, murdered.

And all of us, so many people I know, lined up to be next.

'Let's help catch whoever is doing this,' he says quietly. 'Let's make this podcast massive. Let's make it so that enough people listen to it that *someone* has to know something.'

But massive means visible, a word that is anathema to me. If it gets Alice back though . . . I picture Florence, Freya. *Mummy's got a bit lost.*

I try to breathe. 'But I'll be in the background? Never mentioned on the podcast? I'd never speak or contribute.'

He frowns at me. 'Sure. Course. If that's what you want.'

I nod.

Okay. Okay, perhaps if that's the case I can do this.

'Amazing. Let's stop that A to Z happening then.'

I put myself in the picture too. Think about how long until my letter. It seems there is someone on this island who plans to take – and likely harm – *twenty-six women.*

'Twenty-two of them can be saved,' Ross says now, interrupting my thoughts. 'Twenty-two of them haven't gone anywhere.' He's watching me closely. 'You can help those women too, Lily.'

At what cost to me though? At what cost to this life, this small life, that I've worked so hard to build?

But this is vastly bigger than me. Twenty-six women – but more than that, so much more than that really. Twenty-six worlds. Twenty-six whole, sprawling lives. This will spread its tentacles across our whole island.

There is a feeling in the air on Aurora since this began, a waiting. A ticking clock. People walk a little too fast back to their cars. They glance, wary, over their shoulders.

The trees are arched, ready. Even the air got the memo – the shrill whistle of the wind that was our soundtrack until last week has stilled, as though it's trying to listen carefully; keep its ear to the ground.

It's hard to do that now, though. Aurora is getting busier. The social media sleuths I saw in Evan's drive and outside the press conference. News crews. I've even heard second-homers talking about renting out their places to journalists: a lot of them don't want to be here at the moment anyway.

'Where are *you* staying?' I ask Ross now.

'Someone's outbuilding.' He grins. 'Bit too near to their beehive though. My dreams buzz.'

He comes close to me, pretending to be a bee, and I recoil.

'Sorry,' he says, but I don't reply. 'Oh God. I'm sorry.'

But it's too late. I am shaking, tremoring at the sudden realisation that I am scared and that women are going missing on this island and that right now I am alone with a man I don't know and nobody knows I am here. I live alone. No one will check if I get home. No one will wait up. No one will care.

What the hell am I doing?

'You need to leave,' I tell him, adrenalin pumping. 'You need to . . . It's . . . Look, I'm not interested in producing your podcast. This was a mistake. Alice is my friend, and I don't even know who you *are*.'

'What?' He looks baffled. 'But I—'

'Leave, please. Now.'

I slam the reception door behind him. And I wait until I hear his car engine turn on before I start to cry.

The next day, Zadie sticks her head into the back office as I'm making tea.

'Earl Grey?' I ask through a yawn.

She nods and peers at me closely. 'Should you be here?' she asks, one grubby Converse up against the door like she's bracing.

She watches me as I look out of the window towards the lake. Next to it, the lawn has been mowed short again, despite Zadie's pleas to let it grow and help the bees.

But the guests don't want to see overgrown things. At Aurora Island Eco Wellness Retreat, flowers never wither and plants never die and lawns never grow and every building is a wooden structure that looks like it sprang up with the trees.

The guests do their bit. Most look like they've been buffed and polished like spoons.

'I still think you should be off work.'

I sigh. 'Alice isn't my wife. There's no compassionate leave for mates.'

'But—'

'You need to get those changed,' I say, glancing at her Converse as the kettle boils. 'Richard'll fume.'

'Is he due in today?'

'Richard has eyes everywhere.'

I top up half of my mug with milk. Stir both of our drinks.

Zadie laughs and slips her Converse off, pulling chunky loafers out of a bag. I take out the teabags. 'Chill, dude, they were only for the walk. Thank you.' She takes her drink from me, and I follow her out to the front desk.

'Right. Let's get this Ukrainian afternoon tea sorted,' she mutters to herself, turning on her computer.

I look up, surprised, as my own computer springs to life. 'Richard went for the Ukrainian afternoon tea?'

She looks sheepish. 'Hoping for final confirmation soon.'

'Zadie . . .' But I haven't got the energy to tell her off for ploughing ahead with projects that Richard hasn't signed off on. Not when my head is full of Alice, Alice, Alice. The Alphabet Women. Alice.

'Hey, I've only just realised it's a Wednesday. Have you swapped shifts with Joy?'

'Kid's got chickenpox. Said her babysitter's had it but is too scared to leave the house because of the missing women, and that her four-year-old's ruined her life.'

'I've never known such a natural mother.'

Even our usual Joy-laughs are lukewarm though. We're both facing forward at our parallel screens but I can tell that Zadie is looking at me. 'God, it's a lot to have gone through, dude. Press conference and being with Evan yesterday and the news about Donna and then *bang*, straight back to organising Hugo Von-Twatface's dry cleaning.'

'I didn't know Hugo Von-Twatface was visiting this week.'

'He's here with his wife, Clementine Jones-Twatface.'

But our enthusiasm for mocking rich people has taken a hit too.

'I tell you what I've got for you,' she says, rummaging in her bag. 'A Marian Keyes. Bobbi told me to give it to you. Said Marian is the only thing that can make her switch off at the moment. I think she's spinning out, realising she's a B and that puts her in the clear but wondering why. How she swerved it. Then everyone who comes into the surgery wants to speak to her about it too. It's a lot.' Zadie hands the book over. 'You head back there with this and I'll come and get you in a bit, k? We're not busy.'

I try to resist but she puts the book in my hand and steers me to the cosier chair in the back office. 'Come out when you're ready. Bobbi says to tell you to enjoy the sexy Joey Armstrong bits.' Then she grimaces. 'Don't enjoy them too much, though. We are at work.'

As Zadie heads back to her desk, she shouts through: 'No rush! At the moment we have zero actual tea for the afternoon, er, *tea*, so consider me occupied.'

'Let me know when you need cakes,' I shout back. '*If* you get sign-off.'

She sighs. 'Still offering to bake, when this shitshow is going on. You're a good person, Lily.'

But I don't know what else to do.

A thought creeps in. *I could do the podcast.*

I sip my tea and rest my eyes. The book falls closed.

'When even Marian can't do it, you're done for,' I say to Zadie, coming out to the front desk and putting the book next to her three minutes later. 'My eyes keep closing.'

She hands the book back to me. 'Keep it. Give it another go at home later.' Her computer pings and she wiggles her mouse. 'Yes! Got the tea.'

I sit down in my office chair. 'Do you need to go and pick it up?'

Zadie looks at the clock. 'I can go later. If you want more time . . .'

'Go. I need to work.'

'Well, I *could* do with collecting this soon.' She gestures at the computer.

'Get your tea.' I smile at her, trying my best to look okay.

I watch the back of Zadie's head as she bounces out to the shared company car we use for errands like this, black slacks trailing on the floor and that long, young happy ponytail.

When she's gone, the smile melts off my face. It's exhausting, pretending not to fall apart. I've got better over the years at not focusing on what I can't change in the past. At thinking instead about what I can learn from it. About moving forward. *Yada.*

But since Alice disappeared, I've been consumed by the sort of thoughts that used to drive me to the depths. What I *could* have done, what I *should* have done, to make sure that Alice was still here with her girls.

Not now.

I can't cry now.

Not when a guest could come in any second and complain about the temperature of the champagne we put in the rowing boats.

The phone on the front desk rings.

'Hello there, yes. Just the breakfast, please, from Tomas. In our cabin. We'll take two of the eggs Benedict, each with a side of sausage.' This man speaks to someone at his end before I've had chance to say anything. 'Terrible business this, with the women going missing, isn't it? Did you know any of them?' He doesn't wait for a response as he talks to someone in the background. 'Sorry, make that two sausages.'

Even when hell's landed, rich people still need sausages.

'No, I don't know them,' I lie. 'Can I book anything else for you? We have some spaces for breathwork tomorrow. I know your wife's attended on previous stays, Mr Delaney.'

After breakfast – which can be cooked for guests in their cabins or taken in The Barn (everything sourced locally barring the olives, and let's not mention that salmon) – guests can do breathwork and cold water therapy in the lake.

There are more comfortable alternatives. Inside the wellness centre, for example, there is a heated pool for those who don't fancy the retreat lake or the sea. There aren't many of those people though. Mostly the indoor pool is for the kids with indents from their goggles around their eyes, arms across their bright yellow woggles as they kick their little legs, determined.

'Yes, Pamela has confirmed that she will come along for the breathwork. Can she book hatha for Friday too?' Under his breath he mumbles, 'Don't mind me . . . just the secretary here.'

On the dot of 5 p.m., Zadie nudges the reception door open with her elbows.

I jump up from my desk and walk over. Take some of the boxes of tea from her.

'Are you leaving now?' I ask her when we've put it all away in the office.

She shakes her head. 'No, I need to do a few things.'

'Then lock the door behind me and *do not* answer it unless it's someone you know,' I tell her, as I pack up my rucksack to head home. I think about Ross turning up when I was here last night. 'We should always do that now, if we're here alone.'

'Got it.'

She follows me to the door with the keys.

Sleep's patchy again that night, and when I wake from a nightmare about Alice falling down a trapdoor at 5 a.m., I check my phone and see an email in my work account from Ross, sent at midnight.

I think this podcast can help to find the women, it reads. *I think you can help to find Alice.*

Manipulative bastard.

But I don't go back to sleep.

I'm going to work early, I type back eventually. *If you get this in time, meet me there at 7am. PS I've told my colleague you'll be there. And we have CCTV. And a dog.*

At 5.30 a.m., he confirms.

When Ross turns up at the office at 7.15 a.m., holding his car keys, his phone and a paper bag oozing grease, I usher him in, Jake wandering behind me.

He smirks. 'CCTV and a dog? What was that about?'

'You're a man who's arrived on our island just as women have started going missing,' I say, eyes on him. 'I'd be stupid not to be careful.'

Ross bends down to stroke Jake's ears but my dog pulls back. Jake's friendly but I can always feel a hint of anxiety in him around a new face. 'Fair enough, Lily. Fair enough.'

I glance at the clock. We have until eight, when one of the Hugos will likely be up in his boat shoes and glasses for some eggs to poach for breakfast.

'Shall we talk then?'

But Ross's phone beeps and he takes it out of his pocket.

'Shit.'

'What?'

'E for Ellie,' he says.

My face contracts. Another one? *No.*

He keeps reading.

'She disappeared from the other side of the island last night.'

The other side of the island. Where they are no major settlements, only little hamlets speckled around. Farms and woodland, wild and free. On the other side of the island, where a branch of Waitrose would seem nothing short of ridiculous.

'How do you know this?'

'The wires again,' he answers, still reading. 'Breaking news. Ellie is . . . let's see . . . not much info but she's from the mainland, has a holiday home here.' He carries on reading his phone. 'Had just arrived for a couple of weeks.'

'And now she's gone.'

A, B, C, D, E.

Jesus.

Five women feels like some sort of tipping point.

And suddenly, I can believe it.

I can believe that this won't end here; that they will keep disappearing and disappearing and disappearing.

Alice Fox missed school pick-up and her own birthday party; my friend who's as dependable as Christmas. And now, four more women, absent from their lives.

I feel like I've been winded.

There are twenty-one letters still to go.

'You really believe this podcast could help?' I ask quietly. 'You think it could stop other women disappearing? You think it could bring Alice back?'

'I whole-heartedly believe that, Lily, yeah.'

I nod.

Okay.

Whatever it means for me, then, and however much I think this decision could destroy my life, it no longer feels like a choice.

Okay.

Okay.

I tell Ross I'm in.

F

'People *know* the alphabet pattern now, that's what's getting me about this one,' Ross says, throwing his body weight backwards into the give of the reception sofa. 'They know. So how could this happen?'

Ross rubs hard at his forehead, as though it's stained. Another one who struggles with a *shoulda woulda coulda* then. The weediest of thoughts, ranging and ravaging.

'What's Ellie's surname?'

He looks up at me, and I can tell he's forgotten again that, on this island, a lot of people know each other. That, despite the space on Aurora, the population is small. We're a tight community.

He says it nervously. 'Halliday?'

I shake my head and walk to my desk, taking my notebook out of my desk drawer. Jake trails behind me, before going back over to the new guy for a sniff.

'Ellie's a bit older than the others,' says Ross, then his eyes flash to my dog. 'Hey Jake.' Jake stares back at him. 'We'll be friends soon, promise. I grow on people. People, and dogs.'

'How old is she?' I ask, sitting down next to him on the sofa.

'Early fifties. Single and apparently loaded. Proper big bucks. Took early retirement, according to the woman I spoke to in the bakery who used to live over that way. Cracking cheese and onion pasties from there, by the way. Let me in early while they were putting the food out.' He wipes a tiny flake from his chin and crumples up the bag.

'It's not even eight a.m.'

'Might go for the meat and potato for lunch, if you fancy?'

I shake my head and my heart rate rises slightly at the idea. I have my lunch packed. I've brought my lunch in every day I've worked here. The idea of a spontaneous pasty makes me feel like a rowing boat wobbling off without oars.

Ross throws the bag at the bin.

'We recycle paper here,' I tell him, prim. My body is still tense around him. My mouth purses, my jaw sets. After what happened to me, it's in-built: do not trust journalists.

'With that much grease on?'

But he's looking down at the laptop that's perched on top of his jeans. The Word document only says a few words. *Ellie Halliday, 53.* Still, next to him on the sofa, I stare at it like it contains the answers.

'I've got a source who says she was out alone,' he muses. 'Why would you do that, now?'

'Because you didn't want someone to chaperone you, probably.' I sound defensive. 'Does it matter? Better to focus on what we can control.'

Otherwise *shoulda woulda coulda* will wind and twist us until all we are is a knot.

'Hello?'

I jump.

Zadie looks at Ross then at me and raises an eyebrow.

'This is Ross,' I tell her quickly. 'He's a journalist.' No point hiding it. 'He's working on a podcast to do with the Alphabet Women.' She, like everyone on the island, now knows the term. Knows the pattern. 'I'm producing it.'

'Like you did with Corinne's?' Zadie frowns.

'Exactly,' I say. 'I'll edit it. Bring it all together to get it on air.'

Zadie nods.

'Suggest useful people to interview, too. Local knowledge is helpful for this one.'

Zadie looks at Ross. 'What's left for *you* to do then?'

'Fair question. Well, I write the scripts and I record it. I'm the host but I also do the research, write the copy. I'm the journalist.'

My body, involuntary, contracts at the word.

Zadie glances at me, then turns to Ross. 'I'm Zadie, by the way. Since Rude Face McRudeness here doesn't seem be introducing me. Sorry if I've interrupted your podcasting.' She looks between us. 'I couldn't sleep, 'cause I'd lost my phone. I wanted to check if it's . . .'

'It's in the back. I was going to message Bobbi but I don't have her number.'

Zadie nods and goes to get it, emerging a few minutes later clutching her phone. 'Crisis averted.' She leans down to pet Jake, who gives her a strong tail wag in return. 'Morning, Jakester.'

I nod down at my dog. 'Even he's confused to see you before nine a.m.' Loathing early mornings is one of Zadie's only concessions to being her actual age.

Ross stands up. 'Am I okay to stick the kettle on?' He turns to Zadie. 'Coffee?'

'Tea, please. It's the Earl Grey next to the kettle,' she says.

Ross raises an eyebrow.

'Yep,' I nod. 'And she's twenty-four.'

She flicks my forehead.

As he walks to the kitchen, Zadie sits down next to me but doesn't take her eyes off Ross.

'Is this okay? Being alone here with this guy when . . . ? Jesus, dude, with everything that's going on. We don't know that more women aren't . . .'

'They have already,' I tell her. 'A woman named Ellie Halliday.'

'*Another one?*'

'Another one.'

'Drinks.' It's a couple of minutes later and Ross is putting three steaming mugs down on the low coffee table, next to the book about not drinking and the book about valuing experiences over possessions. 'You don't have milk in Earl Grey, right?'

'Some heathens do,' says Zadie, with a sniff. 'I am not one of them.'

On the sofa in reception, Zadie leans forward and stares at the images of the five women that Ross has collated on his laptop and then she turns to me, pale.

'This alphabet thing is so dark. And what if it keeps going until . . . ?'

'It won't,' says Ross, in a sure tone. 'That's why we're doing this.'

Sometimes when I look at Zadie, she is so wise, such a force. Other times she's my kid sister on the playground who should have her legs in the air doing a handstand. Now, I feel a fierce need to protect that little sister.

'Why don't you leave this?' I sigh. 'You have enough on, and bloody hell, *I* only got tied up in this because Alice is my friend. It's not your—'

'I want to help.'

'You always want to help.' I smile. 'That's your biggest problem.'

Ross grins. 'Sounds like a good problem. I've got a living room back in Manchester needs painting?'

If you go for cake with Zadie, she has one eye over your shoulder so she can corner the manager and ask if they have jobs for refugees. She is the reason that fifteen dementia patients get together here once for a month for a memory café. Why kids do after-school mindfulness on the carpet every Friday, and it's without charge for anyone who's entitled to free school meals. All of this in between one (badly paid) job and what feels like endless babysitting for Bobbi's son Bertie, while his mum works long hours at the surgery.

I don't mind, dude, is her mantra. *I really don't mind!*

'They're all so pretty,' Zadie sighs, staring at the women. Then she looks guilty. 'I know that's not what it's about. I know it doesn't matter. But they are.' She touches Donna's face lightly.

Donna, with her curls.

'That's another reason the press are having such a field day with this, since they've cottoned on to the story,' Ross says gently. 'Have you seen the front pages today? Even before they knew about Ellie . . . Beautiful women still sell papers. They can't do Page Three anymore but it counts as news if they've been . . .' He sees me wince and trails off. 'Mate, I'm sorry. I didn't—'

'It's fine. Let's just get on.'

But I know what nearly slipped out. The possibility that the women, including my best friend, have been murdered.

'What sort of journalism do you do?' says Zadie, and at first I think she's just trying to change the subject, but then I see her face. Pinched. She's investigating him.

'Well . . . I've sort of pivoted, Zadie, is the answer. I trained as a news reporter – court reports, shorthand, door knocks, old-school stuff – but the truth is, it was dying out even as I was training.'

Zadie looks blank.

'Sorry, yeah, another world. Gen Z wouldn't recognise this weird thing we used to make called a newspaper.'

She doesn't laugh.

'The industry's changed a fuckload the past decade and work's been thin on the ground, especially out of London. So the last couple of years or so I've been trying something new. You listen to podcasts?'

She nods and he nods back.

'Yeah. Me too. So when the company that owns the news site I worked on launched a podcast division, I begged to head it up. Not that many people were interested at the time and we were slow starting. For ages, I was still writing because I couldn't justify the podcasts being a full-time job, but then the numbers started growing.'

'What happened then?'

He chuckles. 'I left and went freelance. I was getting frustrated with the stuff they wanted me to cover. It was stale. Done. Cold cases, stories that were decades old. But what it did give me was some experience, some knowledge, at a time when not many people had it.

'So I left and started my own podcast, called *Gone Girls*. The idea is that we work in real time, like the news does. There's not much else out there like it. I went up to Oban on a punt when these teenage girls went missing and applied a proper journo eye to it, I suppose. Investigated. Did it well. People got on board and it went great guns.'

'Then you decided to come here?'

He nods. 'Yeah. I've been searching for a while for a subject for series two and I saw the news about Alice. I thought the island setting and the fancy retreat and second-homer scene was interesting, but then . . . well, since then it's obviously spiralled. Now I'm not the only one here.'

They are springing up even more now. The TikTok crew filming Aurora on their phones. The journalists asking for quotes from local shopkeepers. When I see any of them, I flee. It's too risky for me. Too likely that one of them will frown at me and point.

Hey, I know you. You're her!

Yesterday, I went to the farm shop to buy bread flour on my lunch break and Beryl, the farmer's wife, was sending a reporter on his way. She looked close to tears.

'It's a nightmare, isn't it?' another woman at the counter said to me – a second-homer, surely, in a floral maxi and expensive perfume.

Alice, Beccy, Corinne, Donna, Ellie.

'Let me play you episode one,' says Ross now, and he clicks into an app called Podbean on his laptop. 'Remember this one is just me, one man band, so . . . yeah, it'll be better when I have you working on it, but this gives you an idea. It's just gone live. I have a name for this season now too.'

He hits play.

'Welcome everyone, to a new season of our podcast, *Gone Girls. This season our subject is the Alphabet Women of Aurora Island.*' He pauses. 'Lately, Aurora has hit the headlines. Lately, on Aurora, women have been going missing.'

Some tinkly, ominous music kicks in, ten seconds or so, before Ross is back.

'This story is ongoing and very fast-moving. We'll be giving you the facts, and an inside view of how it feels to be here, in this strangest of summers on Aurora Island. We will speak to experts, and we will speak to local people. People who know the women.

'We hope we can prove that crime podcasts can be informed, rigorously fact-checked and insightful. This will never be about something salacious or about feeding on misery. Rather, it will be about remembering that the people in a news story – the victims and those left behind – are human. It will be about journalism. It will always, *always* be about truth.

'We hope that we can play some part in getting this story out there and figuring out what is happening to these women. And we hope we can play some part in getting them home.

'I am on Aurora Island now. It's a quiet place. Beautiful. Very peaceful, even with what's been happening. To my eye, it looks normal, but the locals I've spoken to have told me that there is a different feeling here now.

'One thing that is clearly new is these signs I've seen being attached to gates today warning women not to walk alone. For an island like Aurora, where the lifestyle is so outdoorsy and so safe, this is hard to get your head around.

'Our guest today knows all about this. Melanie Ingram-Brown usually hikes solo, but you've posted on socials to find other women to walk with – is that right, Melanie?'

'Yes,' says Melanie, sounding hesitant. 'I've walked up every track on this island hundreds of times – I've lived here all my life – but scrambling to a summit on my own isn't something I would do from now on. If I spotted a man, I would feel . . . well. I would feel scared.' She clears her throat. 'We live here for the walks. We live here for the summits. We live here *for* the solitude.'

As I listen to Melanie speak, my eyes fill. That solitude. Going down to the beach and staring at something that doesn't end. Not seeing another person for hours and hours. That's why *I'm* here.

'One thing I've been wondering about is the *point* of the letters,' mulls podcast-Ross a few minutes later, after the emotive interview with Melanie comes to a close. 'I mean, a gimmick, sure, but why bother? What's the *meaning*? There has to be a *meaning*, surely.'

On the stool in real life now, Ross crosses his long legs at the knee and tries to make his stocky body smaller, and we huddle in together, Zadie and I on the sofa, towards the coffee table, the *Interior Decorating Like the Scandinavians* book shoved aside, and I remind myself, as I feel his breath and hear him clear his throat – as he is that close – and I listen to his gentle voice on the podcast: *Don't trust him.*

Do the work if it can help find Alice, but don't forget not to trust him – a journalist, a man, who arrived just as women started to go missing.

When the episode finishes, Ross leans towards his laptop. 'And now, we get going on episode two,' he says. 'Just checking the wires.'

Zadie looks at me, a question, and I explain what he means. How he's getting his updates from news agencies, so that he knows about breaking news in this story before the rest of us.

I pull my knees up and sit cross-legged on the sofa, watching his face.

He looks up. 'Nothing.'

The room exhales.

'Come back at five, when we close?' I say to Ross as he's leaving half an hour later. 'We could pick up then.' I look at Zadie and feel as though I need to explain. 'I just want to help get Alice back.'

Zadie eyes Ross. She's wary, but nods. 'I'll stay too, then.'

At 5.15 p.m., Ross arrives at the office. Jake yaps, loudly.

'He's warming to you,' I say as I lock the door behind him.

Ross reaches down and scritches his ears. 'Quicker than most, Jake.'

'It's so nice out there,' I say, to Zadie and Ross. 'Can we talk while we walk round the lake?'

We head out.

'Wow,' says Ross, looking around the retreat. 'This place.'

'Sadly, we're barely allowed to enjoy it,' grumbles Zadie. 'Never escape the office.'

We walk past The Barn, a Jack Johnson song trickling out at the part of the day where it turns into evening. Opposite us are the cabins, quiet but likely to get louder later as the evening sessions kick in, especially in the warm weather. The large groups who have come away together will be outside on the terraces, aperitifs poured before dinner.

'Why Aurora, then?' asks Ross, hands in pockets like a teenager. 'This is what I keep coming back to. *Why Aurora?* You're not a city. You don't have any notable tensions in the community, do you?'

I shake my head.

'Why do you two think it's happening here?' Ross asks.

I say nothing but Zadie speaks straight away. 'I've wondered if it's pure opportunity, you know. You couldn't *do* this anywhere that was well populated, could you? Not to this many women. You'd be caught quickly. But so much of this island is uninhabited.'

And it's true. We're one of the most sparsely populated islands in the UK. Fifty miles long, with acres and acres of wild land and space. Our biggest settlements cluster together just off the east coast, but the rest is as rural as it gets. Only farms over that way, really. The odd second-homer mansion.

I'm thinking about something else too though. About that word Ross has just used – *tensions*. About the protests that happened when the retreat opened. The *us* and *them* feeling when you saw second-homers parked in Range Rovers on double yellows outside Waitrose, while residents lugged their babies in a car seat from a second-hand Volvo at the other end of Port St Joseph.

'We have a lot of woodland,' says Zadie, sounding thoughtful. 'There are a lot of places to hide on Aurora.'

Still, though. Those newcomers.

'That's one tasteful kids' play area,' mutters Ross as we come to the slides and swings designed to blend into their natural surroundings.

'No rusting roundabouts for this place,' says Zadie, a little resentment creeping in. 'So annoying I can't bring Bertie.'

'Even though you work here?' says Ross.

'Us and them, my friend. Us and them.'

'The locals do cross the boundary sometimes though,' I tell Ross. 'But the rules are very specific. And kids and play areas aren't on the approved list.'

'What is?'

I tick them off on my fingers. 'Pool, café and gym, but only on certain days and times and far less of them than there could be. I think our boss Richard gets off on the power.'

'Is it okay I'm here now?' asks Ross, with an automatic glance around.

'Not really. But Richard leaves at four on Thursdays and he lives in the middle of nowhere on the other side of the island – he would never come back in the evening.'

'In that case, shall we do another lap and keep talking?' says Ross, standing still and putting his hands on his hips as he looks up. 'This is nearly as beautiful as Lake Maddock.'

'Someone's getting to know the island.'

'No second lap for me, I have to go,' says Zadie, a glance at her wrist as her watch lights up. 'I need to pick Bertie up from nursery.'

'Be careful,' I tell her.

'I could take you . . .' But Ross sees Zadie's expression.

'You're alright. Thanks, *Dad*.'

Ross flushes pink.

'Call me when you get home, Lily,' she says, eyes on Ross again.

We walk round the back of The Barn, and hear the buzz and the elevated voices that come from apéro hour in the sunshine with the restaurant's signature margaritas.

'I've heard online that they're all connected,' crows a regular Zadie and I refer to as Bracey McBrace Face. He comes to the retreat once a year and never realises that wearing red braces when you have an extraordinarily large belly is unflattering. 'All friends. All got a few secrets as well. Truth comes out in the wash.'

Ross looks at me and rolls his eyes. 'Ignore it. You always get those people.'

Then he opens up a voice notes app on his phone and starts talking into it.

'Episode two of *Gone Girls: The Alphabet Women of Aurora Island*, with Lily producing,' he says.

My stomach plunges off a diving board.

Episode one – the one Zadie and I just listened to – went live today, and from the look of the hosting site stats that Ross just showed us, it's doing well. But Ross is ambitious. He wants this to be huge, listened to in cars and on runs and in kitchens across the country.

'Interview with Zoe, who runs the coastal walk group,' he says into his phone. 'She covers the terrain of the island and possibilities for how people could leave it, or if they *haven't* left it, where are the most hidden parts of the island and the most sprawling. She knows the landscape well.'

'Oh, I didn't know you were doing that,' I interrupt. He stops recording. 'When did you do that interview?'

'Last night. She was super interesting.'

We sit down on a bench and brainstorm guests we want to have on in future episodes and what else we want to cover on episode two, and who we can contact about advertising – I suggest Moo ice cream and a few other local businesses – and it's only when I realise that my contact lenses are as dry as Weetabix and it's dark around me that I look at my watch.

'Bloody hell, Ross, it's after nine o'clock.'

He looks up. 'Sorry, mate. Didn't realise I'd kept you so long.'

'It's not that, it's . . .'

I'm mortified to say it. I try to stop the flush that is slapping paint across my face. Life as a blusher is like handing over your diary to everyone, all the time. *Here you go: please know exactly what embarrasses me, what I'm lying about and who makes me cross.* All of it. Just via two cheeks.

I mumble all of the words together. 'It's just that it's down the . . .'

The road to the centre of town from the retreat is long and winding, and cars go fast. When you get there, my little cottage, The Nook, is away from the green and on a tiny lane. A very quiet, tiny lane.

The only other route is along the coastal path, which I take sometimes but won't be taking tonight. Won't be taking anytime soon. That route is even more isolated.

There it is: the light bulb moment.

'Oh mate, sorry. I get it. You're worried about getting back.'

'Not normally, just with . . .'

'Yep. Yep.' He's nodding too much. 'Of course. Sorry, I was being slow. Typical man, not having to think about this shit.' He breathes. 'I've got the car though, I can give you and Jake a lift.'

But at that moment, his phone beeps.

He looks at it, then turns to me. Sighs.

'Another one?' I ask.

He nods. 'Francesca.'

Six of them now, and in me, something kicks in. A grit.

'That's enough brainstorming,' I say to Ross. 'We need to be editing first thing. Getting the next episode up tomorrow afternoon. This is moving crazily fast now.'

I can see it: the adrenalin coursing through him. He's nodding. 'You're right. Forget the extra interviews. Zoe plus the news updates – an E and an F – are enough. We can be the authority on this case, but we can't do that if the podcast is lagging hours behind the news apps.'

But they still need to be human. Even if we work this fast. We must remember that each letter isn't a letter; it's a human. People aren't news stories.

'We need someone who can tell us about Francesca,' I say. 'Who she is, what she likes. Paint a picture.'

'Absolutely.'

On the bench next to the lake, Ross checks his email and tells me what he knows about her so far – a woman in her early thirties who once abseiled down a hospital for a mountain rescue charity. 'Anything?'

'Well, I deal with the abseiling centre through work. We send guests to them. I can ask, if they know her or can put me in touch with someone who does. It'll be in the morning now though, they won't be there this late.'

He's nodding. 'Yeah. Do it first thing, and let's see if we can find someone who knows her. Fast though, before someone else goes missing.'

A, B, C, D, E, F . . . G.

When I stand up from the bench, I go dizzy.

'You okay?' Ross asks as he sees me lose my footing.

'I'm fine.'

Of course that's what I say. Being dead's not as bad as being rude. But I'm not okay. I'm not okay as it dawns on me how fast this is moving and how big it is. And that not only am I putting myself at the centre of it but I'm also here alone, again, at the furthest edge of the retreat, with a man I barely know, who turned up on Aurora just as women started going missing. Whose podcast – and career – *benefit* from more women going missing.

I look up.

But I have no other choice.

We head for Ross's car.

G

It starts to rain, from nothing to torrential in seconds, and I run with this man I barely know to the top of the lake, then up the path towards the office.

'It was glorious three seconds ago! What's wrong with this place?' shouts Ross as we run. I am too out of breath to reply.

When we reach the office building, we curl off to the side and round the back, into the unlit staff car park. When we reach Ross's battered old Kia, we fling the doors open.

I load Jake into the back seat then close the passenger door behind me. Shake my head like a dog. Ross does the same.

'Lily,' he says, gesturing to the steering wheel and dashboard and handbrake. 'Meet Kev.'

I look at his socks. Of *course* he's one of those people who names their car.

Ross turns the key in the ignition. Wipers on, then the lights. Out of the windscreen, all I can see is the near-darkness of a furious summer night.

I glance to my right.

Now the thought's been allowed in, I'm hyper-aware that Ross and I are alone in a car. That we're about to drive through and close to places where nature would only need a tiny helping hand. The face of a cliff. A murderous wave.

I clip in my seat belt, checking on a sleepy and damp Jake over my shoulder.

'All set?' asks Ross.

A barely perceptible nod.

He's the safest option available. Not necessarily *safe*. But right now, with the other option being to dodge the boxing gloves of those raindrops as I walk down a long and winding unlit road, the safest.

And my dog is here. I glance again at Jake, sleepy and getting old now.

I'm pretty sure I can read his thoughts. *Don't depend on me to get you out of this.*

Ross tries to reassure me, without saying that that's what he's doing. He doesn't lock the doors, of course. He puts light pop music on, Shakira and her hips. He makes small talk.

When he glances away from the narrow road and down at my hands, bare nails and shaking knuckles clutching the sides of the passenger seat, he speaks.

'Call someone. If you'd feel better. I'm not offended. I'm a man, you're a woman. We're living in a shitshow. I get it.'

'Oh no! I'm fine.' I let go of the seat. God, the realisation that I'd rather lie with my throat cut in a ditch than for anyone to think I was calling them something mean, like *murderer*.

Anyway, I think, as my fingers slowly return to their gripping position, *who would I call?* Zadie is looking after Bertie tonight.

I would have called Alice. The only friend, apart from Zadie, that I've ever made on Aurora Island.

That wasn't deliberate. By which I don't mean that I intended to make more friends; I mean that, when I arrived on Aurora entirely alone, I intended to stay that way.

I had a plan in place, when I came to this island, to make no friends here at all.

I had a plan that was the opposite to this one, where the place I live has become headline news and the world is watching; where the place I came to hide has become the most visible place in the country.

I had a plan that has now become untenable as slowly more news crews have arrived and journalists roam our island and phones are held high up in the air to film Instagram Lives and TikTok videos, eyes everywhere. I must be in some footage. And yet, I'm still here.

Because they are the Alphabet Women, and my best friend is one of them.

How can I leave?

'How did you meet Alice?' Ross asks, small talk ready. 'Was it at the retreat?'

I shake my head. 'No. Way before that. I met her when I worked at the library. Before it closed.'

I'd been asked to work late that night, as we had a new book club happening that evening.

'Can't we just give them a key?' I asked my boss.

'Oh sure. Let them rob the place.'

'I think they just want to analyse some narrative structure, Sheila.'

But rules had to be followed, in case the book club came and scooped all the Jane Austens into a swag bag. A member of staff had to be present if people were on site, so while the ten or twelve women held their meeting, I sat quietly on the other side of the library, working through late-return emails.

'Sorry if we're loud.' A woman with slightly crooked teeth was at the desk and smiling at me. 'Who knew contemporary British fiction could get people so *animated*?'

She perched on my desk with her hands on her belly, on her way back from the loo. She was heavily pregnant.

'Oh, you're not too loud,' I replied, eyes landing on her belly. 'You should hear the drumming club.'

'You have a . . . ? Oh.' She looked down, sheepish. 'I'm Alice Fox. Apparently I don't understand jokes. I run the book club.' She glanced back towards the table. 'We've been doing it at people's kitchen tables for ages – we're so glad to have a proper home. Especially one like this.' She gestured at the shelves around us. 'Surrounded by books! What a privilege.'

I smiled.

'Anyway, we'll try to keep it down. I'm sure you know way more than you need to about this novel.'

Us, they were reading. David Nicholls.

I paused. I knew what was likely to happen if I said what was on the tip of my tongue, but I did it anyway, which was unlike me. Usually I told the hairdresser that I had no holidays booked and the dentist that I had no plans for the evening.

'Actually, I'm halfway through it.'

'No way! Book karma! Come and join us. Can you do that? Are you allowed?'

'Oh, well . . .' I grasped for an excuse. 'Spoilers . . .'

'No, don't worry. Ginger Sue isn't finished either, so we're being careful.'

Ginger Sue.

She saw me note the name. 'Important to distinguish from Sweary Sue.'

'And there's also work I need to do . . .'

She looked at my screen, where I'd finished my emails and was now – very clearly – playing online chess.

I'd run out of excuses so I joined them and I couldn't help it: I had so much to say about that book that, for the next hour, I talked non-stop.

By the end of the session, Ginger Sue seemed to be under the impression that I was now a regular member. Sweary Sue added me to the WhatsApp group. My heart pounded. What an idiot. This wasn't what I was supposed to do. This was the opposite. This was dangerous.

When I got home, I cried quietly in a bath that came up to my nose. I cried because I had made such a mistake but I also cried because I hadn't noticed that I'd been lonely. I'd been here, working hard at being alone, for eight years.

Sweary Sue messaged the next day with details of the next meet-up, and the book they were reading, which she'd drawn out of the hat. *A God in Ruins* by Kate Atkinson. When I was at the library for book club that second time – still technically working – I didn't even turn on my computer.

Six months and six books later, Alice told me about a dog her elderly neighbour couldn't take care of anymore. 'I don't know why,' she said. 'But I have a gut instinct that Jake is your dog.'

My world expanded because of Alice.

'All okay?' asks Ross in the car, now, after I tell him a more basic version of my bookish meet-cute with Alice.

'Yeah. Just thinking about her.'

He says nothing as we turn off the retreat road, bordered by those low walls we have all over the island that are made from local stone and which always look like they are half fallen down.

In front of the car, the rain thrashes down, even heavier now, livid and tropical. I can only just make out the lights and sign with the little cow outside Moo, where they make the award-winning vanilla ice cream we stock at the retreat. The higgle-piggle of farm buildings and large tractors that I know make up most of the scenery along this road I head up and down most days are obscured completely.

'Here.'

We're outside my front door.

'Thank you.' I undo my seat belt.

'I'm not leaving until you've shut it!' he yells from the open window of the car as I unlatch the gate and run up my short path. Once inside, I slam the door closed, and go to the window, flicking the lights on. I put a thumb up in the air, and Ross's car pulls away. After I lock the door, I check it three times.

I am leaning against the kitchen worktop waiting for the kettle to boil and towel-drying my hair when my rucksack vibrates. I rummage in it for my phone.

Night, Doris, the message says.

I laugh. He's funnier, now I'm not worrying he's going to kill me.

Outside, the rain thumps the windows.

V v glad my name's not Doris, I type back to Ross once I'm in bed. *Not just because I'm further down the alphabet. But also because my name's not Doris.*

I am in bed by 10.30 p.m. I am alone in pyjamas with a very milky cup of tea. And in this unlikely set-up, I seem to be as close to flirting as I have been in years, with a podcast nerd in bright socks.

Until I have a word with myself.

Until I remember that I need to be careful, always. That this podcast nerd is a stranger who looks at me, occasionally, for slightly too long. That I worry that this podcast nerd may recognise the real me.

I turn my phone off and leave Ross's last message unread.

Then I try my best to get some sleep.

When my alarm goes off at 6 a.m., the rain sounds like it's attempting a break-in.

If this goes on much longer, the crossing will be too dangerous and the ferries will stop.

I don't know if that's better for Aurora's women, or worse.

It depends, I guess. On whether the danger is on the inside, or on the outside.

I'm only due in to the retreat at lunchtime today – time owed from a weekend shift – but there is work to do at home now, for the podcast.

I didn't have the best sleep and I stagger, exhausted, to my laptop. Take it downstairs with me and make a pot of coffee. And then I open the email that Ross sent to me at 2 a.m. and get to work, editing his copy into his interview with Zoe.

At 9 a.m., I take a break and call the abseiling centre to get a name and number of a friend of Francesca's for Ross. I send him the contact, with a message.

For episode three now, I guess? I type.

Yeah, he replies. I'll get in touch. But I want to get ep two live asap so let's not wait for it.

The rain is still coming down at 12 p.m. when I need to leave for work. When I have sent what I have worked on for episode two back to Ross, I put on a waterproof jacket and waterproof trousers over my uniform. 'Sorry, Jake,' I tell him. But though he's sniffing at the crack in the door and looking unimpressed, I know he'd rather do a walk in the rain than be left alone all day. Begrudgingly he follows me out the door.

Friday afternoon is one of the weekly slots where island residents can come into the café, and when I walk past, I see the usual crew, using it like a workspace. White-collar workers whose income is made via headphones and Zoom and five-quid lattes.

They're the ones who leave the island more regularly than most; the ones who care if the ferries stop running. Who read news that isn't local. They are people who'd think nothing of spending a tenner on a sandwich smeared in nduja and sourcing an organic corn-fed chicken breast from the farm shop in the next village. Most of them arrived on the island – or bought a second home here – looking for space, and they love that but it can't be their whole world; they still need to access their old life for work.

Many of them moved on to the island for work/life balance or to improve their mental health but have brought their city habits with them. If you say the words *supermarket wine*, their body gives a tiny, involuntary shudder.

They're well catered for. In the towns, bougie farm shops and high-end delis have sprung up in the last couple of years. Port St Joseph has a wine shop; regular Chablis tastings. Syford's market is more about artisan chutney than three-for-a-fiver knickers these days. One restaurant has a Michelin star.

Alice works in the café a lot, often at the same table. It's occupied by someone else now. I picture my friend, long legs crossed at the ankles in her gym leggings as her brow scrunches and she stares at her screen. She has good posture, Alice; she looks like she's being pulled upwards like a puppet. Then you see the moment it comes – when the garden she's designing starts to take shape as she's working on the 3D visualisations, the scaled drawings of the spaces.

They have a little community here, the local home-workers. They're almost colleagues. I look at the ones who are here today.

Do you know her?

As I stop and peer in through the door, no one looks up. I'm invisible. I've perfected this over the years. My voice is low and it apologises. I wear neutrals; my skin is as dull a colour as my hair. I don't add jewellery or make-up. I am short, slight, B-cup boobs, no notable bum.

I don't splash colour or pattern anywhere. I move slowly. I fix people's issues without drama. No one would remember who they spoke to when they speak to me, only that whatever they needed sorting was sorted and that someone – 'Maybe she had brown hair? Not old. Not young' – sorted it.

There's not a lot of me, and what there is, is muted.

I head back to reception.

Jake lies beneath my knees, and I knead his fur under my desk.

It's a miracle, to be honest, that Richard lets me bring my dog to work when he's such a stickler for rules, but I think he decided that it fits with our ethos as a countryside retreat; somewhere that's close to nature. Less of a palaver than buying chickens.

So Jake, now, is not just my dog but the retreat dog. Sometimes Richard puts him on the posters, which I don't love, but that's the price I pay to have him here and not to have to walk into my house at the end of each day to a sad dog eyeballing me or a massive bill for Pet Pals.

'Tea?' I ask Joy.

'Oh, hark at this! She's making me a tea!' she shrills.

I hide my eye roll. 'I'll take that as a yes.'

I fill the kettle. When I open the cupboard, I take out the same mug that I took out yesterday, and the day before, the 'I am FIGURATIVELY dying for a cuppa' one Alice gave to me a few months ago to say thanks for looking after the girls while she and Evan went to her dad's funeral.

Then I take out a plate and lay two of my homemade macadamia biscuits in parallel, so close they almost touch, sugary twins.

My phone rings.

Evan.

I tell myself to be strong, no matter what the news is. It doesn't work.

'They have a boat out, Lily,' he says, flat. 'They're searching off the coast, in the strait.'

Are there worse sentences? I don't know what they'll be looking for, taking a boat out after this long. Nothing with a breath of life left in it, that's for certain. I hear myself cry out.

'Campbell just called too,' he says. 'Lily, *another* woman's gone.'

'Yeah. Francesca.'

'How d'you know that?' he asks, sounding confused. 'Campbell said it hadn't been made public.'

'A . . . friend told me.'

'How did she know?'

'He. He's a journalist.'

Evan is quiet for a second. When he speaks his tone is ice. 'Have you been talking to *journalists* about Alice, Lily?'

'Of course not. But there's this one guy – he's making a podcast . . .'

My phone beeps. Ross. It's just gone live.

Episode two of *Gone Girls: The Alphabet Women of Aurora Island* is now up. Episode three – with Beccy's partner, Graham, in conversation with Francesca's best friend, who Ross made contact with earlier after the abseiling club helped us out, searching for common ground or similarities, trying to dig deep for a link – will follow in the next couple of days. Ross is doing the interviews today. We are working fast; the Alphabet Women our pacemakers.

'You're producing it, then, I take it?' asks Evan. 'That's why you're involved with this true crime thing?'

'It's not—'

He scoffs. 'Yes it is, Lily.'

I pause. 'Have you listened to it? He's a journalist, with an investigative reporting background, and this is straight news, thoroughly fact-checked. Hard reporting.'

Silence.

'How is it helping?'

'What?'

'How does he want to help? What's he doing? Has this podcast found Alice?'

'No, but he's . . . we're . . .' I falter. Doubt myself. Am I doing the wrong thing, getting on board with this?

'Has he got any leads, Lily?' Evan pushes. 'Suspects?'

'I'm just trying to do something to help.' My voice is quiet. 'And can you stop talking to me like that, please.' My sentence doesn't have a question mark at the end.

There is a pause. 'I've lost my wife. I'm solo-parenting two traumatised and scared kids. Give me a fucking *break*, would you?'

'You're right, I'm sorry.' Then I pause. 'Evan, you haven't lost her.'

'In a very literal sense, Lily, I have lost her. I can't find her. I've looked in every cupboard. I have absolutely zero fucking clue where she is.'

We are silent.

'I'm going to go,' he says.

'I'll come over after work,' I say. 'I can bring cake.'

'*Food is fuel*, Lily.' He's quoting Alice and trying to lighten the tone and I'm supposed to laugh but I don't. Instead I sit, trying not to be the one who cries.

Oh, Alice.

Alice, who is always telling the girls that food is not comfort or love but fuel to make our bodies work.

'Food is fuel, Freya,' as that little hand goes back into the biscuit tin.

'Food is fuel, Florence,' as Flo tips the crisp packet upside down to get the crinkly crumbs.

'I can come *without* cake?' I say to Evan now. 'If it helps, I can come with a giant bag of vegetables and a couple of rice cakes?' I'm joking but there is also a desperation: *I will come with anything. I will do anything. I'm like an auntie to those girls, please don't stop me coming.*

'To be honest, I'm going to do a spag bol and try to make things vaguely normal,' Evan says. 'The house is like a train station and it's too much all the time; it's not *normal.* I need it to be normal again.' Something hard slips into his voice. 'They're searching the strait, Lily, and we all know what that means. This may be what normal looks like for us now. We need to get used to it being us three.'

His voice breaks on the last word and something in me breaks too, because I *long* for normal and routine, I need it, and this is everything that is not. I hate it for them but I also hate it for myself and my simple, easy life and my routine and my good sleep pattern and my anonymity and my hard-fought-for sanity. Tears roll.

'You won't.' My voice snaps like a bar of rock. 'You won't have to get used to that.'

He sighs. 'Read the stats, Lily. I'm being a realist. I need to prepare myself. And you know what – you do as well.' Then, with snark: 'Maybe you could do an episode of the podcast about it.'

It's like a slap, and another one follows. *Thwack.*

As I get off the phone, I have a message from Ross. One word.

Gemma.

But alongside *that,* something that is even harder to read.

A message from someone who knew me before I came to Aurora. Before I wiped the first couple of decades of my life clean.

Before I began lying to every single person I met.

H

'When you have this many women going missing, you *have* to be looking at more than one perpetrator,' an investigator called Dale Gibbs-Lamb says on episode three of the podcast, which drops on Sunday. 'A partnership, most likely.

'I would also say that I think it's likely someone who's committed a crime before. This is too bold for a beginner. So I presume police are looking hard at anyone on Aurora Island or with any sort of link to Aurora who's on the database.'

I'm working a Sunday shift – we have a rota for weekends – and a customer comes into reception.

I reluctantly press pause on my final listen-through before we upload. Remove my headphones.

'How can I help you?'

But my mind is never in the retreat, not anymore.

My mind is with the women. My mind is with *Gone Girls*. The podcast has even stopped me thinking about that message.

Ross is hiring someone to run the podcast's social media. A sound engineer too. More ads are coming in. Our listening figures are on a steep upwards trajectory. Just like he wanted, people are starting to view *Gone Girls: The Alphabet Women of Aurora Island* as an authority. The scripts Ross has written for the intro, outro and middle give me goosebumps. He's a gifted writer and his voice helps: that low Manchester lilt.

The morning's rain has eased to a light drizzle, and at lunchtime I head out with Jake for a walk. I have to cajole him when he sees the rain battering at the window. *Come on, surely you can't fancy this either.* Once he's out he's less reluctant, though his eyes do wince with every raindrop that falls into them.

We hit the coastal path, passing posters with the women's faces on them in plastic wallets pinned to trees. I see Alice, Beccy, Corinne; the more recent ones are not up yet.

Then I hear a voice shouting my name.

Ross appears next to me, scoops up Jake's ball and throws it, my dog immediately running ahead. Rain forgotten.

'You don't mind if I walk with you, do you?' Ross says. 'Good chance to discuss episode four anyway.'

The sign in front of us says *Wildlife Conservation Area* and we climb up the steps to the stile. Ross has one leg swung over the top of it when his phone rings in his back pocket. Safely on the other side with a dog who did a better job of this climb than either of us, I watch Ross climb, large and unwieldy, one hand to his ear, bright green socks visible where his jeans have ridden up.

'City boys, honestly,' I murmur and he sticks a tongue out at me, straddling the gate, as he says 'Hello?'

I look up at the sky. The rain's stopped completely now, the sky clearing to blue, and this feels like a walk with a friend. I have to remind myself that that's not what this is; that's very, very far from what it is.

'Okay, send it over,' Ross says into the phone. 'We'll take a look.'

It's not just the wires that keeps Ross ahead of the game with women who have gone missing. He has strong, confidential contacts through his years in journalism. A police contact is sending the photo of Gemma. The photo is always what comes next. We find a bench that we can sit on next to the gorse bushes, and we wait.

First name, surname, photo. First name, surname, photo. First name, surname, photo. First name, surname, photo.

It's often a repetitive disaster. Mindful chaos.

These are the moments before the photo is released and the face is everywhere. The people who love her could be anyone, anywhere, doing deals with God or the universe that they will do anything, *anything*, if they can have her back. They may be having cruel thoughts too, selfish thoughts, desperate thoughts. *Anyone but her.*

Around the curve of the path ahead of us, there is a one-man tent perched on a cliff top. A man is draping a wetsuit on a rock next to it.

'The dream,' I sigh quietly, picturing that perfect isolation, waking up to birdsong and stillness.

'The nightmare,' replies Ross, looking at me aghast. He throws the ball again for Jake. 'Imagine if you fancied a balti and a couple of bhajis.'

He refreshes his email and holds his phone out. 'There we go.'

Gemma has a thick, dark fringe that belongs in a shampoo advert. From underneath it, big brown eyes flash with cheek. Her nostrils are a little wide, like they're smiling. She's coming up to forty, maybe, but she's kid-silly. She loves whoever is taking the picture. I'd guess they're a child.

'She's beautiful.' I pause. I shake my head and look up at him. 'No. I've never seen her.'

Ross nods, business-like.

'Can we walk back via the bakery?'

'Ross, *no*. It's nowhere near. And you need to break your addiction to those pasties. I'm not enabling this.'

'They're what I'll miss most when I leave Aurora.'

'Charming.'

We clamber over the next stile with little grace, toddler lambs looking at us with big eyes and spindly legs and still managing to be less clumsy than Ross. His limbs get everywhere. A few seconds later, he mutters: 'Second-most.'

I glance at him, then away quickly.

Did he mean . . . ? I shake my head. Of course not. But then I remember the flirting the other night. The idea that I am up for anything romantic, for letting anyone – especially a journalist – into my life like that is way, way off the mark. I need to make that clear.

We walk on, quiet. The sea comes into view. There are a few swimmers out there – dots of multicoloured neoprene bobbing on blue.

'Meet you after work?' he says when we get back to the retreat.

He sees me hesitate. But then, as always, I think of Alice.

A nod. 'Yeah, we didn't get the chance to talk about the pre-roll ads anyway.'

Somewhere public though. Not the retreat office after hours, quiet and empty.

'Do you know the Beach Bar?' I ask.

I give him directions. The Beach Bar is next to the retreat's private stretch of sand.

'See you there at six?' he says.

'Eat before you come,' I tell him. 'It's my best advice.'

'Mate, remind me – why are we going to this place again?'

I shrug. 'Views are nice. Dolphin will be rammed now the sun's coming out again. And you sort of . . . get used to how shit it is? It's almost comforting after a point.'

Later, Ross and I sit out on the still-damp terrace of the Beach Bar. I move a local newspaper off the table that has been left by another customer, the Alphabet Women's faces spread across the front of it.

'Just tea, remember,' I warn as the waiter approaches while Ross types. 'Do. Not. Eat.'

Across the room, one woman is suggesting her avocado came out of a tube and someone else is refusing to pay their bill because 'you can't in your right mind call that a mushroom'.

'Not even the tapas?' asks Ross, turning from his laptop to glance at the menu.

'Definitely not the tapas.'

Next to us, a family comes in and sits down; the two very small children are coated in sand and goosebumps, buckets and spades bumping bare knees.

'Can we get extra milk, mate?' Ross asks the passing waiter. The waiter ignores him. 'Wow.'

'The service is the only thing worse than the food.'

Once we've finished working on the episode, Ross looks up.

'Hey, they do takeaway ice cream,' he says, nodding at the sign on the wall as he swipes his card on the machine. 'I'm starving. Get one for the walk home?'

We head for the counter.

'Two 99s, please, mate,' Ross says to the teenager playing something on his phone behind the counter.

Begrudgingly, eyes are dragged upwards.

'We've got no flakes and no cones.'

'A tub?'

The teenager nods without looking up this time. 'Yeah, you can have a tub. But we've got no spoons.'

'I, erm . . . I think we're going to leave it for today, mate.'

Outside, Ross turns to me. 'Do you think anyone took him up on his offer to scoop ice cream out of a tub with their bare hands?'

As we walk down the road that leads to Port St Joseph, the sun sneaks out again and a few birds give us a brief song.

'I think that might finally be it for the mad rain,' I murmur.

But as we turn off the beach road and into a residential street, the quiet yells despite the upturn in the weather. No one is in their front garden on their knees pulling up weeds. No one is fighting with their brother or sister over who won their driveway scooter race. No one's watering or mowing or washing the car. When Steve rides past us with his dog in the sidecar and beeps, I jump.

The island feels different in other ways, too – shaken like a can of Coke.

Normally we plod and we amble and we pause. Now we zip and hurry home. Apart from the people who come from out of town to film for their socials, the people we pass walk fast, heads down. If they have headphones in, their heavy facial expressions make me suspect most of them are listening to *Gone Girls*. The whole community is focused only on the missing women.

'Lock every door when you get in,' Ross says as we turn into my lane. 'No risks.'

'We're only on G.'

'Still.'

'Premium listing,' says Ross, then. 'Fancy.'

I look up to see The Old Dairy, the large detached old cottage next to the Sea Glass Craft Gallery on my lane, and a 'For Sale' sign in the drive. 'Must have just gone up. Wasn't there yesterday.'

The front of the house is covered in a carpet of poppies and there is a children's play set visible down the side of the house.

'Thinking of putting an offer in?' I ask.

'Sadly out of my price bracket.' His voice dips. 'But probably not a bad time to get a bargain on Aurora.'

I wince. Is that what's happening? Are people getting out of here before they disappear too? It would be hard to blame them, because you see it in people's eyes. Hear it in the conversations in the queue at the farm shop or at the retreat. Fear.

And if being alone or isolated on this island is now frightening, there's not much point being here. And then what happens? To our community. Our businesses.

'They will figure this out, won't they?' I ask a few seconds later, breaking the silence. 'Even if she's not . . . we will find out what happened to Alice?'

'I think so, yeah,' he says, fingers on his chin. 'Remember what the investigator said on episode three. It's too ambitious. This many women . . . they'll slip up. And it's so *measured.* This person has a certain personality.'

'Obsessive.'

'Arrogant.'

'Pedantic, too.'

'Let's get a psychologist booked for an episode at some point.'

A lone dog walker passes on the other side of the lane and raises a palm. Ross waves back.

'Oh, get you, local now.' I look down at his muddy trainers. It's dry now but the fields are still boggy from that crazy rain. 'What next, Ross? Walking boots?'

STAY HOME, SAVE LIVES, says the leaflet that lies on my 'Welcome' doormat on Monday morning, along with the new paper TV licence I've told them repeatedly I want sent by email not post.

'Tell it to the dog,' I murmur, picking the leaflet up and sticking it straight into the bin.

I don't want women to stay at home. I don't want us to have our lives curtailed and controlled. But if I'm honest, I *am* scared. I hear the words *serial killer* mumbled when I'm buying hummus.

I see people packing up vans with suitcases and duvets and piling kids into them, knuckles white on steering wheels as they get the hell off the island.

And closer to home, that message confirmed to me: Aurora being more visible makes *me* more visible. Aurora's mystery is wrapped up in my own. Which means they can unravel together as well.

It's too much for a mind that normally has the dullest of preoccupations. *What's for lunch? Have I sent that work email? What cakes will I bake this weekend?*

I can walk the dog for you, says Ross, when I take the leaflet out of the bin and send him a picture of it.

'I want to walk my own dog!' I rant at him in a voice note. 'And I leave the house for other things besides walking Jake anyway. I have a bloody job.'

That's about it though, to be honest.

Book club – which moved to the retreat once the library closed – disbanded without a word when Alice disappeared. Beyond that, work and Jake, most of my life happens in the kitchen with a mixing bowl and a bag of caster sugar.

'I could walk to work and back with you?'

I scream down the phone.

'Alright,' grumbles Ross. 'Only an offer. Not necessary to burst my eardrum.'

'This could go on for months though! I'm not a debutante, I don't need a chaperone.'

There's a beat.

'*Debutante?*' says Ross.

'It's not funny.'

'Right. I know he's getting on a bit but Jake does still love a run around that field. You need a solution. Pro dog walker?'

'But only male ones get the business now, right? Because it's too risky for female dog walkers to be in empty fields. This thing just gives and bloody *gives*.'

That morning, I don't walk Jake across the fields or down to the beach like I normally would on a day off.

I avoid his heartland where he can chase birds and roll around in the grass or the sand, and I never see that face he pulls – a smile, of sorts – when he's lying in the shade, exhausted from fetch. Instead we walk quickly down our quiet lane, then up and down the residential streets of the village, past the closed pub and the shops and the post box and the primary school.

But by Wednesday the sun shines again, brighter, and it's warmer now, the forecast telling us that a heatwave is coming. The thought of sticking to laps around the village when I walk Jake after work is too sad. My dog stares at the front door like it's the wardrobe to Narnia.

You can walk with us, just this once, I message Ross. Jake wants to climb a big hill. Outside mine at two?

I'm there.

For the first time it hits me that Ross is away from home, from friends, from his whole life. He barely mentions home. He doesn't say he's missing mates. I know he lives with a flatmate and that he doesn't have kids or a partner, but beyond that, I have no idea about anything to do with his life.

'Your chaperone, m'lady debutante,' he says, with a slight bow at the corner of my lane. 'Though if you don't mind me saying, I think you may be more likely to find a suitor if you changed your name from the rather old-fashioned Doris.'

We turn right at the end of the lane – rather than the left which takes you to the village – and head up towards the retreat, but before we get there we turn off, towards St Nicholas's Church. There we pause. This is where you can start the climb up Ben Fell, one of the only big hills that's walking distance from my house. Most of the others are on the other side of the island.

'Sure you're up for this?'

'I don't want to show off but . . .' He looks down and wiggles his feet. 'How could I not be up for it when I'm rocking these bad boys?'

'Ross! You've bought Aurora shoes!' His filthy city trainers have made way for khaki walking boots.

'Been out walking a fair bit,' he says with a shrug. 'Time to get the gear.'

'You love Aurora.'

'Do not. I'm a city boy. I love chain bars and white shoes.'

'Avo toast.'

'Only if I can have it with an oat milk flat white soya thingy.'

'*Happy with a brew* is such a ruse! Your skin's crawling for an indie coffee shop.'

Laughing is a stupid idea at the start of a climb. We're both out of breath in seconds, huffing alongside each other.

Stop doing this, I tell myself. *Stop getting close to this man. Do the podcast and help Alice but that's all.*

But we carry on laughing, and my brain forgets the message.

'Go on then,' I say, as the terrain flattens out and we fall into step. 'Where have you been getting to on these walks?'

And I couldn't swear to it, but I think I see a look of panic cross his face then.

What was that about?

He recalibrates quickly. Tells me about driving to the top of the island for a thirsty scramble up Great Garth and a loop around Lake Maddock and how he's thinking about getting a new rucksack; he's seen a good one at a place he wanted to tell me about actually, it's called Go Outdoors?

'Oh, Go Outdoors. I've never heard of them. Are they a start-up?' I laugh. 'You know what you'll need next,' I say a few minutes later, pulling at the sleeve of some obscure band t-shirt he's wearing today. 'Waterproofs. You're alright today but you can get caught out easily on Aurora. It rolls in off the strait fast.'

'Lily, be honest with me. Was it a mistake to turn down the Go Outdoors loyalty card?'

'Catastrophic.'

When I get in it's 8 p.m. but I still check my emails. At evenings or weekends, even when we don't work, we're often on call or at least expected to be checking emails.

URGENT: NEW BUDDY SYSTEM.

From now on we're going to have a rota system at work to make sure no one walks home from the retreat alone.

I reply all. *Does Jake count as a buddy?*

No. The answer comes quickly. *Jake does not count as a buddy.*

It's Joy who's been put in charge of the rota.

Not sure why I'm bothering to put myself on it, she writes to me then on our work messaging system. *A kidnapping's the dream, to be honest. Finally, a rest. Day without doing a dark wash.*

I am still simmering over the new rule when Ross calls as I'm picking my bag up to leave work the next day, with Tomas the chef allocated to drive me home.

'Ep four needs an update,' Ross says. 'H has gone.'

'Oh God. Who?'

'Helen Taylor?'

No.

'Lily?'

'I'm here.' I swallow. 'I know Helen.'

Helen swims in the pool at the retreat often. Her front crawl's an impressive sight; when she was eighteen, she was nearly picked for the GB Olympic team.

'She's a dentist?' I say, swallowing hard, confirming just in case. Even in a population our size, you could feasibly get two Helen Taylors.

'That's the one. Actually, we have a photo now too, here you go.' He sends it to me. 'I'm so sorry, Lily, is she a friend?'

No, I only have two of those and one's already gone. I think about Zadie, all the way at the end of the alphabet, and feel a huge relief. For now, she's safe.

Then, inevitably, I think about my own letter. That one's closer. A lot closer.

'Helen swims at the retreat,' I tell him, dragging my focus back. 'That's how I know her.'

'Okay,' he says. 'I'm sorry. Well . . . I don't know a lot yet but I know that she was on her way to the dental practice when she went missing yesterday. To work.'

This will be used as more evidence: women can't go about their usual business. Women must be chaperoned and curtailed.

I look at the cake tin next to the kettle, which contains the berry bakewell I made at midnight when I couldn't sleep.

'Dog walk?' I ask him. 'I'm just leaving, I was going to take Jake to the beach anyway. Want to pick me up, then we'll go? Tomas was going to take me home but if I'm going with you, they'll let me off the chaperone.'

We ring off and I message Tomas. Tell him he's absolved of his duties.

'I called Helen's friend Radhika on my way here,' Ross says when I meet him at the entrance shortly afterwards. 'Tried to get her to chat to us for the next episode.'

I wince. Even though I understand how fast we have to work if we're going to keep the podcast current enough, I hate that we have to approach people when they are still processing what's happening to people they love.

'Don't worry, she wasn't offended. I'd had a tip-off that she was the kind of person who would want to talk, would want to do as much in public as she could if it helped get Helen back. She's very active on socials too. Do you know her? Radhika?'

I shake my head.

'Well, she's in. We're recording later.'

'Zoom?'

'No, location. At her place, actually.' He glances at his watch. 'Seven o'clock. We've got everything else we need for episode four with the historian, so I can send Radhika's audio to you afterwards – what do you think? Can you work on it tonight? So we can get it uploaded to Acast this evening?' I nod. It's going to mean a late one, but I'm committed now. The speed is important. 'Want to come to the interview with Radhika?' he asks.

Another person knowing me, another person thinking about me.

I shake my head.

'Radhika said Helen would rather take her chances than be accompanied to and from work,' Ross says. His phone beeps and he looks up. 'Oh. They found her bike.'

'I remember her seeing me on my bike one day and telling me that cycling was one of the reasons she moved here,' I say, remembering. 'She moved from . . . was it Liverpool, maybe? A city, for sure. But she wanted to live somewhere she could bike to work. No commute, no motorway.'

But Ross is still looking at his phone, a frown etched across his face. 'This is weird, though. The bike wasn't on her route to work. Her bike was found in Syford.'

'Syford?'

Not Port St Joseph, where Helen lived and worked. Where she would have cycled through that day.

But a town she would have no reason to pass through.

Alice's town.

Evan's town.

And suddenly, I let in a thought. I think about how low Evan's been since the record shop closed. How I don't know how he fills his time. I think about the resentful way he can sometimes speak about Alice's career flying while his has died.

I think about how much he doesn't want me to do this podcast. How much he doesn't want this podcast to *exist*. How much sometimes, even before any of this happened, I would see his eyes, glazed, and wonder where he was. How I had a feeling, even if she didn't say it, that things haven't been good between him and Alice.

There are questions, looming.

Do I trust Evan?

Could he have hurt Alice, despite the alibi?

Is it always the husband?

Are the swathes of TikTok videos right to question Evan?

And if so, where the hell do the other women fit in?

I

As Ross and I carry on walking, a whippet flashes by, fast car in the outside lane.

'How can anything move that quickly in *this*?' asks Ross, staring after the dog.

It's only twenty degrees, but Ross is made for chilly November days and a layer of city smog that doesn't let real weather in. His skin is close to translucent. His glasses slip off his face, sweat gathering under his eyelashes.

'Summer, Lily, is officially Not My Thing.' He points to his face. 'Nordic heritage.'

He watches the whippet.

'One of Alice's twins, Freya, calls every dog that goes that fast "Fast Dog",' I tell him. 'She talks about "Fast Dog" like he's one dog even though he's been a whippet, a Dalmatian, a Jack Russell and a good few more.'

Ross smiles. 'Cute. Though to be fair I have no idea what any breed of dog is called, and every time anyone says one, I just smile and nod.'

'You must know some breeds. The obvious ones.'

He nods. 'Yes, I know "big dogs", "scary dogs", "nippy dogs" and "those dogs Paris Hilton used to put in her handbag". Four breeds for you, right there.'

'You'd know what, say, a *Jack Russell* looks like, though?'

'Not a clue.'

'Wow. Sometimes I forget how out of place you are here.'

'That's because of these.' He wiggles his new boots, which are now daubed in enough sand and mud to look convincing. 'And this.' He twirls around to show off the new rucksack on his back.

'Yes, your Island Native fancy dress costume is impressive.'

We move again, a wide expanse of beach either side of us as the tide is at its lowest.

'Hello!' waves Derek, my neighbour, doffing his flat cap as we turn off the beach, stomping our feet to leave the sand behind, and head into the little lane where the Beach Bar serves up its dubiousness. I do my usual scan for the conspiracy theorists of TikTok who live-stream and film from all over the island, but the terrace only has three people on it – sparse. No one is filming. The owner's sitting at a table scrolling on his phone.

I turn back to Derek.

'How are you doing, Lily?' he says.

'Not bad, Derek. Are the grandkids over?' His three grandchildren live in South Wales and they visit every school holiday so he can help with childcare. 'Hope you've got the biscuits in.'

Every time his grandchildren come, I spot him, lugging around a scooter and wiping ice cream off their faces, his beautiful golden retriever, Albert, up ahead.

'You've met the grandkids, haven't you, Lily?' he says every time. 'How are we finding island life, little guys?'

And then they shout and squeal and tell me how much they love it here. Beach days with Pops, late nights and ice cream sundaes.

Now, he stands in front of us. 'Derek, Ross. Ross, Derek.'

Derek's liver-spotted hand is pumping Ross's.

'Ah, the kids aren't coming this week,' Derek says, bending low to pet Albert and explain the delay. 'Just two minutes, Albs. Quick catch-up with Lily and Jake. You remember Jake.' His dog sniffs Jake's bottom. 'Yes, it looks like you remember Jake.'

I laugh. 'Oh, that's a shame about the grandkids, Derek. You look forward to those visits.'

A cloud sweeps his features. 'Their mum is worried about them being on the island, truth be told, Lily. Ash – that's my son, their dad – Ash is telling her she's being overprotective. Though I think he's panicking about how much they'll have to pay at these holiday clubs or whatever they call them.' A wry smile, then he sighs. 'I don't blame her. It's awful around here, all this going on. I'd avoid it if I could. And sending the kids here when . . .' He shakes his head. 'Makes me sad. I always felt like I give them a safe, lovely place to come and stay and have an island adventure. Now I can't do that.'

'There'll be other holidays.'

He nods. 'Not a lot of them though. Kids grow fast. And I'm seventy-nine in September, love.' He turns to Ross and regroups. 'Anyway! I don't recognise you, my man. What are you up to round here?' I hide a smirk when I see Derek clock the bright blue socks that poke out of the top of Ross's walking boots with suspicion.

We have black socks on Aurora, I imagine Derek saying. *Grey at a push. Explain yourself, my man.*

'No, I live in Manchester,' says Ross, with a wide grin. 'What a home you've got here though, Derek. I'm converted, what a place.' He gestures to his feet. 'Lily's even got me in the old walking boots! If my mates in my local boozer in their Nikes could see me now.' I look up in surprise, at this much detail from home.

Derek looks down, bashful, as though he moulded Aurora with his own hands.

'And I'm a journalist, Derek – that's what I'm doing here,' says Ross, still smiling with his hands in his shorts pockets. 'Trying to tell the story of what's going on, I suppose.'

I steel myself for Derek's reaction.

I should know better.

'Newspaper man?'

Ross nods. 'I write, yeah. But mostly now I'm making podcasts. They're a sort of—'

'I know what a podcast is, Ross, I'm seventy-eight, not dead.' Then he gestures to the headphones around his neck. 'Lovely one on here about the Tudors actually. Bit more relaxing than the Alphabet Women one the whole island is . . .' Derek looks up and I see the light bulb moment. 'Ah! I thought I recognised your voice. That's you?'

Ross nods. 'Nice to talk about another podcast for a change, though. Come on, Derek. Did Richard III kill those boys in the tower, or what?'

'Anyway, good for you, my man,' says Derek a few minutes later, after some long-winded chat about Edward VI and who is and who is not a Tudor. I'm lost. 'Important profession, journalism. My father wrote the obits in *The Times*. Started life down in London myself. Whole childhood. Roamed around West Hampstead with no adults when we were seven or eight. A different time.' He chuckles. 'Never catch Ash letting the grandkids do that these days. Anyway, keep going at it, Ross, we need facts and the truth. We need journalism. God, all this stuff that's popping up on my phone, stories based on one thing someone in deepest darkest wherever posted on the internet. What nonsense. The podcast's the most trustworthy news source on this thing, if you want my feedback.'

Ross's grin is wide. 'That means an awful lot, Derek. An awful lot. Thank you.'

Albert pulls hard on his lead. 'Right, this one wants a swim,' says Derek, leaning down to knead his fur. 'Anyway, good to chat.' He nods. 'Lovely, that. See you again soon, Lily.'

'Well, I did not know that about Derek,' I say as we walk away. 'Huh! Londoner. And the obituaries . . .'

'You learn something new, eh?' Ross says lightly. 'Nice guy. And there's you saying you don't have friends.'

Something odd happens when he says that. Out of nowhere, I am biting my lip to stop myself crying. I don't know Derek's surname. There's decades between us. But what's the definition of a friend? I'd care, if something happened to him. I would care.

'Lily,' says Ross, turning to me, confused. 'What did I say?'

I shake my head.

Derek and I speak most days. I know his granddaughter, Harper, is autistic and I know that he thinks it's brilliant that we recognise neurodiversity these days, and that we don't write these kids off as 'naughty'. I know his wife's knees are bad, and there are issues with her lungs too, but also he thinks she could push herself more and not give in to it and perhaps some air would help. I know that she doesn't agree. I've not seen her in a year or more.

I know he makes me rethink my presumptions about generational differences, about old men in small villages.

I know he would be one of the first people to notice if I weren't here.

I have a pang then, a gut punch of missing Alice. She'd be *the* first to miss me.

She *would have been* the first.

And that's why doing the podcast is worth the risk. Why it's worth worrying if Ross recognises me or a newcomer in the farm shop looks at me for a second too long. It's worth it, to find Alice.

I make a decision.

'While we're so close by, I'm going to call in on Evan,' I say. We're only a few minutes from Alice's road. Since we had the conversation about Ross last week, Evan has barely spoken to me and I'm desperate to see the girls. But I'm also desperate to see his face. His expressions. To watch him.

'Okay,' says Ross. 'Sure you're alright though?'

'The grandkids. The whole thing. It's—'

He puts a hand on my arm. 'Yeah. It is.'

Then he envelops me in a hug, while I stand frozen and straight like an ice pop. A few seconds later, he releases me.

We approach Evan's house. I scan, relieved to see that there is no one filming outside today.

'I'm here now, so you'd better . . .' I shift uncomfortably as we near the top of Evan's path.

He grimaces. 'This Evan guy really isn't into me, is he?'

'Not you, exactly, but your . . . kind.'

'My *kind*! Wow. I'm pretty sure journalists are the last group of people you're allowed to stereotype like that. Mate, we are the ultimate maligned minority. I tell you what this Evan Fox is, he's journalist-ist.'

I look towards the house. 'I'd better . . .'

'Yep yep. Got it. Bye, Jake. Bye, Doris.'

I walk up the drive with a half-smile on my face.

'Oh, Lily. Hi,' says Evan, when he lets me in. Then he frowns over my shoulder out of the front door. 'That the podcast guy?'

'Yeah, that's Ross.' I shift, awkwardly. I look back at the path. 'Where are the others? Drone crew departed?'

'Moved on. I think Helen's husband is being berated from outside his own home as we speak, maybe they think he's a "crisis actor" or part of a government sodding conspiracy too. But I'm safe for today.' He shuts the door behind me. 'Poor bastard.'

Even though I don't look online, I see them, phones out and filming in the farm shop to show where the victims buy their groceries; where they were last seen. Apparently The Dolphin has a huge problem with them. I even had to kick a young woman who was trying to live-stream from The Barn out of the retreat a few days ago.

'Can I do anything?' I ask, wincing. What is wrong with these people?

'Stop talking to that journo guy?'

I sigh. 'It's completely different to . . . Have you listened to the podcast? I'm really hoping it can help get Alice home.'

A scoff. But it's true. I do hope that. New social media manager Shannon is a machine and our listeners are spreading further and further afield. Three per cent of our listeners even come from outside of the UK. My stomach plummets when I think about that, even though I know it's a good thing for the women, at least. Because surely finding the women is a numbers game; someone must have information.

In the kitchen, I press play on the rough cut of episode four and the gentle tones of Lizzy Noble-Parkin, a historian who wrote a book about Aurora Island, answering Ross's questions on the island's past.

'I'm not interested,' says Evan, filling the kettle. 'Turn it off, I'm not interested.'

'Please. Just a bit. Tell me it sounds like tabloid junk after you hear this.'

'How do you think the role Aurora Island played in trade in the 1800s influences the island now, as a society?' asks Ross's voice, tinny from my phone.

Evan grimaces.

'I think it makes Aurora very self-sufficient,' Lizzy says, thoughtfully. 'It's only a few decades since one person was sent to the mainland for the newspapers every day because it was the only thing they needed. Everything else was there on the island.'

'I've been living on Aurora while we make this podcast,' says Ross. 'And a lot of people still feel like that, I would say.'

'Oh, absolutely. You can be born and die on Aurora and never leave, and in between you can have a very lovely—'

Evan reaches over and pauses it. 'I don't have time for this. I need to prep food for the girls.'

But he is leaning on the kitchen worktop and doesn't move towards the fridge. I start collecting the sea of mugs and hummus-smeared plates, leftover Alphabites spelling nonsense words in potato on the table. Those girls must wonder what has happened to their neat home with its organic vegetables and fresh flowers every week.

Evan has never been the most domestic – I know it's a bugbear between him and Alice – but the house is disgusting. The flowers in the vase are from before Alice went missing two weeks ago and they are rotting, fetid. I throw them straight into the outside bin, then come back and squirt washing-up liquid in the vase, before I carry on cleaning.

Why has no one else done this? But Alice and Evan have no extended family and I can't imagine Evan's cycling group spraying lavender Method across the surfaces.

I look at Evan. 'You should speak to Ross.'

He says nothing.

'Hear what he has to say. He's getting the word out there. I think we need him, Evan. Better than the people spreading conspiracy theories on socials.' He flinches. 'Otherwise the next story will come along, and it'll be new and it'll be on the mainland. And we'll be forgotten about.'

But I also want Evan to come on the podcast so I can watch him. So I can listen to him. So I can analyse him. So I can stop thinking about that bike in Syford and about that deep, simmering resentment that he's had for years now over his career tanking. About toxic masculinity. About those faraway eyes. About whether something dark has burrowed into Evan's psyche, and if that could be our answer.

I'm holding what I guess to be the remnants of the girls' after-school snacks from yesterday. 'And Alice—'

Evan interrupts me. 'Alright.'

'What?'

'I said alright.' He sighs. 'Fine. Whatever, if you think it will help people not to forget Alice. For them to keep looking for her. And I do hate the stuff they're posting on TikTok . . .' His face flushes red. 'I'll speak to Ross. I'm not agreeing to an interview, but I'll hear what he has to say at least. I trust you.' He looks defeated and I feel bad for being suspicious, bad for thinking he's anything other than a man living in hell.

That's what this nightmare does, though. It makes you question everyone and everything.

I call Ross.

'Do you have some time before you have to get to Radhika's?' I ask him. 'There's someone who's willing to chat to you.'

He says he can fit it in.

When he arrives, Evan lets him through the doorway with the air of a teacher who's having a meeting with a kid who's had seven detentions already this term. *Well, well, well, what do we have here.*

Still, they shake hands.

'I was at that gig,' says Evan, nodding at Ross's t-shirt.

'Yeah?'

'Legendary night. Coffee?' Evan asks. He looms over as Ross bends down to take off his walking boots.

'A tea would be great, mate, thanks. Same as Lily has it.'

'I'll make them,' I say, pleased to have something to do.

'Oh, and I forgot I brought cake from work on our walk,' I say to Ross, rummaging in my rucksack. 'It's still in my bag. I'll split it between the three of us. They're massive slices anyway.'

‘They’re always massive slices,’ grins Ross, two hands to his belly, and I smile back and then see Evan register it: how familiar Ross and I are with each other already.

As I stand at the kitchen work surface slicing cake and sucking crumbs off my fingers and rummaging for plates and filling the kettle and tidying, I keep my eyes on the table.

‘There we go,’ I say, awkwardly jolly as I put the drinks and cake down in front of them. Coasters, of course; I’m thinking about Alice again.

I struggle not to smirk at the sight of them. Two stags circling one another, if stags circled over milky tea and chocolate cake.

‘Aren’t you sitting down, Lily?’ asks Ross.

I see Evan register the familiarity in the tone again and feel a blush smear itself like cheap make-up across my face. I’m getting too close to Ross. I barely know him. I need to be careful.

‘Two minutes,’ I say. ‘I like a potter.’

Evan doesn’t object to me scrubbing his kitchen. Doesn’t take offence. I don’t think Evan cares if anyone does or doesn’t load his dishwasher.

‘Beautiful picture, mate,’ says Ross, standing up with his tea and walking towards the shelf on the left-hand side of the room.

Our eyes follow Ross’s. The picture is of Alice, alone. Her hair was shorter then, a long bob tied back in a scrunchie as she held a paintbrush in her hand. Before they had the girls, when they were renovating the house. She looks happy and she looks shattered.

Ross turns to Evan. ‘I’m sorry this happened to you.’

Evan nods. ‘Thank you.’

He waits for Ross to sit back down. I think about what we normally sit around this kitchen table for. Roast chicken and jugs of gravy and catch-ups and summer plans.

Finally, when someone's been persuaded to eat the last roast potato, I'll peel myself up to have a kickabout with Freya in the back garden or reread *Kensuke's Kingdom* to Florence on the sofa.

Alice will make a pot of ginger tea and I'll sniff at it suspiciously then ask for a milky English Breakfast. I'll bring brownies for Evan's sweet tooth and rainbow-coloured cakes for Florence, who calls anything that's multicoloured 'unicorn'.

'Thank you, Auntie Lily!'

While we eat, the girls will hop on and off my knee. They deliver little treasures – Lego builds or pictures they've drawn. They put on shows, find costumes. The house vibrates with their giggles.

'I want to do everything I can to help, honestly, that's my aim here.' Ross's bright, warm face is open.

Evan has his arms folded. His chair is pushed back so that one of his legs can be crooked across his thigh in a way that feels, with his length and stature, a little confrontational.

'Will you come and talk about Alice on the podcast, mate?' asks Ross.

Nothing.

'It'll be prerecorded.'

'So you can take out any bits I don't like? Edit it?'

Ross looks awkward. 'That's copy approval. It's not . . . I mean, it's the antithesis of good journalism. Also, we upload it fast, there's no time for back and forth with guests.' He sighs. 'I get it, I know there can be paranoia, some concern, but no one's trying to trip you up. You speak in your own words. We'll represent you accurately. Fairly.'

Silence drops into the room, heavy.

'No. I'm not doing it unless I can check it.'

Then suddenly, the girls are here, the front door flung open – purple rucksacks, Chupa Chups lollipops, Barbie magazines and shoes discarded behind them like they're deliberately leaving a trail

– and everything else is forgotten because it's the first time I've seen them since their mum went missing and my arms snake around them wide and tight. I'm not a tactile person with anyone else in the world. But the girls are different.

'Auntie Lily!'

'Billy's mum dropped us off. We went for a playdate!'

'Did you bring cake?'

I am crouched down with my head buried in Freya's hair when I say: 'No, I brought onions.'

Florence shrieks. 'You did not bring onions! We don't even like onions, do we, Freya?'

'Oh no,' I say, hammy. 'This is bad then. I've only got onions.'

She turns to Freya. 'She's tricking us.'

'Tell us the truth.'

'Pinky-promise you only have onions.'

I stand up. 'Okay, fine, I brought cake.'

They turn to each other and in unison say: 'YES!'

'Can you stay?' Freya asks, still wrapped around me even though I'm standing up now, at the same time that Florence says: 'Do *you* know where Mum is?'

I look at Evan, who's reading something on his phone.

'We're about to eat actually,' he says without looking up. 'Maybe tomorrow, girls.'

I whisper into Florence's hair so the start of my tears is left in there: 'I don't know where she is yet, but I know we'll find her soon. I know it. And she'll be missing you two like *crazy*.'

'I'm going to head,' says Ross, eyes on me as he looks up from his own phone. 'I need to get to Radhika's. Walk you home?'

I accept, begrudgingly.

On my way out, he reaches over to touch my arm.

'The letter I, already,' he whispers. 'Issy. Just pinged in. Jesus Christ. It just keeps . . . Someone on this island *has* to know something, Lily.'

'Do we know anything about her yet?' I ask Ross. 'Issy?'

He checks his phone. 'Surname is McCulloch? She lives in Syford.'

I shake my head. Nothing.

'Why did she go out?'

'Appointment for a mole she needed removing at Aurora Community Hospital. Made the appointment but never made it home.'

Ross reads on his phone.

'Her fella was on a shift – he's a carer. He's taken on extra work because they're saving to buy a house. Car's been found in some random spot next to Lake Maddock.'

I am swigging water. I look up.

'What?' he asks.

'That's miles from her route,' I say. 'That makes no sense.' I speak slowly. 'Because Issy's home is in Syford and the health centre is in Syford. Lake Maddock is nowhere near.'

J

A gull shrieks loudly overhead, wings outstretched and coasting.

It's Monday now.

The weekend brought another disappearance.

Jameela, barely eighteen.

We have lost ten of our island women.

Over the weekend Ross and I worked hard, either side of my Saturday shift, and the most recent episode of the podcast is about to go live – the jarring opening of the ice cream advert giving way to an emotive interview with Jameela's best friend, Osian.

I have a day off today and I am listening to it – one last run-through before we upload – with headphones on at the beach. Ross is next to me.

'Tell me about the last time you saw Jameela,' says Podcast Ross, gentle. 'It wasn't long before she went missing, right?'

'An hour,' says Osian, in a timbre that straddles child and adult. 'That's what I'm kicking myself about. If I'd just walked her home after our coffee . . . We'd talked about her being a J but she said it was the middle of the day. She'd keep to main roads. She just had to nip and pick something up and then she'd go straight home.'

Ross's voice is more curious now. Searching. 'Pick something up?'

'A package? She was super into fashion, Jameela, and always getting sent a new pair of jeans she'd bought for a fiver or some weird new cardigan. I presumed she was going via the post office in the village which is super busy, loads of people around. Then her house is all main roads from there.'

'But the post office said she never turned up there and they didn't even *have* a package for her, right?'

'Exactly.'

'So perhaps she picked it up from somewhere else?'

Ross and I are aiming to have this episode uploaded by the time we leave the beach.

I swig some water, and laugh as I watch Jake swooping into the waves, tail wagging, flicking water high into the air. Jake is not a fan of the sea but the sea today isn't what it usually is. It's relief; today the sun burns hard enough for him to run towards the water like it's Mecca.

Ross takes a banana out of a side compartment of his rucksack as my phone rings. I pause the audio.

'Sorry, I know it's your day off but this is important,' my boss, Richard, barks into my ear. 'I can't have you hearing it from someone else.' A beat. 'We're closing.'

'What?'

'Instructions are clear. Don't come in tomorrow. Retreat's in lockdown.'

'You have to be kidding me.'

Ross bites the banana and frowns at me. I shake my head.

But haven't I half been expecting it? Women are putting themselves under self-imposed house arrest when their letter is approaching. The entire island is living under a cloak of fear.

'Are you still there, Lily?' Richard says.

'Sorry. Yeah.'

'Well, the thing is that we can't in good faith encourage people to visit Aurora. We can't even encourage second-homers or locals to come up to us when they would be safer working at home.'

'What about the guests who are already booked?'

'Every stay cancelled with immediate effect. People here now are packing up. Then we close the doors.'

And then I find my voice. The one I lost so many years ago that it's a shock to hear it doing something other than agreeing, apologising, accepting.

But I think about that message, and the letter that followed it. Both of them written to the old me, thinking she still existed. And suddenly she does.

'Without any guests, there's no job for me, Richard. For a lot of us. You know that. We exist *for guests*.' My voice is firmer. No hesitation.

Richard sighs. 'You'll still be working, this isn't lay-off time,' he says. 'Just from home for a bit. I disagree about there not being a job without the guests. It's not like there isn't stuff to do. Planning. Christmas. Then, when this is done, we can come back with a bang.'

But the thought of that routine disappearing makes a pulse spring up around my belly button. The thrill of speaking up has dissipated and the charge is different now. It's not adrenalin.

It's just panic.

Richard sighs. 'It won't be as full-on as being in the office, no. But maybe you could see that as a *good* thing? You'll still be paid.'

'What if this doesn't stop soon? You won't *keep* paying us to do nothing.'

Silence.

'Richard, could the retreat close?'

What would I do? What the hell would I do?

The silence stretches on and I think Richard may be consulting notes. *Will we close and will Lily lose her job and/or sanity? See stock answer on page seven.*

Richard sighs. 'What do you want me to say, Lily?' His voice contains human emotion. That's a shock. 'I have no idea. I don't imagine we will close close, but if we did, I'd be as fucked as you. More so, probably, because not to pull the "as a parent" card, but I do have swimming lessons and endless fifty-quid-a-pop school shoes to pay for, and Soph's tablescaping business earned approximately forty-six pence this year, and escaping to this job was a fucking *lifeline* for me living on this arse-end-of-nowhere fuck-off island surrounded by my motherfucking in-laws every time I walk into a pub or a shop or the motherfucking dentist.'

My mouth is hanging open.

'Sorry about that language there, Lily.' He sighs. 'It's all fucking true though. Fuck fuck fuckkkkkkkk.'

I sit and wait for him to stop saying 'fuck'.

'This doesn't have a precedent,' he says, quieter now. 'We're just acting with the information that we have *at the moment,* and it might change and it might not but all I can do is pass it on. I am sorry, though. I really, really am sorry.'

Afterwards, when I've looked at the picture of the most childlike of the women so far, Jameela, and told Ross I don't recognise her, I put my head back against the sand and process what I've just experienced.

Richard, having mundane, everyday problems like in-laws and a wife who wants to live somewhere he's not into. Richard, saying 'fuck'.

The next day I wake up at 5.45 a.m., and though I try to go back to sleep, it's pointless. Usually when this happens, I make myself tea and take a flask and Jake to the beach. My dog eyes the cold, angry waves with deep suspicion as they charge over the stones at the water's edge that make it look like a graveyard. No one bothers us. Only nature makes noise.

Today I can't do that.

I log on at 6.30 a.m. Send an all-staff email.

> Day one WFH! Let us know what you need us to do, Richard.
>
> In the meantime, I hope it's okay but I've made a brief list of what we could use this time at home constructively for, including:
>
> * Brainstorming how we can bring people back to site safely
> * How we can make this work for local people if no visitors arriving
> * New revenue streams. Ideas?
> * Letting all regular groups know about cancellations (overnight guests already informed)
> * Dealing with complaints/questions (I have started on this in the contact email account)
> * Christmas planning – let's make this the best one yet!
> * Ditto Halloween!
> * I can and will hand deliver cakes
>
> Perhaps we could all add to the list with our thoughts? I'll put it in a Google doc and share.
>
> Thanks,
> Lily

There are a few half-hearted reply-alls, but mostly there are just people messaging me privately to tell me about this thriller they're binging on Netflix. And also: will I bring them blondies?

I bake and bake, but then: what am I supposed to *do*? It's too much time in my own head, and that is a terrible thing for me.

By 9 a.m., I am holding on to the back of a chair with Jake looking up at me, wide-eyed and worried.

I reach down to try to anchor myself with a hand burrowed deep into that soft fur on top of his head. Around his ears. I try to remind myself of the basics. *Breathe, breathe, breathe. Stroke your dog and breathe.*

But that thing that used to happen is back. I have forgotten how to breathe. My brain snatches at worry, in any direction it can find it.

Alice, holding her spring rolls.

Helen, on her way to work.

Jameela, so young.

Donna, whose sister's birthday cake I'd been due to make. She hadn't told me yet what design she wanted. We were still arguing over her wanting to pay me. And then, nothing.

Everything paused.

These women. All these women.

I lose control of my breath again and I cry like an exhausted newborn. That doesn't help me to remember to breathe.

They used to come so often. Now though, it's the first time in a few years that I've had a panic attack so awful that, in the midst of it, I am so sure I would bet my house on it that I am going to die.

Well, says my brain. *Look at what's happening on this island. You probably are.*

And at that moment Jake barks to tell me: there's somebody at the front door.

K

'Oh. It's you.'

Just an assistant from the retreat – male of course, the only ones with any freedom on this island now – delivering my work laptop from the office.

I let my breath go like a balloon.

'Just being cautious, Harry,' I mutter, undoing the chain. He hands over my computer without making eye contact and I double-lock the door behind him, wondering if I did a good enough impression of someone not in the throes of a panic attack.

Over the rest of the week, more places on the island close, or send staff to work from home. Only the essential industries will keep going. I wonder how you decide what's essential. If Moo can stay open to produce milk, but not ice cream. Small businesses on the island are bolstered by the retreat. Now what happens to them?

It doesn't help that the heatwave that's been promised for a while now has landed on the island and inside feels rotten. I fling the windows open, then close the larger ones again. The back door that I normally prop open on warm days stays locked.

Breathe.

Most days are the same. I sit in mismatched pyjamas watching old episodes of *Extreme Cake Makers*. It's comforting and easy, a yellow custard of a life.

Outside the sun shines but it is wasted and unloved.

When I walk Jake, dressed in shorts and flip-flops, we don't see the sunsets on the beach or the views across to the mainland from the hills. Instead we stay close; heading up and down and up and down my lane past the rows of terraced cottages and the mansions set back with their tiny vintage cars in the drive, rows of greenhouses down the side.

I keep my head low, so people don't say hi. That comes naturally.

I stop trying to create work. Why bother? I go back to bed in the afternoons, lying on top of my duvet, because I'm lethargic from the heat, and because I am bored and sad and scared to my bones.

Sometimes I forget to breathe again, and the panic attacks come.

Even reading takes too much effort. *Extreme Cake Makers* it is again, then. There's a series they made in Bulgaria. I make a note of some ingredients I've never heard of. Not that I'm baking a lot, because that takes effort too.

I could be anywhere, I realise. Without the smell of the sea and the sound of the cormorants, my little cottage, The Nook, in Port St Joseph – along with Syford, the only place big enough to call itself a town on the island – could have been plonked down anywhere in the world. I am placeless. I have no anchor. I float, untethered, and that unclips something in my mind too.

The only positive thing is that it seems to be working. It's Thursday now; no one has gone missing since Jameela on Saturday. A longer gap than usual.

'Why weren't you picking up before?' asks Ross when I finally answer, the sixth time he calls. 'Mate, I was worried.'

'Why? I'm not a K.'

'No. But . . .' *Not far off.*

'Just work, Ross. It's been busy.'

That, and remembering to breathe.

He knows I'm lying. I am ordering food deliveries, and not flour and butter but Mr Kipling and McVitie's, the processed stuff I normally balk at but I'm now eating in place of meals.

'Meet me at the beach. Please.'

And then he tells me: there's been a K.

First name, surname, photo. Mindful chaos.

I go to the beach for Kris Rex-Rehman, and for Jake. I go to the beach for Alice. I go to the beach with Ross without either of us mentioning: the next letter is L – L for Lily.

'Let me tell you what we know about Kris,' says Ross, as Jake sprints towards the sea like the sea is his long-lost puppy. It's hot enough again that this dog who normally cringes away from the waves runs towards them. 'Went out to buy vodka for her alcoholic dad.' Something crosses his face. 'God. This is going to be a heart-breaking one to cover.'

He's trying to get me to engage with the podcast again, but I stay silent.

Eleven women.

Breathe.

'And cereal for her ten-year-old sister because no one had bothered to feed her all day.' Ross winces. 'Fuck.'

Jake returns, chewed old ball in his mouth, and sits in front of Ross, not me. His tail flicks and wags. Ross throws the ball for him. Again. Again. Again.

'We need to get episode six out,' he says, quietly. 'I can't wait any longer, Lily.'

'You can get another producer. Everyone wants a piece of *Gone Girls* now, Ross. Everyone's talking about it.'

He shakes his head. 'That's not my point. I know I can get a producer. But I want *you* to produce it. You're local. You make it authentic. You stop me making stupid mistakes. You make sure it's always about the women.'

Jake comes over with the ball. Drops it at Ross's walking boots again. I reach over and pick the ball up.

'Come on. Let's head back.'

Ross watches from the end of the path until I've locked my front door, and then I get back into bed and eat three lemon fondant fancies. I cancel plans to see Evan tomorrow, telling him I'm ill, but he asks if the girls can still walk Jake – they were looking forward to it – so the next day they come to collect him.

After they head off on their walk, I put on another episode of *Extreme Cake Makers*.

I wanted to see the girls properly but it feels too much, all of it. Watching Evan. Wondering. Watching Ross. Wondering. The girls. The women. The podcast. Too much, too much, too much.

This TV show and its cakes is not too much.

This TV show is safe. Small.

And I think about the message again.

Are you ok? This Alphabet Women thing is happening on the island you live on, isn't it? I'm listening to the podcast and I'm worried about you. Please can I come and visit?

The problem wasn't that it was mean. The problem was that it was unbearably kind. Kindness can hit harder, when you're trying to build a wall.

I deleted the message, then stuffed the letter that followed it – a longer version of the same sentiment – into my wood burner. Kind kindling.

That message wasn't meant for me anyway, not really. I had been another person, in another life, and it was meant for that person, but they don't exist anymore and so there's no point in replying. No point.

For the next few days, I stay at home and lock the doors. Jake wanders around my small back garden in lieu of a walk. Investigates the dahlias. Looks up occasionally to shoot me tiny daggers.

The girls and Evan take him for more walks over the weekend, and I tell Evan I'm still not well. He doesn't push it: he's too distracted to care.

Ross isn't.

'Just get another producer,' I snap when I finally answer the phone on Sunday.

'Got one, thanks, mate,' he says, annoyingly cheerful. 'That's not what I'm calling about. I'm worried about you. Work's not busy, Zadie told me. What are you doing for all these hours?'

I'm falling apart. That's what I'm doing.

'It's none of your business, Ross.'

He sighs. 'It can be hard, living alone. Especially now. It can send you into your own head too much. Is that what this is – is it getting to you, not being in work?'

'Don't be patronising, Ross,' I spit. 'And don't analyse me. You barely know me.'

The next day, he messages me a picture. A protest gathered outside Waitrose. Rudimentary placards.

She was only going to work.

We aren't babies. We don't need babysitting.

They're right. Why should adult women have to be accompanied? Infantilised? And yet I've become used to it quickly, and I'm too scared to go back.

This is not the first time my life and the national news agenda have converged, and I'm scared of that too. Of Ross's role in everything. I used to have the same thought about Corinne. That industry, that world: in the background, I always wondered if she knew. Now is there a chance *he* knows?

The quieter I am and the more I retreat, the less chance they have of working it out. All these journalists around, all of these people scouring social media. All of these people trying to find out everything about everyone on our island. Especially those linked to the Alphabet Women. They leave no stone unturned, and I can't risk being turned over.

I realise it now: I made a huge mistake getting involved in this podcast. A huge mistake putting my head back above the parapet.

Because if Ross or Zadie or Corinne or Evan or Derek or even *Alice* knew what I had done to be headline news all those years ago, they wouldn't just be upset that I'd lied, or shocked I had secrets.

They would find me repellent.

And not one of them would be able to look me in the eye.

L

Since I moved to Aurora Island, I've not been twenty-four hours without seeing the sea. Now, I haven't been outside for three days.

I prescribed myself the horizon when I decided to move here. I didn't care how big the house I rented was, or how run-down, but I did care that it was less than a ten-minute walk from the beach.

Anushka said it was a good idea.

'It'll be good for you. Remind you that you're not a very big deal.' That dazzler of a smile. 'The sea does that.'

Anushka thought it was a wise decision to move to Aurora Island, even if it meant I could never see her again.

Now, as I finish looking at the picture of the protests and put my phone down, Jake's eyes are on me.

I could admit the panic attacks. I could admit how all of this is tipping me off my axis. I could admit that I'm flailing and that that can't happen. That equilibrium is essential to me.

But how can I do that, without having to tell people the things I can't ever admit?

Breathe.

God, I need to leave this house, whatever bloody letter we're on.

I pull walking sandals on to feet that are no longer used to being contained by anything and head out, blinking like a newborn in an island heatwave that's become even more intense while I've been inside.

When Ross touches my arm, I startle like a newborn too.

'Oh. Didn't mean to make you jump. Of course it would . . . now . . .' He takes a careful step back. 'Just came from the other direction. I was going to call round and offer to walk Jake after I sent you that message, if you didn't want to come out. With it being . . .'

'Okay, Ross, you don't need to spell it out.'

K has gone. We're on L.

I ignore him and keep walking – *breathe, breathe, breathe* – but he falls into step next to me.

'Have you listened to episode six yet?' he asks, eager as a toddler.

I shake my head. 'Not yet.'

I glance left and watch him bite his lip; try to hide his disappointment. 'Well, it's good. Listener numbers are up. Feedback's brilliant. I don't want to be a show-offy twat but, mate, the Apple reviews are better than I could ever have imagined. This is a million times bigger than Oban. We're getting episode seven up soon.'

When we walk across the grassy dunes, Ross stops and reaches down his shin. He hasn't asked if he can come for a walk with us, but that seems to be what's happening.

'One sec,' he says. He pulls off his boots and his socks and carries on walking in bare feet. 'That's better.'

On impulse, I do the same with my sandals. Then Ross walks away from me, towards the sea, pulling the t-shirt that commemorates yet another nineties gig in Manchester off as he goes and discarding his boots and socks as well as his top at the water's edge. Jake bounds into the water with him and I notice it for the first time: they have a similar gait.

I stand next to the pile of clothes.

This was what I came here for. *Remember you're not a big deal.*

I watch Jake galloping, basking in the relief from overheating, lurching through the shallow sea, fur sodden and heavy. The sun feels threatening now. Bearing down and dominant, like a master. It must be thirty degrees.

My dog's body moves up and down, up and down in the water like a dolphin. Next to him is Ross, in his shorts. He's put on a little weight since he arrived, and as he wades in the water, he grabs his middle in two hands. 'Aurora pouch is out!' he shouts.

A smile inches across my face.

'Like a tattoo! Marks my time here!'

And suddenly, I can't resist it either. In shorts and a plain black t-shirt, I throw myself under a wave that crashes in.

You're not a big deal.

This is what you came here for.

I close my eyes and stay under for a long time, and when I surface my dog's face is close. I laugh, properly from my belly.

When we're sitting outside the Beach Bar with two Sprites an hour later, my clothes have dried out and Ross picks up a chip from the bowl that sits between us. We thought that we couldn't go wrong with chips but they seem to have tipped half a pot of generic Italian flavouring on to them, and I cough up oregano every time I swallow one. We've tried to mask it with ketchup.

As well as his chin, Ross has some on a rogue hair that sticks out at an angle from his right eyebrow. And about half a teaspoonful in his beard.

'Even the *ketchup* is odd.'

'They make their own.'

'They shouldn't.'

He digs into his pocket and takes out his phone. Reads something and frowns.

Here we go. It was too much to expect to hold on to this feeling. To enjoy the lightness.

'Hold on,' he says to himself. Then he looks up, still frowning. 'I just need to speak to someone. Make sure this is . . . that this is right. Hold on.'

He walks off the terrace and I reach down to bury my fingers into Jake's black and white fur, drenched in the sea but already dry thanks to the heat. Then I look out.

You're no sea, I tell myself. No ocean.

You're no big deal.

A few minutes later, Ross jogs back on to the terrace.

'Rose Vandenburg?' he says, pulling out his chair and making eye contact. 'Does the name mean anything? Rose Vandenburg?'

When I was working on the podcast, Ross did this each time, an initial check about whether I knew the woman before he talked about them in that more disassociated, removed way he had to in order to stay sane.

'No. Nothing.' Then it dawns on me. 'Hold on, *Rose*? We're not on R. We're on L.'

L for Lily.

'Yeah. Exactly.'

He dips a chip in ketchup, then shoves it down, before he speaks again, with his mouth half full. 'Lives in that tiny hamlet that you can pretty much miss, just before the port.' He swallows. 'Apparently though, the family don't *call* her Rose. She's not a girly girl, and she's always hated it. They call her Lee, it's her middle name.'

My heart starts to hammer. So now *nicknames* are in play. It's also unclear whether this means L has passed, or not. What does this mean for me?

'It feels like he's messing with us.'

'Whoever he is.'

'They?'

'But not she?'

Ross stares out, off the coast. The sea is at its highest now and Little Aurora, the small island off ours that's inhabited only by twenty-two varieties of birds and some seals, looks far away – even though at low tide you can walk out across the sand towards it.

Maybe when I came here, I should have gone further. To Little Aurora. Lived there, set up a tent. Embraced the solitude.

The birds can't make such a mess of things as we do. As far as I can see, they rub along with the seals without drama.

It all works when you don't let humans get involved.

Humans create chaos. I learnt that a long time ago.

It's happening again.

M

The heat the next day has the persistence we normally expect from the wind, or from the endless rain that bounces down on to Aurora Island in the autumn.

As I crouch outside in my garden to check the herbs that have been quietly going about their business while I've been locked inside, the sun hits the back of my neck like a laser. I spread my palm across it, scant protection. Even minutes in this heat feel like they'll leave you red and scalded.

We're a tropical island now, by the looks of things. It's hard to imagine us ever pulling on our bobble hats again. Zipping up our coats. Hot water bottles and bowls of soup start to seem like comedy ideas; artefacts collected on another planet.

It's climbed up to thirty degrees today. Hotter, apparently, than Tel Aviv.

'You're okay,' I whisper to the rosemary like it's a small baby. 'You're okay.'

Then I get distracted by the basil; thoughts of a lemon and basil yoghurt cake. *That's the end for us, Mr Kipling.*

Oh. Something's shifted.

I'm clutching a palm full of basil and about to put my key in the door when my back pocket vibrates. Jake plods away from me, around the small square of front garden. 'Hey Ross.'

'I'll be passing yours in a bit,' he says. 'Just wondered if it would be okay if I called in?'

He sounds breathless. I can't work out if he's excited or scared or riding a bike fast up a hill.

'Are you riding a bike fast up a hill?'

'What?'

'Nothing. Has something happened?'

He sighs. 'Well, a woman named Morwenna has gone.' He tells me her surname and waits for me to confirm that I don't know her. 'Picture should be over soon. But that's not what I was calling for though. I just . . .' I hear the swallow. 'Swimming was fun yesterday. The beach. All of it. I wanted to see you.'

He lets the words settle and I shut the front door behind me. I get Jake some much-needed water with one hand then stand in the hall while he heads for a doze on his mat by the back door.

'Okay,' I reply.

I want to see Ross too, I realise. I have gone from not trusting this man – this new arrival on our island – and a bloody *journalist* as well – to realising that he means something to me. That I want to tell him the truth.

'You don't have to work on the podcast,' he says. 'I mean, I love having you working on it, obviously, but we have a team now. We can keep the freelance producer if you want. I'm not coming round to persuade you to work on it.'

I nod. It's a relief. The podcast is a beast now. Everyone on Aurora listens to *Gone Girls: The Alphabet Women of Aurora Island,* but it goes far beyond us – 93 per cent of the listeners are outside of the island. Ross has a whole team on board now: a booker, a social media manager. People are clamouring for advertising space. It's number *three* in Apple's podcast chart.

But that just made me more visible. I was right to get out.

'Just thought I would say hi.' Then he repeats it: 'I wanted to see you.'

I'm alone but my cheeks are crimson. Bloody hell, they don't even need an audience.

I look around the hall at the discarded socks and dog balls and hair bobbles and a single paper Mr Kipling case balled up in a corner.

Every instinct in me screamed to keep Ross at a distance. That at best he was an archetypal scumbag journalist and at worst something darker. And yet somehow, we've become mates. Somehow I've started to find comfort in having him around.

So has Jake.

If I want to keep Ross in my life, though, I have to open the metaphorical door, but first I have to open the literal one and I have to tidy up because he's going to knock on it any minute. I'm not a big swearer but I mouth *fuccccccckkkk* silently while shoving things in cupboards with the phone still at my ear.

'How far away did you say you were?'

'Ten minutes? Maybe fifteen because, as you know, Lily, I move slowly in extreme temperatures.'

'We've not hit forty-five degrees, Ross. It's not Delhi.'

'Viking heritage, remember. This is extreme. See you in a bit.'

Ten minutes later, after I have thrown clean socks into washing baskets and dirty socks into drawers and wiped up that stubborn dried-on cake mix on the kitchen table and got rid of the Mr Kipling Wrapper of Shame and sprayed enough jasmine room spray to persuade someone they have arrived at a boutique country spa, my phone rings.

Zadie.

I answer, in case it's about work.

'All okay? I can't stay on long.'

'Why?'

I pause. 'Lily?' She sounds worried. 'What's going on?'

'Nothing! Nothing bad, I mean. I'm at home. Safe. It's just that Ross . . . Ross is on his way over.'

There is silence. Then: 'Be careful, Lily. I know you're getting close. And I know we've technically had our L but . . . dude, I still don't trust him. There's something so *off* about him arriving here just as the women started disappearing. And Bobbi said she saw him drive past her when she was on her way to an out-of-hours shift at work at, like, five o'clock in the morning. She said he looked like he'd been up all night.'

I sigh. Pull off a rubber glove as I squash the phone between my ear and shoulder. 'He's fine, Zadie. He's just Ross. Nerdy podcast guy, Ross. Stop worrying. You're not the big sister here, that's my role.' The doorbell rings. 'Right. Have to go.'

When I open the door of The Nook, Ross is standing on the doorstep.

'Hey.'

'Hey.'

His forehead sweats profusely. I blink into the bright sunlight. Ten seconds later, we're still standing on the doorstep.

'Am I coming in or . . . ?'

'Oh! Sure.'

I close the door behind him.

'Mate, it smells good in here. That's not for me, is it?'

I deliver a withering look. 'Ross, this is just how my house smells.'

'Well, it's lovely,' he says with a grin, then he looks around. He fights a yawn, and I try to block out that story Zadie just told me about him being out all night. Bobbi was probably mistaken; it was just someone who looked like him. 'As is your house. As, also, are you.'

It's impossible to know for certain that a person is loaded with goodness and that they are not at their core bad. People can live with someone for a lifetime and not know it; they can be blindsided by a secret life. And I know what Zadie thinks. But I look at Ross and against all the odds, I think: *I like you.*

Against even longer odds*: I want to let you in.*

'It's not too much?' I ask. 'The smell?'

He thinks. 'Nope. It's exactly as floral as the home of a woman named Lily should be.'

Just one problem, I think. *Lily's not my name.*

Without a podcast to make, without a horizon or a mountain to look at, the atmosphere between Ross and me is suddenly awkward. Our arms dangle, not sure where to put their weird hanging lengthiness.

'Do you want a tour?'

Ross looks around. A wide smile sprawls itself across his face.

'I would *love* a tour, mate.'

I feel the singe of my cheeks settle to a light pink and put a hand on my bloated middle. Bloody Mr Kipling.

'So, living room,' I say, walking into the first room off the hall. 'Probably obvious. Weird to put a sofa in any other room.'

'Bathroom sofa might be cosy?'

'Imagine the soggy cushions.'

'Bet there are bathroom sofas in some corner of Pinterest.'

'Deviants.'

A gasp. 'Lily, are you on *Dark Pinterest*?'

'People are freaks. Some of them put bifold doors on their en-suite.'

Seeing him chuckle as he lolls against the door frame in my living room makes me smile.

It goes against everything I thought about him, every feeling of mistrust, every worry Zadie has confided to me, but somehow I can *picture* him staying here, watching *Eternal Sunshine of the Spotless Mind* or *Four Weddings and a Funeral* with me on a Sunday afternoon. The odd baking show. I can picture him putting the kettle on. I can imagine telling him things. I can imagine telling him my secrets. My worries.

I can even imagine telling him the truth.

Jake is happy to see him now too, and he stays close like Ross might try to leave if he doesn't monitor him. Ross crouches down, hand in that soft fur I love to stroke between his ears. Petting him, hugging him, murmuring to him.

'Well. This is the definition of *hugeggggeee*,' says Ross, looking up from his best dog pal eventually and referencing the Danish trend we all went nuts for around 2016.

'I'm sorry, *what* was that?'

'Look, it's not my fault if you're uncultured. I'm a global citizen, Lily.'

'It's not *my* fault if you're trying to pronounce a Danish word that loosely translates as "cosy" but you're pronouncing it wrongly because you've only ever seen it written down.'

'Oh hello, someone's confident. Go on then.'

I clear my throat. 'Hyoo-guh.'

He nods. 'Fair play. No idea if it's right but it sounds convincing.' He yawns again. 'Hyoo-ger. Better?'

'Marginally.'

I look around my living room, still laughing, and see the place through Ross's eyes. It is hygge, snuggling into itself. In the centre of the wall is my little wood burner with a decent stack of logs making a home for the spiders next to it, and a battered metal bucket spilling over with kindling.

If the heatwave announces its sudden end and Aurora weather returns, I'll be ready.

A thick, dark wooden beam runs across the top of the fireplace, loaded with scented candles and spider plants and tiny mirrors and art.

Ross's eyes move to the walls, a rich, deep green against all the online advice that suggested that dark colours make a small room look even smaller. I love it. The dark walls make me feel encased. Safe.

My own eyes go to the grey sofa and second-hand velvet grey armchair. To the ottoman that's filled with blankets and sits in front of the fire like a coffee table, on top of a big, tasselled dark green rug.

I evaluate it all through Ross's eyes.

When I look back at him, though, he has stopped scanning the room. His eyes are on me. And something I've barely let myself acknowledge creeps into the dynamic between us.

I walk quickly down the short hall. 'Next stop, kitchen.'

Even Alice hardly ever comes inside my house. I go to her, it's easier with the kids. Either that or we go out; meet for roast chicken in one of the cosy pubs in the smaller villages where I take my old mint tin full of condiments and Alice reaches across the table and shrieks at the new additions.

'And what would we use this bad boy for?' I picture her asking, a sachet of sriracha between her fingers as her other hand combs through the truffle oil and sea salt and local honey.

'That would be if you wanted to, say, zhuzh an egg.'

'*Zhuzh an egg?*'

'Sometimes an egg needs zhuzhing.'

And Alice would laugh so hard and so loudly and then lean over and kiss my cheek. 'I *adore* you.'

Now, Ross touches my hand and I'm zipped back out of the pub and into my kitchen.

Here he is, another one. These tactile people I somehow find myself around. The ones who put up with me flinching and wincing and freezing. Who touch me anyway but do it gently, when I'm ready.

I look around. It's not just Alice who has barely stepped foot in here. Has *anyone* else been in my house, if they're not being paid to fix something? I can't picture anyone leaning back on my sofa but me. I can't picture a meal for more than one person being eaten in my kitchen.

That's not an accident: I've shut them all out.

The kitchen doesn't have the hygge of the living room; it's airy and bright, high stools up against the kitchen worktop and hundreds of spices, flours and sugars lining the shelves on the walls. Jake lies on the mat by the back door.

'Mate!' he says again. 'What a place! This smells of every cake you've ever baked, somehow. All at once.' He shakes his head. '*Mate.*'

Mate.

I pull a tea towel off a wire rack. 'I was about to make a basil and lemon yoghurt cake when you called but there are peanut butter cookies there.' Another one. 'And banana cake.' Another. 'Oh, and just a small batch of blondies.'

He blinks, fast. 'I only told you I was coming twenty minutes ago.'

I cringe with embarrassment. 'I didn't make this all for you! I was just . . . I've been bouncing back from a baking drought.'

Ross sticks his bottom lip out. 'You could have pretended. Who *were* they for then? I don't want to tell you what to eat, Lily, I know that's not the done thing, but that's a lot for one woman.'

I point at the cookies. 'Evan.'

The banana cake. 'Farm shop.'

'And the blondies?'

'Fine, *they* were mine.'

He grins at me. It gives me the same feeling as eating cake, actually, when he does that.

'Talk me through this baking drought,' he says.

I rearrange my face to be serious. 'Well, I've been doing something I'm ashamed of.'

His face drops. 'Okay.' He takes a deep breath. 'Do you want to talk or . . . ? Should we sit down?'

'I've been eating Mr Kipling fondant fancies.'

'*Fuck*, mate.'

'Even the yellow ones.'

'No.'

'I know. But look.' I nod to the cakes. 'You can see it's over now.'

He chuckles.

It's a new thing, seeing The Nook and my bakes through someone else's eyes. I made a home this beautiful and it smelled of butter and sugar and vanilla and the fire blazed and the sofa was soft and I didn't share it with *anybody*.

But that wasn't the point of it. I think about Anushka, and that last conversation we had before I left. I remember what she said about comfort zones. The *point* was that no one came. The *point* was that it was my bolthole. The part I forgot was that you're meant to retreat to a comfort zone to recharge, but it's not meant to be where you stay, always and alone.

'Right,' I say. A gulp. 'Shall we carry on the tour?'

But my terraced cottage is small. After a quick 'there's the loo' finger point, the only place left to tour is upstairs.

I remember my earlier thoughts about Ross. A man I haven't known for long. A journalist. Is it okay, no matter how relaxed I'm feeling now, to take him up there? I hear Zadie in my head: *Be careful, Lily, be careful.* I think about all the women from our island who are gone.

Ross puts a hand out to let me go up the stairs first and follows me up, then past the bathroom and the spare bedroom, sticking his head into both.

'And that's my . . . bedroom.'

It's awkward. A step too far, and unnecessary, and we both know it. He pokes his head round the door and says 'lovely', then clears his throat.

Ross is the first downstairs, and he heads for the sofa, crossing one bare hairy leg in his shorts and socks over his knee. We're back to normal. Now that we aren't looking at beds or toilets.

I go to open another window.

'You okay?' asks Ross, as I stretch up and turn the stiff key.

I prise the window open then turn and stare like I've never seen him before. I am not sure how it happened, but in my bolthole is a man who has left his huge walking boots by the front door in a very neat pair and is sitting on my sofa. The sock on the foot that dangles is a luminous yellow. He looks comfortable.

'Yeah,' I tell him. 'Think so.'

He grins. 'In that case, tell me where the teabags are, eh, and I'll whack that kettle on.' He stands up. 'Consider this my heavy hint to crack out those blondies. I could really do with a sugar boost today.'

Why? I think about that 5 a.m. sighting. Shake my head to get rid of the thought. Then I follow him into the kitchen and I open the back door that's been closed for so long, all the way through this heatwave, then I sit down while Ross potters around in his dopamine socks, making us two cups of identically milky tea.

'Do you want me to . . .' I go to stand up and he comes over and gently pushes me by the shoulders back down on to the chair at my little wooden kitchen table.

'Nope.' His eyes are right on mine. 'I want you to sit there and I want to make you a cup of tea.' A pause. 'And then, I want you to eat a blondie that you, er, made yourself anyway but which I will at least put on to a plate.'

I smile.

Tell him.

I've wondered often if I'm not the only one here who's done it: come here to disappear. I look at faces and I wonder, as I see something cross them, something I recognise, if I'm not the only one who is pretending.

It's not just the way we are cut off, sometimes, with the weather. It's not the Wi-Fi signal that would embarrass the year 2008 (I always thought it was smart of the retreat to make a USP out of what could have been every guest's most negative feedback on Google). It's a place to escape. Where you can reduce the noise; ignore a large chunk of the world. Live in a low-fi kind of way. Get to the bare bones of things.

As Ross opens a drawer and rummages around for a teaspoon, I force myself to leave him to it. His eyes dart regularly back to mine.

I'm going to tell him, I think. I'm going to tell him the truth. Otherwise how can we move forward?

And I want to move forward.

As I drift away into those thoughts, Ross opens a cupboard. He slams it shut and turns to me.

'Yikes, I've found your biscuit tin.' He raises an eyebrow. 'Can I look? I find biscuit tins as juicy as most people find playlists.'

'I'm not sure it'll be that interesting, but sure. Knock yourself out.'

He flings the cupboard back open and takes out the biscuit tin, ceremonial. Then he pulls something out and inhales.

'*Homemade cinnamon cookies?*'

I nod.

'You're kidding me. These can't belong in a biscuit tin.'

'Why not? They're a biscuit.'

'I'm looking for a Bourbon. A Hobnob. This is . . .' He shakes his head, then he keeps rummaging. 'Hold on a second.'

I start laughing, knowing what he's found. Left over from the illicit stash.

'Now! This is more like it. We've got a custard cream!'

I feel my middle shake with laughter as he finds a plate and lays everything he can find – the blondies, cookies, custard creams – on it so it looks like it's feeding a table of ten people, as the kettle comes to a boil.

The bloating in my middle – panic and Mr Kipling – has deflated now, jiggled out by laughter. Ross puts a cup of milky tea in front of me and one in front of himself, and we talk. When he asks me a question, I don't blush, and when he touches my arm, I don't flinch.

I arrived as a little mole, burying myself in Aurora's soil. Staying safe underground. Then I met people I loved. Alice. The girls. Zadie. Derek.

Ross.

When Ross kisses me for the first time, across the table where meals are eaten usually by one, we don't taste of homemade blondies or cinnamon cookies but of the sugar and comfort and processed crap of custard creams, a little of which – as most of Ross's food does – has found its way into his slightly overgrown beard.

We taste of milky tea.

My bedroom is no longer an awkward place.

We eat the blondies with our fingers and I make lemonade, slicing extra lemons to go in it, then I load it up with ice and we take it into the garden.

Later, I light candles. Fancy ones.

Ross stays over.

We talk.

We talk more.

More.

The picture changes.

I realise my comfort zone's comfy enough for two. This is not an invasion.

The next day, Ross is still there and I walk in bare feet to the kitchen and I make breakfast, or perhaps lunch, or an unnamed anytime meal of Marmite on thick slabs of homemade bread which we eat in bed, licking our fingers clean. We boil the kettle. We drink more milky tea. He makes it just right; he always has. I spot a little Marmite in his beard and scoop it up with my little finger.

Ross goes home to grab some fresh clothes but he's going to come back after that and I suspect that, at some point soon, he won't ever leave. I don't want him to.

I tell Jake I won't be long and I cycle to the farm shop to buy milk – we get through *a lot* of milk, Ross and me, it's the tea – and also two lemons and some courgettes.

I'm cooking for Ross tonight – an early tea because he can't stay over, something to do with work again – and the two of us will eat together at the table and I am going to make—

PART TWO: ZADIE

N

Lily disappears on N, and it makes sense to no one.

On the doorstep, as I try to catch my breath, I take my ringing phone out of my pocket and stare at Ross's name on the caller ID.

'Hey.'

It's odd for him to call me. We only know each other through Lily. He surely gets the vibe – barely hidden – that I don't trust him, that I am not his mate and that I don't buy his schtick.

'Zadie,' Ross says, not commenting on the fact I'm panting – I've just run home from babysitting for Bobbi's friend for some extra cash. I told Lydia I felt fine about the walk; that it was light outside. I didn't tell her that Bobbi and I have been learning self-defence on YouTube when Bertie is in bed. I didn't tell her that Amazon Prime delivered us two cricket bats this week.

'Lily's gone.'

My middle nose-dives to my toes and I fight the urge to drop to my knees. To catch it and scoop it back in through my belly button.

'No.'

It's the only word my body is making, and it *is* my body that is making it. It comes up from my gut. Sinew. Atoms. *No. No. No. No. No.*

Again. 'No.'

Ross says nothing. I hear him breathe, shallow and hurting.

'Well, it's not an Alphabet Women thing. We already had L.'

'Zadie, I need you to think. It might be like Rose. Is there a nickname?'

'I don't . . . I don't know?'

He sounds impatient. 'You must know.'

And technically, he's right. I must know. I spend most days with Lily. But I realise how little I know – about her past, her family.

'This is pointless, Ross. It doesn't matter if she had nicknames because she isn't . . .' I scoff. 'It's not an Alphabet Women thing. We're edgy and we're freaking out but people go off radar. She'll turn up. That's *all this is*.'

When Ross speaks again, his voice is gentle. 'They found her phone, that's how they got hold of me, from recent messages.'

I try to think.

I think about what Lily told me, when we spoke on the phone a few hours ago. That something had happened between her and Ross last night. And even then, how I had that feeling: *This will lead nowhere good.* Lily may have stopped being wary of him. I haven't.

'If you're telling me she really has gone missing,' I say, 'on the *day after* something happened between you two, then there's only one person I'm suspicious of here, Ross.'

O

There is a beat – a silence down the line. Then: '*What?*'

'Something happened between you and Lily last night, right? And then suddenly – the next day – you say she's missing. And Bobbi saw you . . . she saw you driving round in the middle of the night.'

'That's . . . it's . . . it's work, Zadie.'

I scoff. 'What sort of work do you do at five a.m., Ross? Lily should never have trusted you.'

He says nothing.

I can hear traffic in the background, and then a dog barking.

'Have you got Jake?'

'No, that's just a big dog that's passing. Her next-door neighbour had a key, so we got Jake but Derek's taken him.'

'Who's Derek?'

'The neighbour. You know, the old guy. The one Lily likes. I'll explain—'

I cut him off. 'I spoke to her earlier. She was fine then.' My voice is accusing.

'When did you speak to her?'

I look at the time on my phone. 'Three hours ago? Just over, maybe.'

'Yeah. That's when she went to the shops, while I left to . . .' He pauses. 'When I went home to get clothes. But when I went back, she wasn't there. Jake was at the window. I waited for ages, called her . . . Nothing. How was she when you spoke to her?'

When I spoke to her, Lily was cycling from The Nook to the shops.

'She was . . . stupidly – really fucking happy.'

I hear Ross swallow.

'I knew she was alone,' I say, almost to myself. Quiet, like Lily. 'I knew. And I didn't tell her to go home.'

He sighs. 'The nicknames, Zadie. Have a think.'

But there's nothing, and suddenly I look at my friendship with Lily through a different lens. Lily has an accent that's not quite London but not *not* London, and I know she didn't grow up on the island. But I don't know where she was born. How can I not know where she was born?

When you ask Lily anything about her life before she landed on the curve of Aurora Island, though, she bats it back and asks a question. And I answer them, all of them, thinking: *She's so caring, she's such a good listener, she's so selfless.*

Or just so secretive.

I think our age gap fuelled the dynamic. There's eleven years between us. Lily's always been a mentor and advisor, sage and wise. A surrogate big sister, for me who's never had one. The only person – to be honest – who's ever mothered me. Looked after me.

Now, that excuse feels pathetic. She isn't my mentor. She isn't my big sister or my mother. She's my friend, and I know nothing about her.

'Are you inside, Zadie?' Ross asks now. 'Are you at home?'

'On my doorstep.'

'Please get inside,' he begs.

I roll my eyes. Ross, protector of women – sure.

I push my key into the lock but the door jams.

'Hold on, front door's being weird.'

'Weird?' His hackles are up. 'Zadie? Zadie, is someone there?'

'Not human weird, just letter-wedged-at-the-bottom weird.'

He exhales. 'Wedged letters we can cope with. Stay on the phone though.'

I hold the phone under my chin and shove the door up and over the letter.

'Shut.' I put the bolt on. 'Locked.' I walk to the bottom of the stairs and shout. 'Bobbi?'

I'm the most junior member of the admin staff at Aurora Island Eco Wellness Retreat and the salary isn't enough to afford my own place, so I rent a spare room in Port St Joseph, the same town as Lily. I live with my housemate-cum-landlady Bobbi, and also with Bertie, her four-year-old who starts school this September.

I used to try my best to give them family space, not to intrude, not to use up the last of the rice noodles. To be as close to invisible as I could be. Over time though, that changed. Now, I am family. I babysit Bertie without asking to be paid, though Bobbi still insists on it. Even if I could afford to, I wouldn't want to move out now.

I sleep in the tiny box room I call my 'Harry Potter cupboard', after evenings with Bobbi on the sofa with a tube of Pringles and a ham sandwich (me) and unsalted nuts and oatcakes (her), both wearing our glasses and watching back-to-back episodes of *The Traitors*.

'Is she in?' Ross asks.

'Not yet.' I slip my Converse fully off now, without bending down. 'She'll be picking up Bertie from nursery.'

As I'm talking, I reach down for that post that blocked the door. There's my name and address, handwritten on an envelope. But I shove it, folded, into my back pocket. Too consumed with Lily to think about it now, no matter how weird its presence is.

'How long is Derek keeping Jake for?' I ask. 'If Lily's not back tonight . . .'

'He's happy to have him for as long as we need. Hold on.' When he speaks again, his voice is defeated. 'Message just came through. Another woman's gone. O for Orla.' He pauses. Swears under his breath. 'Somehow, Zadie, Lily definitely counts as the N.'

When I'm silent, except for my breath which comes heavy and wheezing, Ross becomes softer. 'I know. I don't get it either. But you need to stay home, Zadie, the rules have changed. In fact until we know different, there are no rules. There is just some psycho, taking women from Aurora Island.'

'You're really not someone I would turn to for advice, Ross,' I snap.

He sighs. 'Lily would want me to make sure that you—'

'Lily *would* want! Jesus. She's not dead, Ross.'

Although, it's what everyone really thinks, isn't it? If they go, there is a strong chance that they aren't coming back.

'I didn't say she was dead.'

'Lily was *extremely* suspicious of you, until you tricked her into bed,' I tell him. 'She just let her guard down, that's all.'

'I know I'm not going to persuade you of this, Zadie, but I'm not the bad guy. I care about Lily.'

I say nothing and he sighs.

'I have to go,' he says, sounding agitated. 'Call on the other line.'

When I hang up on him, I throw all of my favourite swear words at the wall of my room over and over – glad of the empty, child-free house – until I am spent. Then I lie on my bed and try to make my thoughts less muddy.

N.

N.

Does Ross have a nickname for Lily? Something cutesy and gross that begins with N?

Something digs into my lower back and it's only then I remember the letter I shoved into my pocket. Very, very little post comes my way, what with me renting a spare room and the fact that this is 2025 and I am twenty-four and a stamp costs twenty quid or something, and I stare at it like a relic.

The envelope is still folded in half and I unfold it to flat and smooth it out.

My name. My address.

I don't know what I'm expecting when I open it but this isn't it. At the top of the sheet of lined paper is the date, I presume, that it was written on. Like we did at school, on the top of every work page.

That date is March, two months before Alice went missing.

And the *writing*. Gorgeous calligraphy, like it's a wedding invitation. Except it doesn't say anything about carriages or canapés. Instead, apart from the date, it says only three words.

The Alphabet Women

Still clutching the piece of paper, I see my belly rising, falling, rising, falling, too fast. Too fast, too much. It shouldn't look like that. Lily shouldn't be missing. I shouldn't have this. Those words shouldn't – couldn't – have been written in March.

Alice went missing in May, the rest of the women in June. How could they have been written in *March*?

My heart thumps, a heavyweight's fists, as I realise what this means. What this letter's been sent to tell me. The term is not new and it didn't start with the missing women. Someone was using the term the Alphabet Women *before* Alice and the others disappeared. Someone took this paper and carefully wrote it down, months before any women went missing.

Thump.

Someone wrote it down.

And I know who.

Because people come to Lily, always, for cakes. But they also come when they want handwritten wedding invites. They come for Lily's beautiful calligraphy.

P

Bobbi walks into the living room where I am staring at the TV but not taking anything in. She pulls off her headphones, her face set into a grimace. 'Any news?'

I shake my head. It's Thursday; Lily has been gone for twenty-four hours. Just as with all of the other women who have gone missing in the last three weeks, there has been no news. No sightings. Nothing.

Bobbi perches on the edge of the sofa. 'You're still feeling wary of Ross?'

I scowl when I think of him. 'More than wary. I just keep thinking about that thing you told me, about him being out in his car in the early hours. And there are other things. He leapt off a call to take another one, even though we were talking about Lily, even though it was crucial. I just feel convinced that he's hiding something, Bob.'

She nods.

'He's messaged me again,' she says, tentative. 'Same thing. Wants you to do episode seven. Talk about . . .'

'Talk about Lily, *as her best friend*. I know. He's messaged me too.'

Ross always invites friends of the Alphabet Women on to the podcast to make sure they don't become *just letters*. To make sure listeners remember that they are human. He wants me to be that person for Lily. But how can I, when I know about the note? When I'm still trying to process what the hell it means. Where it fits.

Bobbi pauses. 'It might help?'

'Why would it?' I sulk. 'It never has before. None of the other interviews have got the women back. And anyway – how can I sit and chat on a podcast now, with him?'

'Cheese and onion pasties,' Ross says, brandishing a greasy paper bag when I open the front door five minutes later.

For God's sake.

'I like junk food more than most people, Ross, but pasties won't swing this for you.'

'What if it could help though, Zadie?' It's Bobbi, behind me.

Judas.

What if it could, though?

An hour later, my voice shakes as I sit in a quiet booth at the Beach Bar.

Ross asks: 'Zadie, welcome to *Gone Girls*. Can you introduce yourself?'

And I explain that I am Lily's friend, Zadie, and that I'm as confused as everyone else.

'I spoke to her right before she went missing,' I say. 'She sounded normal, she sounded happy. She didn't say anything that made me worry.'

'Lily went on N. Do you have any idea why that might have happened – out of sequence like that? We'd already had an L.'

'I have nothing. There isn't a nickname for her, or a middle name that begins with N, as far as we know,' I tell him. Tell the listeners. At the same time, I eyeball Ross across the booth of the Beach Bar. *Do you know?*

'And you're one of her closest friends, right?' he pushes. 'You would know?'

'Of course.'

But as I say it, I feel like a fraud. A liar. What would I know since I realised that I barely know Lily at all?

When we finish my interview, Ross rubs his forehead, exhausted.

He's looked like this a lot lately, I realise. Exhausted. No wonder, if he's driving around Aurora at 5 a.m. Where do you go?

'I'm going to record a couple of lines to reference Paola, bring it right up to date,' says Ross, as he presses pause on his recording. The call about Paola came in just after I got here. 'I'll work on the copy at home tonight, and then it should be ready to send to Gav.'

Ross snaps his laptop shut and puts his Zoom microphone away. I unclip the microphone from my top and pass it to him.

'Who's Gav?'

'The producer on the mainland that took over from Lily. Used to work in radio, top bloke. After he's done, I should be able to upload it first thing tomorrow.'

My stomach does extensive gymnastics.

Tomorrow.

Would Lily hate this? Being spoken about in a public forum? My gut says yes. But she would also get it, wouldn't she? If it could help, she would get that I have no choice.

'I'll drop you home,' says Ross, downing the last of his tea and retching. 'Mate, even the tea. This place.'

It's 8 p.m. and not long after midsummer. I've got a while before the sky will darken, and my instinct is to grab at a hint of freedom. To meander home in my Crocs like I'm on a fortnight's half-board in Majorca.

He sees me pause. 'Call Bobbi. Tell her we're leaving now, and where we are. What time we're due. Tell her you're with me and that I know you're calling her. I am not doing this, Zadie. I swear to you, I am not the one taking the Alphabet Women.'

A muffled noise comes out of my throat.

'They aren't sticking to the letters.' God, the complacency of a man who thinks I could forget that they aren't sticking to the letters. Who thinks I could, after we've lost *Lily*, my friend Lily, be anything other than terrified every single second, without even the pattern of the letters to reassure me. Who doesn't have to live with my most secret, selfish thought: *I wish I was an S.* I wish I had a more common letter. I wish they'd take someone else, anyone else, but me. I run through anyone I've ever met on this island who's a Z – there aren't many – and on some level, I am hoping that one of those women disappears. Probably by doing that, I'm wishing her dead. And what sort of person does that make me? What sort of community does that make us – all of us wishing each other dead, as long as we can be okay?

'Just accept the lift, mate, would you?'

'Fuck YOU,' I say injecting the words with as much rage as I can. Then I call Bobbi and stomp out towards his car anyway because what choice do I have?

In Ross's old Kia, bloody *Kev*, I look down to see my fists balled in my lap as nineties Oasis blasts out of the speakers. Ross presses something on the steering wheel and the volume's turned down on 'Live Forever'.

A couple of minutes later, his eyes land on my lips, mouthing the words.

'Would have thought this was a bit old-school for *the yoof*.'

'The way you say *yoof* is in your top ten cringiest attributes.' I look out of my window. I hope he doesn't see that my hands are shaking. That, despite the call to Bobbi, I'm still wary of being in a car alone with him. I hope he thinks I'm just sparring with him.

'What are the others?'

'Naming your car.' I turn to him. 'You're so old that your music taste has come back around by the way.'

'*Already?*'

'Yep. Look. Nineties.' I gesture to the scrunchie that ties up my hair and the *Friends* t-shirt I'm wearing with my cycling shorts. *Just keep the small talk going. Keep it light and get home. Stay safe. Stay alive.*

'Christ, I'm done for.' He turns his neck to the right. 'I am *old*. Check my crown. Is it a Prince William situation?'

I look over. Fight my smirk. 'You're alright for now.'

The music is interrupted as a call comes through on Bluetooth from someone named Barry.

Ross is ignoring it. 'Aren't you going to get it?'

But he shakes his head. 'I'll call him back when I get in.'

I frown and wonder what he doesn't want to talk about in front of me. What he's keeping from me.

When the call goes to voicemail, Ross says, 'Go on then. Why Zadie? I mean, you had one hell of a moniker going on already with a surname like Christmas. It's a bold parental move.'

I scowl at him.

'I love it,' he says, defensive. 'It's lovely. Just unusual, that's all. Not a Claire, is it, or a Rachel?'

'You're such a Ross, wanting every girl to be a Rachel.'

He glances at my t-shirt with a smirk. 'Touché.'

His eyes are back on the road now and he says: 'Wondered where it came from, that's all.'

'Well, here's the thing, Ross. My mother was a huge reader and obsessed with Zadie Smith's *White Teeth*.'

He nods his head. 'Cool. Great book. So I'm, er, told.'

'None of that is true. But that's what *Lily* presumed, because Lily would, and I thought it sounded deeply cultured, once I'd googled Zadie Smith and *White Teeth*. So I went with it. Zadie Smith was actually called Sadie when she was born, by the way. She changed her name.'

'Nice fact. And the truth about how *you* were named? If it was nothing to do with Zadie Smith?'

'My mother *misheard* the name Sadie, Ross . . . If you must know. Lorna Christmas was not one for detail.'

He looks at me with an expression somewhere between amusement and disbelief.

'Are you serious?'

'Deadly. Someone told her just before she registered me, but by then, she'd decided she liked it with the Z.'

He watches me for a few seconds, eyes flicking back to the road intermittently.

I have my keys in my pocket and my fingers on them. One move and I'll scrape them down your face and run.

I carry on looking out of the window, wondering what conclusions he's making about a mum who didn't bother checking she'd spelt her child's name right before she allocated it to her for life. But then, what do I care? Who is this man to me? Who's he ever been, other than someone I think Lily was wrong to fall for and wrong to trust?

'There we go,' says Ross when we pull up outside my house.

I unclip my seat belt.

Ross is staring straight ahead, thoughtful. 'It felt hopeful with Lily, if that's not too cringe a thing to say.'

I sit in silence for a few seconds. 'That one's not cringe at all, as it goes.' That's how Lily sounded on the phone yesterday too – *hopeful*, despite my own cynicism. But then lust can do weird things to people. And it can definitely override judgement.

'I like Lily a lot,' he says as I reach to open the car door. I see Bobbi looking out from between the curtains.

I nod. 'I asked her a while ago if it was a romantic thing,' I tell him, taking my fingers off the door handle and looking him right in the eyes. *Go on, persuade me.* 'She said you called her *mate* so it couldn't be.'

He looks aghast. 'I call everyone mate!'

'Exactly.'

He groans. 'I'm thirty-six and straight and I live with an adult male I barely know called Colin. You might guess that I am very, very bad at this, Zadie.'

I go to respond but Ross is already speaking again. 'I get why you're weirded out that she went missing straight after something happened between us. It was the first time and then . . . yeah, straight away, like *straight away*, she's gone.'

'When it wasn't her letter.'

'When it wasn't her letter.'

I watch his face, etched all over with being human. Hurt and worry and guilt and silly jokes and a podcast and being a friend to the dog and a goof and a suspect, all of them jumbled, balled together like socks.

And I try to work out who he is really; which parts are the fundamental parts.

I stare at him. 'Goodnight, Ross.'

And I walk inside to Bobbi, thoughts still muddy. Judgement still veering widely in both directions, a drunk driver at the wheel.

'Oh, excellent,' Bobbi says through a mouthful of toothpaste, appearing at the top of the stairs. Glasses and dressing gown. 'Ross didn't kill you.'

'Not yet.'

I hear her spit into the sink and then laugh as I walk up the stairs. 'Night, Zee.'

From my bedroom, I take out the envelope that was delivered yesterday, and the note with that March date on: *THE ALPHABET WOMEN*. 'Actually, Bob,' I say, appearing in the bathroom doorway as she massages oil into her face. 'Can I show you something?'

Bobbi splashes water over her face. 'Course.' She pats her cheeks dry.

'Give me,' she says, hand out for the paper, the other still holding a towel.

When she sees it, she frowns. Looks at me. 'What is it?'

'I think Lily wrote it.'

A light bulb moment. 'Oh my God, of course. The calligraphy. The wedding invites.' She looks at it again. 'But it's . . . ?'

I nod and pull my ponytail tighter for something to do with my hands. 'Yeah. It's from before any of them went missing.'

She turns to me and frowns. 'I don't get it. How is that *possible*?'

I look at her. Swallow hard. 'It's not,' I say. 'That's the problem. It's not possible.'

Q

In the bathroom, we look at each other.

'Is Lily *involved*?' I say, because I can't come up with anything else.

'Oh God, Zee, of course not.'

But what's the alternative?

'Mummy!' Bertie calls.

'I'll probably end up falling asleep with him,' Bobbi says, heading for her son's room, apology all over her face. 'But if I don't catch you tonight, we'll *definitely* talk about this in the morning.' She kisses my cheek. 'We'll figure this out together, okay? Night, Zee.'

In bed I lie awake, thinking about Lily, about Ross, about the note that's tucked away now in my knicker drawer, about the rusty window that doesn't close properly in my room. Opened fully, it's big enough for a small adult to squeeze through. Can I ask Bobbi to replace it? Money's always tight though; she still has so much student debt. I give myself a talking to. *Stop being ridiculous. No one's going to come through the window.*

In my Harry Potter cupboard, contact lenses tapped out, my glasses on, my phone lies propped on my knees.

Q has gone, says Ross's message. We always wondered what they would do at Q. It's a surname, Quinn. No first name yet. Ringing any bells?

But I don't reply. Because, on my laptop on the bed next to me, I've just seen something else.

A TikTok DM that says: *She's not called Lily. She's called Natasha.*

N.

I watch this message like I would watch an egg poaching, on alert for it to boil over or fall apart. I watch it and I watch it and I watch it. But nothing happens. Nothing falls apart. Nothing boils over.

When I click on the profile that sent it, it's faceless, a sea of numbers.

Of course it is.

It's probably rubbish.

One of the thousands of strands of nonsense and misinformation and conspiracy theories and speculation and rubbish that have been shared about what's happening in this strange summer on Aurora Island from the people who film TikTok videos on the beach and next to the 'Welcome to Aurora Island' sign.

But Lily disappeared not when we were on L, but N. And that repetition doesn't make any sense. It never did.

It also fits with something else: that there is so much about Lily that I have never known.

God.

I am out of my depth. Drowning.

And so I make a decision.

I pick up the phone, and I call the direct line I've been given to the police. When Campbell answers, then sends someone over to collect the note with the calligraphy as evidence while I forward the DM, I feel the palpable relief of emptying myself out. The palpable relief of telling him absolutely everything. Of coming up to the surface for air.

R

Friday, and the local news says that today will bring the highest temperature ever recorded on Aurora Island. The heatwave shows as much sign of abating as the disappearances.

'I'm going to get straight to business this morning,' says Ross through my headphones as I sit on the beach looking out to sea, listening to episode seven of *Gone Girls: The Alphabet Women of Aurora Island on my day off. I haven't got to my part yet; that's up next.*

'Two have gone now in quick succession. Whoever this is, they're speeding back up. First, we had Barbara Quinn. And now, we have had confirmation that Rita Rowe is the latest woman to have gone missing. These two, our Q and our R, were within *sixteen hours* of each other.'

That familiar looming intro music begins, and then the adverts.

'We price-match on thousands of products. Cheaper than you think; try us today.'

And then Ross is back.

'Today we are extremely pleased to have former police detective Mark Williams on with us,' says Ross, with a slight clear of his throat. 'Mark, thanks for joining me. I know you have your own pod, *From the Archives*, where you look back at historical unsolved crimes. I am a big, big fan of it here at *Gone Girls*, and it was a huge inspiration for me when I launched the first series on Oban.

'But today you're coming to help us out on our podcast. Tell me, from your experience: should we be worried that these disappearances are particularly close together?'

'It's a good question, Ross. Let me break it down.'

And in they dive. But while I'm usually gripped by every word of every episode, this time my mind is meandering.

I've told Campbell about the note, but I haven't told Ross. Which means I'm omitting evidence that could be covered and dissected on the podcast. Could have been in this episode. Maybe it's the right thing to do, to leave it with the police only. Or maybe it's catastrophically wrong.

And then.

'Jesus!'

Someone is lifting off my headphones. Someone is way too close to me.

And on the beach, I scream.

'Sorry. Did I make you jump? Just spotted you and wanted to ask a couple of extra questions for the pod.'

I stare at him. 'Maybe think about not creeping up on women on this island right now, Ross? Not a good look.'

But while I sound annoyed, what I really am is trembling head to toe in terror.

I don't trust this guy. Still can't shake the feeling that he is hiding something huge. Something that is fundamental to this whole thing.

Ross sits down. 'You're right. Sorry. But I tried to speak to you and it was quite hard to get your attention when you had headphones on and your eyes were closed and under those giant sunglasses.'

He rubs sweat away from his forehead.

'Maybe not a good idea to sit on an empty beach with headphones on at the moment though?'

But there were plenty of people around when I sat down. Or a few at least: the early crowd who were here for a swim before work. When I look around now though, I see that he's right: we are on our own.

'Lily said there was no way Aurora would get a proper heat-wave,' says Ross, oblivious to my internal fizzing.

'Lily lied,' I mutter, putting my headphones in my bag.

'What?'

I shake my head. 'Nothing.'

But she did, didn't she? Lily did lie. And not just about the weather.

'Even Jake doesn't want to move,' says Ross, flopping down, supine on the sand, next to the dog.

When we got down to the beach half an hour ago, Jake headed straight for a sea that was as still as a building. Now, soggy and sated, he lies panting at our feet. When he does move, Jake's gait in this heat is teenage – a fifteen-year-old hauled out of bed to go hiking with his parents. *Mu-uuum.*

Suddenly, there are people. Yoga mats being unfurled in front of us; a sound system being lugged on someone's shoulder.

'Friday beach yoga.'

In front of us are eighteen or twenty locals and second-homers rolling out mats for the weather-dependent class. More join them, until eventually there are about forty or fifty people.

The music kicks in, and they start to move.

Slow.

Graceful.

We sit and watch. Faces under baseball caps look towards the sun, arms are slightly out to the sides, toes are spread and clad in toe rings, dipped into the sand. For a few minutes, these women aren't thinking about disappearances and warnings. They aren't listening to the podcast or passing on the information they've heard about the latest letter. They're not whispering the words *serial killer* to each other in the queue in Waitrose while they pick up fresh olives, or watching police boats search for bodies while they walk their Labs.

'Sun salutations,' Ross whispers, nodding towards them. 'Beautiful.'

'Oh, *of course* you do yoga.'

'Mostly, on the beach, though, I do my tai chi.' He starts waving his arms around at sharp angles.

I stare at him. 'You're an acquired taste, aren't you, Ross?'

He nods solemnly. 'I am, that.'

He kneads his fingers in Jake's fur. 'Was Derek sad to say goodbye?' he asks.

I nod, peeling a banana that Bobbi, shouting something about UPFs again, shoved at me as I walked out of the door. 'A bit. Mostly he's just desperate to hear some good news about Lily though.'

I picked Jake up from Derek's this morning, along with his bed, food and approximately seventy-five chew toys. He's going to live with Bobbi, Bertie and me, until Lily comes home (Bertie thinks that's fair: two boys, two girls).

Now, Lily's dog rolls in the sand, then settles at my feet. I offer Ross half of my banana but he shakes his head.

'Would rather have something madly processed with shitloads of additives,' he says. 'How can *ultra* anything be bad? Ultra's cool, right?'

I start to laugh then stop myself. *Don't laugh at him. Don't take your eye off the ball.* That's what Lily did. She started trusting him, buying into his innocent-Manc-with-a-podcast-and-stupid-socks schtick. Look how that ended.

The yoga class is done, the yogis supine too now, faces to the sun, tattooed feet lolling at the ends of their mats. I do the same on the sand. It could be the Caribbean. Right now, it's impossible to imagine how cold that sleet feels when it sneaks down your neck as you battle your way up Ben Fell, wind pushing you back with two strong palms.

Five minutes later, I've answered Ross's podcast questions and he's gone and I am lying on my back in the sea. I float, pretending I am in Tahiti or Mauritius or Barbados. I head far out with a strong front crawl. I drape an arm across an inflatable swan that's not claimed an owner, then cruise around on it like I'm on an 18–30 in Kavos.

I act like there's no podcast, no Alphabet Women, no danger of disappearing, no note, no message, no secret that is being kept, no problem. I try to block out thoughts of the friend who I am trying so hard to find, even when the evidence is battering me over the head that my friend has never really existed. Even when I am angry with her. (Thinking someone might be dead doesn't stop you feeling angry towards them. Humans are complicated.)

After I dry off, I have an urge to stay out, not to go home – for this long day to stretch out even further – and I head off on the long walk to The Dolphin. Bare legs, full pint, sand scratching the backs of my thighs. I order a pint of cider and sit in the beer garden out the front.

When I finally get there, The Beatles tell me what I already know: 'Here Comes the Sun'. Steve lollops outside, takes the mike as he likes to do, and I smile and hum along.

'Another pint?' Steve asks, when the singing and my drink are finished and he is back to barman duties. His hand combs through his long, grey beard. He is slightly out of breath.

I hand over my empty glass.

'Serious multitasking going on here,' I smile. 'That was brilliant.'

He nods his head in thanks. 'Appreciate that. Just trying to bring a bit of joy.' He takes my glass. 'Hang in there, love,' he says, giving my arm a squeeze. 'We'll find them.'

While Steve is getting my drink I sit there thinking about all those women who should be here on a Friday afternoon, drinking cider too fast on an empty stomach like me, and eating chips for dinner instead of that sensible salad they'd planned. I look around. Today it feels like everything is heightened. Everyone is drinking faster, laughing louder. Maybe we're doing it on their behalf.

When I walk through the door at home at 6 p.m., Bobbi laughs and pinches my face. 'Cider cheeks!'

'It's sunny,' I pout.

She raises an eyebrow.

'Bit of both?' I concede, touching what is admittedly an extremely warm face. 'One cider cheek and one sun cheek?'

She hugs me tight. 'I'm glad you switched off.'

Then, as she pulls away, she pauses.

My body tenses. 'What is it?'

'Nothing bad, don't worry. No one has . . . no one's gone.' She bites her lip. 'But I do have something to tell you. Did you ever meet Susie, who goes to book club with Lily and Alice?'

I shake my head.

'Well, she came into the surgery today.'

'Okay.'

'She said that just before this all started, they had a bit of a change at book club.'

'Right . . .'

'Their book club started apparently as a few mates with no real plan about what to read in the library. But like lots of things

on Aurora, it grew and there's a lot more . . . well, I guess, external influences in it now.

'Lots of the women – and Susie said it's only ever been women – were at other book clubs that had names and themes, stuff they specialised in. They decided to do the same and after a brainstorm, they decided that they'd aim to read a book from every letter of the alphabet, in order.'

I look at her.

'They renamed their book club, and they called themselves—'

'The Alphabet Women,' I whisper. 'Jesus.'

Bobbi nods. 'Susie said that she and the other women mentioned it but the police were sure it was just a coincidence. Said there was no way the two things could be connected. She said they were dismissive of the idea of a book club being of any sort of importance, mocked it a bit to be honest.'

I look at her. Wise, wise Bobbi. 'But what do you think?'

She considers. 'I thought it would make sense if that's what the note was,' she says slowly. 'Like Lily wrote it to put up in the retreat on the noticeboard or something to advertise the book club? Didn't get round to finishing it, putting on the details of the book club, so it literally just had the name. I don't know. That was the most I could get it to make sense. But a coincidence, on this same island, seems . . .'

I'm nodding. 'Yeah. Agreed.'

My brain is working overtime. Bobbi puts a bowl of leftover pasta in front of me at the kitchen table. I am ravenous and eat a mouthful of anchovies and olives and also swallow down relief. This is it: an explanation for why Lily was writing about the Alphabet Women. An explanation that doesn't mean she's somehow tied up in this.

But it only clears up one part of things. Because there is still the question of who sent the note, and why.

Ross?

I twizzle another forkful of spaghetti, heart hammering the whole time. We're getting close, aren't we? I can feel it. The connections might not quite link yet but they will.

'You okay?' Bobbi says, coming back into the kitchen. She's changed into a white vest and cotton pyjama shorts, hair in a messy ponytail. Her thick black glasses are on. I love it when Bobbi is in this mode: the day's done, the juggle's over, the hatches are battened. Tonight, it's even more reassuring. 'Sorry, I know you didn't need anything extra to think about.'

I look at her, adrenalin coursing. 'Bob, there's something I haven't told you.' And I tell her. The DM. Lily, not Lily. Natasha.

Bobbi's lovely eyes widen.

'Jesus Christ,' she mutters. 'Did you respond to it?'

'I thought it might be a nut job. It's not like there aren't a lot of them about. I thought it was another online faker, just stirring because of the repeat of the L. But the more I think about it and the more I think about how much Lily hid . . . You know what, it would make sense.'

Bertie shouts and Bobbi's upstairs for twenty minutes. I go into the living room and lie on the sofa, picking up where I left off on the new episode of the podcast at the beach. When Bobbi comes back down, I pull off my headphones.

She nods towards my phone. '*Gone Girls*?'

'Yeah. Just got to my bit. Nothing better than listening to your own voice.' I pretend to shudder.

Bobbi laughs. 'Do you want to keep listening?'

I shake my head and turn my headphones off. 'No. That's enough of my awful voice for today. I want to hang out with you.'

She leans over and hugs me. 'Just one thing before we do the Netflix scroll of doom. I know you're wary of Ross – I'm wary of Ross too, don't trust that guy as far as I can throw him and that middle-of-the-night thing was shifty as hell – but if he is innocent . . . hear me out . . . *if* he is innocent, then he's doing a good job getting this story out there, Zee.'

I nod. 'I know. It's just . . .'

'Yeah. I get it. But honestly, everyone who has stepped foot into the surgery is talking about *Gone Girls*. This woman told me today how her friend lives in *France* and said that even all the ex-pats in her village are listening to it. Ross is doing the opposite of what all those TikTok posts with their conspiracy theories are doing. He's making sure people know the facts and remember they're human. Everyone knows these women's names.'

'Except for Lily's.'

Bobbi purses her lips. 'Well. Maybe. But we have no evidence that that's true, Zee.'

She picks up the remote control. '*The Traitors*? I don't think I can do a whole film.'

But just then, tiny feet patter down the stairs.

'Here we go,' Bobbi says, putting tea that's still nearly full down on a coffee table that's filled with *Fireman Sam* magazines and *Paw Patrol* figures.

'Mummy, my tummy hurts.' Framed in the entrance to the living room, his tiny face is tilted to the side, like he knows his cutest pose is his best chance of not being sent back to bed. The eyes blink, the long eyelashes flutter.

'Hmmm, always hurts at bedtime though, baby,' says Bobbi, head tilted to mirror Bertie's – I wonder if that's deliberate or something that just happens. 'And never when the chocolate buttons are open.' She grabs him for a cuddle and kisses his cheek. 'Back up to bed, monkey.'

His eyes turn to me. 'Auntie Zee?'

'I'll take him up.' When it's Bertie-related, I'm weak. I also grab at distractions at the moment and Bertie's the best one by far.

When I come back downstairs after a very complicated teddy-arranging session, Bobbi smiles. 'Our luck was in the day you rocked up here. When I think who we could have got.' She sips her tea and nods to the coffee table where there's a steaming mug for me, too. 'I hated the idea of having some stranger in the house, especially with a kid, but it's not been like that. And it's not been just about rent money.'

I reply in the same whisper she's using, both of us trying not to disturb Bertie.

'When I think about who *I* could have got too though,' I say, with a shudder. 'It's a lifeline having you two.'

Bobbi reaches across the sofa and squeezes my hand. We drink our tea in silence, both listening out for Bertie, but he's quiet.

'I'm so glad neither of us is living on our own through this,' she says, eventually. 'It's having such a massive impact. Looking over our shoulder, having to be on high alert for some psycho all the time. The news being constantly bleak. One after the next going missing.' She pauses while she sips her tea. 'I'm finding it hard, Zee,' she says, her face tired. 'Having to be positive in front of patients. Everyone knows someone, everyone's feeling it. We're too small an island not to. And then trying to keep it all from Bertie when I know he's picking up on bits . . . This isn't in the parenting books. I'm struggling.' She looks up. 'Sorry to moan.'

I squeeze her hand back. 'Sorry it's been rough.'

'I'm starting to see other stuff in practice, too,' she says. 'Just *fatigue* with it all. Anxiety. Loneliness. Heart palpitations and chest pain in all these young, healthy women.' She pauses. 'I feel guilty, sometimes.'

'Guilty?'

'That I'm a B,' she says quietly. 'No one even *knew* the alphabet pattern at that point. I feel guilty that I haven't had to live with that level of fear, like you do every day.'

I go to protest, but she gets there first.

'I know you do, Zee. I see your face when you walk in the door, the relief that you've made it through another day. I saw your expression just then listening to the podcast. Not that I'm not still scared – it doesn't feel completely safe being a woman on this island, whatever your letter. But I know it's not like how you must feel.'

She looks at me like I'm a painting and sighs.

'And I know how much you're missing Lily.' She leans her head back on the sofa, her own tea nearly empty now. 'We took it for granted, didn't we? Normality. Lily popping in for a cup of tea when she dropped off one of her lemon poppy whatsit loaves. Bliss. Normal, boring bliss.' She breathes out. 'In the absence of the lemon poppy thing though, shall I make toast?'

She comes in a few minutes later with two plates of hot toast smeared with still-visible butter.

'Mummy, it *still* hurts and I have tried for *ages* to get to sleep.'

Bertie is standing at the living room door again, tiny pyjamas on tiny limbs.

When Bobbi scoops him up, he looks at me over Bobbi's shoulder and his big brown eyes narrow. The eyelashes go again. 'Hey, you're having a midnight feast!'

It's 8 p.m. but the two times – 8 p.m. and midnight – are the same to Bertie. All of it happens after he goes to bed, in the Official Adult Hours, and the idea that you can eat in those hours is nothing short of magical.

'*I* want a midnight feast. And I'm still too hot.'

'The seventy-five teddies you have stacked around you probably don't help,' I laugh, holding my arms out for a cuddle. He doesn't know how much I need one. 'Maybe getting rid of a few might cool you down.' I look at Bobbi. 'I could read him a story?'

Bobbi wrenches him out of my arms and shakes her head. 'No. Too late.' She buries her head in Bertie's neck. 'Bed for you, mister.

Stop taking advantage of Auntie Zee.' A warmth spreads through me every time they call me that.

Hold on to those things. Hold on to them.

As Bobbi steers Bertie back out of the living room door, grabbing a slice of toast from her plate with one hand and taking a bite, she looks at me. 'I might stay up there, you know. I'm shattered.'

I nod. 'Sure. Night, Bobs.'

When she's gone, I check on Jake, who is already zonked out in the kitchen, and then I head to my room as well. It's too hot to sleep and I know listening to the rest of the podcast before bed will give me nightmares. I turn on my iPad. Look at the message again. Still no comment.

In my DMs though, there is another message from an anonymous account. A different one this time. My heart thumps harder.

I know I shouldn't open it. I know it'll probably give my laptop a virus. But after that last post, the title's too tempting.

My hand shakes as I click on it.

That name again: Natasha.

But this time, a link.

I put my headphones on so I don't disturb Bertie, and so that Bobbi thinks I'm sleeping. So she doesn't hear this, whatever this is.

A video.

My body is rigid as I click play on what looks like . . . a reality dating show? A vintage one, judging by the fashion and the adjectives. I peer more closely.

I let the monotony of the programme wash over me, the *babes* and the *huns* and the *dudes* and the arguing and the flirting and the sunbathing.

What the hell is this?

Most of the women on the screen are about my age. A group of them loll against a kitchen worktop in tiny bikinis, pink, green, leopard, matching hair to their matching waists. I touch my own hair. Long too, but not like theirs.

'Like you've been living in the woods for a few years,' Lily concluded once, about my knots. 'And somehow on you that looks incredible.' She tells me I'm pretty but I don't see it. My cheeks belong to a chipmunk and I'm scared of doing anything to my eyebrows. I am only just five foot which means as soon as I put on a few pounds, I look kind of *round*.

I pull at my clothes a lot, trying to get them to cover something or enhance something or fit better or sit differently. If my clothes were more expensive, that might help. But once rent and bills are paid, there's not a lot left.

The women on the screen don't have these hang-ups.

One of them stretches for something, barefoot on tiptoes so that her arches are invisible heels, like a Barbie doll. She tells her new friends that she has hair extensions – they all do – but I can't tell where they begin in the long, highlighted hair that touches her barely there bum. A bikini that makes it clear which wax she went for.

She's as far removed from waterproofs and wellies as you could get.

And yet.

I peer closer.

No. Couldn't be.

This woman has the wrong name for starters.

And then, the alarm bell fires loudly and with clarity.

And in that moment the question about why I know so little about my friend Lily – that woman I think of as a sister, but who has told me nothing – is answered.

Natasha, they call her.

Whoever sent me that message is right. Lily is not Lily. She never was.

Lily is someone else entirely.

S

Sweat drips down the small of my back to the waistband of my underwear and beneath.

There have been so many times when Lily was vague. So many times when she's swerved the question and dodged the details, unless we talk about things that have happened since she moved to Aurora. As though that is when her life started.

And now I know why.

Because Lily's life *did* start then. Before that, she was Natasha.

'Natasha,' I murmur, trying it out. 'Natasha.'

I peer at her again, closer, closer.

There are a gaggle of reasons why this woman on my screen can't be Lily. Those *arches*, for starters. When I picture Lily, she's always in her walking boots or her wellies. Staid office flats. I've never seen her wear anything approaching a heel.

Natasha is close to naked on national TV and I've barely seen Lily's shoulders.

I can't take my eyes off the screen.

I watch her talk, move, frown. Watch her smile. So much of it is similar.

But hold on: she could be a cousin of Lily's. Even a sister.

Then the camera zooms in and I see her eyes and I know it. I know it with a jolt of certainty. This woman isn't Lily's cousin, and she isn't Lily's sister. She is Lily.

My brain throws thoughts and memories around like a bingo machine. The message, about her real name. The TV show, still playing now in front of me. The note with that beautiful calligraphy. I thought she was my big sister but I didn't even know her.

I press play again. I watch a man cook a woman an extremely basic sausage sandwich and receive a lot of praise for it. I see women who are barely adults walking very slowly towards stairs in very big heels. And all the time, there she is. Swimming or sunbathing or talking or sipping from a water bottle in the background.

Natasha.

And then, this Natasha walks slowly in her very high heels to the bedroom. When the camera is back on her, she has changed into red lingerie and different heels. A group of other women in bikinis clap as she presents herself on the landing and walks, even more tentatively, down a spiral staircase.

A hulk of a man in small red swimming shorts takes her hand. Gives a tiny, barely perceptible lick of his lips.

There's an ad break then, and afterwards we go straight to Natasha and this man, Andreas, in a room that is entirely black and gold. I grimace.

I've watched these shows before. I know what's happening, and I know what happens afterwards – to the women, anyway. A tiny noise comes from my throat.

Don't do this, Natasha . . . Lily . . . Whoever you are . . . Don't do this. You can't take this back, and they'll punish you for it.

Natasha is in the room, alone now with the red shorts man. There are cheap-looking pink rose petals sprinkled on a bed, and as they talk, you can hear the gurgling plastic mass of a hot tub outside.

Natasha and this man drink something fizzy from champagne glasses, and I hear myself make the noise again. They say a few very scripted lines about their feelings for one another. And then Natasha climbs with her super-smooth Barbie limbs under a duvet and has sex on TV with a man who laughed earlier to another man who was lifting weights next to him about how he didn't really fancy her.

I turn my iPad off and pull my headphones down to my neck, my face contorted, and just then my phone pings. Ross.

Wires reporting that S gone. Her name is Sana? No more info yet.

But I can barely react, not even to news of a missing woman. To yet another human being lost, along with my friend. Along with lovely Alice Fox who loves ABBA and is never late to school pick-up. Along with Issy. Rita. Paola. All of them.

All I can think is *Natasha. Natasha. Natasha.*

Lily.

And something else, an uncomfortable truth. If this woman on my screen hadn't been Lily, I would have carried on watching, possibly pausing the show to grab some crisps. If Bobbi had been around, I'd have called her in, told her it was a good episode and she had to see this. I'd have seen it only as entertainment.

I wince.

How did whoever was in charge of that show let that *happen* to girls? I know things used to be bad. I know there didn't used to be any mental health support on these shows. But seeing it play out like that . . . What must have happened when women realised they'd been thrown to the wolves? When they realised what people had seen, and slowly – horrifyingly – grasped that it would be out there forever? That this would always be who they were.

They ran away from it, I suppose.

They ran from themselves.

They found a remote island and they cut their hair off and they quietened down and they bought staid office flats.

Oh, Lily.

I google the woman I just saw on my screen, using her real name. Natasha Goldstein had just turned eighteen when this show was filmed, seventeen years ago.

When she came out of the show to a barrage of offensive and sexist headlines, *she* – who had the face of a kid who'd just done her GCSEs – issued an apology. The man she'd had sex with – who was twenty-five and had a three-year-old daughter – did not.

I keep reading.

The consensus was that Natasha had let her family down. She'd let her friends down. She'd let the producers of – what the fuck? – *Ultimate Bakes,* which she had won the year earlier, down.

I stare at the words on my screen.

What?

Natasha had been the youngest-ever champion of the huge reality show *Ultimate Bakes.*

Now, I feel a tiny smile inch across my face. Okay, this is more like it. A part of her that I do know. That crosses the boundary line between Natasha and Lily. That she hasn't been able to edit out, because it's at her core.

I laugh out loud.

All those cakes! The ones Lily makes for everyone at work on birthdays or often on not-birthdays. Just because it's Friday, or loads of people have been off sick this week or because it's the school holidays and she knows the gardeners or the cooks or the cleaners are juggling childcare and work and that they might fancy a slice of red velvet.

Since Ross has known Lily, he's sneaked on about half a stone. You can't refuse her cakes.

She does the fancy creative stuff too. Detailed piping. Has the patience and skill to turn her cakes into art. On Bertie's birthday, she whizzed up a *Paw Patrol* masterpiece and refused to be paid.

Of course she's good enough to win *Ultimate Bakes.*

I keep clicking.

On my screen, next, in a huge, bright kitchen, Lily is there again but now she's somewhere between Lily and Natasha; a little closer to the woman I know.

She is wearing plain white trainers and she has an apron on and is holding a giant bunch of flowers. She is sandwiched between two famous chefs whose names I can't remember. Hiding in plain sight. Hiding in *Google*.

Lily must wonder constantly if people know. Ross, for sure – she must worry that a journalist would recognise her. Corinne, who used to work in the entertainment industry, who was always name-dropping celebrities she met and parties she went to back in the day. Did she ever do a double take? Or can anyone hide, if you change the context enough? I wonder if Lily has changed her name formally, by deed poll.

I open another tab and keep reading.

When Natasha left the dating show, this champion who aced her showstoppers and technicals and signatures week after week and beat the best bakers in the country when she wasn't even *eighteen*, had her *Ultimate Bakes* title taken off her because she'd had sex on TV.

She apologised, saying she felt ashamed of herself and knew that she didn't deserve to be *Ultimate Bakes* champion. That by having sex with this man on TV, she'd brought the cosy baking show into disrepute. She apologised for being a bad role model.

(Still nothing from the guy, by the way.)

I feel my fists curl into little angry balls as I keep reading. I want to stand up for Lily, but all of this happened *seventeen years ago* and it's too late, and no one cares, and no one knows who she is anyway.

I feel something warm on my chin and realise I've bitten my nails again. Too far down, so that they pinch and bleed.

On the screen, another image. A picture of Natasha, clothed now in a black work suit that should never be worn by an eighteen-year-old. She poses awkwardly, hands in her lap, regretful and sheepish.

Clutched in her fingers, there is a letter of apology that she wrote and posted on Facebook. Underneath the picture, it's transcribed: *Sorry. Regret. Shame. Guilt. Don't deserve.*

Suddenly, something occurs to me. What if it was *Lily* who sent me the message about her real name? Maybe more. The post. The clip. What if *Lily* wants me to make the connection, because it will help solve the mystery of the Alphabet Women? If that's true though, I am doing a terrible job of it.

I pick up my phone, to use my direct line to Campbell and tell him about the dating show. But this time, something stops me. Lily changed her name and changed her life. She hid it from everyone. She worked so hard to build something on Aurora and start again.

And if she is sending messages, she's sending them to *me*. Not the police. Me.

I've told the police about the note and I can't take that back. But from now on – even if I have a thousand questions – I think I need to hold Lily's past close. Keep her secret. Until, at least, I know more.

In the morning, I walk to the retreat, Jake in sync at my feet, to get some notes I need for work. But all I can think about is what

I watched last night. The images feel like they are etched on to my retinas.

Bobbi is the only person I'd tell but she was out early to take Bertie to his swimming lesson. Instead, the information just rolls round and round and round inside my mind. I swipe my pass and walk through the gate towards the office. Outside the doors to reception, there is a strong smell of lavender from the bushes that used to sit neatly in pots, trimmed and restricted. Now the lavender is starting to sprawl, wild and crazed, with no one here to rein it in.

There's no one here to rein anything in anymore. And when things aren't reined in, they get wild.

It's a Saturday. If the retreat were still open, the weekend crowds would be here and there would be a scrum of people waiting to pick up picnics that had been made on site that morning. Tomas and his team would have been in the kitchen from 6 a.m. prepping them: herby olives and tomato bread, wheels of brie and oily hummus. The smell of homemade scotch eggs drifting with them out of the office door. Proper napkins and good champagne.

'Like the Famous Five grew up and won the lottery,' Lily once murmured. Like a lot of her book references, I didn't really get it.

If the retreat were still open, our lake would be swarming with everyone who hadn't carried their large Waitrose shoppers down to the beach this morning – laden with beach tennis and rounders bats and footballs, inflatable kayaks and paddleboards and woggles and rubber rings.

I put my key into the office door.

Today, it doesn't smell of herby olives. Today, it smells of nothing. Or something a little more sour than nothing. In the office, I put pens in pots and swipe off dust that's built up while we haven't been there. The cleaners, of course, are staying home too.

It's not just the grime. We're still showcasing a spring candlelit yoga flow and the posters advertising an orange wine tasting that never happened feel eerie. Abandoned and frozen, the world's fanciest war zone. Like everyone fled one day with only their passports, clutched tight in their hands, though *maybe* they had time to grab a couple of bottles of Chablis on the way out.

'Okay, Jake,' I mutter, as we stand in that sour nothing of the office. There are three dead flies on the floor. 'Okay, okay.'

When I have the notes in my backpack, Jake heads towards the lake, one of the places Lily used to walk him most around the retreat, stopped ten or twelve times per lap by kids who want to stroke him.

'Go on then,' I say. 'Just a few minutes.'

The only noise is from the gulls circling, probably wondering where all the sausage rolls have gone. Except, for them, everything is immobile.

I know I shouldn't be here. That I should head straight home. But I am so sick of being scared all the time and I am so sick of following the rules. I tilt my neck back to let the sun bathe my face as we walk around the water. A few seconds later, I take off my shoes and socks, slipping my feet into water that feels fresh but – for once – not unpleasant.

'You're okay to wait there for a minute, aren't you?' I ask Jake.

He looks at me. *What's this plan, then?*

It's a fair point. I'm not sure why but I take off my clothes, down to my underwear, and for the first time ever, I swim across the whole width of the lake.

I can swim properly, a strong front crawl – it was one thing my mum was insistent about teaching us all – but today I don't do that. Today I do a deliberately slow and upright breaststroke so that, as I swim, I can look up. A sky that's almost cloudless. A sun, not hot yet but warming up for us; running on the spot and doing its stretches.

From the shore, Jake keeps a close eye on me.

I've not felt this calm in weeks. Even though I am alone in a lake. Even though Lily is missing. Even though I watched that video last night, and can't get the images out of my head. Even though we are starting – surely now – the approach to my letter. To my Z.

But I look up and I'm not looking at a rusty window feeling fearful or lying still on a bed in a tiny room.

No. I'm free, actually, so fuck you, whoever tried to make sure I wasn't. Fuck you, whoever you are who is taking our women and hiding them and making the rest of us live in terror.

I shout it, loud. 'FUCK! YOU!'

And then someone is standing next to the dog, and a shadow falls across the water and I am too scared to shout anymore. My *fuck you* feels stupid. I fall silent.

T

'Jesus Christ,' I say, treading water as I look up at Ross, my hands shaking. '*Again*, how about not creeping up on people?'

But even as I'm scowling at him, I'm thinking – *don't antagonise him*. If it *is* Ross, if he *is* involved, then I need to keep him on side. Report anything he does to the police, but in the meantime make sure that he thinks I'm being friendly.

'I didn't *creep up*. I didn't know who was swimming, did I? I came over quietly in case it wasn't you and it was, like, Richard or someone and I needed to back away and do a runner.'

'Do I look like Richard?'

Richard is a forty-nine-year-old man.

'Only around the nose hair area.'

I ignore him and heave myself out, dry myself ineffectively with my jumper then slip my clothes back on while Ross plays with Jake and averts his eyes.

'Why are you here? Did you follow me?'

'Not follow . . . But I was out for a run and I saw you and Jake heading up here and I . . . well, I was worried, to be honest. That you were out on your own. It's pretty isolated up here, Zadie.'

I scoff.

'There's also just been a T,' he says, ignoring the noise. 'I suppose that made me more nervy. And I thought you might want to know.'

'Who is she?'

'A woman named Tijen?'

I shake my head. I don't know her.

'Beautiful name, huh? Turkish heritage. Didn't turn up to her job at the island cattery this morning and she would never miss a shift. Known for being Mrs Reliable. Family and friends haven't heard from her. Police are sure she's the next Alphabet Woman.'

I nod.

'Look, there was another reason I came.' He looks oddly nervous. 'I wondered if you wanted to listen? To the next episode, before it goes live. I know you're not a part of this one so it's not a . . . I just miss getting Lily's local feedback.'

I bite my lip.

Nod. 'Okay. At the Beach Bar, though.'

Here is too isolated. I can't ignore the fact that I still find Ross a threat. That I'm convinced he is hiding something.

I need to be around other people. Quickly.

When we sit down on the terrace at the Beach Bar, I exhale. He says: 'Bad night?'

'Struggling,' I admit, this part true at least. 'Barely any sleep at all.'

'You don't drink coffee, do you?'

I shake my head. 'Just tea.'

'I don't think we're going to see any significant boost from an Earl Grey.'

I order one anyway.

'Right,' he says, taking a sip of his own black coffee – not like the usual milky tea he drinks – as he clicks something on his laptop. 'Sent to you. About to upload. Episode eight, if you can believe it.'

'How are the reviews?'

'Reviews are incredible.' Ross nods. 'Wish Lily could have seen the latest ones.' He shakes his head clear of the thought. 'Anyway. Just check it over from the local perspective, make sure all the geography's right, that I don't sound like some interloper who doesn't get it.'

Ross reaches down and scratches his ankle just above his luminous green sock. I watch him drink his coffee and I watch him scratch his mosquito bite and I watch his ridiculous socks and I try to read him.

'Okay. Let's channel this into something positive.' Ross claps his hands.

You're the type of person who has a gratitude journal and a quote from Winnie the Pooh on your wall, I think.

'Wallowing isn't going to get us anywhere.'

Who carries a couple of crystals in your back pocket. Wears bright colours so that you 'bring some joy' to the day.

I put my headphones on.

'Victoria, welcome,' says Ross's voice in my ears.

'Hi, Ross.' She sounds nervous.

'You're one of a group of women from Aurora Island that we have on today. It's important that we speak to the detectives and the psychologists and we love having those experts in their fields on, of course – it's a privilege – but our aim with *Gone Girls* has always been that we show the *human* side of things, and that that comes direct from Aurora.

'You're here, Victoria, you're in the thick of it, you're still having to go about your daily life while having this hanging over you.

Can you tell me how you feel, knowing your letter hasn't come round yet, but that it's imminent?'

A beat. 'Well . . . scared?'

'Of course. What's your strategy? Are you staying home or getting on with life?'

'I'm still doing the essentials. Picking the kids up from school, running them to climbing practice. But when we pass U, I'm stopping all of that and my husband is going to do it, even though that's going to be a nightmare, juggling all of that with work. But I'll be staying at home, full time, until we pass to W, and someone will be staying with me all the time too. Family or friends.'

'Will you do the same when it's your letter, Wendy?'

There is a tiny cough. 'No. Um. No. It won't be possible for me.' I turn the volume up to hear her. 'I mean, my kids are grown – even my grandbabies are grown – so I don't have that issue but I live alone. There are things I'll have to go out for.'

'I'm sure friends would help?' says Ross. 'There are groups, I hear, where people deliver essentials to their neighbours when it's their letter. Take turns.'

'I'm in a farmhouse by myself, Ross, right out in Aurora's sticks. There are no neighbours.' She sighs. 'But also, I'm eighty-five, petal, you know and I've . . . I've lived through a war. I'm not having this, being scared to leave the house because of some psycho with an ABCs fixation. If it's my time, it's my time. But I'll give him a good fight if he comes for me, I'll tell you that.'

Ross chuckles. 'Oh, I bet you would, Wendy.'

When I've finished listening to the women and take off my headphones, Ross reaches his hand down to Jake, who is lying under the table. He avoids my eye contact, nervous.

'So?'

'It's brilliant,' I tell him. 'One of the best yet. Absolutely got me at the end when Vanessa cried. She's right. What *is* she expected to do when she has a midwife appointment and she's single with no family nearby? Broke me. You're doing a good job.'

And yet the praise is delivered reluctantly. Something about Ross still niggles at me; a gut instinct that he is lying about something. Hiding something.

'How's Jake doing?' he asks, nodding down at Lily's dog.

'He's good. I'm relieved Bobbi was up for us having him. It was a bit much for Derek. He's seventy-eight and Albert, his own dog, was put out by the new arrival. This works better.'

Bobbi has said we can look after him until Lily comes home. 'Comes home', like she's got a Jet2 deal to Rhodes and will be rocking up on the 3 p.m. flight next Saturday.

'He's missing her,' I tell Ross.

Ross pulls the dog into his chest. 'You and me both, Jake,' he murmurs. He looks up at me. 'I'd love to help with walks, if I can? I need to get out. And Jake's about my best mate on this island. What a loser, eh?'

The cuddle's covering up tears.

Genuine – or is he just a good actor?

I look away.

'Does your landlady not mind?' Ross asks, with a cough. Changing the subject. 'About the dog?'

I laugh at the word *landlady*. Bobbi has considerably cooler music taste than me and we watch *The Traitors* together in our dressing gowns and glasses, our hair in ponytails, fingers splayed around tea mugs to warm our hands.

She's eight years older than me, but apart from being a mum and able to afford her own place – as long as she rents out the spare room – we feel as adult as each other. Equal.

'No. Bobbi's an Aurora Island native, which means she likes dogs better than people. Only reason she doesn't have one already is that she's a GP and works long hours.'

'And she's a single mum too, right?'

'Exactly. There's never been capacity for a pet. But I'm doing the bulk of looking after Jake. I'm working from home, and let's face it: there's fuck all else to do.'

'Bet the kid loves it.'

The kid does love it.

I grin when I think about Bertie's face when we brought Jake home. 'He goes *nuts* for him, Ross. I think we're in trouble when Lily comes back, he's going to campaign hard to keep him.'

When Lily comes back. We dodge each other's eye contact. None of the Alphabet Women have come back. Not many women who disappear come back. Why would Lily be the exception?

'Do you want kids?' Ross blurts out, then looks horrified, like he's asked what knickers I'm wearing.

He actually *slams his hand over his mouth* like he's in GCSE Drama trying to convey the very specific emotion of Regret Over What I Have Just Said.

I start laughing.

'I don't know why I asked that,' he says, moving the Hand of Shame away. 'I know it's not okay, my sister struggled to get . . . She always told me not to ask women. I'm so sorry, mate, ignore me.'

'It's fine, Ross, chill out.' I nod. 'Yeah, I reckon I want them.'

He looks thoughtful. 'But I suppose it will be . . .'

'Hard without a penis involved? Well, a little, but you may have heard that there are ways for lesbians to have children, Ross. In *the modern age*.'

He knows it's time to shut up.

'Do *you* want them?' I ask. Ross is still so unknown. This man, who specialises in missing women. So much so that he created a podcast entirely dedicated to the subject. Maybe getting to know him more is the key to finding Lily. Do some digging. Like a journalist would. Like *he* would.

Ross grins and nods. 'Oh yeah! Tons of them. Or, er, maybe two. Mate's got four boys. Looks like he wants to come at me with an axe when I tell him I had a lie-in at the weekend.'

Lily has never told me, I realise then, if she wants kids. Yet another omission.

'You babysit a lot for Bobbi's kid, right?'

I nod. 'I'm a pro. I have five sisters.'

'Let me guess. You're the oldest?'

'How can you tell?'

'You give absolute eldest energy.'

I shrug. 'Well. I basically raised them.'

'Where were your parents?'

'Wouldn't know my dad if he served me Bourbons in Lidl. And Mum is . . . a romantic.'

'Not the worst thing to be?'

'No. Unfortunately it's combined with truly awful taste in men and not much maternal instinct. Sometimes that meant date night was higher up the agenda than feeding her six daughters.'

'So you did it.'

'So I did it.'

We sit in silence for a while, Jake's bulk between us, both of our hands delving under the table into his blanket of fur for comfort.

'How about now?'

'I feel bad being away from them. There's no stepdad at the moment but I don't know if . . . Mum says she's around, she says they're all fine . . .' I shake my head. 'But I can't put my life on hold anymore. I do only get one, don't I? That we know of. I needed to get out of north London. I would have gone under.'

Ross looks closely at me. 'Why Aurora, then?'

I shrug. 'I like it.' I smile. 'And after years of being the oldest, I met Lily and it was like I'd finally got my own big sister. Which was the best thing.'

'A way from London though. What brought you here in the first place?'

Ah. The journalist probe. It brings me up short and reminds me who he is. Reminds me that I shouldn't be opening up to this guy; that I don't trust him. Time to stop. 'Long story.'

He sits back. 'It's embarrassing how much time I have, if you want to tell it.'

I stand up. 'I need to get back.'

Anyway, this story isn't for him. But I came to the retreat three years ago as part of a placement scheme they were doing for young people from lower-income families to get work experience in the tourism industry. I'd been waitressing and doing bar work since I left school. I'd gone back to college to do a travel and tourism course which I'd nearly finished.

The retreat had volunteered to take on two young people as part of the scheme. I wanted an excuse to leave London and I put everything into that application that I had never bothered putting into school work or exams or much else apart from my sisters.

Right place, right time.

When the placement finished, a job was made available for an admin assistant in the office. Minimum wage and nothing glamorous. But I'd proved myself and I got it over the other work experience guy, Marcus. And I flung myself into that too, like a rich guest into an icy lake.

'You liked it enough to stay, anyway, however you got here.' Ross nods, thoughtful, at my silence. 'I can see why. I like it here too. It's a special place. You and Lily became friends through the retreat then?'

I picture Lily and me the first time we hung out away from the front desk, swapping our work shoes for walking boots I'd just cut the label off – I was as out of my comfort zone as Ross back then, used to Saturdays on Oxford Street and clubs in Brixton – and heading to the edge of the retreat's parameters. There, we skipped over the wall and out into farmland, before cutting across the dunes and letting Jake run ahead and down to the beach.

'You said it was thirteen degrees!' Lily shouted, trying to make herself heard through the hoods we'd pulled up to protect ourselves from the chill.

The waves were charged and weighty and Jake edged away like they might come after him. He likes the sea when it cools him in a heatwave. At thirteen degrees with a wind chill? He was as likely to go for a swim as I was.

'That's what the app said!' I shouted back.

'Wind chill factor . . . ?'

I shrugged. 'I'm not a meteorologist, Lily, I just looked at the number.'

When the wind eased up, we sat down on the dunes. It was high tide but we were far back enough from the water to avoid the spray.

'You're not like other twenty-one-year-olds, are you?' Lily said as Jake brought his ball back and dropped it at her feet. As that tail moved like a windscreen wiper.

I turned to her as she raised her arm and threw it. 'Well, you're not like other—'

'Humans?' she interrupted with a laugh.

I was experienced in little sisters. Lily was my first big sister.

That's why I have to find her. That's why I have to hang out with Ross, keep him on side and be friendly. It's why I have to keep Lily's secrets and why I have to do whatever it takes to bring her back, even if she's been lying to me now for years.

I have to trust that it was all for a good reason.

'Doesn't bode well if it's this bad already,' she murmured that day, staring out at a sea uninhabited by boats or people. Listening to the wind whistle, orchestral around us. 'It's only October.' She paused. 'October on Aurora though, I guess, not real October.' Island weather can be brutal. She turned and smiled at me. 'Do you think Aurora is like us? *Not like the others.*'

'Maybe that's why we're here.' I looked at her. 'Do they call it a pathetic fallacy? Is that what that means, am I using it right?'

'I think so?'

'You read so much, you must know. And didn't you go to uni?'

She laughed. 'Not quite.'

She didn't say anything else and I always knew – always had the instinct, without realising – when we had strayed to a place she didn't want to go. I retreated.

Now, I go over all of those chats looking for the clues that I missed.

Of course there was no university. Look what Lily – Natasha – was doing when she was university-age. What she was dealing with.

I remember something I saw Lily reading for book club once, *The Scarlet Letter.*

How could Natasha have turned up in a lecture hall when her classmates would have seen her dragged over hot coals, a contemporary . . . what was her name, Hester someone?

Now, as we stand up to leave, Ross's eyes keep appearing over glasses that need tightening.

He pushes them up. They slip down. And repeat.

'You're distracted. You haven't heard anything, have you?' he asks. He watches me closely.

I hesitate. Just long enough.

'Zadie, has she been in touch?'

Has she?

'Of course not,' I snap.

Suddenly there is a sound, loud and shrill.

'Fuck me,' says Ross, yanking his phone out of his pocket. 'Sorry, no idea why the volume's on that loud.' He glances at the screen and his expression drops. 'Just one sec, though. Have to take this.'

He heads out of the door. His laptop's open and I click out of the podcast. I need to check something that's been on my mind since I saw the video. To look at the guy's face more closely. I want to double-check that I don't recognise him and that he's not been on the island. Because with the message and the link to the show, I'm convinced that this programme, this past of Lily's – even if I don't know how – is connected to the Alphabet Women.

The first video that comes up when I search for that year's show on Ross's laptop is the one where Natasha has sex with this man, Andreas. Andreas likely sprinkles steroids on a four-egg omelette for breakfast. His smile is a snarl. Natasha's eyes are kind and innocent but – as I peer closer – they're vague too.

She's drunk.

I turn the sound right down. Natasha moves towards Andreas across the rose petals. The producers probably bought that lingerie set. Dressed her in it like a doll then fed her vodka.

I shiver.

No *wonder* Lily came to Aurora Island. No wonder her urge now is for Tupperware and thermals. Imagine having this on record no matter what you do afterwards. No matter what you did before.

You *would* put a fence around yourself and make yourself small. You *would* start again. You would change your hair and shoes and nails and home and life and friends, and yeah, you probably would even change your name.

And then another thought drips in. What if that's not the only time? Lily might have reinvented herself again. It would be a smart ruse. If you felt like it was catching up with you, using the missing women to slip away – everyone thinking you're an Alphabet Woman, presuming there must be a nickname that starts with N

– when really you are just feeling too exposed. The messages might be her way of letting me know that, without alerting the police.

I look at the screen, frozen now in a pause.

Is that what you did, Lily?

Then I notice something. The tiny counter in the corner. 'You have watched this video 17 times.'

What?

Seventeen views of Lily having sex on a reality show seventeen years ago. Seventeen views of Lily being Natasha.

Seventeen views, from Ross's laptop.

I've been keeping Lily's secret and protecting her real identity. I've been lying to Ross.

But he's also been lying to me.

Because he already *knows* that Lily is Natasha. And what the hell does that mean?

U

Ross walks back on to the terrace and heads towards me.

'Hey.'

I close the laptop window.

My chest rises. Too high, too fast, too visible.

Finally, I reply. 'Hey.'

I move along and he sits next to me in front of his laptop.

My thoughts race. Perhaps Lily has *told* him who she is. Perhaps she's even showed him the TV show.

'You okay, mate?' Ross is frowning at me.

Mate. Ugh.

I choke out a reply. 'All good.'

If it was innocent, he would have told me. Showed me. Sharing this with Lily's female best friend is very different to sharing it with a guy she's just slept with for the first time.

Unless he already knew. Unless he's known for a long time. Unless that's why he's here and why he's involved in all of this in the first place. Unless there is a link between Lily and that TV show and what's happening on Aurora this summer and Ross.

My brain whooshes and whirrs.

I'm close now, I can feel it.

Ross is near enough to me that he must be able to feel the heat from my body as adrenalin charges through me. Bare leg against bare leg, bare arm against bare arm. We are both wearing few clothes because of the weather, and it feels like another thing that's exposing me. Pounding heart, visible through thin t-shirt.

Ross nods to his phone in his hand. 'U.'

I hear 'you'. 'What?'

'U. The letter U.'

'Oh. Right. A surname?' I try to keep my voice steady.

He shakes his head. 'Actually, no. Ute. She's originally from Germany.'

The horrible truth is that I can barely concentrate on the latest missing woman, even when Ross shows me her picture and I register – on some level – this woman, Ute, with her striking green hair who teaches at a secondary school on the island and who does look familiar. Maybe she uses the retreat's gym?

But I can't think about her. All I can think about is Ross. How I have a secret from him, and he has a secret from me. He *knows*.

'Zadie?'

And yet, we keep pretending.

'Sorry. Yes, I recognise her. But I don't know her.' I feel my teeth drag over my bottom lip. 'I need to get back soon.'

'Already?'

His eyes flit back to his laptop and I watch the side of his face. The maddening way he shoves those tortoiseshell glasses back up over and over and never thinks to just go to the optician and get them tightened. The hair, slightly too long now, a little wild with the hint of a curl. Dark circles under his eyes that hint at late nights playing computer games. All of it adds up to this picture of him as this endearing geek.

I think that's what Lily started to believe he was. And I did, too, to an extent.

Did we all stop being careful, when the reality is that Ross is what we worried he was from the beginning – someone who isn't helping to find the women, but is part of the reason they have gone? Who started making podcasts about missing women, as the darkest double bluff.

Ross's eyes flit to the window and he frowns. It's only 11 a.m. but the beach is already bathed in sunshine and light.

'Yeah. Already. I forgot I'm babysitting.'

He sighs. 'Alright, I'll give you a lift, then.'

'I can walk.'

'Oh, come *on*.'

Go along with it. Don't let him think you suspect him. Do what you would normally do. Anything else is too risky.

'Okay, thank you.'

In his Kia, I'm careful with my body language. With my tells. My nails stay in my lap, away from my teeth. I feel my chest rise, then hold it, hold it, hold it like breath before I let it fall. I even try to hum along to his shit nineties indie. He drums fingers on the steering wheel. Opens the window and rests an elbow on it.

But I watch him. Out of the corner of my eye, I watch him. My keys are in my pocket. My hand is on them, the sharpest one out and ready.

'Where's Bobbi going?'

'What?'

'You said you have to babysit?'

'Oh. Yeah. Lunch, I think? Old school friends.'

I clutch my keys tighter, my finger running over that serrated edge. *I will shove this in your eye if I need to. I will shove it anywhere. I will shove it hard.*

We turn the corner, and Ross steers right. My house is left.

'Where are you going?' The chill I've been demanding from my voice is gone. It's given way to pure panic. 'Why are you going this way? This isn't the way.'

He turns to me. 'Erm, roadworks? Did you not see the sign?'

But I was too busy watching him, feeling his body language, fingering the keys, everything inside this car charged and crucial. Outside – everything beyond the route home – was a blur.

'Oh. Fine then.'

Only a minute later than planned, we pull up outside my door.

'Thanks for the lift.'

'No problem, mate.' But is it my imagination or does he frown as I step out of the car? I'm watching him. But he's watching me too.

My brain whirrs. What is the best thing to do, for Lily?

And then I make a decision.

'It's about the Alphabet Women,' I say to Campbell, cuticle bleeding on to my phone. A tiny drop of blood drips on to the white tile of the floor. 'Sorry to call at the weekend but I thought you would want . . . I wanted to report someone I think could be relevant. Could know something.'

Campbell offers to come to my house but I recoil, thinking of Bobbi and Bertie and their faces if a police officer walked into our kitchen. 'No. I can't do that, I don't live alone.'

'You could come to the station?'

My nerves drip down the phone line.

He sighs. 'Is this on the record or off, Zadie?'

'I'm not sure.'

His voice softens. 'Would you rather meet somewhere you're more comfortable? How about a café?'

'Do you know the Beach Bar? It's down by the beach.'

'Surprising.'

I get to the Beach Bar early and choose a table at the far end of the terrace. My drink arrives, shortly followed by Campbell.

'Just a black coffee, ta,' he says. He puts his hand out to me. 'Hello. We've never met in person, have we, Zadie? Police Constable Campbell.' A light Scottish accent. Someone who's been away from home for a while.

I shake his small, damp hand and he lands, light as a feather, in his seat.

'Nice to meet you. And thanks for this.' He looks after the waiter with trepidation. 'Not going to lie, I've heard dodgy things about this place. But nowhere can mess up a coffee, surely?'

'Give them a chance. Lily ordered a flapjack that tasted of cheese once.'

I picture her, looking a combination of confused and horrified as she chewed, but still too polite to complain.

'Speaking of Lily . . .' he says, a barely there glance at his watch. 'You had something you wanted to tell me. I presumed it was to do with her. You two are pals from the retreat, right?'

'Yes, that's right. We work together.'

He looks at his watch again.

'Sorry if I'm keeping you.'

'Oh, not at all. It's just got a wee bit busy around here lately.'

'Surely you've been sent back-up?'

'Been watching Netflix, have we?' He looks at his phone, out on the table. 'You said you had some information?'

'Well. I don't know if it's related but . . .'

'But?' His tone softens. 'Aye, go on. Everything helps build the picture.'

'Can I get you another drink?' the waiter asks as he puts the coffee down in front of Campbell. He gestures to the pot of damp-looking sugar sachets.

The Earl Grey I ordered earlier is sitting undrunk because it tastes – and who even knows how this is possible – like bad coffee. And I don't even like good coffee. 'I'm okay, thanks.'

Campbell pushes on. 'You don't know if it's related but . . . ?'

'Is this between us?'

'It's between you and the Aurora Island police force, if that's what you mean.'

While I sit in silence, he looks out towards the sea and points. 'Hey, look. A buzzard.'

'Mmmhmm.'

He sighs and sips his coffee – winces, too hot – then trains his eyes on me. 'Look. If you have information, it will help build a picture and it may help get these women home. Whatever you're worried about, I would think that it's worth that.'

It is worth it *if* it gets Lily home. If it doesn't, all it does is change how everyone views her. All it does is ruin the life and identity she's worked so hard to build.

'I was watching TV . . .'

'How any good evidence should begin.'

He disarms me being jovial but I suspect he's trying to put me at ease. I take a deep breath, a swig of the tepid coffee-tea, and then I tell him about the woman who had sex on reality TV. 'Her name is Natasha. But I think she's . . .'

He blows his coffee then tries it again. It seems to have cooled enough. 'You think she's . . . ?'

I am barely audible. 'I think she's Lily.'

He goes to speak but I cut him off. 'Hold on, that's not the only thing, let me keep going before I wimp out.'

I look around the Beach Bar terrace – what was I thinking, coming in here? Ross, like me, is now a reluctant regular.

'Don't worry, he's not here,' he says, following my eyes. 'I never stop looking around. Part of the job.'

He sees my surprise, that he knows who I'm looking for.

'This is about the podcast fella Ross as well, yes? I was surprised you didn't come with him, and I presume if you didn't, and if it's something you're so worried about . . . well, it's my job to look for clues.'

I nod. Take a deep breath. 'Ross knows. About Natasha. He's never mentioned it but he knows. He's watched the clip of her having sex,' I wince. 'He's watched it *a lot* of times. But he's never said anything to me.'

Campbell is scribbling something down in a notebook.

'Why wouldn't he tell me? I'm a woman, her friend. It wouldn't be like me telling him, a guy she's involved with.' I look up. No point keeping secrets now. 'You know something happened between them? I keep thinking . . . Well, what if Ross's arrival here isn't a coincidence? What if he's involved somehow, in what's happening here this summer?'

It's out now, I may as well carry on.

'What if he has her somewhere? What if this is all him? What if what happened in Oban with the first series of *Gone Girls* was really him too? Jesus, what if he engineers situations to give himself material for his podcasts?'

Campbell lets me ramble, then sits in silence. I exhale, hard, like the whole speech was delivered on one breath.

When he finally speaks, it's after downing a slug of his hot drink. He turns to me as he gestures to the waiter for the bill and the card machine.

'We knew she was called Natasha already, Zadie,' he says, business-like, while we wait. 'Aye, we also knew about the dating show, and about what happened to her on there, and about *Ultimate Bakes*. Whole lot.'

My mouth falls open.

'There are a lot of police on this case, we're all working hard,' he says. 'And something like *this*, about one of the missing women, especially one whose name comes out of sequence like that . . . it wouldn't have gone under the radar. We know a lot of information about all of them.'

Campbell is tapping his card on the machine. 'So you can stop beating yourself up about that part of things, for starters. Zadie, we *knew*.'

'Then why didn't you . . .' I half ask.

'Same as you. Because we are trying to protect Lily's right to privacy, even now she's front-page news, the same as we're trying to do for all the Alphabet Women.

'We've learnt from . . . mistakes that have been made in the past by other police forces in high-profile cases that sometimes . . . well, often shouting about people's personal lives doesn't go well. I don't know whether we can *keep* protecting Lily's secret, by the way, and sometimes there are instances when you do have to share information and that's best for the investigation. But we'll do our best.'

I nod. 'Can you be subtle?' I ask. 'If you speak to Ross. About it being me who told you.'

'I'll do my best.' Campbell takes a sip of coffee and winces. 'God, you weren't wrong. That is really shit coffee. Granules and hot water. How can it go so wrong?'

He's on his way out of the door when he turns.

'Time to get this podcast fella in for a chat then.'

V

'Another bottle?' asks a grinning Bobbi later that night, hopping up off the picnic bench outside The Dolphin. I bite my thumbnail. Look down at my lap and glance at my phone.

I'm drinking white wine under a sun that's still high at 8 p.m. Ross is likely to be asking for a glass of water and a lawyer in a windowless room in the police station.

Good. That's what he deserves.

He might be Lily's new boyfriend. He might host a successful podcast. But I am 100 per cent sure he's also a liar.

Five minutes later Bobbi leans across me – brown shoulders freckled in a vest top – and puts a cold bottle of Pinot Grigio down, then swaps the empty one out of its ice bucket.

'Bloody hell, that *queue*,' she mutters. 'Ordering cocktails! In The Dolphin. You have to be quite the optimist to think you're going to get a decent margarita out of the barman who looks about fourteen and works in the local boozer.'

'Probably one of the TikTok crew,' I reply.

They're still here. Phones at the ready, filming to camera, posting with theories around this whole thing being a government cover-up. Apparently Beryl, who owns the farm shop, caught one of them trying to scale the fence at her farm the other day as they had a tip-off the women were being hidden there.

'Maybe,' nods Bobbi. 'Definitely can't be anyone who actually knows how things work on this island.'

I reach for the wine. The wine is helping to distract me from those thoughts of Ross.

'Have you not thought about getting out of here?' she says, picking up the conversation we were having about my same-age mates before she went inside to the bar. 'You're so young, Zee. You could skip this nightmare summer and go and get off your face at some festival in Berlin?'

'You talk like you're eighty-three. You're thirty-two, Bob.'

'Oh, I stopped being young quite some time ago, whatever it says on my passport.'

I smile. 'Not true.'

But she does pour our wine like a sensible adult, halfway up the glasses, then plops the bottle back in the bucket.

'So?' she pushes. 'Why not? You could do with a blowout. What's stopping you?'

'Cold hard cash? But also, it doesn't feel right this year, with everything. Next year, maybe.'

She stares at me. 'You know the Alphabet Women are not your responsibility?' she says. 'It is not up to you to fix this.'

Then she looks out across the green. 'I went to Cambodia when I was twenty-four. Three months. Backpack *hummed* by the end. Best weed I've ever smoked in my life.'

'Dr Simpson, I'm sorry to bother you. But do you know if my bloods are back yet?'

Bobbi looks at me and I cover my mouth with my hand and shove my laughter into the centre of my palm. 'I don't, Sheila, I'm sorry. Call the surgery on Monday though and they should be able to let you know.'

This woman shakes her head. 'Forty-first in the queue, I'll be, Dr Simpson. Shambles, it is, absolute shambles.'

Bobbi looks at her, unblinking, for slightly longer than is comfortable. 'I'm going back to my drink now, Sheila. Enjoy your weekend.'

Sheila looks at our wine and points. 'Three units in that glass.'

The laughter's escaped my palm before she's stalked away as far as the next table.

'She thinks the Pinot's bad. Imagine if her hearing was better and she'd picked up on that *excellent Cambodian weed*.'

'Zadie!' Bobbi hisses, with a glance at the back of Sheila's static grey bob. I take a long slug of wine.

'Excellent Cambodian weed!' I say, taunting Bobbi. 'EXCELLE—'

Bobbi clamps a hand across my mouth and this time my giggles are muzzled by *her* palm. But she's laughing too.

When she takes her hand away, I top my glass up and go to top up Bobbi's but she covers her glass with her hand. 'I'm alright for a bit,' she says. Then she stage-whispers, '*I think I'm drunk.*'

I stage-whisper back, '*Me too.*'

Neither of us are big drinkers. But Bertie's grandparents are visiting from Shropshire – they moved over to the mainland when they retired a few years ago – and we never get to do this.

It's also still twenty-six degrees at 8 p.m. and I've just reported Ross to the police and . . . we're here. We're here, and a lot of women on our island are not here. Alice is still gone. Lily is still gone. Tijen, Helen, Kris. Lily is not even Lily anymore. Nothing is how it is supposed to be. I drink the wine.

Only an hour ago, a forty-something named Vickie who was born on the island and recently moved back here with her own husband and teenage daughter was named as the latest woman to go missing.

My silly, drunk smile falls away when I think about Vickie. About all of the women who are missing. How there is still no trace of any of them. Still not a hint of what has happened to them on this island.

'Oh, go on then,' says Bobbi, moving her hand. 'Just a small one.'

I top her up and open the packet of salt and vinegar crisps she brought back with her from the bar. I rip it down the side.

'Mmmm, dinner,' she says, hand grabbing at the pile.

'You're an exemplary doctor. Really walking the walk.'

She shoves crisps in her mouth and sticks her middle finger up at me.

'Lily thinks you're such a saint too, it's always *Bobbi* wouldn't approve of this, *Bobbi* knows a UPF when she sees one, *Bobbi* would want you to eat a nectarine.'

'A *nectarine*?'

I shrug. 'Or whatever.'

'I'd be happy if I saw you leave the house with a peach, for the record, or indeed any stoned fruit.'

'Plum?'

'Plum would work.' A minute later, glass lolling in her hand, Bobbi says, 'You know what I was thinking when I heard two patients chatting about the podcast in the waiting room yesterday? They were there for so long, we were nearly closing up. But they needed to talk. And I was thinking that people *want* to come together. They need to be together, to be a community. We've always done that well on Aurora but now we're all so isolated. I wondered if we could organise a memorial for the women?'

She sees my face. 'Not memorial! No. Wrong word. Something less . . .'

'Something less dead?'

'Yes,' she concedes. Swig of wine. 'Something less dead than a memorial.'

'Just getting people together to say we're still thinking about them, we're still hoping they come home? That we're still missing them. That we remember them.'

Bobbi nods. 'Exactly. It would be good for people on the island too. A lot of my patients are really struggling with loneliness through this.'

I reach over and squeeze her arm. 'You're a good person.' But I'm thinking about something else. This memorial could be another way to watch people. To see how people behave. It could be an attempt to catch someone out.

'A good person when I'm not smoking weed in Cambodia or drinking my second bottle of wine or eating crisps for dinner?'

I tilt my head. 'Bobbi, serious question. Have you ever considered a nectarine?'

When I look up a few minutes later, Bobbi is staring at me.

'Hello?' she says.

'Sorry.' It was too tempting to check my phone to see if I'd heard from Ross or Campbell. 'Sorry, what did you say?'

She raises an eyebrow at my phone, as I slip it into my back pocket, then at me. Then she speaks. 'I *said* maybe we could hold it – the non-memorial – at the beach?'

'Wouldn't we need permission from the council?'

'Oh. Good point.'

'Unless we used the private beach at the retreat?'

Bobbi's face lights up. 'Oh, yes! Awesome idea, Zee.'

I take my phone back out, but this time I open the Notes app.

'Just to keep track of ideas, promise,' I tell her. 'I'm not checking anything else. Local businesses are so good with donations. They were amazing with the Ukrainian afternoon tea.'

'Don't ask the Beach Bar though,' says Bob. 'No one needs to make the situation worse.'

I laugh as I top up both of our wine glasses – no objection this time from Bobbi.

'How about we have loads of stuff specific to the women? You know, things they love. Homemade cakes for Lily . . .'

Surely whoever is doing this won't hide in plain sight, slapped in the face with all that they have taken away. We'll see who on this island doesn't show up. Who makes weak excuses.

My brain goes back to him. *Will Ross come?*

'Chuck some axes for Beccy!'

'Plant stall for Alice?'

Bobbi and I go on like this, so intent on planning that we don't notice that everyone else has left the beer garden, and that the staff are tidying up sticky pint glasses and crisp packets and wiping down tables all around us and that our wine has all disappeared, like a magic trick.

I don't notice.

I don't notice that the sun's gone down.

I don't notice anything.

Until I see the tiny pale goosebumps that sit on top of the birds and the flowers that snake up Bobbi's arms.

I lean over. 'Hey. You're chilly.'

And it happens in a second. Bobbi cups a hand around the back of my head and nestles her palm deep in the waves of my long and messy hair. And I lean in, and I kiss her.

'We're closing up now, ladies,' says Eleri a minute later, ten minutes later, who knows, her lovely New Zealand lilt lifting over the sound of the glasses clinking in her hands. Crocs, three-quarter-length leggings, a huge Rolling Stones t-shirt and socks, and somehow the coolest woman I've ever seen.

She doesn't acknowledge that she saw us kissing, although there is a giggle dancing across her face.

'I'll be back for your glasses when I've taken these in. Sorry to break up the, erm . . .' She gestures around awkwardly and walks away.

Bobbi picks up her denim jacket and slips her arms into it. I stumble slightly as I stand and Bobbi reaches for my hand.

'Bye ladies!' shouts Eleri. 'Take care getting home, both of you.'

She's grinning but then a frown takes over – the reality of living on an island where woman after woman is going missing. She opens her mouth to say something else then stops herself.

It's almost 11 p.m., but Bobbi and I walk home with a lazy gait, with the cockiness that this day will last forever. Our fingers mesh.

'Come on then,' Bobbi says. 'What were you waiting for tonight?'

'What?'

'You're not a phone-in-your-lap-in-the-pub type person,' she says gently. 'You've clearly been checking on something or someone tonight. Is it to do with Lily?'

Her warm fingers squeeze mine.

I pause. I've wanted to tell her all of it, all night. But even if it's Bobbi, it's Lily's secret – not mine to tell. 'Too long a story for the walk home.'

A split second. 'Let's take a detour then.' She nods in the direction of the beach, and pulls me behind her. Some part of me registers that it's not a good idea. That women are going missing. That we're living on an island that now has something bad lurking at its core. But then sensations – that hand in mine and a belly full of wine – take over from thought. I feel another tug on my hand, and we swing a left. As we hit the sand, we slip our sandals off and walk barefoot, sea lapping quietly, *don't mind me.*

We don't think about it being dark here. We don't think about how quiet it is and how isolated. We're too drunk and we're too together and as I talk, Bobbi's fingers mesh tighter, tighter, tighter with mine.

The evening stretches out and out and out; an elastic band of a day.

And I tell Bobbi everything about the video. About Natasha and the older guy. About *Ultimate Bakes*. About Ross watching it so many times. About calling the police. About being in the Beach Bar with Campbell.

'Why didn't you tell me, Zee?' she says when I've finished. 'I can't believe you've been dealing with all of this yourself.'

'Because this felt like the most private thing ever – this is who Lily *is*. It just didn't feel like my place. I told the police in case it was relevant, in case it could help. But other than that . . .'

'*Me*, though.'

'Even you. It's not my secret to tell. And it's *Lily*.'

And Bobbi nods; gets it. There is no one I'm closer to than Lily. No one who's more like family to me on Aurora. Then Bobbi looks around, and through the darkness I just about see a frown cross her face. That conversation has burst our bubble.

We should get back,' she says. 'This was stupid. I'm a mum and I'm . . . We shouldn't be out here. Not with . . . whoever around.'

We cut back up from the beach, walking faster now with the odd glance behind us, not speaking, and as we head towards home, Bobbi's fingers close around mine again, and even in the midst of hating how much I can see her fear, her nerves, the panic across the face of this strongest of women, I think *oh, the reassurance of having an ally*. A teammate.

I look down at our hands. What does *this* mean, though?

Just comfort, this summer. Or something more?

When we get home, there will be grandparents who are staying over and a dishwasher to empty and Bertie's tiny, dirty socks dotted around the floor. There will be us, *real us* – landlady, tenant. Mates.

Tonight's a mini break.

When we turn into our road, we both release our hands from each other's without a word. Mini break's over.

'Hi, girls,' whispers Bobbi's mum, Jane, relief coating her face when she opens the door as Bobbi is about to put her key in the lock. She puts a finger to her lips. 'Keep your voices down, Bertie's just got up.'

Jane puts cups of tea in front of both of us a few minutes later. I don't tell her it's the wrong kind for me.

'Dad was about to send out a search party,' she says, with a hammy *tsk* and a smile. 'Dirty stop-outs.'

'Mum, it's not even midnight!'

'I know, baby,' she says, her face such a replica of Bobbi's beneath her bob. 'But I was listening to the podcast tonight too, that episode with all the women whose letters haven't come round yet, and I was in floods, and at the moment, on this island . . . I just panicked, Bob.'

We all drop our gazes. *At the moment, on this island . . .*

Jane sends an accusatory glance at Bobbi. 'And you weren't replying to messages.'

'Right,' I say, most of my tea still in the cup, leaving them to it. I try to sip a little more and gag. I can feel a hangover kicking in. 'Time for bed. Thanks for the tea, Jane. Night, Brian. Sleep well, both of you.'

A little glance at Bobbi as I get myself a glass of water. What would have happened if there hadn't been tea to drink, and if there hadn't been Jane and Brian, still up in their slippers at the kitchen table?

And what would happen *now*, if Bobbi wasn't sleeping on the air bed in the living room so that her parents – over from the mainland, where they moved when they retired – could have her bed? I lie on top of the duvet in my own room, heart hammering in my chest, asking those questions. Knowing the answers.

The air is stifling even with the window open, and I picture Bobbi, just downstairs. Tattoos running and flying down her arm. Ponytail in her hair. Gold stud in her nose.

Nope. That wasn't a mini break.

The next morning I walk into the kitchen to find Bobbi in her Talking Heads pyjamas and her glasses flipping a pancake, Bertie barefoot dressed as Batman with his mouth wide open, staring upwards and waiting.

'Stand back, Batman,' Bobbi says to him with a grin. 'It's going to be a big one.'

When she's successfully flipped the pancake, Bertie drags a chair up against the cupboard. Then he goes on a mission to locate some Nutella, with the various pots of cumin and rosemary that Bobbi cooks with spilling in the process.

As I scoop up a handful of cinnamon, my phone rings on the kitchen work surface.

'It's him,' says Bobbi, glancing at it. We both stand and stare at the little vibrating machine.

'Call him back,' she says quietly to me, when the cumin's swept up and the pancakes are on the table and Bertie's face is smeared top to bottom with Nutella. Jane, Eric and Bertie are deep into a game of Snap. 'Whatever's happened, you need to know.'

She looks at my hand, leaning on the counter next to where she is wiping the surface clean of egg yolk. She stops and picks my hand up. It's a lifelong habit, the cuticle-nibbling and the nail-biting. But they're particularly bad now, red raw and screaming for help.

'Call him for the sake of those cuticles, if nothing else.'

'Hey,' says Ross, when he answers the call. Neutral tone and impossible to read. 'Fancy a cup of tea?'

We arrange to meet at the Beach Bar.

'Don't go anywhere else with him though,' Bobbi says, keeping her voice low so her parents don't hear. I know she doesn't want to give them any more worry. 'Stay in the café. Promise me.'

I nod. 'Promise.'

I borrow Bobbi's car to drive to the Beach Bar, and ten minutes later I'm looking around for a waiter. There is a sign that says **You Don't Have To Be Mad To Work Here . . . But It Helps!** opposite another that says **Best Café On The Island . . . Says Our Mum**. The gags are still better than the food.

I look at the menu that I find on the counter – still no sign of any waiting staff – and try to work out what the Beach Bar can mess up least. I'm hungover and want a full English but I have dark thoughts about what this place could do to an egg. The thought, as I sit waiting for this man I now think is involved in my friend going missing – in all of the Alphabet Women going missing – makes me nauseous.

When Ross walks in, I've just ordered an Earl Grey and two slices of white toast. He's barely sat down when they ask in very unfriendly tones, like he's an absolute imposition, what he wants.

He grabs the menu from the table and scans quickly. 'Full English and an Americano, mate, thanks.' He stifles a yawn and I watch him, carefully. *What were you doing last night, Ross? Where do you go in the early hours of the morning? What's with the new coffee habit?*

Then he turns to me, his face a question.

'I've already ordered,' I tell him.

'Just that then, mate,' he says, turning back to the still-unsmiling waiter.

Ross looks out of the window. 'You didn't want to sit outside? Lovely out there.'

'Nah, I'm alright.' I tilt my neck backwards. 'I like the air con.'

He squints at me. 'This is a subtle look from you today.'

I am wearing neon pink cycling shorts with a matching neon pink t-shirt and a black bum bag. I scowl.

He holds his hands up. 'I like it! Just saying. Wouldn't miss you in a crowd.' Then, when his hands are back down, he squints at me. 'Are you okay? I was only joking. I'm just jealous because I'm nearly forty and I'd be laughed out of town if I went within three feet of a bum bag.'

He looks down at my hands, which are shaking lightly. Then Ross leans forward so our faces are close. Close enough to see the dark circles under his glasses. I recoil.

'What the hell are you doing?'

He sniffs the air then pokes his finger in my direction. 'You got drunk!' His laugh is packed with glee. 'You did! Hurrah, Zadie finally acts like a twenty-something!'

I'm po-faced. 'I had a few glasses of wine in The Dolphin with Bobbi, Ross. This is hardly my rebel phase.'

When our drinks arrive, he murmurs: 'And you still order Earl Grey on a *hangover*, you nut job.'

Ross pushes his glasses up on his nose. They have a ridge of thick tortoiseshell along the top of them, which makes it look as though the upper half of his eyes disappear into the glasses.

I stare at them.

'Two slices of white toast and a Full English.' The waiter slams the food and drink in front of us with some grubby cutlery and walks away.

Ross aims a finger at his plate. 'That's a powdered egg if ever I've seen one, and I've seen a lot of powdered egg because I stay in some very shit hotels in this job.'

I watch him closely as he says that, and I question all of it. Whether he even is a journalist. Whether any of it is true. Whether his identity is as fictional as Lily's.

'I will enjoy my food!' he yells across the room towards the waiter. 'Thanks, mate!'

I look at Ross, chewing toast that's passable at least, as the waiter ignores him, offers us zero condiments, and returns to the kitchen possibly to open another tin of limp mushrooms. I frown at Ross.

He isn't acting like someone who spent last night being questioned. Isn't acting like someone under suspicion.

As I stare at him, he pokes at something that may be a tomato, but also possibly beetroot.

'It was you, then.' He says it as a statement of fact, looking down at his food as he reaches for the ketchup bottle and squirts an extraordinarily large circle of sauce on to his plate. 'You who spoke to the police about me.'

I say nothing.

'I don't mind,' he says, chopping up a concerningly pale sausage. 'I'd rather you told them anything you were worried about, you know that. But can you tell me *why*? I couldn't really establish that from the questions the police asked. What did I do that spooked you?' He examines the sausage closely, then seems to decide it's passable and puts a piece of it into his mouth, meeting my eye as he chews.

I still don't answer. I'm not ready. Not quite.

'They let you go then?' I say instead.

He puts his knife and fork down and shakes his head. 'Nope. Unfortunately, I did get life.'

He waits.

'If you want to change the subject, I do have one question. Lily's the blusher. Why did you go so red and weird when you mentioned your landlady before?'

'None of your business,' I mutter.

'Well, that's that question answered,' he says with a grin and a victorious clap of his hands. 'And fits with the hangover too.'

I say nothing until the waiter asks if the food is okay, just as our plates are already empty.

'Just the bill, please,' I say.

'The egg particularly was delightful,' Ross adds. 'Not to mention the mushrooms.'

The waiter bows and puts his hands together as though in a prayer of thanks and doesn't pick up on even a hint of sarcasm.

Then, as Ross reaches for his coffee, I say it. 'Lily. Natasha. You knew.'

He sits back slowly. Puts his drink down. Nods.

'I'll get this,' he says.

As the waiter goes to get the card machine, he leans his forearms on the sticky Formica of the table.

'I did know about Natasha, yeah. I didn't mention it because I didn't realise that *you* knew. I would never have shared something that Lily clearly wanted kept secret.'

I stare at him. 'You watched that video seventeen times.'

Something flies across his face. 'It wasn't in a . . . Ew. Bloody hell, mate! She was eighteen and she'd been plied with booze and coerced by a TV show. That's not *sexy*, if that's what you're getting at?'

When he speaks again, his voice is quieter and he sounds – for the first time since meeting him – angry. 'For the record, I fancy Lily, who is a strong thirty-five-year-old woman who can outpace me on a mountain. I don't fancy *Natasha*. But yeah. I did watch the video, quite a lot of times. Seventeen, if you say so.'

'Why?'

'Because I hoped it would give me answers, Zadie!' He pauses while he taps his card on the machine and leaves a pretty generous tip when you consider what he just lived through with the powdered egg.

'And did it?'

He pauses and looks at me. Then, slowly, he nods. 'Yeah,' he says. 'Actually, it did.'

'Ross,' I say, watching his face and slowly, slowly realising something about this man who arrived on our island a stranger, then inserted himself so deeply into Aurora's consciousness. Who has become the voice of our island, the authority on the Alphabet Women. Slowly realising something about that feeling I've had. *You're lying about something.*

'Ross,' I repeat. 'You know where the women are, don't you?'

W

He stares back at me for a few seconds before he replies.

'I don't know anything that I can safely tell you,' he says, carefully.

'What the hell does that mean?'

He sighs. 'It means . . . can you wait, Zadie? Not long. But can you wait?' He pauses. 'If I told you that it won't be long and that I can tell you something then? Could you do that?'

Fuck. Fuck. *Fuck.*

'Are they alive?' My voice comes out as a breath. 'Is Lily alive? Is Alice . . . ?'

'I don't know,' he says, and I spot it: he takes a quick look around him. 'Zadie, keep your . . . Honestly, I don't know. Stop . . . Can you . . . But I think I will . . .' Pure panic crosses his face. 'Please, Zadie. Will you trust me on this?'

'No,' I tell him. 'No, I won't trust you on this, or anything else. I barely know you. My best friend went missing the day after she slept with you. You've watched the video of Lily – Natasha, whoever – having sex seventeen times, and you knew she wasn't who she said she was but you didn't mention it and now you say you . . . I could go to the police with what you've just said.' I stand up. 'Actually, fuck this, I am going to the police with what you just said.'

But his eyes flash, suddenly dark, and he tugs at my arm and pulls me down.

'Get the hell off me,' I hiss. I shrug him loose. The waiter looks over.

'If you do that, I am telling you that you will be putting people in harm's way,' he says quietly. He locks his eyes on mine. 'That will be on *you*, Zadie.' He pushes his chair back with his body weight. 'I mean it.'

Then he stands up and leaves.

'You alright, love?' asks the waiter. I nod.

And I sit, shaking all over. Stuck. As stuck as I have ever been.

That will be on you, Zadie.

Lily trusted him. Should I?

At home, as she stands at the kitchen worktop chopping onions, I tell Bobbi what Ross said.

'He could have found something out through the podcast?' she says, frowning, knife poised. 'Something that has led him towards the women or given a clue or something. But I guess he just needs more time?'

'What, though?'

'I don't know – something from a source? A listener? It does happen, crime podcast sleuthing.' She looks up from her onions, eyes weeping. 'Christ. Sorry. Maybe give him a few days? See what happens?'

'Do we have a few days though?'

I think of it again. My Z. Inching closer.

That evening, Bobbi is in the kitchen making us a cup of tea when she calls me in from the living room.

'Zee! You have to hear this.'

I walk into the kitchen. Bobbi unpauses her phone. The A and Z logo of *Gone Girls: The Alphabet Women of Aurora Island* podcast is on her screen and Ross's voice rings out.

A new episode?

Already?

My stomach drops. He didn't ask me to listen to this one before it went up. I have no idea what's on it. No idea what he's going to say either.

'Okay, so some odd things have come to light this week which is why this episode follows so quickly from the last,' says Ross. 'We have a lot to catch you up on. This one is particularly odd.'

And then, the music.

'"The Alphabet Women" feels like a new term, one we all started to use to describe the missing women, as a collective,' says Ross, when it finishes. 'But that's not the case. Actually, it was already the name of an Aurora book club that two of the missing women – Alice and Lily – belonged to. I've got another member of the book club here now. Welcome, Susie. Can you explain?'

I look at Bobbi. 'What the fuck?'

And Susie, hesitant, explains what she told Bobbi a couple of days ago, about the book club's name change.

'I was there, when Lily wrote it down that day, at our March book club,' she says, her voice shaking a little. 'In that lovely fancy writing she did, once we had decided on it, she started doodling our new name – the Alphabet Women.'

'And what did she do with the piece of paper?'

'I have no idea. Last thing I remember it was just on the table in The Barn at the Aurora retreat.'

'Then the next thing we know, the Alphabet Women happens,' says Ross. 'And that same piece of paper – the one Lily innocently doodled on at book club – is sent to a friend of Lily's. To their house. Pretty weird, right?'

My heart pounds. What is he doing?

'Some other clues have emerged too,' Ross continues.

'Oh God,' murmurs Bobbi.

'It's been suggested that one of the Alphabet Women has another identity. If you know anything about this – or *anything* to do with the Alphabet Women – do message us and let us know.'

My heart races. Adrenalin sweeps through me. I hold on to the kitchen worktop.

'How could he?' I say, quietly. He might not have mentioned Lily by name but people will suspect – she went out of sequence. 'What the hell is he doing?'

'Maybe he's trying to root someone out?' says Bobbi, coming up behind me, slipping her hand over mine, after we listen to the rest of their conversation, which doesn't go on for long. It's a short episode, clearly made to be released quickly. 'And at least he didn't give details about Natasha.'

A few minutes later we are sitting down in the living room and I fling my head backwards on to a fluffy green cushion. I'm not feeling any less pissed off. In fact, my rage is building.

'Fuck him,' I say, sitting up. 'I'm calling the police. I need to tell them that Ross knows something. That he basically admitted that to me.'

'I think there's a chance he *is* nearly there though,' says Bobbi, gently. 'That this is part of it. Frightening them, showing them how close he is. And what if we ruin that?'

I appreciate the *we*.

Almost a week goes by, and despite what I said, I don't go to the police.

On Saturday we hold Alphabet Day, the fastest turnaround non-memorial event there has ever been. Aurora Island Eco Wellness Retreat is a sunburst, lit up and shiny. Out of hibernation, for today only.

Over the last six days, I have distracted myself by calling everyone. I have asked for every favour. I have pulled up weeds and I have baked cakes and I have put up gazebos and I have mowed lawns and I have muttered apologies to the bees and I have begged and pleaded for tea and bouncy castles and chairs and I have cancelled my plans and I have neglected the basics like sleep in quite an extreme way.

'Are these in the right place?' Alice's daughter Florence asks me, as she lines up more paper cups next to the water cooler.

'Perfect, chicken! Thank you.'

Her tongue pokes out of the side of a mouth that does a little grin, proud at being helpful.

'Would you like another job, Florence?'

She nods. 'Yes! I love jobs. Can I do it with my sister though?'

'Sure.'

She runs off and comes back with Freya.

'Okay, you ready, girls? I need you to write a sign to go next to the hook-a-duck with the price on, please. Best handwriting. There's the paper. It's fifty pence per go, or three for a pound.'

'We've got it!' they tell me in unison.

Florence skips off to a nearby table. She's wearing a pink tutu and ballet shoes. They're a useful aesthetic; a clear and shiny reminder that we aren't mourning anything or anyone today. How can we be mourning? No one is sad. No one is weeping. The only person wearing black is my friend Jas, whose whole arse I can see out of the corner of my eye as she queues up for cake in a thong bikini. No one mourns in a thong bikini.

I turn up the music. Scan around. I've had no contact with Ross and so far there's no sign of him.

But I don't want to think about Ross. I want to think about the women. The women who now include – I heard whispered around here earlier – a reiki teacher from the east side of the island named Wren.

W.

Which means only two letters are left. And then, we will come to Z.

'What a shocker that Ross isn't here,' I say to Bobbi, rage building as I look around. 'He's fed me such a line.'

'Just remember,' she says quietly, standing next to me as we watch Alice's girls run off. 'Alphabet Day was our cut-off. If we don't get evidence from him today that he's making progress, that he's found the women or at least that he knows something concrete, we go to the police and tell them what he said. He's had long enough then. So try and enjoy it today, Zee. Try your best to forget about him until then.'

But I shake my head. How can I do that? I look around again. 'I can't believe he's not here.'

It feels like every other person on the island is, though – spilling down towards the sea or putting up tents and umbrellas on the sand. The weather has played ball; we all worried the skies would open but the heatwave marches on. The gates of the retreat's grounds have been flung wide open for an hour now, since midday, and humanity is flashing its best side every way I turn.

For today, we're trying our best to block out its other face.

Bobbi makes a noise, a scoff. 'After ignoring your messages for six days? I can believe he's not here.'

I have asked and asked and asked. *What did you mean? Tell me what you know. I won't go to the police but please please please just tell me.*

I have begged. *She's my best friend, Ross. I need to know if she's alive.*

Nothing.

Five hours later, I tap my toes in Crocs to Steve and his folk band, who have bowed to pressure and are now performing – rather against genre – some early Taylor Swift. Steve growls and I try to enjoy it and sing and lose myself in the music and switch off. My brain has other ideas.

What does Ross know?

'Is it just me or is this version of "Love Story" weirdly brilliant?' Eleri asks me on her way past. 'I mean, I know I'm biased . . .'

'You're not.' I smile. 'It's epic.'

Florence and Freya's sign lies half-finished and abandoned, a pen discarded and drying with its lid off next to it. Florence is twirling her sister round with the confidence of a *Strictly Come Dancing* pro as the pair of them sing along.

A gaggle of adults dance alongside them, singing Taylor's words back to Steve, mostly higher-pitched, less growly, as he sticks a microphone out towards the audience.

Through the crowd, my eyes are everywhere. There is no one I don't look at today. No one whose absence I don't notice, no one whose smile I don't monitor, no one whose words I don't second-guess. Today is for the Alphabet Women, but for me, too, it is research.

Jas and Erin – my 'young people friends' (™ Bobbi) – both used to work at the retreat during their university holidays. They got back from travelling yesterday, and are home for a while to save up some money before the next leg. I glance at the schedule on my phone: the two of them are taking over as DJ J'Erin at 6 p.m. Everyone's found a way to pitch in.

'Coming in the water, Zadie?' asks Jas, fit and tanned next to me in that tiny black thong bikini.

Erin stands beside her in a sportier bikini top and denim cut-offs. 'We're being brave, Zade. Going in with a paddleboard.'

'Which I should add is especially brave as that did *not* go well in Sri Lanka,' says Jas.

'What happened in Sri Lanka?'

They exchange a glance and smirk. 'It's a long story,' says Jas. 'Crux of it is: don't mix interesting cigarettes and water sports.'

'Especially when you haven't slept for twenty-four hours,' winces Erin.

'We'll drag you out for a wine at some point while we're back, Zade, and we'll tell you the whole mad story. Also involves a man named Aubrey who's a distant relative of Zara Phillips but . . . anyway! Another time!' She gives a little pull on my arm. 'Come on, into the water.'

'Can't. Jobs to do,' I tell them. 'But *you* definitely should. Put those Sri Lankan demons behind you before the tide goes out.' I try to smile in the way they smile. Relaxed and full. But it's impossible.

I scan the crowds again for Ross. Still no sign.

Right now, it's high-tide and the sea is loaded like a child's bath water with toys and inflatables: paddleboards, kayaks, dinghies and swans. Kids in sopping sun hats and heart-shaped sunglasses run in and out of the water, flinging their slim chests across bodyboards, filling buckets and watering cans until they become almost too heavy to carry.

Adults in sensible swimming costumes tread water and tilt their heads backwards, enjoying the novelty of warm island waters.

We could be in the South of France. It's thirty-one degrees on Aurora today.

The bloom of the early sunshine has given way to thirsty fields that used to be green as lime but are now the colour of sandy beaches. Hosepipe bans have been extended and the sea's a popular place to be today. Jake is in and out of the water with a happy tail, a full Aurora Island cast to play with (as well as the odd inflatable unicorn).

On the small of my back, while I watch Erin peel off her denim shorts and run after Jas's tanned bum as it jiggles its way to the sea, I feel a small hand.

'Ready to head up to the field and throw a few axes?' asks Bobbi, smiling.

'What an offer.'

In the furthest reaches of that parched field, Beccy's business partner is teaching people to throw axes. We haven't mentioned it to Richard. We're not in the market for 'did you do a risk assessment' and 'is it covered on the insurance'-triggered heart attacks, so we're just hoping he doesn't head up that way. It's easy to spread out when you have forty-seven unused acres.

I turn to kiss Bobbi then stop. Since Jane and Brian left the island the day after our drinks at The Dolphin, the kissing – when we're alone – hasn't stopped.

Soon we're going to explain to Bertie what's changed. For now, whatever Ross thinks he knows, I hold the secret tight and close. Because it has to be Bertie first. And because this summer's seen enough chaos. Enough change.

'I'll get to the axes later,' I tell Bobbi now. 'Few things to keep an eye on here.'

She frowns at me. 'Still thinking about Ross?'

I nod. 'Can't stop.'

All the cakes and the axes in the world couldn't boot out those thoughts today.

Me, Bobbi, Bertie and a host of other people have made attempts to recreate Lily's best recipes. Our cake stall is emblazoned with a sign for **LILY'S BAKES**. I make a deal with myself, as I look at that sign. If Lily comes back, I'm going to bug her to launch her cake business for real. To get away from Hugo Von-Twatface and do the thing she was so good at that she won *Ultimate Bakes* when she was seventeen years old.

At the foot of the dunes, there's a bar being run by Donna's partner, Lois, a huge Welsh flag hanging behind it as they serve Donna's favourite beer, Red Squirrel, which is brewed on Aurora Island. **DONNA'S BEER AND RUGBY CLUB**, says the stand. On the screen, a giant of a man smeared in mud runs with massive calves towards a goal. People stand and scream, Welsh dragons across their backs. Some major rugby tournament that Donna would never miss. *Would never have missed.*

My tenses flip around when I think about the women. On a good day, they are still present – away somewhere, somehow, but coming back. On bad days, I am convinced that there is no other explanation than the darkest one. That this is about a serial killer. That they are all dead and that police are right to search the strait, that the best thing we can hope for are bodies to bury. That they're not coming back and we're doing this for the families, now, not the women. That it is too late for the women.

I meet Lois's eyes.

'Thank you,' she mouths back. Then she blows me a kiss.

I stifle a sob. Then I remind myself. Not mourning. Celebrating. Present tense.

I blow a kiss back.

I've done okay today. I have had a grin on my face for most of the time. I have blown kisses and given hugs and high-fived kids and sung along. I have laughed and I have danced and I have talked and agreed: it will all be okay. Of course they will come back! Behind it all, though, are the real thoughts.

Ross. The women. The past tense. And my letter, fast approaching.

Not many people's names begin with an X or Y. They may just get missed out. Realistically, I may not have long at all.

Lois's eyes are still on mine. 'You okay?' she mouths, forehead contorting into a little frown as she hands over a pint to a guy in a sun visor and mirrored shades.

I nod. Reapply the grin like lipstick.

At one end of the sand, we've set up a Minions bouncy castle and a game of rounders for the kids. Freya and Florence play alongside Beccy's boys and an older girl I think is Vickie's daughter, and a gaggle of other bouncing, shrieking, sugar-fuelled kids in bare feet.

If you look at them from across the beach, you can believe that they're kids whose mums haven't disappeared off the face of the earth.

Don't look at their eyes, though.

And don't look at their dads.

The kids shriek when they catch the ball. They cry when they land on top of each other. They ask for more chocolate ice cream when they still have the remnants of the last one across their faces; they ask for it even though they have started to feel sick because they're kids and they don't *want* to moderate or be sensible and because, because, because they're just kids.

Doing what kids do.

Just a normal day. Just kids.

Blur your eyes a little, make today go fuzzy, and you won't notice the drawn faces of husbands who fear the worst and children who had terrifying nightmares last night.

Make it go fuzzy and you can roll your eyes at the nineties indie dad who's walking around shoulders-first looking for his kid around the back of the rounders pitch and who's holding a can of lager like he's Liam Gallagher, shades on, swagger in place, stalking the Minions bouncy castle like he used to stalk the Wetherspoons in town.

You could miss the fact that he's scared his wife Ute might be dead. That she may not be coming back. That, yesterday, he couldn't get out of bed.

I look over at Richard, standing by the ice cream van with his wife Liz, the two of them with their 99s. When he catches my eye, his smile is more human than usual. I think he's pleased to see the retreat being enjoyed again. But I even look at Richard closely. Could *he* know something?

We're expecting a lot of people today. They sprawl across every inch of the place. Laughing together in corners, carrying bacon sandwiches loaded with ketchup over to friends. Running into the sea and out again, grabbing cornflake cakes, drinks, a beach ball, each other.

From the water, there's a cacophony of children and noise, but in the middle of it all is Derek, standing shin-deep only a couple of metres from where Jas's boobs are threatening to escape as she wrestles with a paddleboard. Derek doesn't seem to notice. Or he's averting his eyes.

Lily's neighbour has his shoes off and his beige chinos rolled up, his short-sleeved shirt splashed with water as he paddles.

On the shore, an older woman is sitting in a camping chair looking out at Derek.

'Are you Sandra?' I ask her, wandering over. 'I'm Zadie. I think I know your husband.'

She chuckles. 'That man makes friends everywhere he goes.'

I look out at him and smile. 'He is very friendly. We don't know each other all that well but we have a mutual pal.'

Her eyes fill up. 'Oh love, is it Lily?' I nod. 'My goodness he's sad about Lily. I can't get him to switch off from it. He's missing their chats so much.' She looks down, suddenly. Jake has just arrived at my feet. 'Oh hello, Jakey!' she says, and he gifts her a hearty, soggy wag. 'Is it you who has the dog now, love?' she says, as she wipes a little seawater from her cheek.

'That's right, yes.'

'How's he doing?'

And I catch Sandra up on what Jake has been doing, how well he's settled in with me and Bobbi and Bertie, into our little family. How pleased we are to have him until Lily comes back.

We avoid eye contact, like I do with everyone when I say these words. I don't believe them. None of us believe them. Hoping isn't the same as believing.

Derek sees me talking to Sandra, gives me a thumbs up and mouths the words: 'That's my wife.'

I laugh. Return the thumbs up. 'I know!'

Then he waves his hand to gesture to everything around us. To today. He mouths again. 'Lily would be *very* proud of you.'

I nod. Smile a thank you. Another sob, choked down like bad food.

I say goodbye to Sandra and tell her to shout if she needs anything and then I walk away to be alone for a second. Today is turning me inside out.

'You okay, Zee?' Bobbi walks past a second later carrying a huge tray of raw sausages.

'Still mulling.'

She frowns. 'Leave it until tomorrow. Only thing worth mulling today is wine, Zee.'

'That would be a very weird choice of drink in a heatwave.'

'There is that.' She leaves with her raw meat. 'But then so is Earl Grey and I spotted you with one of those earlier, you crackpot,' she laughs, raising her voice over her lovely freckly shoulder. 'Axes were super cathartic by the way! Try and get up there.'

But it's 5 p.m. already. The day is running away. Then somehow it is 6 p.m., 7 p.m., 8 p.m. And I look around and nod.

Yes. It's been a success. Bobbi was the one who came up with the idea of turning today into a fundraising event, raising money for the Alphabet Women's families to spend on investigators, or to help with childcare or whatever they need it for, as long as it goes directly, 100 per cent to them. Split however many ways it needs to be. Twenty-four, twenty-five. Twenty-six. This moves fast.

Over a microphone now comes a voice. Steve. 'Okay, ladies and gentlemen, five minutes and we're back on so grab the drinks, get yourself a processed meat product, and soak up the beers with some carbs. We'll see you back here in five.'

At the top end of the field, Steve is getting ready for a set, his motorbike parked next to him, his beard longer and grizzlier than ever.

Just behind me is a stall being run by Moo Ice Cream and a man named Dennis who is singing the crescendo of 'Unchained Melody' to himself as he hands over a couple of chocolate waffle cones loaded up with mint choc-chip.

When Steve finishes his set, he looks over at me and mouths: 'Good to go?'

My index finger is immediately in my mouth and in seconds I've gone too far again and I taste the metal of blood.

Why did I agree to this?

While everyone around me has queued at the BBQ and eaten a weekly quota of sugar at Lily's Bakes, I haven't eaten anything today. I've been too nervous. About all of it. But mostly about this.

I'm doing a speech.

I am talking for around three minutes about what we've been doing today and what it's for – *who* it's for – before we go back to the music and the bouncing.

Bobbi puts a hand on my back.

'You'll be great,' she says, leaning close to my ear as the buzz and the frenzy of today bounces around us. 'All you need to remember is to breathe. Wide stance, make yourself big. And no matter how fast you think you're speaking, it will always be a good idea to slow-wwwww . . . dowwwwwwn.'

And then Steve is introducing me and I'm clambering up on to a small makeshift stage in the middle of a field in my Crocs and pulling my cycling shorts down my thighs and trying to remember everything Bobbi just said.

'Welcome, now, to Zadie Christmas. Zadie, I think it's fair to say that you're heavily involved in today's event. The brains behind it. Can you explain what it means to the people of Aurora Island to be able to do this for the Alphabet Women?'

And I talk – too fast, I'm pretty sure – but without crying, and even, occasionally, with a smile, about the event and what we are raising money for. I keep it light, in case the kids wander over from the bouncy castle and pick up bits of it.

In the crowd, Bobbi gives me a thumbs up like I'm a nervous kid in a swimming lesson. Derek thinks he's being subtle when he wipes a tear away with a spotted handkerchief. And I wish, I wish, I wish hard that I could look out into that crowd and see Lily.

No one's face calms me like Lily's. I imagine it's how most people feel when they spot their parents.

And then, to a wall of clapping that threatens to bring the sobs back up, I clamber down and sit on the grass in front of the stage where a few hundred people are watching Steve take the mike again. And I wait for my heart rate to return to normal.

It's done.

At the exact moment I realise I can finally eat, Bobbi appears holding a giant sausage bap.

'Oh, I love you,' I whisper as I take the sandwich off her, than panic smears itself across my face. No. We haven't said that yet.

'Love you too,' she says, matter-of-fact. And then she pulls me into a hug that ends up in ketchup smeared down my front, about which I give precisely zero fucks. 'And God, I'm proud of you.'

In my head, I tell Lily: *'You won't believe this. I'm in love.'*

In my head, she hugs me and whispers: *'Good for you. But can you get on with finding me now?'*

Hours later, as the kids who are left fall asleep on picnic blankets and the adults flop down next to them, too much sun, too much beer, too many tears, too much joy, too much butterscotch dressing, no desire to go home to houses that are occupied by one person fewer than they should be, people begin to drift home.

'Go,' I tell Bobbi, who is lying next to me on a picnic blanket with a sleeping Bertie in her arms. The paraphernalia of sausage sandwiches and juice and melted chocolate cakes is littered all around us.

Bobbi has told me she loves me approximately twenty-seven times in the last half hour, and it's been as prolific in the other direction too. Our eyes are centimetres from each other's. 'He needs bed, don't wait for me.'

'I came in the car though. If I wait, I can give you a lift.'

'We could be a while. Look at it. There's so much tidying.'

There is a gaggle of other people left, all pitching in with the big clean-up. Even Richard. Lois comes over holding a bin bag and I put a paper plate in there. 'Thank you. But make sure you divide the recycling. Lily would kill me if—'

She holds up another bin bag in her other hand. 'Plastic and cans.' Then she nods towards the first one. 'Paper and cardboard.' A third nearby on the floor. 'Food waste.'

Then she walks away again, picking up plastic water bottles and paper plates and ketchup sachets and gin cans and halves of discarded sausages and allocating them to the right bags. Whistling 'Unchained Melody'. Segueing into 'Love Story'.

'I'll come home with Lois or one of the others,' I tell Bobbi. 'Get Bertie home, honestly, he's done for.'

She nods. 'How long will you be?' she replies in a whisper, inching up to standing, body tense, clutching Bertie close, soft toy to a baby's chest. 'God, this is like nap time when he was tiny.'

I look around. 'An hour or so? Want to make sure we get it all. Don't leave a rogue Wotsits packet on hallowed retreat grounds.'

I'm smiling when Richard appears next to me, snapping his litter picker around a Coke can. 'Incredibly satisfying, this,' he says. 'Feel like Jaws.'

Bobbi laughs under her breath and nestles her chin in Bertie's hair. 'See you on the sofa for a wine in an hour or so. Might even crack open that super-nice one. You deserve it tonight, Zee.'

I nod and down the last of a can of Fanta. I crumple it and put it into one of the bin bags as various people shout goodbye and thank you and well done as they leave, swallowed whole by the night.

Bobbi leans down to the exhausted and damp dog at my feet. 'I'll take Jake home too.'

'Thank you.'

I watch them walk away, Jake ambling at Bobbi's sandals, low-key tail wags now and keeping a gentle and loping pace with her as she moves slowly so that she doesn't disturb Bertie, who dozes in her arms. My heart does cartwheels and tumbles. Love and love.

Somewhere along the line, after arriving on this island, solo and without my own, I've picked up a family. It's just missing one crucial part: my surrogate big sister.

After Bobbi and Bertie leave, the final stragglers head home too.

'Thanks for coming!' I shout.

Everyone who leaves is effusive. They hope we made a lot of money. They appreciate us giving our time. They just hope it helps to get all the women back. They clutch balloons and brownies and beach balls and hula hoops they won in the raffle. The odd inflatable unicorn.

When we're done tidying the beach, we move to the field. It's nearly 10 p.m. and the light's almost given up entirely now. It's hard to even make out Lois's outline.

I head down to the bottom of the field to where the recycling bins are tucked away around a corner out of sight (retreat guests like aesthetically pleasing things; they don't want to see recycling bins).

'Lois!' I shout when I come back up to the top of the field.

But there is nothing.

'Are you still there?'

Nothing comes back.

'Lois? Richard?'

And then I hear it, in the distance up towards the car park. An engine, turning on. The crunch of wheels on gravel.

The cortisol flies around my body.

Fuck.

I didn't tell Lois I wasn't going home with Bobbi. I didn't ask her for that lift. I just presumed we'd leave together and I'd hop in her car, but the light's faded and I've ambled to the other end of the field and now she's gone and so has Richard and I'm alone and we are so close now. So close to my letter.

X, Y.

Z.

As I run towards the entrance of the retreat in the near-blackness, heart thumping, brain whirring – *idiot, idiot, of all the times to be alone in a field* – I see no one. Nothing. They have all gone. I stumble over an empty drink can but don't reach down to pick it up.

My brain is firing 999 messages. *Go. Now.*

This is too close for comfort. Far too big a gamble.

Run.

I move faster, breath coming fast and painful, a burn in my chest.

Towards the entrance.

Fuck.

But I slam into something.

The gate is closed. They've shut it behind them. They think I've already gone.

I shake it but it won't budge. I don't have my card.

I clamber over it, getting stuck, briefly, before I fall and land on the floor. But I scramble straight back up. There is no choice.

Now there is only a long, dark and isolated road ahead of me. I need to walk fast. I need to calm down. And I need to hope hard that there is no one following me.

I check my phone even though I know it's pointless. Of course there's no signal. There never is in this kind of radius of the retreat.

Stupid place.

I run.

And after a few minutes, my pocket begins to vibrate.

'Hello?'

I am half jogging as I talk, relieved for the call, relieved that I can pick up a tiny bit of phone reception. But the line is terrible. I slow to a walk; strain to pick up words.

'. . . Winterbottom.'

I frown. The police officer? Why would he call me? If I speak to anyone, my contact is Campbell, but even he never calls me.

'Zadie. Sorry . . . call so late. How did today go? Sorry I couldn't make it . . . shift . . . Can you talk . . .'

The line is so patchy I can barely catch meaning.

'Can you pick me up?'

I describe where I am.

'What's that, love?' he says.

He can't hear me.

He's saying something to me, though. Nearly audible. I catch one word. *Email.*

'What did you say?' I shout. 'My email?'

I take a punt. Shout my email address a few times down the phone. I have no idea if he can hear me.

'It's coming now,' says Winterbottom, clearer. 'Take a look, then call me back. I'm giving up on this ruddy line. Hopefully you heard that.'

And he hangs up, before I can try and ask for a lift again.

As I keep walking and click the symbol for my email, I see the most recent message has been sent from an Aurora Island police account. It contains no words, just an image that lands slowly, painfully, through the weak 3G of our island.

I can't wait. Can't stand still. Not out here, in the darkness.

So I carry on walking.

I slip into a jog when I can. Walk when I am too out of breath.

There is no pavement on this stretch of road so I need to keep looking up; a car could come out of nowhere if I'm not ready to move right in.

Even so, I sneak a glance down at my phone.

What could it be? This image?

But it's still not loaded.

I look around. Walk faster.

Glance back down at my phone.

And finally, the image loads.

What the fuck?

The image is dark and there are only two things I can make out. One of them is a sign, on an easel and when I read what it says, my breath pulls in, sharp. My heart races, faster, more, until it's too much surely, too much for a human body to take.

The Alphabet Women Project, *the sign says.*

And next to the sign is a face I know.

It's been inevitable, really, hasn't it? I've known in my gut he's been lying. And there he is, next to the sign. Ross. A part of this Alphabet Women Project, whatever it is, all along.

I go to call Winterbottom back, then remember that I'm alone in the darkness. That Ross is out there. I can call the police back when I'm home but for now I need to focus on getting there. I need to focus on making it.

I break into a run.

Running as fast as I can, I look out towards the sea, to where I know the bay curves. In the black, I can't see it but I hear the waves lapping, lapping, lapping. The odd croak of a cormorant. Then I turn and I look back inland. The quiet hums in my ears.

From Steve crooning 'Love Story' and kids spread-eagled in swimsuits across bodyboards. From pop music in the sunshine and kids dancing across a Minions bouncy castle in tutus, chocolate ice cream on grinning cheeks, to this. Conversations with police officers. Images loading slowly on an old phone. Cortisol shooting itself around my body like a Class A.

I *do* want, I realise as I run and gasp for breath, to be Jas or Erin. I *do* want to be twenty-four and light. What is it about me, that I attract this and not a paddleboarding disaster after too much weed on a hot day in Sri Lanka?

When my phone rings on a sharp bend, I slow to a walk and hit accept.

It's him. Winterbottom.

'What is this?' I ask. 'What is this picture?'

'The answer, perhaps,' says Winterbottom. 'We're hopeful.'

'And why are you calling *me* about it?' My reception dips. I don't hear his reply, and then I have a new question. 'Where is it happening? This project?'

'From what we're told by the tech guys, the picture was definitely taken on this island,' he says, clearer again now.

'On the island?'

My chest hurts.

Were they here, the whole time?

We have no major cities. We are so *simple*. But we have space. Wasn't that what hit me when I first came here? *All this space.* So few people, and so much space. Maybe that space is the thing.

The space where Jake can run off his lead for miles. The space where I walk to work, tabard in my bag, and can easily not see anyone for a mile, two, along the coastal path. This underpopulated space – even with the second-homers and their sprawling new-builds, we're still sparse – with so few settlements. Swathes of space, but it's always felt safe. It's going to be a struggle, whatever happens next, to feel safe.

'Are they alive?'

'We don't know. But at this point we're not ruling anything out, Zadie.'

I look all around me, into the blackness, across the thirsty fields of Aurora, parched from the heatwave. Behind me are the wild dunes and beyond that, a still, quiet sea that's black now, invisible. It doesn't matter though. I know this landscape with all parts of me. With my bones that have taken on Aurora as their home. I can always find my way, on this island.

'We'll be acting swiftly,' Winterbottom says, breaking up but just audible. 'I'm sure you can imagine how delicate this is. For now, Zadie, I need you to keep this one hundred per cent to yourself. And I need you to act naturally with Ross. Not like you've seen him in this picture at all, okay?'

'Yeah.' I find my voice. Just.

'What I said before. Why are you calling me about this?' I ask again.

He pauses. 'Because you know Ross, probably better than anyone else on the island now Lily's gone. Because I know you suspected him. And because I saw lots of stuff posted on social media today, Zadie, from people who were at the event. You're the face of it. The face of this whole thing.'

I huff. 'Not really.'

His voice is gentle. 'I'm afraid you are, love. Like it or not.'

I am silent.

'You were on *Gone Girls* yourself, speaking. You're personable. You're relatable. You're also . . . well, there's the thing that we're not saying, isn't there?'

I swallow.

'I wasn't there today, Zadie, but I did see the masses of stuff that was posted on socials. I kept abreast of it all.'

'And what?'

But there is a feeling in those Aurora Island bones, now, of deep foreboding.

'They must be thinking about these final letters now,' he says. 'They're going to be hard ones to hit. X, Y.'

I swallow. He's the first one who has said it to me, so explicitly.

'X, Y. And then Z.'

I say nothing.

'You are all over socials, love. *You.* Steve introducing you. Pictures of you speaking. Your name, everywhere. Your name, with its Z.'

My name. The one I hated so much at school when I was so desperate to be called *Chloe* or *Olivia* but that over the years I've warmed to. That name that I've started to embrace.

My unusual, wrongly spelled name. My Z.

'You asked why I'm calling you, Zadie. I'm calling to tell you to be careful. I'm calling because I think more than anyone, you're visible and you're a likely target.

'I'm calling because I think Ross has been involved in taking twenty-three of our island's women as part of something called The Alphabet Women Project, and I think that he – possibly him and some others – have hidden them somewhere on Aurora.

'I don't know what we will find when we work out where it is, or what he wants these women for, but I'm telling you now that it won't be pretty. And being blunt, Zadie, the obvious point is that you're a Z. The worry is that you're on the list to join them soon.'

He pauses. I've known it, all along. Especially lately, as we edge closer.

And yet something about it being spelled out to me makes my heart hammer and hammer and hammer and I look around, through the blinding darkness, and I can't speak.

'I'm telling you because even more than other women on this island, you're in very current danger.'

Instinct kicks in.

'Can you . . .' I begin, but what's the point? I'm not far from home. I don't want to wait for a lift. I don't want to be in someone else's car, even if it does belong to the police.

I feel like I can't trust anyone, or anything, barring my own body, my own grit.

When Winterbottom hangs up, I start to run.

I will go hard, and I can do this in less than ten minutes.

But a minute later, someone is standing in front of me, blocking my way.

Of course.

Ross.

X

Here he is then, finally.

My phone is folded tightly into my palm, like the filling in a sandwich. Minutes ago I was exhausted but not now. My fibres are lit up, shop windows at Christmas.

Think, Zadie. Be normal. How would you act, if you hadn't seen that photo?

'You took your time,' I say, through the wheeze of someone who never normally sprints for her life.

Act normally, act normally.

The worst thing I can do is let Ross suspect that I know he's involved. If he knows that, I don't stand a chance. If he doesn't, then there's no need to go for me, not yet. Not until my letter.

'Are you okay?' he says, noticing how out of breath I am. He doesn't wait for an answer. 'I'm so sorry I couldn't make it today. It's . . . Long story.'

'Another one you're not willing to share with me?' *Act normally, act normally.* And this is what I would normally do. Answer him back. Stand up to him. I tuck my shaking hands into my pockets and start to walk, fast.

'How did it go, then?'

'It was amazing,' I say, defiant. 'Everyone did brilliantly. Everyone pitched in.'

He nods. When I sneak a glance at him, he looks embarrassed.

What have you been doing today? What have you been doing that's more important than Alphabet Day when the podcast about the Alphabet Women *is your life? Your bread and butter? When your girlfriend – if that's what she is – is one of the missing women. What could possibly have been more important?*

All the times I've thought: *you're hiding something.* Now I know what.

'Why bother coming now then?' I ask. *Keep him talking.*

I walk around him. March even faster.

'I was on my way to the retreat,' he says, keeping pace with me. 'Thought I might make it for the end. That it might still be going on.'

'Well it's not.'

'I can see that.'

He walks alongside me. Keeps up with my march. I bite my lip.

A minute later, Ross takes his glasses off and rubs at the lenses with the bottom of his crumpled t-shirt. While they're off, he digs a knuckle into the crevice of his right eye.

'Any thoughts on the next ep?' he asks. 'Anything you'd like to hear more of? Any new angles we should be covering?'

You, as the perpetrator.

I look straight ahead. Keep walking. 'Not that I can think of.'

As we keep going, Ross looks up at a sky dotted with stars, hands dug deep into his shorts pockets. He sighs. 'Tell you what, the sky never looks like this in Manchester.'

I say nothing.

'Okay, what's wrong?' he asks with a snap, a quick glance at me as we walk along the winding road between the retreat and Port St Joseph. 'Come on, tell me – what's up?'

He turns to look at me but my eyes duck away.

'Fine. Got it.' He sighs, frustrated. 'Will you let me know when you're next walking Jake? I'd love to see him. Or I could walk him for you?'

'Mmm-hmm.' A large, dilapidated farm is in total darkness on our left. I watch Ross to see if he looks towards it but he doesn't seem to notice it. My neck cranes to see how many acres they may have. How possible it would be to hide twenty-three women in there, dead or alive.

Ross's elbow nudges into mine as he takes a long swig from his water bottle then replaces it in his backpack. We curve around the bend, not a car or person in sight. We've passed the farm, the looming shadow of the hills making it feel like we're cut off from everything, like it's just me and Ross, two miniature figures hidden behind a giant, imposing wall.

I stare at him, with his Cheshire Cat grin. I listen to the stomp of his new walking boots. *Lily trusted you*, I think, fists balled. *She let you in. What did you do?*

'You alright?' Ross asks, after a minute or so of quiet.

'Yeah.' Keep talking, keep talking. 'Actually, I feel as though I'm hungover and I wasn't even drinking.'

'Probably just exhausted,' he says. 'Like, to your bones exhausted. All the planning and turning today around so quickly and the pressure of it . . . Zadie?'

While he's talking, my phone pings with a news alert. Another Aurora Island woman has gone; her middle name was Xanthe. And suddenly I am standing at the side of the road, hands on my knees, hot dog from earlier about to come back up.

'Zadie?' Ross repeats.

He takes my water bottle from the side pocket of my backpack and hands it to me. The bottle's almost full. I don't think I've drunk any liquid today other than an Earl Grey and a can of Fanta. The temperature's been in the thirties and I've barely been in the shade.

'Did you know?' I ask him, my breathing too fast, holding up my phone.

X.

Y.

Z.

'About X?' Ross nods, looking at the news story. 'Yeah. But it felt cruel, to tell you today.'

Or perhaps he had another reason for keeping it secret. Either way, we only have Y left now. The layer that protects me – those couple of letters – has just been sliced in two. Just one woman between the Alphabet Women and me. And then what happens?

I drink half of the tepid water before we start walking again, this time at the speed of tired pensioners. It's all I can manage.

Ross keeps his eyes on the road, alert for any cars that wouldn't expect to see us there at this hour in the pitch black. Cars that would be on us by the time we were spotted.

I feel it again, the sensation dripping down my limbs. Like I'm boneless and could crumple. But I'm on the side of a road without a pavement with Ross. *This is not a time or place to crumple.*

I want to be at home with Bobbi, with the stacked rings on her fingers whirling into my hair, round and round and into a massage on my scalp as we sit close together on the sofa. I want to be anywhere but here.

Today, Jas and Erin asked if I want to go to Southeast Asia, to join them for a couple of weeks once they've saved up enough money. I was in the middle of making forty-three excuses about why I couldn't go when Bobbi overheard and said that all of my excuses were bullshit and that I had to go, that I had to smoke some excellent weed on her behalf and then come home and tell her all about it.

'Make her,' she whispered to my friends, conspiratorial. 'She's basically off work anyway. I'll pay for the first day's drugs.'

'You're a *doctor*,' I murmured while Bobbi did a 'well, what are you going to do?' shrug at the girls.

Erin put her arm around Bobbi's shoulders. 'I love this woman,' she said, no clue about what is happening between us but always a good judge of character. 'Can't you come to Cambodia, too, Bobbi?'

'Book me in for 2038.' Bobbi nodded, serious. 'I'll bring Bertie for his gap year.'

Now, I want to be in Sri Lanka, or at least in the sea here, in our sea. I want to be floating on a dinghy on the edge of Aurora Island with a collie and a kid, waving to a pensioner on a paddle-board and his proud wife in a camping chair. I want to be barefoot on sand. I want to see Jas's bum cheeks wobbling happily in my peripheral vision.

But I have to accept the inevitable. I can't leave this alone. This summer for me isn't about a trip to Asia and adventures. It's only ever been about the Alphabet Women.

'We can stop again if . . .' says Ross from behind me, but I am pacing ahead now, even with the exhaustion of today, even with the nausea, with only one thing on my mind. Home. I stumble, slightly, on an invisible branch. And I picture it again: Ross, in the photo with the sign saying **THE ALPHABET WOMEN PROJECT**.

Ross, who is behind me now in the pitch, pitch darkness of Aurora Island at night. Six-foot something, as I am weakened and spent. There are no farms or houses now, just woodland sprawling on either side of us. There is no one else around. We walk together, down an empty road that feels now like it is devouring the two of us in its darkness.

Like we are going together, into a cave.

Y

Except for the stars, the darkness is total now. Despite us edging into hedges and walls, not a single car has been down this road the whole time we have been walking. Without headlight beams, there's nothing to give us a break from the darkness.

We aren't a well-lit island. We've never needed to be. Street lamps were for other places, where the bad things happen.

Until we started living this horror movie of a summer.

Now, I see Ross's eyes stray towards that denser woodland. To the part where you need your walking boots, even in summer. The part that is so chock-full of bogs and mud that you don't walk but wade through it, sinking like a doomed ship and rescuing yourself with each footstep just in time, as the furthest edge of panic sets in and for a brief second you imagine yourself drowned and stuck with not a tiny particle of air left in your lungs.

My eyes follow his towards the nothing.

'Bob will be sending search parties out by now,' I say, to fill the silence. To warn him too: *someone will notice*. 'She'll be stressing about me.'

He presses something on his watch and it lights it up. 'She'll be asleep, more like,' he says, with a light laugh. 'Didn't you say Bobbi can't stay awake past ten p.m.? She'll be well out for the count by now.'

My hand reaches round and touches my phone through my cycling shorts pocket. What would happen, if I called someone now and if I said, out loud: *Come. Help me*? I wonder what Ross would do. What there would be time for.

Occasionally as we walk, Ross's bulky walking boots stray closer to me and I feel my body tell on me – muscles tense, breath held.

I give myself little talks. *Even if he is involved, it will be too obvious if I disappear when I'm with him.*

But another voice chats back. *Lily disappeared the day after she slept with him. He didn't think that was too obvious. And people don't even know you're with him.*

We pass a row of pebble-dashed terraced cottages and the bend where I know, despite the dark, from the map of the island sketched in marker pen across my mind, that there is a sign that warns of high winds.

Tonight, though, there is no wind. No rain. The air is silent and still, not a sway of movement and bone-dry. All I feel is heat. All I hear is the rhythmic thud, thud, thud of Ross's walking boots. I can see nothing, hear nothing, and all I can do is move, one shaking and weak leg at a time, into the spot I can see in front of me.

All I can do is trust instinct and memory.

It's 11 o'clock now and the night's still the kind of warm you get in Majorca in August. I'm in a t-shirt and cycling shorts. Ross and I both have sunglasses propped up on our heads, as though we expect the sun to nip out for an encore.

I turn to him there, on my left next to the road.

'Will you go back to Manchester?' I ask, to keep him talking, something filling the space that isn't darkness and stillness and aloneness, until we see the lights of Port St Joseph, the lanterns outside The Dolphin. The head torch of a late-night dog walker. Warm lamplight from someone who forgot to close the curtains.

All of that is still a way off.

Usually, I love Aurora Island's solitude, but at this moment the opposite seems idyllic. A sweaty department store, the stark lighting of a packed train. CCTV and hordes of people.

'You mean when this is over?' Ross asks. 'Well. Bloke who's subletting my room wants it permanently. I'm thinking about telling Col to say yeah.'

I want to scream at him: *I know! I've seen the picture. Stop bullshitting me, I've seen the picture.*

But I need him to think I trust him. That I am lapping everything he says up as truth. 'Then what would you do?'

'Fuck knows, mate. But going back would feel weird now. I'm here. Aurora's got under my skin.' A pause. 'Lily would laugh at that.'

'She wouldn't be that surprised though. She has seen your walking boots.'

He nods (I hear that too). 'I'm committed now, mate. Caved and got the Go Outdoors loyalty card.'

A low laugh. Fraudulent and desperate.

How long? How long until those lights? I would guess four or five minutes. I try my best to speed up.

'Hey, I wondered if you'd help me with some stuff on the podcast tomorrow morning? I can sling you a hundred quid if you could bring your Gen Z brain to help me share some audio clips on TikTok? Apparently, we're missing a trick not doing it.'

'I thought you had someone doing your socials?'

'Yeah, we do. Shannon. But you know this content so well. And . . .' He sounds hesitant. 'Okay, full disclosure . . . You were so natural when you came on the podcast, Zadie. I wondered if you wanted to come on and talk about being a Z. How it feels to be at the end of the alphabet. To be waiting.'

Something dawns on me then. Just because I haven't heard about a Y going, it doesn't mean it hasn't happened. We could be on Z now. The buffer could have vanished already.

Just agree with him, Zadie. Let him think he's going to see you in the morning. That everything will be normal.

I'd guess we have three or four minutes left now, until we hit Port St Joseph.

I need to let Ross think he'll have another shot at getting his Z. That he doesn't have to do anything now, if he's thinking about it.

'Sure, let's do tomorrow,' I say, forcing levity into my voice. 'How's it going? The podcast?'

'Brilliant,' he says. 'It's flying.'

But I don't hear this like I would have heard it before. I hear another version. Every woman that goes missing, Ross's success is growing. Who benefits from women going missing as much as the man whose career hangs on the success of a podcast all about them?

I googled what happened in Oban. It was never solved; they never found the girls.

Three minutes now.

'What happens when we get to Z?' I ask, willing time to pass, trying to ignore the throb in my ankle. 'Does the podcast keep going?'

'It depends whether *this* does,' Ross shrugs. 'Unfortunately, we're not in control of this. Any of it.'

Bullshit, bullshit, bullshit.

We turn the corner. Stop at the junction to check again for cars.

That image is seared on to my brain. Ross, in front of that **Alphabet Women Project** sign, in the Arctic Monkeys t-shirt I've seen him wear now so many times – a limited wardrobe when he had no idea he would be staying this long. Or maybe that's bullshit too. Perhaps it was all planned. Perhaps there is a packed wardrobe.

We try our best to tuck in to the side of the road. Past a house again, now – this one set back with so much space in front that it's more like something I'd imagine being in the US, not off the coast of the UK on our island. A Confederate flag flying; rocking chair on the porch. I picture a big man and a gun and my mouth is wrung out again, sawdust.

I take my water bottle out of my rucksack but the bottle is empty now. Ross holds out his own drink. Two minutes now, perhaps. Dragging. Slow.

I swig and swish the water around my desert mouth.

And as I do, Ross lunges at me, hands on my arms, and I am pushed hard, deep into a thick, spiky hedge.

I make a noise, but it's not loud. Why am I not loud? There is a house there. Be loud and they'll come. But I make barely a whimper.

I wonder if this is what happened to the other women. You hear about it, don't you? Being too shocked to scream. The noise trapped in your throat.

I thought I was prepared. I knew he would come for me and I knew it would be soon. I was primed, for this whole walk. But still I'm acting as though I am in shock.

I try again. Nothing.

Then there *is* a scream. But it doesn't come from me.

'Dickhead!'

Ross's scream falls into nowhere.

'Sorry,' he murmurs, putting a hand out to help me up, as I wipe leaves from my shorts and touch a spot on the back of my leg that's been scratched by branches and is bleeding. 'Didn't mean to shove you. But fuck me, mate, that monumental *dickwad* was so fucking close to hitting us.'

Ah.

His scream wasn't aimed at me. It was aimed at the driver of a car with a speedboat on the back that must have been doing 60 mph on a pitch-black 40-mph road and whose trailer swung dangerously close to us as it took the bend, but who is gone now, long gone.

My brain hasn't got that memo though, and I straighten and snatch my hand from Ross's. I move away from him. Wrap my arms around my body. Watch him, wary. Fear whips round my body like a storm.

I picture those hands, coming at me.

Get away.

Get away.

'Really am sorry, mate,' he says. Then he looks at my face. 'Shit. Are you okay? Are you faint again?'

That would explain my shaking and my nerves and I need something to explain it. 'Yeah, faint,' I answer. 'And just a bit shocked after that car thing.'

He nods and we stumble on.

We walk past a field where in the daytime there are usually six or seven local owners' horses who will wander over to say hello, to see if you've brought food. My nose wrinkles at the pungent smell of manure. Blinking, I can see the faint outline of a tractor left to snooze for the night, before its early start in the morning.

A little more visibility. I try to get my bearings. We're on the edge of town now; the home straight. The road curves and I know it's the stretch with the sign on. **BADGERS CROSSING**.

One minute now, perhaps?

Not long, not long.

Come on.

Ross whistles. 'They're fancy.'

I don't have to look up to see what he's talking about: three beautiful holiday homes with glass fronts and first-floor balconies that let their owners see far out to sea. To the cormorants and the waves.

On the corner of a lane, there is a small bench that's been placed there for the view of the sea too. I know the plaque on it is dedicated to a woman named Susan, who lived to ninety-three and loved to look out at the boats. She died two years ago. Lucky Susan, missing all this madness. Lucky Susan, who got to feel safe when she sat alone and hushed on a bench.

'You're breathing heavily, you know,' he says. 'And the way you couldn't catch your breath before, with that car . . . I'm worried you have sunstroke. Or you're properly dehydrated.'

'Maybe.' *Just get home, just get home. X has gone. Y may have gone. Just. Get. Home.*

And then, more lights.

A few more.

Come on.

A hand on my arm. I flinch.

'Maybe get Bobbi to check you over?' he says, brow furrowed. 'You really don't look right.'

'Mmm-hmmm.'

Come on. Come on.

And then, finally, the island is released out of its darkness.

There are porch lights and people and the odd dog walker and street lamp, and we turn into the lane where I live, and finally, *finally*, I exhale and I feel a burst of energy and I speed up even though my bones ache with exhaustion and we turn the corner and I am home. I only realise my nails have snapped back to between my teeth when I take them out.

Outside my house, Ross turns to me.

'Well done today, mate,' he says, throwing his arms around me for a hug. I freeze, Lily-style, at the touch. 'Sorry again I didn't make it.'

I release myself. Fall through the gate. My hands shake as they push it closed.

Home.

Alive.

Safe.

'Bye then?' Ross says with an attempt at a laugh as I shut him out. 'Take a Berocca!' he shouts after me. 'And if Bobbi's got any rehydration stuff, get one of them down you too! You deffo look peaky. Hope you feel—'

Slam.

I lock the front door behind me and then the real shaking starts, as the adrenalin leaves my body. I see my hand tremble as I take a glass from the clean dishwasher and head straight to the wiped-down and spotless tap that Bobbi's clearly scrubbed since she got in. And I drink and drink and drink, because Ross is right about one thing – as well as everything else, I am probably dehydrated.

And then, when my mouth no longer feels like it contains what's been swept up with a duster, I sit down at a kitchen table piled high with Duplo and drawings of superheroes and crayons and I lean back on the chair. My thighs bounce lightly on the seat.

'Hey superstar!' says Bobbi, eyes glimmering as she puts her head round the kitchen door. 'Bertie's unsettled so I'm back in with him. But I'll be down when I'm done. Wine's in the fridge.' She frowns. 'Just wanted to say well done though, and also hi.' She looks at me shyly, as we've started looking at each other lately.

I smile back at her, and this one's real, made of relief. 'Hi.'

Bobbi comes closer and puts a hand on my forehead.

'Hey, you okay?' She looks at my hands. 'Zee. You're shaking like crazy.'

'Mummy, I don't want to be by myself.' A voice through a yawn from the stairs.

'Sorry, I'll . . . I'll be back soon,' Bobbi says, squeezing my arm as she puts a topped-up glass of water in front of me. 'Don't move. Call if you feel ill.'

I nod.

As she leaves the kitchen and I lean my head back against the chair, my phone rings.

'Zadie,' Winterbottom says without waiting for me to say hello. 'Me again.'

'So Ross is involved?' I reply.

'There's a lot I can't tell you right now, Zadie, I'm sure you understand that. We're dealing with an ongoing investigation.'

Why is he calling then?

I lean forward on to the kitchen table, bow low among the melee like I am praying to the gods of Lego sets. *Save me, Batman.*

And I know, half a second before he says it. I know and it's inevitable and still it's a heavyweight punch to my middle.

'A Y's gone,' he says. 'I thought you should know. Yola. Youngish lass by all accounts. Just got word. No more details yet.'

And so now we're there, where I've dreaded being for so long: *Z is for Zadie.*

'Okay.'

And it's time.

'Look, Ross implied to me that he knows where the women are. He wouldn't say anything else. I was going to tell you but we wanted to wait until he'd had a chance to . . . But now . . .'

Winterbottom whistles out his breath. 'Right. Right. Zadie, this might be a play. Something to get you to go with him somewhere. Keep us *constantly* in the loop when he contacts you, especially now we're on Z. We'll have eyes on him anyway now. When did he tell you this, about the women?'

I pause. 'A while ago. Sorry. He made out that if I told you, I would put the Alphabet Women in harm's way.'

He scoffs. 'Right.' He pauses. 'Course he did.'

When we dial off, I sit with my head in my hands. He thinks I'm stupid, believing Ross. I am stupid. But now I need to focus. Me keeping Ross close could lead police to the women. It could save people. No, scrap that. We're on Z. Me keeping Ross close could save one person. *Me.*

I drag the kitchen chair around the room and wiggle the lock on each window, then I feel something warm and damp trickling down my forearm. Another cuticle, bitten so hard and so violently without me noticing while I was on the phone, that it is bleeding on to my wrist.

I move the chair back to the table and sit down, picking up the tiny Batman, with the tiny cape. There he is, the little good guy, taking on the bad. On the table a tiny Joker beams, red-lipped and cruel. Sometimes it's that simple. There's good, and there's bad.

And now, after all these weeks of wondering, I know which one Ross is.

My phone beeps. Him. Hope you're okay. Still on for the morning?

I type with shaking fingers.

Course, I reply. See you at the Beach Bar at 11.

Because we might be on Z but it's not just about me. I owe it to them to meet Ross. To keep up the charade, so they can be found. I owe it to them. I owe it to the Alphabet Women.

Z

A, B, C, D, E, F, G, H, I, J, K, L, M, N, O, P, Q, R, S, T, U, V, W, X, Y.

Z.

There are no more buffers. No more human shields.

When Bobbi walks back into the kitchen, I have put my phone down. My breathing is ragged.

It is time for Z.

'Just water for Berts,' Bobbi says, holding up a Spider-Man water bottle, and she's in a rush to go up to him so she doesn't look at me closely. Doesn't see.

She shouts over her shoulder, 'Love you, Zee.'

'Love you too,' I say back.

But my bones hurt and my heart, mostly – oh God, my heart hurts. I don't want to die. I don't want to disappear. I don't want to be an Alphabet Woman. I want to stay here, with Bobbi and Bertie, and I want to go to Asia with Jas and Erin and I want to laugh at Joy at work with Lily and I want to swim in the sea and I want to drink cider outside The Dolphin and I want, I want, I want to live.

I pull the blind down and head up to my room. Check my dodgy window.

Whether it's the window that gets me or not though, it feels inevitable now. There are women out there, across the island, who are called Zoe or Zara. Perhaps there are women out there with surnames that start with Z, or middle names that start with Z or nicknames that start with Z.

And yet, for a while now my gut has told me that this thing is chasing me down. That me and my Z are where this will end. That *that's* why I can't walk away from it. That that's why it's my cuticles between my lips and not a spliff on an Asian beach.

That I am part of this, just like Lily is. Just like Alice is.

That all of us are part of it, for reasons we don't yet understand. That we have always been Alphabet Women.

The adrenalin keeps me awake until long into the morning. When my phone rings, I feel like I've only just gone to sleep. I look at the time. Seven fifteen.

My first thought is: *Ross. Making sure I meet him. Making sure I don't try to get out of it. Changing the venue to somewhere more private. Somewhere more isolated.*

My second registers that the name flashing up on my phone isn't Ross's.

'Have they found them?' I answer, grabbing at it. 'Are they back?'

I answer like I've been drugged. No pleasantries; confused and flailing with the oddness of this name and this hour. This name that never calls me. This name that is only connected to me through the Alphabet Women.

I picture that sign. **The Alphabet Women Project.**

'No, no,' the voice on the phone says quickly. Then it is quieter. 'No. Sorry to make you think that. And sorry to call this early.'

I rub at the corners of my eyes, and even when I'm 90 per cent asleep and a rollercoaster of stress hormones are whizzing around my insides, I still say 'that's okay' to Evan Fox. When does the politeness reach its limit?

Evan speaks again. 'I wondered if you could come round? I can't come to you because I have the twins. I struggle with babysitters now. Lily was . . . well, Lily was the go-to. But there's some stuff I need to show you. Important stuff. I wondered if you could . . .' He sighs. 'Zadie, it's about Ross.'

I sit up fully.

'Okay. What time?'

'Well, I have police coming round for an update later, the girls dancing lessons before that so it wouldn't be until this afternoon.' He pauses. 'Unless you could come now? Before dancing?'

It beats the tiredness. It beats the exhaustion. The curiosity over what he has to say about Ross beats everything.

'Yeah, I'll come now.' My voice is grainy and I am stumbling out of bed, bare feet on carpet, eyes still half-closed. 'Give me twenty minutes.'

I don't shower, though after yesterday I need to, badly. I slick on extra deodorant. I don't brush my hair or swipe on mascara.

Instead, I pull on shorts with the t-shirt I've slept in, and I slip my feet into Crocs, and my eyes open a few more millimetres and I blink, over and over, and I cycle to the next town, to Syford, to Evan and Alice's lovely family home.

I go because I want answers.

I go because he says: 'It's about Ross.'

I go because I owe it to the Alphabet Women.

'Coffee?' asks Evan, as I step in my Crocs over a violin case and a ballet leotard and a slim, muddy pair of green football boots.

'I'm okay, thanks.'

I keep my arms close to my sides, convinced that skipping the shower was a mistake, but to be honest the odour's as likely to be coming from Evan. It doesn't look like he's washed in a while.

'Sure? I'm doing a pot. It's already on.'

'I'm okay, thanks.' I consider the request before I make it, but whatever is coming next, having a drink I like would make it easier. I could really, really do with a cup of tea. 'Though, if you have Earl Grey . . . ?'

Evan bites his lip. 'Earl Grey,' he repeats. He rummages in the cupboard, then in another one and another. 'I've definitely got normal tea, but I'm not sure if—'

'It's fine,' I say. 'Don't worry if you don't—'

'Bingo!' he says, bringing out a lone teabag. 'Phew. Must be Alice's.'

'I don't want to drink her last—'

'If Alice comes back, come round with a box of Earl Grey, how about that?'

And I duck my head, accepting.

We make small talk for a while. He preps the drinks and takes a packet of cookies out of the cupboard. I presume that he is building up to it, whatever *it* is, whatever he wants to show me, so I let him potter around and I sit at the Foxes' kitchen table, looking up at a picture of Evan and Alice and the girls – much smaller versions of the girls – at Peppa Pig World.

I gear myself up to look shocked if he shows me the same picture that the police sent me. If that's what this is about.

It's going to be a warm day again, but the sun, like my eyelids, is still not fully up. There is a chill in Evan's old house, in the big space up to its high ceilings. My bare legs goosebump. I wrap my arms around myself. And I wait.

Evan shoves a football trophy and a book that says *School reading record – Freya Fox* and a banana skin and a glass of milk that looks about a week old out of the way – but doesn't actually take any of it off the table – and puts my drink into the small gap in the middle.

'You don't want a biscuit?' he asks, looking at the packet that's sitting on the table in front of me, between a wrinkled grape and a tiny Porsche made out of Lego.

'Bit early,' I say, nodding to the clock that now says 8.10 a.m. 'Even for a junk food addict like me. I haven't had breakfast. Thanks for this though.' I try to smile, then I sip my tea.

'I'm surprised the girls haven't smelled biscuits,' I say. 'I live with a four-year-old and Bertie's like a sniffer dog with chocolate.' I smile. 'Where are they? The girls?'

'Just getting ready for dancing.'

But now Evan has sat down and the kettle isn't boiling, I can hear just how silent the house is.

I've lived with five sisters. I *live* with Bertie. I know that kids don't stay that quiet, especially in the morning when their bodies are recharged and their bellies are hungry and the house is a whirl of lost socks and extra slices of toast.

'Do you mind if I say hi?' I ask, putting my mug down. 'I met them at Alphabet Day. Such sweet kids. It would be nice to see them.'

His eyes don't move from his coffee cup. He picks it up; waits until he's sipped his coffee to reply. 'I'd rather you didn't. They need to get on.'

'Oh, I wouldn't disturb them, just a quick—'

This time the coffee is down and his words are delivered faster, sharper, fired out like bullets. 'I said I'd rather you didn't, Zadie.'

I nod, shocked, and Evan stands up.

'Right, I'll get the iPad. Then I can show you the stuff I mentioned.'

He stands up, a hulking six foot plus in what look like cycling clothes. A lot of Lycra, top zipped up to his collarbone, socks halfway up bulging calves that are covered in a light ginger fuzz.

'Okay,' I manage. 'Great.'

While he's out of the room, I slip my hand into my back pocket and take out my phone to message Bobbi. I didn't tell her where I was going – she and Bertie were in their beds when I left – and I don't want her to walk into my room and panic. She knows there isn't a lot I get up early for, especially after a day as full-on as yesterday. Soon she'll check the news, and know that we're on Z.

Before I get chance to type though, I see a message from Ross, sent five minutes ago. I frown at it.

> Stay away from Evan Fox. Explain all later. But stay away.

What?

'All okay?' Evan asks, standing behind me.

And then I feel it. Breath on my shoulders.

I flip my phone over, chest thump-a-thump, then I turn to him. Did he see the message?

He stands close, holding an iPad, and his breath still comes too fast. It's stale – unbrushed teeth and late-night snacks, the remnants of which are *everywhere*, Pringles tubes on the work surfaces and biscuit wrappers under the table on the floor. I look around. Actually, everything is a mess.

Evan's beard is overgrown, uneven and as out of control as this table. As chaotic as this whole room. The place smells too – days-old food and dead gladioli and breath and armpits and a room that's been kept closed and insular for weeks.

It doesn't smell like family life.

There is still no sound from the girls.

◆ ◆ ◆

When I start to realise that I'm feeling dizzy, I can see pictures of Evan and Alice's twin daughters in lovely ornate frames. I can see the outlines of vanilla ice creams stuffed with fat flakes in pale hands; I can see grins that are missing front teeth.

I hear myself say their names. I think I say their names.

Florence.

Freya.

I look down at half an inch of Earl Grey left in an empty 'Kitchen Disco' mug that I presume is Alice's, and at my phone in front of me on the table with my new screensaver of Bobbi and Berts, and it all add ups, slowly, slowly.

Too slowly.

Just that second too late.

Evan picks up my phone and moves it away from me and I don't have the capacity to reach out for it, or to protest.

But it's different to yesterday when I was exhausted and faint.

It's impossible to challenge Evan. It's impossible to move. Everything is impossible. Is this how they all went? Is this what happened to the other twenty-five women?

I open my mouth to ask Evan. *Was it never Ross? Was it always you? Did you do this to all of them, starting with your own wife? Or are you in it together, and Ross is trying to pass the blame?*

But no words come out.

Evan pulls up a chair.

'I'm sorry, Zadie,' he says. His face is swimming in front of me but it sounds as though he is crying. 'I'm so sorry. Swear to God I'm so sorry. I had no choice. They gave me no choice.'

They.

Who?

But that word doesn't come out either.

Only one thing does. The letter, my letter.

'Z,' I whisper.

A, B, C, D, E, F, G, H, I, J, K, L, M, N, O, P, Q, R, S, T, U, V, W, X, Y.

And now, inevitably, I am Z.

He nods and repeats it. 'Z.'

My eyes droop and close.

A to Z.

There's a peace that comes with that thought.

With me, at least, it ends.

When I open my eyes, I feel the comfort of a palm in mine. But then I'm in a . . . What is this? There is an IV attached to my right hand.

I let go of the palm and try to sit up.

'Oh! You're awake,' Bobbi says, standing up from the white plastic seat and knocking a bottle of water that was in her lap on to the floor. She cups my cheek. 'Don't worry about talking. Just rest, Zee. You're in the community hospital. On the island. You're safe.'

I can see the worry etched on her face.

I don't feel like I can manage many words, so I prioritise the most important one. In case they don't know. In case I fall asleep again.

'Evan,' I say.

'It's okay,' she says, hand on my shoulder now, another squeeze. 'It's okay, Zee. We know. Now rest, my love, okay?'

My eyes droop and I sleep again.

When I wake up the next time, a nurse sources a rogue Earl Grey teabag at Bobbi's insistence. I take a sip and wince, shake my head and put the mug down.

'Still nauseous?' asks the nurse, checking the IV.

I nod.

'That might take a while to pass.'

'What happened?' I ask Bobbi. Panic rises from my diaphragm. 'What did Evan do to me?'

Bobbi puts a hand on my arm. 'Nothing, Zee. The police got there right after he'd slipped sleeping pills into your tea this morning. He didn't get a chance to do anything.'

This morning. I look at the clock on the wall. Six p.m. – I was at the Foxes' house ten hours ago but my last memory is when I was sitting at their kitchen table. The time between then and now is blank.

'I thought the tea tasted a bit off,' I murmur. 'Just presumed no one drank Earl Grey and the teabag had been knocking around for ages.' I pause. 'I didn't want to be rude and leave it.'

She puts a hand to my arm, but Bobbi is distracted. 'He'd been prescribed temazepam after Alice went missing,' she says, biting her lip. 'He couldn't sleep for even a minute.' She ducks her head. '*I* prescribed them, Zee.'

'You were just doing your job.'

'I know. Didn't make it easier when it dawned on me what he'd given you, though.'

'How did the police know I was at Evan's?' I ask her.

'Ross, as it goes.' She raises an eyebrow.

Then I remember. The message Ross sent to me this morning about Evan. But the big picture feels like a *Where's Wally?* – answers buried beneath something I should be able to see but can't.

I sit up slowly. Sip water. Bobbi's phone pings and I watch the swallow in her throat as she looks at the message.

'What is it?' I ask, wiping my mouth with a tissue. 'Is there news?'

Bobbi shakes her head. 'No, but there is a new *Gone Girls* episode. If you wanted to . . .' Then she answers her own question. 'No, not now, hey. You rest.'

'I want to listen to it.'

'Oh now, I'm not sure she's up to that,' says the nurse, who's just popped in to top up my water jug, with a glance at Bobbi's phone.

But as soon as he leaves, I nod, and Bobbi – knowing there isn't any point arguing and, I know, also desperate to hear it herself – presses play. The two of us wait through the advert for Moo ice cream.

'I'm a podcaster, but first and foremost, I'm a journalist,' Ross is saying, twenty seconds later. 'And anyone who has ever been a journalist will tell you that whatever they go on to do, what they are, *deep down*, is a journalist. It's a core part of my identity.

'I like answers. I like telling the truth. I like digging. Asking questions. If you've got a biscuit tin, I will rummage in it. I'm nosy.

'Something about journalism buries itself deep into your being. Even people who haven't done it for decades will tell you that.' A small laugh. 'Shout out here to my friend Derek's dad.'

Ross's deep breath is audible.

'I came to Aurora Island to report on Alice Fox's disappearance and to make this series of the *Gone Girls* podcast. But lately, I've started to feel like *Gone Girls* isn't doing enough. The journalist in me has kicked in – I want to go deeper. I used to do a fair bit of undercover and investigative work, back in the day. It's time to get back to it.'

The music starts. I look at Bobbi. 'What does he mean?'

She shrugs, and Ross's voice comes back on.

'Before she went missing, Lily – who regular listeners to the podcast will remember is the Alphabet Woman who went missing erroneously on N – said she had something important to tell me.

'Lily and I had become . . .' He coughs. 'We were friends. She was going to tell me this thing the day she went missing. She never got the chance.'

He clears his throat. 'I had an instinct that whatever Lily wanted to tell me was connected to the Alphabet Women. I was also convinced it was something to do with an envelope I'd seen at Lily's house, addressed to a name that wasn't hers. That name begins with an N. Some listeners might remember that I mentioned one of the Alphabet Women having another identity on a previous episode of *Gone Girls*. I can now tell you that was Lily.'

From my hospital bed, I turn to Bobbi. 'Oh my God. He's talking about Natasha *on the podcast*.'

Ross continues: 'One thing I've never got – especially when you consider an island is a finite land mass – is why we couldn't find the Alphabet Women. I know, I know. Most people thought they had left the island or were dead. But I was convinced that the Alphabet Women were alive, and that they were still here on Aurora. It seemed too much to me, the idea that someone was transporting women off the island when so many eyes were on them. When there's only two ferry crossings a day, and the port is being watched so closely.

'I joined every local group, every local message board, and I tried to look for something – *anything* – weird going on. Something that might ring alarm bells. But there was nothing. No patterns I could see. Just the usual local chat.'

Ross pauses. 'Until I stopped being me.'

In the hospital, I look at Bobbi. She shakes her head; she has no idea what he's talking about either.

'I thought I'd work backwards,' Ross continues. 'What would whoever was doing this need most? I figured that if I was right and they were on the island, there must be some serious security in place to stop them being found, and they would need more and more of it as they took more women.

'I set up a new profile as a security guard. Helpful that – sorry, I know you can't see me, listeners, but I'm a pretty big guy. Mostly because I like pasties but there is the odd muscle lurking under there too.'

Bobbi rolls her eyes. 'Get on with it, Ross,' she mumbles.

'Like I say, I have undercover and investigative journo experience,' he says. 'Which means I have good contacts to help me look convincing as a hire. I hung around local sites. Posted that I was looking for work. Eventually – after a couple of jobs that went nowhere – there was an interesting bite.

'I was contacted by this bloke who said his name was Barry. Promised decent money to do security at this mega house on the other side of the island. Deep in the woodland to the north of the island, away from Aurora's biggest settlements, Port St Joseph and Syford, or even the other smaller villages. I was told it was a celebrity who was living there so I had to sign an NDA. That's standard for Aurora these days, with the kinds of super-rich people who are arriving on the island, but something about it felt off. My spidey senses were pinging.

'Even after four shifts though, I'd seen nothing. Got nowhere. Unsurprising, since I wasn't allowed inside the perimeter fence or inside the huge security gates. Instead I was just charged with manning the entrance with ID and vehicle checks, watching for any suspicious movement,' says Ross. 'We usually worked in pairs. We had a security booth, and access to the external CCTV, but there was zero way of knowing what the hell was going on inside. That wasn't our business. We were just first line of defence.'

Bobbi squeezes my hand and I look up in surprise, remembering where I am. As often happens with *Gone Girls*, I am so consumed by the podcast that I forget what's happening outside it. My mind is there, entirely. That's Ross's skill.

Something pops into my head then. The strong coffee, the dark circles. *This* is why Ross has been so exhausted lately. Not because he took the women; because he's been working nights undercover as a security guard.

'The other security guards didn't ask questions,' says Ross. 'Clocked on, clocked off, happy to be paid cash in hand, do their patrols, watch the CCTV, then leave. It didn't seem to cross their minds that this was about the Alphabet Women. They just thought it was rich people guarding their wealth – that that's why we were there, to stop masked robbers nicking diamonds. Since the second-homers arrived, there'd been a lot of this surveillance work and these blokes were old hands. This was no different to them. Just a job.

'They also – when the subject of the women *did* come up – thought the same as most people had started to, over time, even if we tried our best to stay positive. That the Alphabet Women had been taken off the island, or were dead and gone.

'I watched and waited, and eventually on my patrols I found something. Round the back where it was all woodland, there was a blind spot in the cameras. It was still risky. I didn't know what I'd find but I needed to move things on, so one night I went for it. I disabled the electrics, and I scaled the fence.

'The house itself was old – Victorian maybe? I'm not good with architecture but stuff growing up the sides, beautiful but run-down. *Secret Garden* vibes. Not one of the more WAG-y, super-modern ones that have sprung up lately.

'The *grounds though* – even in the dark it was obvious they were something else. They had acres and acres. I mean, for someone who grew up in a terrace on the outskirts of Manchester, this was . . .'

He trails off.

'The weirdest thing, though, were the sheds that ran down the back of it. Very small and new, crammed in. Spidey senses again, listeners.

'I started walking between these sheds. If anyone had seen me, they'd have thought I was stark-raving nuts, muttering to myself as I walked up and down, up and down, at three a.m.' Ross pauses. 'But I was muttering because something, slowly, was dawning on me.'

I look at Bobbi with a silent question: *What?*

When Ross speaks, it's in a quieter voice. 'There were twenty-six sheds.'

'Fuck,' says Bobbi, standing up, holding her phone out in front of her like it's a bomb. 'Fuck, Zee! Twenty-six! A to Z. They were there. He was right.'

Under the thin material of the hospital gown, my heart thumps too hard for a patient who's having their blood pressure checked at regular intervals. An impatient patient.

'I went looking down the narrow passages between them,' says Ross, both of us staring at the phone now like Ross is addressing us directly from its screen. 'For something, *anything*. And I tripped over this wooden stick. When I picked it up it was attached to a sign, like an . . . easel I guess? When I picked it up and shone my phone torch on it . . . This sign had four words on it: The Alphabet Women Project.'

The podcast lets a little of its ominous theme tune play before Ross carries on.

'What the actual fuck?' murmurs Bobbi.

We stare at the phone again. Wait.

'I was convinced then – even more convinced than I had been – that the women were *there*, or they had been at some point,' says Ross's voice. 'Now I just needed to find out if they were alive, and who the hell was behind this. I was suddenly very aware again that

I was in danger just being there. And that what I might be about to stumble across could be something very, very dark.'

'Are you sure you . . .' begins Bobbi.

I nod and move the phone so she can't hit pause. I am so desperate for the long-overdue answers to this most bizarre of mysteries that I can't stop now, whatever this brings. However dark it gets. Whatever it is doing to my heart rate and my blood pressure.

'I stood the sign up and took a picture, with me in it,' says Ross's voice. 'Thought it would prove I was there, that it was me sending it, I guess. Validate it. And then I got the hell out of there.'

I turn to Bobbi. 'Hold on . . .'

That picture that Winterbottom sent me, when he said Ross was involved. That must be what Ross is talking about now.

That *Where's Wally?* image swims in front of me again.

'When I got home from a shift last Wednesday, I sent the photo to the police,' Ross says. 'I called and explained that I was undercover, that I needed a little more time to find out who was responsible but that I was nearly there. The officer gave me a brief telling-off about taking matters into my own hands and told me to keep this to myself for now – to only go through him. Keep the circle small.' He pauses. 'I knew how much could depend on what we did next. How it could be the difference between the women making it – if any of them were still alive – or not.

'It was only twenty-four hours until my next shift. but I felt frustrated every second I wasn't there,' says Ross. 'Getting inside the fence *still* hadn't been enough and I hadn't found a trace of the women.'

Bobbi squeezes my hand tighter as my body becomes a run of goosebumps.

'Then it was finally time for my next shift. I went on my patrols, disabled the electrics again, headed for the same blind spot.

Quick as I could, straight down to the sheds. And that's when I saw her.'

My breath quickens.

'Ute. Our U. Face pressed to the tiny window of one of the sheds, looking out at the stars. She didn't see me but I had burnt the faces of *every one of those women* on to my retinas. I'd looked at the photos so much, so often, in such detail. I'd researched these women. I knew them. And I knew it was Ute. She was alive.'

I look at Bobbi.

'I knew if one of them was alive, any of them could be,' says Ross's voice with a little crack of emotion.

Lily. Lily.

I put a hand on my hospital gown. Try to press my heart into slowing down; the doctor will be in to check my vitals again soon. But it's no use.

'It was a reason to keep going, and it was *evidence*: I'd been right.'

The music kicks in again and I turn to Bobbi. I know doctors would tell me to rest; that listening to this now is a terrible idea. But how can I stop?

'What I found odd was that . . . I knew it was the middle of the night but . . . Well, I had always expected that if I found the women alive, if I found any of them alive . . . that they would have to be restrained. Because doing the podcast, I felt like I'd got to know these women and they'd *fight*. But Ute wasn't being restrained. She was alone, from what I could see, and she wasn't fighting.'

'Something's not okay,' I say to Bobbi, frowning, hitting pause, blood pumping. 'What were they doing to them to make . . . Because Ross is right. There *would* have been anarchy. Corinne would have fought, and Donna. *Lily* would have fought.'

The room spins.

'Lily can't have been there, then,' I say. 'Lily can't have been . . . Most of them can't have been . . .'

Bobbi speaks then. 'But they're women, Zee,' she says quietly. 'They don't need to prove their might with fists. Maybe they were doing it with staying power. Let's listen.'

I nod and press play. Feel my heart race again, that beating power beneath the slither of hospital material.

'I was desperate to go and speak to Ute, but I knew it was stupid. I had no idea who was around, what this was. I couldn't storm in by myself. I needed to get out of there. Make a proper plan and speak to my police contact. But when I was about to get back over the fence, I heard it. A voice.'

I look at Bobbi.

'I stayed hidden,' Ross continues, 'pushed myself right up against the fence. My heart was hammering because it was obvious the voice didn't belong to one of the missing women. It was someone talking loudly, almost manically, *about* them. About The Alphabet Women Project. I caught snippets of words but it was hard to hear all of it. One phrase kept coming up, though: *The End*.'

The End. My stomach drops. What is *The End*?

'When I got back out, I told Darren, the other guy on shift, that I'd been to check out a noise. He barely looked up. I turned the electrics back on and carried on as normal until my shift was over. I knew I couldn't break my cover until I knew who was doing this, who I'd heard . . . That was the whole point. So that when I figured this out, we could see it through. That I'd be able to get a conviction.

'But I knew whoever I heard had to be the person – or one of the people – who had taken the women. And what was weird about that was that . . .' Another beat, before he speaks again. 'It was a woman.'

My eyes flick to Bobbi. A *woman*? That has to be impossible.

'And actually, there *was* a woman the blokes talked about. This woman whose diamonds we thought we were protecting,' says Ross. 'Who I never would have dreamed in a million years could have been involved. She was the only person we ever saw leaving the house. Shopping, the blokes presumed. Spa trips. Her mates came round but we didn't see them, they drove straight round the back into the garages and disappeared inside for lunches or whatever, their cars driving away a few hours later. The blokes were scathing – *rich bitch, wouldn't know a hard day's graft if it hit her in the face*.

'She was *small*, though. Well dressed, head down and meek. I knew there was no way she could be behind it all. I still ran her through a Google Image search. I'd sneaked a photo of her through an open car window one day but it was another dead end. Or it felt that way. On the third page of Google, though, when I was about to give up, I found something interesting.'

In my hospital bed, I sit up from the pillow, back arched. It's too fast though and I feel dazed. Light-headed.

'A picture of her on a TV set. A backdrop I recognised.'

A TV set?

Ross's voice is careful. 'The show was called *Date Me*.'

I look at Bobbi. 'Is that . . . ?' she begins. I nod. The show Lily was on, yes.

'This picture was taken at the wrap party of the TV programme. This woman was glammed up, holding a glass of champagne.'

My brain races to connect the dots.

The Alphabet Women.

The reality show.

Lily.

Natasha.

This small, rich woman.

The wrap party.

Lily wouldn't have been at the wrap party, of course. Lily would have been busy issuing her apologies and atoning for her sins in a trouser suit, a modern-day Hester whatsit. The room swims again and I close my eyes for a second, but when Bobbi asks if we should turn it off, I shake my head. *It's fine. Carry on.*

Ross speaks again: 'The woman who lived at the house was called Minnie Rushby. She was the exec producer of a show Lily went on when she had her other name, Natasha – and Lily, I should say, has given me permission to tell you this, listeners. Minnie Rushby was the person who made the final decision not to edit or censor the scene where Lily had sex on that show. But to let it play out in full and go for the ratings, at the cost of someone's lifelong mental health and infamy. She got a record audience, that night. *Six million people.*

'And now she was on Aurora Island producing her next TV show. Her next show, starring the Alphabet Women.'

But I don't register any of that. Even though it is important. Even though it is at the heart of everything. Because all I hear is this: if Lily gave Ross permission to talk about Natasha on the latest episode of the podcast, which only went live *today*, just now, then Lily is with him.

Lily is alive.

We can only press play again after my blood pressure has been checked and I have lied that I don't feel faint and the nurse has left with a frown on her face and vows to be back soon.

When my sobs have abated.

When the doctors and nurses are far enough away that they don't know what we're listening to.

Bobbi hugs me hard.

'She's okay,' she mutters into my hair. Matted and smelly. 'Lily's okay.'

'What was the new TV show?' I ask Bobbi as she pulls away, with a feeling of deep foreboding as my brain makes space for something else and this part begins to register. 'What show did Minnie want to make?'

But it's not Bobbi who has the answers. She clicks play, and Ross's voice rings out again.

'This is what we know, then,' he says. 'From what she told the women, and from what a bit of digging has told me, Minnie Rushby had become heavily involved in activism.

'In the last few years, Minnie had barely worked in TV, despite being hugely successful. Instead, she dedicated most of her time to her other passion. She was part of an organisation that protested against climate inaction.

'And there's nothing wrong with that, right? We all want to save the planet. But hold on, because then you look into this organisation she is part of. A lot of you may have heard of The End Rebellion? Yeah. Okay. So they had become, over the years, the most extreme of any of these groups. And behind the scenes that was going further.

'They were planning for the next phase of action. They believed that, for world leaders to listen, they had to agitate harder. Escalate. They had hit the headlines before – tampering with pipelines, rooftop banner drops on high-profile buildings, blocking roads, there had even been the riots down in Bristol, remember – but it wasn't enough. Now they were looking for more media attention. And they were going to do that with bolder action, which would hit headlines all over the world.'

Bobbi murmurs, low: 'Oh my God.'

As she looks at me, Ross confirms it. 'And that meant,' he says, swallowing audibly, 'coming to Aurora. And one by one, despite the families left behind, despite the pain, taking – kidnapping – these women.'

There, finally, is our answer.

'Minnie believed that the only way to get the kind of attention their cause needed was to do something radical,' says Ross. 'But she also wanted to use her TV background and turn whatever action they took into a documentary. Minnie knew TV, she was very good at TV. And because of that, she knew the importance of a strong USP.'

I look at Bobbi, a question. 'Unique selling point,' she says, hitting pause. 'Something to make it stand out.'

She presses play again.

'Aurora ended up on Minnie's radar when she came here in March – we all know the island's become very "in" lately, and she came for a weekend at the retreat for her wedding anniversary.

'She started thinking that Aurora would make a great setting for action, and the documentary. Partly because it's so wild. Partly because it perfectly illustrated their cause: sadly, the island of Aurora is likely to be one of the first places submerged in UK waters because of rising sea levels.'

I look at Bobbi. 'Is that true?'

She shrugs. 'Not one for now, Zee. Focus.'

Ross carries on. 'Regular listeners will know that Susie, who goes to the retreat book club, came on to the podcast to talk about how they had written their new name – the Alphabet Women – on a piece of paper. On her visit there, Minnie found that piece of paper.

'Now, frankly, she didn't care about the book club, she isn't a reader. But she was working on an idea for this new radical action, and something about the term *Alphabet Women* sparked something. She pocketed the paper as a reminder.

'Now Minnie's mind was working in overdrive. She was thinking about this USP, this structure, this island setting, and slowly, slowly, a plan was coming together. The End Rebellion would take these women to a safe place in the wilds of Aurora, create this huge news story about them going missing, and then post the documentary online, with a voiceover of The End Rebellion's aims, and a warning. Act on climate change, or we will take people or – next time – we will do worse.'

Ross pauses. 'And that's how The Alphabet Women Project was born.'

Bobbi pours us both a glass of water. 'Jesus Christ,' she murmurs.

From Bobbi's phone, Ross carries on speaking. 'Minnie did wobble. When she saw the women crying and when she realised how big this was getting, that there were press conferences, podcasts . . . But she believed in this *whole-heartedly* as a cause. She believed this was for a greater good: the future of humankind. How could they not disrupt if it literally saved the human race? To Minnie, this was a temporary, small price to pay.'

Ross pauses. 'Minnie Rushby was a force. Always had been. Hugely successful – rich too, hence how she could afford that house. And whatever she did, she did to the extreme. Now she was determined to agitate more than anyone had agitated before, then, after Z, bam: she'd release the women, then post the documentary. But by then she'd be long gone, starting again.'

Suddenly, I am parched. I gulp down my whole glass of water in one.

'From the women we've spoken to today, it seems like they were all told the same thing,' says Ross. 'At the end of this, you can go back to your lives. But if you don't go along with it . . . well, according to the women we've spoken to, this was when Minnie's husband was allegedly sent in. He was also a key member of The End Rebellion and a scary guy, we hear.'

Ross's voice drops low. 'A narcissist who thrived on attention, by all accounts. Knowing he was behind the headlines and the pain and *all* this police resource . . . Unlike Minnie, he never wobbled, all it did was fuel his ego.' A beat of silence. 'Next, we're going to a part of the podcast that may be hard to listen to. It's something I recorded earlier, on location.'

Bobbi pauses the episode and looks at me, brow furrowed. 'We don't know what we're going to get here, Zee. Are you sure you're up to this? Want to take a break? Sleep and come back to it?'

'No,' I tell her. 'Press play.'

But when the first thing I hear from the phone is the most piercing scream, I grab hold of the sides of the bed and brace, like my plane is heading for destruction. Bobbi peels one of my hands away and grasps it. Then she slips her Sambas off and climbs on to the bed with me.

'Budge up then,' she murmurs. We lie side by side, railway tracks.

'I'm recording this on location,' says Ross's voice, out of breath. 'I want us to have a record, if it turns out that I'm right. And even if I don't . . . perhaps this is evidence. Hopefully this is evidence. It is Saturday, sixth of July and I am at a settlement deep in the woods of north Aurora where we have found . . . we have found the Alphabet Women.'

Someone shouts a word that I can't make out. Bobbi grips my hand tighter.

There is the crunch of leaves, and Ross continues. 'Security guards have been taken for questioning and police have entered the grounds. So far we have found Ute, Donna, Yola, Gemma, Issy and Paola. All of them are alive and seem well. They tell us the others are safe. But there is no sign of the couple who we now have reason to think have been taking the women. Alerts have been put out to airports and of course the port.'

'Ross!'

The sound of a scuffle then. I turn to Bobbi. 'What's happening?'

'Oh my God,' comes Ross's voice. 'Oh my God.'

And then there is the kind of melee of bangs and white noise that suggests a recording device has been dropped or manhandled, and even though I pick up the phone and put it to my ear, Bobbi leaning in close too, I can't make out a thing.

'What's happening?' I say again, panic rising. 'What is it?'

But when I turn to Bobbi, alarm on my own face, she is frowning in concentration.

'Listen,' she says. 'Listen properly. Didn't you hear . . . ? I think he left it like this even when he edited it with the other recordings, for authenticity probably. Listen.'

And when I do, I can just about hear a voice I recognise.

'That, there . . .' says Bobbi, smiling. 'I think that's the moment that Ross found Lily.'

Lily's voice comes out through the phone, emotional, frenetic. 'They're alive, Ross,' she says. 'They're all alive.'

A little noise comes from my own throat.

They're alive.

Alice. Corinne. Lily.

The daughters, the mothers, the wives, the sisters. The humans.

All of them are alive.

Each sob feels like it's been wrenched from the deep. Bobbi passes me some water and rubs my back until I can speak again. And then Winterbottom walks in.

'I was going to ask if you'd be up to a chat,' he says, then he nods to Bobbi's phone, clutched in my hand with the podcast logo, its A–Z, visible. I pause it and he sighs. 'But it looks like you've already listened to the podcast.'

'Can I talk to her?' I ask. 'To Lily?'

'Not yet,' he says. 'They're being looked over. Then, if they're up to it, they'll be interviewed while all the evidence is fresh. But soon, love, I'm sure.'

He looks at his phone.

'You told me Ross was involved,' I say. 'But he's a good guy, right? He *solved* this.'

Winterbottom flinches and he nods. 'I know that now. But what I was told at the time, love . . . That was different. That ruddy beanpole I get stuck with all the ruddy time was sowing the wrong seeds. Even sent me the picture of Ross there without telling me he was undercover, so I thought he was involved.'

He sees me look confused.

'The other officer? Campbell?'

'That's the one. Attached to his phone most of the time, now we ruddy well know why. It seems my colleague has been taking bribes to pay off his apparently quite substantial gambling debts.'

'Bribes?' says Bobbi. 'Police Constable *Campbell?*'

'Same as your own colleague, Zadie – Joy, is it? Apparently *she* served up a nice long list of names before this started happening – women from the island . . . most of whom she didn't like or found irritating.'

'*Joy* gave them names?'

'She had no idea what she was doing at that point, to be fair, but still – she didn't bother to ask why anyone would want this information.' He sighs. 'Just took the cash and ran. Tale as old as time, love. A lot of people have a price. Just very embarrassed I didn't see it happening in my own ruddy force.'

He pauses. 'We've arrested Minnie. Just now. Heathrow Airport.'

'And the husband?'

'Not yet.' He looks up. 'Have you got to the part about who the husband is yet?'

I *know* him? I shake my head.

'A ruddy arsehole even then. But now . . . next level.'

I still don't get it.

'Three years after that wrap party for *Date Me*,' he says. 'Minnie Rushby married the man Lily had her . . . erm, relations with on the show.'

He pauses.

'Minnie Rushby married Andreas. And The End Rebellion was born.'

SIX MONTHS LATER

Bobbi holds Zadie's tanned hand snug in hers, as they amble in their wellies and padded coats along the wide expanse of Port St Joseph bay. Up ahead, Bertie sprints in the Spider-Man wellies and matching raincoat he got for Christmas. He runs alongside his other Christmas present – a sausage dog who is the exact colour of well-cooked sausages.

It's still a novelty for Bobbi to have Zadie back from what turned out to be a month in Cambodia and Thailand before Christmas, and for them to be together, officially.

It's late afternoon and the sun that kicked off the year so brightly this morning is less bold now. The sky's ink is slowly shifting. Darkening. Each minute it turns an inch angrier, the clouds mushrooming out and out and out and out and out. They'll burst in the end; inevitable as mortality.

With her spare hand, Zadie checks an alert on her phone.

Under her breath, she murmurs to Bobbi: 'It's up.'

'It's up!' Bobbi echoes, and Lily and Alice turn their heads in symmetry, and walk quickly back towards them.

'Would you mind taking the kids, Dad?' Lily asks her dad, Duncan, who's spent Christmas exploring Aurora Island and getting to know his daughter again. 'Just a bit further up the beach, so they can't hear while we listen to the last episode.'

'Course, love.'

'I'll help,' says Bobbi. She turns to Zadie. 'I can listen later, it's not going anywhere. I'll take Jake too.'

The girls run ahead with Duncan and Bobbi, Florence cartwheeling, muddy lemon leggings and high-tops sticking up like spring flowers high into the air as Freya dribbles a ball up the sand, trailed by rival player Jake.

Lily, Zadie and Alice head for the rocks and sit down. Zadie presses play.

'This episode of *Gone Girls: The Alphabet Women of Aurora Island* is brought to you in conjunction with Moo Organic Ice Cream,' says Ross's voice, that advert that was so incongruous in the first episode, but is white noise now. 'The creamiest, freshest treat from the island that we all love.'

And then, that ominous theme tune that is so synonymous with last summer. That will forever make them feel like they are back there.

'Hi everyone, and welcome. I know *Gone Girls* has been silent for a while. I know you have waited a long time to hear the story of the final Alphabet Woman – Zadie – and what happened next after the last episode, which went live the same day that she was targeted.'

Zadie feels herself shrink. How odd, to hear yourself spoken about like this, after an advert about ice cream.

'And of course, of what happened *after* the alphabet was completed. Once charges were made, we had to be very cautious with what we reported on. Now, though, the trial has finished, so we can tell you a lot more. It's time for our final episode of the podcast.

'We all know now of course that, six months ago, the Alphabet Women were found, and *every single one of them* was alive and healthy. We know Minnie Rushby was arrested, and that straight after that someone – we presume Andreas – posted the Alphabet

Women documentary on YouTube, with footage of the women after they had been taken, and a voiceover warning that, if The End Rebellion's climate demands weren't met, they would play out more rebellions like this one, or worse. That the world was roasting – this was filmed, a handy coincidence for them, during a heatwave on normally chilly Aurora – and this was about survival; they would stop at nothing to get world leaders to listen.'

Ross pauses.

'Now, in a world exclusive, I'm speaking to a number of the women.

'Firstly – and I think this is appropriate as she was the first woman to go, our A – I have Alice Fox.'

On the beach, Lily sees Alice suck her breath in. They recorded this together last night, in the office at the retreat. They know what they're going to hear. But that doesn't make it any less terrifying.

Lily grabs Alice's hand. She's got better with touch lately and they're tied together now, the Alphabet Women. Sometimes Alice can feel it like it's a real tie, a belt that expands wide to spread around them all and pull them in tight.

'Alice, welcome to the podcast,' says Ross's voice from Zadie's phone. 'Thanks for coming on when I know you were at the verdict today and must be exhausted. This can't be easy. Can you tell us what happened to you?'

'Well, I didn't disappear from an alleyway, as was reported,' Alice says. 'I got a notification after I'd been shopping that I'd got some loafers from The Row that I wanted for my party for a hundred quid, but the seller said they were pick-up only.'

'Can't blame you,' Corinne says, with a whistle. 'Hundred-quid The Row loafers, come on.'

'I drove to the address,' says Alice. 'Very specific instructions. Use the garage entrance round the back. Fanciest house I'd ever seen *in my life*. This woman – she said her name was Sally – met me there, huge grin, bare feet and a gleaming pedicure. It's bad how money can make you think you're safe, isn't it? Not one thing about it felt off.

'She said she was waiting for her husband to bring the shoes down and took me into one of the sheds. It was brand new and done up nicely, though, could have been a quirky little Airbnb. We made small talk. I asked if they rented the sheds out to tourists and she told me no. That they were actually for this documentary she was making. Then she started . . . I mean, would *preaching* to me about climate change be over the top? No, I don't think it would.

'I said sorry, I'm all for sustainability but I haven't got time for this conversation, I'm having a party and I just want the loafers. And then when they didn't turn up after ten, fifteen minutes, I tried to leave. But then her husband arrived and . . . well, that's when the mood changed.'

'Changed?' Ross says.

On the beach, Zadie squeezes Alice's hand. 'He was threatening,' her voice says from the phone.

Ross is careful. 'In what way?'

'It was made clear that I was staying, and if I did that I'd see my kids again – *soon* as well, this wasn't a long-term thing. If I tried to leave . . .' Alice's voice cracks. 'We never knew exactly. But he was a very intimidating man.'

There is a pause before Ross speaks again.

'Lily, can you tell us how *you* became an Alphabet Woman?' he asks.

'Kids' scooter.'

'Okay . . .'

'I went to pick up a kids' scooter for Freya's birthday that Minnie – well, she said her name was Annie to me – was selling on a resale app. Thirty quid, absolute bargain, pick-up only again. I got the notification while I was food shopping, thought I might as well go and get it. I was on my e-bike which can do some decent distance so I cycled over there. I was going to strap it to the back. I spoke to this woman on the phone and she sounded . . . sweet?'

Corinne's voice pops up next. 'Andreas wasn't front-facing. It was all Minnie . . . and Minnie . . . well, she wasn't who we were looking out for. She was a woman in an Aligne dress and glowy primer, who smelled of Jo Malone. She didn't look scary or threatening or guilty. She didn't look like a bloody eco-terrorist.'

'We should say that no terrorism charges were brought,' says Ross quickly. 'Right. Helen is working today so she couldn't record with us, but we now know that she went out to Minnie's place on her bike to collect a particularly generous donation she'd been promised for the raffle she was organising for her work gala. Her bike was then left somewhere else as a decoy, like the cars often were. And you, Donna?'

'Waitrose hummus aisle.'

'Waitrose hummus aisle?'

'I was on speaker to my wife about buying a small property to rent out for the tourists – lots of people are doing it now on the island, it can be a great investment. I have a loud voice, Lois always says it, and when I put the phone away, this woman said sorry for listening in but she had a farm and she was putting some of her outbuildings up for sale, blah blah, and it sounded like it'd be the kind of thing we wanted. Rural setting.

'She said her name was Poppy – said I could go over and see them now if I wanted. I *jumped* on it. Then she smiled at me and told me it was easy to make that hummus with the jalapeños on top at home, and it was *yummy*. It sounds stupid now but nothing about that conversation seemed linked to what was going on. Nothing. She was just some rich woman lurking round the hummus in Waitrose using words like *yummy*. That doesn't ring alarm bells, you know?'

'And what happened when you got there?'

'I drove straight into the garage, like she said. She showed me round the sheds. Then she sent the bloke in.

'But obviously by this point . . . well, unlike Alice I wasn't the first and it dawned on me quite quickly that this was connected to the missing women. I was terrified. So when he said it was about taking action, a rebellion, an uprising, I could have total freedom if I went along with it. . . I was . . . relieved, I suppose? Seconds before, I'd thought I was about to be murdered. It was weird but it was . . . well, it was better than dead in a ditch, I guess. I just agreed and shut up.'

'Same.'

'Same.'

'Same.'

'We were given a timetable, like we'd gone to rehab,' Alice says. 'It was very routine. As more women arrived – God, it was such a relief and so awful at the same time when you saw someone you knew – we were split into groups. But we were all doing the same sort of things. Filming to camera from the scripts they got us to read about climate change. Or making the posters. "THE A–Z OF CLIMATE CHANGE" was a major theme – I think they liked using the symbolism.'

She pauses. 'That moment they found us was the first time I let myself fully process what it was, I think,' says Lily, a lot quieter than Corinne, the difference in their voices pronounced. 'Electric fences, guards, cameras, the lot. We'd been abducted. Used as human fodder for a cause. And we'd been imprisoned.'

The music comes on, a break in the flow. When Ross speaks again, the mood is a little lighter.

'Explain to me how the letters worked,' says Ross. 'We know that, Lily and Zadie – your colleague from the retreat gave them a spreadsheet of names. Other than that though, how did they find them?'

'Small communities have a lot of communication and a tight network,' says Lily. 'But there is also a presumption, a trust that everyone in that community, in those groups, is who they say they are. It's easy to infiltrate.

'Who checks that the twenty-two people in the Pilates class WhatsApp group are all who they say they are? Minnie was on a *load* of local island groups – the am dram group that do the panto, cardio tennis, modern pop choir, kids' cricket, watching out for who needed a raffle prize or a donation or a new house. Everyone assumed everyone in there was known. But no one ever checked. A friendly profile picture that looked generally the same demographic as everyone else's and a quick message – *I'm interested, can you add me* – and bam, you're in. No one's got time to police these things.'

'She did all of it with different non-threatening personas too,' said Donna. 'Even the names . . . *Annie, Sally, Lucy, Poppy*. She was always just there – sweet, innocent, but lurking and observing people. Then finding ways to appeal to them.'

'She just looked,' says Corinne, 'like the absolute definition of a basic bitch.'

'Let's move to another crucial part of the project,' says Ross, suppressing a laugh at the words *basic bitch*. 'After Minnie contacts her first victim – Alice – she realises something. She sees the photo on Alice's WhatsApp and realises that the friend Alice is posing with on it is familiar. *You*, Lily. Had you not met her when she came to the retreat?'

'No. Apparently she was only there for two nights and I wasn't on the rota. We never crossed paths. Otherwise, I'd have recognised her, even if her style is pretty different to back then. And I'd have definitely recognised Andreas.'

'So, she recognises you in this picture . . .'

'Yes. Me. Or to Minnie, she recognises who I used to be. Natasha. After the TV show, I moved to Aurora Island and changed my name to run away from that identity. Every letter that passed, I was terrified – not just the fear of being taken but because, if I was, it meant that people would *research* me. Find out about me. Talk about me. And I knew that even if whoever took me didn't *know* I was Natasha, and I went on L, it wouldn't take long before other people figured it out.'

Lily pauses.

'Now, though, I think it's the best part of last summer for me,' she says. 'I'm *glad* I was exposed. I used to think I was disgusting, that I had ruined my own life and was entirely to blame. I cut myself off from my poor dad – my lovely dad – even though he sent me messages and tried so hard to come and visit me. But I wouldn't let him, because I couldn't look him in the eyes without feeling ashamed.'

On the beach, Lily's eyes go to Duncan.

'Now I know that I did nothing wrong. I was a kid, and I was taken advantage of by a TV show and producers, and by an older man who was extremely manipulative. He still is. We're pretty sure he was the one who contacted Zadie about my real name, who sent the video and that piece of paper Minnie had taken. Enjoying inserting himself into things, I guess.'

'He liked being the puppet master.'

'Exactly.'

'Can we talk next about what happened for the letter Z?' Ross says, after an advert for an introductory offer on free bets. 'It was a little different to the others and it's the one letter we've never told our listeners the story of.'

There is a pause. On the beach, Zadie slips an arm around Alice's middle. Even Lily goes for an awkward hand-hold.

'This isn't easy, sorry,' says Alice's voice from the phone. 'But it was my husband Evan who spiked Zadie's drink with temazepam and planned to take her in his car up to the farm and hand her over to Minnie.'

Ross whistles. 'Very different to what normally happened.'

'Yeah. Andreas contacted Evan after Y and told him that if he did this, if he brought them this Z – Zadie suggested by name – he would get me back. Didn't tell him anything else. Just said he had me and I would come back if he did this and kept it to himself.'

There's a pause.

'Evan said he took one look at the girls and made his decision, and I'm not saying it was *right*. But I am saying . . . I just appeal to everyone not to be too harsh on him. What would you do in that situation? What would any of us do? Evan didn't know what was really going on there. He thought Andreas would kill me.'

On the beach, a fat tear starts to run down Alice's face as she hears her own voice on the podcast crack and falter.

'Full disclosure: it was me who sent the police to your house that day,' Ross tells Alice. 'Who sent them after Evan. I was on an early shift the day after Alphabet Day and I got inside the fence again. This time, though, I needed to go further.

'There was a door unlocked to the main house. On a table in the hall there was a piece of paper with a phone number on it and the letter Z, underlined. I took a picture of it, and when I got back over the fence, I sneaked down into the woodland and called the number. When someone answered whose voice was familiar, the penny dropped. I'd *met* him. It was Evan Fox. Unfortunately, I wasn't quite quick enough. Zadie was already at his house. And she was already in trouble.'

Evan had sent the girls for a sleepover at their friends' the night before. Then he called Zadie and crushed the temazepam into her

Earl Grey (the *relief* when he found that teabag, after the worst odds ever: finding a twenty-something who doesn't like coffee).

'He was charged?' says Ross.

'Yeah,' says Alice quietly. 'No custodial sentence though. Previous good character.' She pauses. 'He was just a man, Ross, who was desperate to get his wife back. *And* he was being blackmailed.'

'What's devastating, of course, is that Andreas has *still* never been found,' says Ross. 'We can't bring you any conclusion there, which is extremely frustrating.'

On the beach now, Florence runs over to Alice, and Zadie quickly hits pause. 'Mum? Are you coming to play with us yet?' Florence asks.

'Sure, chicken,' Alice says, kissing her daughter on her head. Inhaling her.

She turns to Lily and Zadie. 'It's just goodbyes and thank yous after that anyway, isn't it? Let's put this away and go and get chips.'

'Is Ross meeting us in The Dolphin?' Zadie asks Lily as they walk, seeing the half-smile dart across her face that usually means Lily is thinking about her boyfriend. The kids bound ahead again.

Lily nods. 'Speak of the devil,' she says at the shrill ring of her phone.

'Hey,' she says to Ross.

And everyone sees it. The moment her face registers the news. The moment it is, finally, over.

'They've arrested him, Lily, they've arrested him,' Ross tells her, out of breath as if he is walking somewhere, although Lily suspects it's just adrenalin. Ross has waited for this for so long. He has put everything into getting them back. Into securing justice. 'I suspect the trial has reignited interest in the case; maybe it's meant someone recognised him or—'

'Where?' she interrupts.

She means: Is he near here?

'They found him in a bloody *bothy* near Fort William if you can believe it.' She hears Ross breathing heavily into the phone. 'That's not all, Lily.'

Lily steels herself. Alice and Zadie don't know what's happening on the other end of the phone but they can see her face, and while everyone else subtly leaves them to it, they sit close to her, shoulders touching on both sides, Alphabet Women tied together. Strong rope.

Then Ross continues, softer. 'My source says they have evidence to link him to at least *three* other crimes.'

Lily sucks in a breath. Alice looks at her, a question, and she puts her phone on speaker.

'The End Rebellion network is sprawling. These are people who didn't fit in the other groups. Who wanted to go further than civil disobedience. There may be more arrests to come as well; I suspect that some of this network may have helped with what happened on Aurora. Behind the scenes. Logistics. I suspect the guy who first contacted me about the security work – Barry – was one of them.'

After they end the call, Alice, Lily and Zadie sit in total silence.

Lily stops it, just the second before the sob comes out.

'You met a very bad human,' says Zadie. 'You met him *twice*. But you survived.'

After a few minutes they stand up and they walk on in silence among the squawks of the cormorants, eyes ahead on that scramble of kids and dogs and limbs and raincoats.

Lily thinks about how she could leave, now, if she wanted to. The Alphabet Women no longer need her. She could avoid standing up in front of Andreas in court – would they force her? She isn't sure – and she could go to the Arctic or she could go to another island or she could go to a city, even, to disappear in a different way, into a huge sprawling crowd.

But she realises something. She doesn't want to.

Aurora Island is in her soul now.

To the human brain, the same outcome can feel worlds apart depending on one thing: whether we have control over it or not. If we do, fine. If we don't, the wheels come off.

And Lily, as she walks on that beach on her island and sees Aurora's sky turn to black, knows one thing. She has control over this. And she will face Andreas down.

Lily, like the rest of them now, is an Alphabet Woman.

She doesn't need to prove her might with fists. But she will prove it with staying power.

ACKNOWLEDGEMENTS

Firstly, thanks to the women.

I've been lucky enough to know, be friends with, drink wine with, play netball with, analyse books with, and often work with a gaggle of brilliant, smart, funny women in my life, and I name-checked quite a few (but disclaimer – not all) of them in this book.

Halfway through *The Next Woman*, I realised that having a cast this large with all of these character names was a chance to say: we might not keep in touch, life might have pulled us apart a little, but I'm thinking about you. Or a chance to just say: you're great. Under the guise of, er, missing women. Niche, I know.

To the readers, old and new. I appreciate every one of you. I'm a reader too, and, as a writer, all I ever want is to write books people can't put down. I hope, hope, hope I've done that.

As usual, lots of people helped with this book. Firstly, my podcast experts, Daisy Buchanan and Alison Perry. Thanks for answering all of my questions, and not thinking any of them were too ridiculous. Or at least not telling me you thought they were. Any errors are, of course, my own.

To Katy and Suzanne for police questions. This won't be the last time. And you live too close to escape me. Ditto the errors.

To the Glasman/Hallams for letting me write their late dog Jake into this book, and especially to Pete for the lovely personal detail. Thank you.

Nat and your tin! I love it when I can sneak ridiculous bits of real human detail into books, and when I was laughing so much I couldn't speak in the Ferrero Rocher bar (if you know, you know), I knew your tin was going in. The holy water was a step too far, though.

From the same crew, thanks to my super-talented pal Lucy Stowell-Smith, who helped me out with lovely detail on Alice's job. There was a man who lived locally to me named Steven Spark. I didn't know him but he used to ride his motorbike with his dog in the sidecar and wave at my children as he passed, and they loved it. Lots of local kids did. When I read the news that he had died in a motorbike accident, I thought a lot about how odd it is that these people who we know but don't know can touch our lives. He brought us joy. Steve, the owner of The Dolphin, is not based on him but is meant to pay a small homage.

The character of Derek was formed in a similar way. I have many chats with the dog walkers local to me – again, knowing and not knowing – and I was thinking about the nature of friendship. Derek was my grandad's name. My grandad was also a very good friend of mine.

To Emma Ledger, for the beautiful illustration of fictional Aurora Island. I had tears in my eyes when I first looked at what you had created, Emma; how magical to see something I pictured in my own head for so long brought to life. You're such a talent. Emma does commissions – follow her on emma_ledger_ on Instagram.

Journalists and the changing nature of journalism play a big part in this book. Like Ross, journalism formed me and continues to form me. It's why I ask a lot of questions. It's why I value privacy highly. It's also why I get irate when journalists are portrayed in fiction as moustache-twirling meanies, and why this book is dedicated in the way it is. To the journos, then: lifelong friends, near or far, and the staunchest allies to have on your team. Whip-smart and super-funny with *the best* stories. They're always working on a side hustle. They'll champion you hard. They will rally, when needed. Most of them don't even have moustaches.

(The Britney trip that became a twenty-four-hour drinking session in Paris happened, by the way. Funnily enough, I can't tell you much more about it. It's a little blurry.)

I'd really like to thank Russel McLean for making editing such a laugh once again, and teaching me that birds have wings. Sometimes we need to get back to basics.

Gemma Wain and Ian Critchley, there is no limit to how many thank-yous I owe you both for sorting out my nemesis, The Evil Timeline, especially on a project of this size, with a cast this big. This book was quite an undertaking, and I couldn't have pulled it off without you.

To writer friends and all the writers who've been so supportive along the way now I am six – six! – books in. Special mention to my good pals Rachael Tinniswood (AKA Jessie Wells), Tabitha Lasley, Daisy Buchanan (second mention, you win a prize!), Lucy Vine and Harriet Johnson.

To Emily Hayward-Whitlock at The Artists Partnership, for your incredible work on TV options and for one of the most exciting chats of my life (and I speak as someone who has interviewed Beyoncé – but that's a story for another time . . .).

To the awesome teams at Riot and Tandem, especially legendary Lex and my new local lunch buddy Lucy, for all the amazing work you do on the PR and marketing front to get my book out there to readers. It's hugely appreciated.

To the booksellers who have been so supportive and – as ever – wonderful Cheshire West and Chester Libraries. I believe passionately that, more than ever, reading is fundamental for our mental health. Thanks for everything you do to support that. Let's use our libraries and not lose them like Lily did. (I also referenced our children's laureate, Frank Cottrell-Boyce, who does so much for children and reading in this country, just because he's brilliant.)

To the RLF, who are such a support for writers. I adore working for you.

To the many talented authors I've interviewed this year and to the bookshops that have allowed me to do that. Special mention to my adored local Linghams, Waterstones Liverpool and The Mold Bookshop.

To the whole awesome crew at my agency DHH, and especially Diana Beaumont for, you know, the small matters of my whole career in publishing and the preservation of my sanity. If it helps, I tell everyone how wonderful you are on pretty much a daily basis.

To my publisher, Thomas & Mercer. Two books in now, and working with everyone on this team is such a dream. Thank you, Nicole, for the constant support. Thank you to Vic Haslam, for acquiring *Tiny Daggers* and for everything that you have done on that book and this one. To Hannah Shaw, the transition since Vic went on leave has been so seamless, so wonderful, and that's testament to your brilliance. I can't wait for what's ahead.

To Mum, Dad and Gem, for the kind of unwavering support and love that makes a person feel secure for life.

And to Simon, for – actually, the same thing. How lucky am I? Thanks for talking me down when my writer brain spirals. Thanks for doing school pick-up when I'm hunched over my desk and close to weeping over *that bloody timeline*. Thanks for approximately ten thousand other things.

And my boys! Old enough to read acknowledgements these days – if not quite the books yet, sorry guys – so I need to up my game. When I was planning this book, we did a recce to a real-life island to help create a picture in my mind of the place that would become Aurora. I asked you to shout out to me as we explored the island: what you could see, hear, smell. I scribbled it all down and so much of that magic from your minds made it into this book. Let's keep reading, writing and nosying around the world yelling 'SEAGULLS!' together forever ♥.

Another psychological thriller by CAROLINE CORCORAN.

Loved *The Next Woman*? Here's a sample chapter of Caroline Corcoran's incredible psychological thriller *Tiny Daggers*. Available now.

THE BODY AT THE CHAMPAGNE BREAKFAST

Emergency services called to luxury Florida beach resort

Police and ambulance services have been called after a body washed up on a private hotel beach in the Florida Keys.

The body, which has not yet been formally identified, is believed to be that of a guest at the exclusive 5 resort of Turtle Bay in Islamorada.*

The idyllic resort is one of the most photographed on social media, and regularly plays host to celebrities and influencers.

A member of staff at the resort who did not wish to be named said: 'We were setting out the champagne glasses for the breakfast mimosas, when one of the waiters spotted the body.

'He screamed the place down. It was only a few metres away, over by the jetty where the guests take the sea kayaks out. It's going to take a long time to get over the shock of seeing a human corpse at work in the morning.'

One star who has been staying at the resort for the past week with friends but did not wish to be identified, said: 'We're not sure what's happening but we came down for brunch before our yoga class and there were police everywhere? I mean everywhere. Man, have you seen this place? It's hard to get your head around something so ugly happening somewhere this beautiful.'

More information to follow when we have it.

PROLOGUE

ISLAMORADA, FLORIDA KEYS

Here we are then. The two of us: Good Holly and Bad Holly. When they tell you which one is which – and, oh, they will when they find out everything – don't believe them. It's not as simple as that.

A mosquito comes close and I swat but miss, then I look for it as it hovers around me waiting to try again, but it is impossible in this darkness. It's late. Or it's early.

They have no teeth, you know. Mosquitoes have nothing so prosaic. Instead, they come at you with mouths lined with forty-seven tiny daggers – concealed but lying in wait; ready to puncture your skin and thieve your blood. Get this for a paradox: their daggers are so sharp that you barely feel the bite.

'Holly!'

I hear my name – the name we have in common – and it takes my attention away from the mosquito.

In that split second, I look at her. That's *you*, Holly. That's what you are. A bloodsucker. A mosquito.

It's okay to hurt her, because she is a pest. She lands and she sinks in her daggers, but she doesn't give a thought to the damage that she does or what impact she has. And we know the rule, don't we? Idolise the bees, don't hurt the spiders, but *always* take down the mosquitoes.

A memory consumes me. An inconvenience, an annoyance. Girls in crisp white shirts standing on tiptoe, the block heels of their black leather loafers lifted off the ground to see round the side of the geography block; the scent of cheap body spray. Shock painted across teenage faces that were loaded with muddy lipstick and thick face powder that had been ripped off the front of magazines on the way to school. The whispers.

'She was on the front of my dad's paper.'

'She was on the radio when we were having dinner last night.'

'Mum reckons *our Holly* is the biggest news story of the year.'

I shake my head. I can't think about this now. But I'm distracted anyway, by something humming, lightly and close to my ear, and I turn my attention back to that, the real mosquito, bugging me and still out for blood.

I am fuelled on adrenalin.

I won't miss, I know that.

Thwack.

'Yes,' I murmur, pleased with my kill. 'I got you.'

Next, I turn my attention to Holly. Mosquito number two.

PART ONE: HOLLY JONES

DAGGER 1

MIAMI, FIVE MONTHS EARLIER

On the day I saw her sitting with my group of expat friends outside my favourite brunch place in Coconut Grove, the humidity made the air teeter on the edge of fetid.

As I watched her from a few metres away, she clinked a bulbous glass with the woman next to her. The neon of her orange juice popped against the paleness of her arm.

Then she threw her head back and laughed, and I was back there. Laughs don't wrinkle with age, and that familiar cackle carried its way over, over, over to me. Now, we were adults in Miami. Then, we had been at school in north London. More than two decades earlier, teenage best friends.

My old school friend was sitting under that canopy with the group of women I was closest to in Miami, the city I'd lived in for over a decade. But they were women that, as far as I was aware, she had never met.

Objects started to lose their edges. I was dizzy. A prickle of sweat leapt up from my armpits, even though I was used to the Florida climate.

When the people and tables came back into focus, I started to move again, slowly, towards them all. In those seconds, I took in everything about her. The glimpse of a shell tattoo behind her ear, as she pushed her hair back. On the t-shirt she wore under her sundress, you could just make out She-Ra from *He-Man*. Her trainers were pumped up on air pillows, as neon as the orange juice.

A line of sweat formed around my hairline. When she put down her drink to push her hair back again, I saw sweat on her own hairline too. Relief. A trace of imperfection.

The stickiness of Miami follows you under canopies – under anywhere – especially when you aren't used to it. The only escape is the air con of a shopping mall, or flinging yourself into the Atlantic. I imagined Holly would love to fling herself into the Atlantic. She had been a county swimming champion back in the day – a lithe fish doing length after length after length as the rest of us fussed about chlorine in our eyes, or thighs we were self-conscious about, or the heavy period that soaked through tampons.

Turn, repeat, turn.

Even after more than a decade in Florida, I'd not become a good swimmer. I pictured Holly, heading further out from shore and taking on the ocean, strong and able as ever.

Turn. Repeat. Turn.

Something ominous sat in the lowest part of my belly as I approached the table. Even the warm bath of the Florida air felt different. Oppressive. Like it wanted to suck me under in its current and drown me. I felt more sweat on my body, this time a cold drizzle meandering into the small of my back. I tasted the rot of overripe fruit.

And then she saw me too. I held my breath and my old friend held on to my gaze. Her grin didn't wane.

My own body angled and stiffened, sensing danger like a cat, and my gut called 911. *She shouldn't be here. Get her away from them. Get her out of here.* Still, I kept walking towards the table. What was the alternative?

'Pancake stack? Who ordered the pancake stack?' a waiter yelled, doing his best to be heard over the hum of the table. 'Guys! I've got some pancakes here that are desperate to be eaten! They're gagging for it! Begging!'

I was close to the table when my phone slipped from my fingers, and I felt my thighs dissolve to juice as I scooped it up. This was my most frequently visited brunch spot, where I put extra sugar in my cortado and people-watched with my friends from a terrace we could spend hours on. This was my world. The sight of her drinking with my friends and the sound of that throaty laugh, amused at things that *they* had said, felt as incongruous as a shark in a nightclub.

Step.

'Smashed avo with soft eggs!' shouted the waiter, brandishing a plate on one giant, pumped-up arm. 'Someone help me out here and claim the smashed avo!'

Then her voice, confident over the noise. 'That one's mine,' she said, with that smile that spread itself wide and fat across her face. And still not taking her eyes off mine: 'Whoa, looks good.'

Step.

Step.

Step.

I was so close that I could see the red birthmark on her chest, and had a flash of memory of her borrowing my Rimmel concealer to try to make it disappear like a spot, in the school toilet next to our form room.

When I reached the table, she was the first to stand up. Arms that were more sinewy than they used to be snaked around me. I wondered if she could feel the tremor in my arms. Or the heart that pressed against her collarbone and was beating too fast.

Next to her, my friend Sofia stopped sawing at her French toast.

'Wait, what?' Sofia put her knife and fork down and licked her fingers. 'I was about to do introductions. But you already . . . ?'

Next to each other, Clair and Violet looked up. Violet's neat, dark eyebrows – such a contrast to the Scandinavian-blonde wisps of her hair – were furrowed. 'You two *know* each other?'

I looked away from both of them and took a deep breath. Then I turned back and nodded. 'First met in London when we were . . . fourteen?'

My old school friend confirmed my memory, pointing to her face with a fork. 'New girl.' The fat grin was back. 'Holly got me in with the cool kids.'

Me: I'm Holly Jones. Her: Holly Wild. At school though, we'd been one entity, *The Hollys*. Inseparable. Best friends.

'Give me a break,' I said. 'Look at you. You *are* the cool kid.'

She was relaxed, as though she were sitting in an old squishy armchair. Her hair was far longer than it used to be, surfer-chic, pushed over to the wrong side so that it answered its parting – brown roots growing out down into dark blonde waves. The navy sundress looked new, and one spaghetti strap slipped off her shoulder. I touched my own tousled brown bob. Neat. Just-so.

I struggled to catch my breath. The juxtaposition of her there, an old friend in amongst my new friends, tangled wires in my brain.

As Holly Wild sat back down, she folded one leg over the other, and an ankle bracelet with a tiny dolphin glinted at the bottom of a slim calf. I was still standing and I tried to look away but something about her pulled my eyes back. She hadn't taken her eyes off me. Another trickle of sweat, heftier this time, like a leak, made its way down my back.

At school there had been a five-inch height difference between us – me, the gangly one who could get served in the darker and more dubious Camden drinking dens; Holly, dinky like a child – that still

existed now. A difference in eye colour: mine are two identical round nuts, hers have always been that serious, don't-fuck-with-me grey.

But that wasn't what they'd used to distinguish us. There was no 'Tall Holly' and 'Small Holly'. No 'Brown-eyed Holly' and 'Grey-eyed Holly'. Instead, they boiled it down to what everything boils down to in the end, whether it's *Harry Potter*, *Star Wars*, *Lord of the Rings*, *Batman*. World wars.

Right, wrong. Yes, no. Good, bad.

The memory of it hurt.

One of us was *Good Holly.*

One of us was *Bad Holly.*

You become what they say you are.

ABOUT THE AUTHOR

Photo © 2022 Dan Bentley

A former journalist across magazines including Grazia, Marie Claire, Stylist and several of the UK's national newspapers, Caroline is now a *Sunday Times* bestselling author. Her work has been translated into multiple languages and sold around the world.

Her novels, often described as psychological thrillers, are also very much books about the female experience, tackling themes such as infertility, domestic violence, motherhood, sexual assault and mental health.

When not writing, Caroline is usually reading, going to book club, or interviewing fellow authors at her local bookshops. Some people might say she needs more varied hobbies.

You can follow Caroline Corcoran on Instagram at @carolinecorcoranwriter and on BlueSky at @carolinecorcoran.bsky.social.

Follow the Author on Amazon

If you enjoyed this book, follow Caroline Corcoran on Amazon to be notified when the author releases a new book!
To do this, please follow these instructions:

Desktop:

1) Search for the author's name on Amazon or in the Amazon App.
2) Click on the author's name to arrive on their Amazon page.
3) Click the 'Follow' button.

Mobile and Tablet:

1) Search for the author's name on Amazon or in the Amazon App.
2) Click on one of the author's books.
3) Click on the author's name to arrive on their Amazon page.
4) Click the 'Follow' button.

Kindle eReader and Kindle App:

If you enjoyed this book on a Kindle eReader or in the Kindle App, you will find the author 'Follow' button after the last page.